THE ESCORT

In the Service of Women

Shayne McClendon

The Escort: In the Service of Women by Shayne McClendon
The Escort: In the Service of Women
Original Copyright © 1999 and Beyond Shayne McClendon

Published by Always the Good Girl LLC
www.alwaysthegoodgirl.com

All rights reserved.
ISBN: 9798884426573

This is a work of fiction. Names, characters, places, and incidents either are the product of the author's imagination or are used fictitiously, and any resemblance to actual persons, living or dead, business establishments, events, or locales is entirely coincidental.

Please don't steal my work. I put my soul into it.

NOTE FROM SHAYNE

In the Service of Women was the first full-length erotica novel I started writing in 1999.

It took me *years* to finish because I was working full-time and raising my kids. I also didn't think there was a place for something like this in *polite* society.

I know better now. I self-published it in 2012 and took it down less than two years later when I realized how sloppy my original releases were.

To be fair, I didn't have anyone to read, edit, or critique my work back then so publishing was completely trial by fire.

Not terrifying at all - *ha ha*.

[There was also the *Laptop Crash of 2013* after I edited the book the first time…but we shan't speak of that since I still have nightmares.]

This is one of the most popular stories I've ever published and I've been asked to re-release it over and over again since I took it down. It took me a while to work up the courage.

Know this: *it is not the same story*.

The foundation is the same. Some scenes remain similar. Other than that, it's a different story entirely.

If you have never read the original, I'm glad. I hope you like this wonderful new story I wrote.

If you loved the original, consider this an alternate universe version, keep your old one, and pop into this one now and again.

Fair warnings about what you'll find inside…

I explicitly describe sex between women *many* times, some sex between men and women, a little sex between men, some polyamory, and even a good old-fashioned orgy.

I also deal with some painful topics (though not in gratuitous detail) that include physical, emotional, and sexual abuse, rape, violence, stalking, and severe trauma. To a lesser degree, eating disorders, homophobia, and addiction are touched upon.

In the past, this book was described as the lesbian version of my book *The Barter System* - meaning, it has a lot of sex. It's about an escort. She works in the sex industry. There's going to be sex.

Don't say I didn't warn you.

If you're not into all this, you might want to stop reading now. Otherwise, sit back with a nice beverage because you may get a little overheated.

Happy reading and much love,
Shayne

TABLE OF CONTENTS

PROLOGUE: My Name is Sarah _____ 1

CHAPTER 1: Introductions _____ 4

CHAPTER 2: The Madame _____ 10

CHAPTER 3: Reflection _____ 20

CHAPTER 4: The Interview _____ 25

CHAPTER 5: Reflection _____ 36

CHAPTER 6: My Campbell _____ 39

CHAPTER 7: Devil in the Details _____ 48

CHAPTER 8: Staff & Stable _____ 54

CHAPTER 9: Photo Shoot _____ 60

CHAPTER 10: My New Coworkers _____ 70

CHAPTER 11: The Attorney _____ 77

CHAPTER 12: Monica _____ 87

CHAPTER 13: Big Thoughts _____ 95

CHAPTER 14: The Mystery Client _____ 102

CHAPTER 15: Ilene _____ 110

CHAPTER 16: Reflection _____ 119

CHAPTER 17: Bad Penny _____ 124

CHAPTER 18: Another Birthday _____ 131

CHAPTER 19: Drawing Boundaries _____ 144

TABLE OF CONTENTS *(cont'd)*

CHAPTER 20: The Singer _____ 155

CHAPTER 21: Tricia _____ 165

CHAPTER 22: Reflection _____ 173

CHAPTER 23: Ilene _____ 179

CHAPTER 24: The Model _____ 189

CHAPTER 25: Making Lemonade _____ 202

CHAPTER 26: Plus One _____ 210

CHAPTER 27: The Housewife _____ 218

CHAPTER 28: New Subscriber _____ 234

CHAPTER 29: The Pilot _____ 241

CHAPTER 30: Reflection _____ 252

CHAPTER 31: Masquerade _____ 259

CHAPTER 32: Daily Life _____ 270

CHAPTER 33: The Chef _____ 276

CHAPTER 34: Rookies _____ 286

CHAPTER 35: Unwanted Attention _____ 295

CHAPTER 36: Rage _____ 304

CHAPTER 37: Terms & Conditions _____ 314

CHAPTER 38: First & Last _____ 320

CHAPTER 39: Endings _____ 335

TABLE OF CONTENTS (*cont'd*)

CHAPTER 40: Maximum Release _____ 346

CHAPTER 41: Ebb & Flow _____ 359

CHAPTER 42: Important Decisions _____ 369

CHAPTER 43: Peace at Last _____ 379

CHAPTER 44: A Different Life _____ 389

EPILOGUE _____ 396

EXTRA: The First Night (Max) _____ 401

GOOD GIRL PUBLISHING _____ 1

ABOUT SHAYNE McCLENDON _____ 3

FIND ME EVERYWHERE _____ 5

*When you sell your body,
you can lose little pieces of your soul.*

PROLOGUE:
My Name is Sarah

In 2009, a few weeks shy of nineteen, I became a paid escort for a service run *by* women, *for* women.

I was hired by my clients to wine, dine, and give them orgasms...but it was so much more than that.

In entertainment, there's a common perception of people like me. Women who *make it* on their backs because it's the fastest way to get rich.

Movies show us either falling for millionaires or taking our clients for everything we can get.

To be fair, customers *are* dollar signs and sex workers make no excuses for that - nor should they be expected to. It's a job after all.

I applaud their detachment. Truthfully, I was never particularly good at maintaining detachment. I guess you could say I'm more of a *hooker with a heart* type.

This isn't a book about my *clients*.

It's a book about the *people* I met while I worked as an escort for eighteen months.

I originally dove into this occupation for the adventure. I stayed because of the people.

The money was gravy.

At the end of the day, if money is the main motivation for anything, there's a chance you're going to end up feeling pretty fucking empty.

I don't want to live like that.

I don't want to feel that way.

Instead, I choose to embrace every moment, every experience, for all it's worth. To go through life with my eyes open and do the best I can to be a decent human being.

With that said, this is about my journey from a young woman to a somewhat smarter woman.

A metamorphosis that happened accidentally while traveling a path of luxury and mind-blowing sex.

A world I wasn't cut out for in the end.

Since you're going to wonder, most people would label me bisexual - if I was one for labels. Ten years after signing on to service women in whatever ways they desired or required, I identify as pansexual.

In other words, my attraction to someone isn't about their outer package but the *feelings* a partner inspires.

Courage in youth so often conceals an ignorance of reality…but I knew all about the darkness in people before I ever recognized the light. At the time, I was just going with the flow and trying to figure shit out.

Things can get dicey when you realize even small choices change the course of your entire life.

The Escort: In the Service of Women

My life today is quite different from the one I used to live. However, I'm the person I am now - in many ways - because of the time I share here.

I have no regrets.

I hope you like the journey. If you don't, that's alright, too. My story - much like the sex industry - isn't for everyone.

Sarah Kent

December 2019

CHAPTER 1:
Introductions

November 2009

Entering the sex industry as a paid escort came about on a quiet Friday afternoon at the unlikely location of the law firm where I interned part-time in Ft. Lauderdale, Florida.

The owner was a family attorney named Monica Carter - who was also *my* attorney. I did filing and odd jobs around her office to repay her for waiving my legal fees while I was still a minor.

Monica managed to get me emancipated from my shit show mother during my sophomore year of high school. At sixteen, with no power of my own, dear Paula withdrew me without consent to punish me for leaving her house.

Thanks to Monica, I was able to find a place to live, get back to classes, and ultimately graduate. I even had enough credits to get my official diploma six months early.

Though she repeatedly told me I didn't owe her anything, I didn't like to feel indebted. When the sharp law lady didn't budge, I showed up early as a client one day and befriended the older office manager who'd worked there for years.

By the time Monica was ready for our appointment, I'd learned some basic tasks and gotten coffee for the paralegal department.

I was eighteen then and had been living on my own for over two years. Not much shocked me.

With my childhood, I'd *always* felt like an adult.

A lifelong insomniac, I accomplished a lot more in the course of my day than most people. I kept my place nice, dated when the mood struck, and worked the rest of the time.

Average. Safe. A little boring.

The world was in a strange place socially, politically, and environmentally. *When is it not?*

The rumblings about global warming were getting louder while we continued destroying our planet and stripping her resources one acre at a time.

Doubt that will change anytime soon.

Some prudes on a political mission were making life hell - again - for anyone outside what they felt was normal. I hated everything about censorship, racism, and the insane phobias about the poor, sex workers, the LGBT+ community, and on and on.

Hate of all kinds is just ignorant to me and so short-sighted. It's none of our damn business what people do as consenting adults - as long as they don't take advantage of others or hurt them.

Religion was making a comeback in all the *worst* ways. It had the end-of-the-world groupies foaming at the mouth. I'd been against most organized religion for a long time - for many valid reasons - so this was particularly frustrating to me.

For years, I'd done my best to stay under the radar. I hid from a rough childhood and a few mistakes I made on my own before I knew better.

I'm not writing this to share my sob story. It's pretty depressing and it's finally behind me. While I give you background that's hard to write about later, I want you to know that I'm focused on what's ahead.

I have worked my ass off and vowed to make better choices than my family ever did.

Unlike most people my age, I enjoyed my own company. I preferred to read when I had down time or write stories that came to mind.

However, I sure as hell wasn't going to turn down something interesting if it came knocking.

The unexpected *knock* came one sunny afternoon in the form of a beautiful stranger.

* * *

Vivienne Masters was a former model frustrated with Father Time for sweeping her *past her prime*. It was a complaint I would hear many times over the course of our acquaintance.

When we met, she was thirty-six. Twice my age and twice the audacity of any man I'd ever met. She was five-ten with long blonde hair and bright blue eyes.

She'd been blessed with a body most women would happily commit a crime to possess. Gorgeous breasts and legs that went on forever could make anyone - male or female - beg for mercy.

Within minutes of meeting her, I was sure she was begged for mercy on a regular basis.

Vivienne was alone with Monica in her office for about an hour when she joined me in the closed courtyard area where I took my lunch breaks to read.

From the corner of my eye, I sensed her watching me as she lit a long cigarette.

She was dressed in crème slacks and an electric blue silk top. Her heels were crème leather and added another three inches to her height.

No doubt…a Viking goddess brought to life.

The woman didn't approach me immediately but didn't hide the fact that she was staring.

It didn't take long to make me squirm.

I had dark red hair almost to my waist and light hazel eyes. I maintained a fit body from running and working all the damn time.

My D-cup breasts had been with me since the fifth grade. They were a *real* hit with the asshole boys who teased me endlessly. Suffice to say, I've had my share of staring. I'm *rarely* comfortable with it.

That day, I wore jeans, a soft t-shirt, and running shoes. My hair was braided down my back and I wasn't wearing makeup.

Nowhere near glamorous…but I thought she was glamorous enough for both of us.

I met my initial nervousness head-on by looking directly at her and flashing my friendliest Texas smile - guaranteed to win friends, influence teachers, and make a lot of straight guys hard.

It seemed to do the trick. She came to sit beside me, her heels clicking over the Mexican tile of the outdoor patio. She chose a chair a few feet away, kept her back straight, and crossed her legs with a natural grace I envied.

"What's your name?" she asked. Her voice sounded fresh from a New England prep school.

"Sarah Kent." I responded, automatically putting my hand out to shake.

She gave me a smile as she took my hand. I was surprised she didn't let go right away. She examined my nails, which were short but neat, turned my hand palm up, and ran a polished nail down the center. Her gaze returned to my face.

With a nod - as if she answered an unspoken question - she told me, "My name is Vivienne, and I'd quite like to be your friend."

Schooled early in the harshness of life, I was able to sense bullshit quicker than most. So far, no alarms were ringing in my brain.

"Sure, who can't use friends?" I replied.

"Today is going to be a good day, Sarah. I want to take you with me for the rest of the afternoon. Would you like that? I can speak to Monica." She took a long drag of her cigarette.

Monica was smart, gorgeous, and cool to work for. Still, I didn't feel right taking off with some stranger when I'd committed to doing a job.

I said as much to Vivienne, and she responded with a lovely laugh. "Monica and I go *way* back. We were sorority sisters. She's one of the reasons I'm here talking to you…but we'll discuss that later. If it makes you feel better, you can come with me to speak to her."

She took a final puff and stubbed her cigarette out in the ashtray. Then she met my gaze and waited.

I knew this woman was different from anyone I'd ever met. It seemed an unspoken opportunity had presented itself to me.

Beautiful and sane enough - I could spot crazy from a hundred yards - I found myself curious.

Adding to the curiosity was a familiar stirring in my lower abdomen. I chose male sex partners with care but I was less guarded with female lovers.

I didn't know anything about human trafficking back then but if I had, I knew Monica wouldn't send someone to me with dangerous intentions.

Leaning into whatever Vivienne offered seemed like the smart thing to do.

"I'll grab my stuff while you talk to Monica."

Her answering smile was a bit predatory and it made me pause for a moment. With a shrug, I figured I could take her if things got weird.

CHAPTER 2:
The Madame

Half an hour after meeting her, I climbed into Vivienne's Mercedes convertible and she drove to her penthouse in Miami.

I'd never been to Miami before and that first drive scared me to death. The roads are narrow and the drivers seemed to have a death wish.

Vivienne was unconcerned, drove ninety all the way, swerving between cars like she was competing in Formula One. *Elton John's Greatest Hits* played and she tapped the steering wheel in time with the music.

She made small talk - asked about my life, what I wanted to do, and if I had a boyfriend.

Avoiding bringing down the vibe with my past, I dove straight into talk of the future.

My dream was to be a writer. I didn't tell her I'd lost my chance at a journalism scholarship or even to attend college because of my batshit crazy mother.

I figured the universe had other plans for me.

"College isn't for everyone and that's okay. I'm proud of my brain but even prouder of my common sense." I frowned. "It seems a lot of people are missing that."

"Agreed. And…a boyfriend?" Vivienne prompted.

"No one at the moment. I've had a couple. A few girlfriends." She smiled as she stared at the road. "I don't have a preference or really see a reason to choose a team. It limits your options when you exclude half the world's population."

"I like the way you think, Sarah."

Vivienne maneuvered her car off I-95 and through narrow side streets. She pulled into a parking garage beneath a luxury building on South Beach. She parked and turned to me with a smile.

"This is where I live."

"Nice." I was noncommittal.

Money was important. I took it seriously. However, I didn't live my life in pursuit of it and I never would.

We got out and she walked to a private elevator. On the top floor, the doors opened to a gorgeous penthouse. An entire wall of windows looked out over the Atlantic.

It was the prettiest view I'd ever seen.

The rest of the room was done in varying shades of white. It was a beautiful backdrop for the impact artwork and modern furniture in every color scattered around the room.

There were multiple seating areas with thick rugs over crisp white tile. A faux fireplace adorned one half-wall, a built-in saltwater fish tank decorated another, and both added to the effect of openness.

Vivienne hung my backpack in a coat closet beside the elevator then paused in her living room to turn on the stereo.

Casually taking my hand, she led me to the kitchen. "What can I get you to drink?"

"Just water, thanks." She brought me a bottle from the fridge before making a vodka-cranberry for herself. We sat side by side at the island bar.

Her kitchen was painted in a *shocking* shade of plum purple with matte finish steel appliances and high-gloss white cabinets.

The effect was surprisingly cool.

This room featured another spectacular view and a shaded balcony off the breakfast nook.

I wondered if she ever used the space to actually *cook*. Something told me no…but the design was like something out of a magazine.

"You mentioned you run?" she asked politely.

"Mm. I knocked out five miles this morning." I shrugged. "I'm not obsessive about it like some people. There are days I run more and others I run less. Depends on what I need to work out in my head after I tie my shoes."

"I would *not* have the stamina for that. I'd need a week to recover."

She was slim but I didn't see her being into hard-core exercise either. Still, I seriously doubted she'd ever had trouble with *stamina* in her life.

I let it go with a smile and no comment.

Marvin Gaye's *What's Going On* began playing in the background, one of my favorite old songs.

My music tastes were eclectic. I liked older artists as well as the current hip-hop, alt-rock, and pop most people *my age* listened to.

For twenty minutes or so, we did the small talk thing. It was cool and all but…the suspense was killing me.

Setting my water bottle on the counter, I said, "Um, I think you might want to fuck me. I'm cool with it if you do. I don't mean any disrespect but…you don't have to spend a bunch of time talking me into it."

Vivienne's eyes widened in surprise and her jaw dropped. "You're *cool with it* if I want to fuck you?"

"I mean…yeah. Why not?"

For a moment, I thought I'd read the situation wrong. Maybe she was looking for a nice girl as a charity case or something.

I was ready to apologize when she leaned forward and dropped her mouth over mine.

Thank goodness…I was worried my *fuck me* meter had gone on the fritz. False alarm.

Let's do this.

For a few seconds, I let Vivienne explore my mouth while I learned her style. She was thorough and skilled at kissing. It was clear she had experience.

I hadn't been with a lot of people but I put effort into sex just like I did everything else in my life.

Smiling to myself, I gave as good as I got.

Standing, I turned her body towards me and stepped between her legs. My arm slid along the small of Vivienne's back and I cupped the base of her skull.

I needed to anchor her so I could take control. My tongue coiled around hers as I kissed her with aggression born of a combined need to prove myself to an older, more experienced lover - while maintaining the dominant role.

Only when she was out of breath did I break the contact so she could get some air. Sighing, I kissed a trail along her jaw and down her neck.

Her pulse jumped against my lips and I *loved* that.

Vivienne rested one hand on my shoulder while the other traced the long braid down my back. She found the band, unwound it, and combed her fingers through the length.

I watched her face as she stared at the curls I worked hard to tame without much success. She brought it to her face and inhaled deeply.

No doubt she smelled the coconut product I used.

For a moment, the blonde seemed to exist in her own world. She ran her hands over my arms, back, and ass, lightly squeezing my flesh as she went.

I felt a little like a horse at auction. Later, it would turn out my instincts weren't far off the mark.

Still, I didn't mind. She had a soft touch that caused pleasant sensations up and down my spine.

Besides, I did some exploring of my own. I trailed my lips over her shoulders and dipped my tongue into the hollow of her throat.

Vivienne possessed *incredible* skin that held the soft scent of peaches and expensive tobacco. Living in South Florida, it was obvious she took extreme precautions against the sun.

I burned fairly easily so I made my own sunscreen and rubbed it head to toe after every shower.

Slipping my hands around her waist to pull her closer, I moved beneath the silk top she wore. Massaging her gently with my fingers, I liked how warm she was.

There wasn't a lot of touch in my life - giving or receiving - so I took advantage of it when a chance presented itself.

Frustrated to have fabric in the way, I lifted the blouse over her head and dropped it on the kitchen floor. I felt no hesitation as I removed her expensive bra and tossed it away to join the blouse.

I took in the appearance of my new lover's upper body with genuine appreciation.

Her breasts fit in the palms of my hands. They were firm with pale pink nipples. I watched as the tips furled into little pearls under my gaze.

My head lowered to take one of her nipples in my mouth and she gripped the hair at the base of my neck with a sigh.

The slight roughness turned me on so much that I clutched her hard against me. Cupping her breast, I continued to suckle.

The female body is truly a miracle of design.

Breasts can be so many textures - both soft and firm at once. No matter the size, shape, or age, nipples fit perfectly in the mouth of a person who knows how to appreciate them properly.

I've always appreciated them.

Vivienne pulled at my t-shirt and I was forced to release my treat so she could lift it over my head. When I was free to return, I transferred my attention to her other breast, licking around the nipple several times before I sucked it to the roof of my mouth.

She kissed and bit along the column of my neck as I sucked her. Soft moans escaped her and it spurred me to greater lengths to please her.

Long legs wrapped around my waist and she ground herself against my belly. Even with the fabric of her slacks and panties between us, I could feel the damp heat of her pussy.

I needed to give her attention that felt impossible on a bar stool. It was time to move to a more comfortable location.

A trait that never failed to turn girlfriends on - and intimidate boyfriends sometimes - was the fact that I am *ridiculously* strong for someone of my size.

I cupped Vivienne's ass cheeks, picked her up, and carried her to the living room. Sensing her shock, I was glad she didn't protest.

"Will anyone be stopping by?" I asked and she shook her head. "Then here works."

Taking a seat on a green chaise, I had her straddle my lap and went back to giving her breasts the attention they deserved.

Vivienne's head dropped back on her shoulders. Both hands in my hair, she held me against her and I smiled to myself.

She wanted me as close as possible.

There was nowhere else I wanted to be.

I lifted my face to lick her throat and lightly bit her jaw before gripping the nape of her neck and reclaiming her mouth.

She sucked my tongue between her lips as I ran my hands down her back. Taking her ass cheeks in my palms, I gently separated them and pushed them back together. Feeling the stimulation instantly, she broke the kiss to gasp for air.

I was startled when she suddenly stood up.

Vivienne slipped off her heels and unbuttoned her slacks. Pushing them over her flared hips, when they hit the floor, she kicked them aside. Hooking her thumbs in her panties, she started to take them off.

Grabbing her hands, I went to my knees at her feet.

"Let me do that, Vivienne. It's my favorite part. Like unwrapping a present."

I wondered if she could hear the lust in my voice. It was beginning to cloud my ability to think straight.

Staring up at her face, I was fascinated by her expression. Vivienne's hands dropped to her sides and I winked.

"Thanks."

Rubbing my cheek over her belly, I inhaled deeply. I could smell how turned on she was and knew she was already wet for me.

Disappointing her wasn't an option.

Licking along the band of her panties, I planted kisses on her belly, hip bones, and the tops of her thighs. Her fingers returned to my hair.

I pulled her panties down a bit on one side, then the other, leaving warm kisses on each section of skin as it was revealed.

The tiniest patch of blond curls tempted me. I rubbed the backs of my fingers over them. Goosebumps broke out on her skin and she inhaled sharply in response.

"You're so patient…" she whispered.

Her blue eyes were bright with need. I knew she was alternately curious to know what I'd do next and anxious to receive release.

Ruffling the trimmed curls, I wondered, "Why rush? You deserve to be worshiped as well as fucked. Making you wait now builds the pleasure later."

Her hands clenched in my hair. She was breathless as she asked, "Is that your personal motto?"

"Sure." I laughed. "I just like seeing a lover in a boneless puddle before I get mine. Job well done and all that."

"A bit of competitiveness perhaps?"

"Maybe. Does it matter? Whoever you've had in the past or will have in your future…right now, you're in *my* hands. I don't like to waste opportunities."

Vivienne held my chin between her finger and thumb. "There is something about you…it intrigues me. I want to know more."

"I'm not a complex entity."

"I think that's a lie. I'm certain you know it."

She bent to suck my lower lip between her teeth and I couldn't help but growl a little. Her look was almost feral as she pulled back.

"And if I prefer to worship *you*, Sarah?"

In answer, I went back to lowering her panties. "Isn't there a saying about it being better to give than receive? I always liked that idea. The more you give, the greater," kissing the crease of soft skin just beneath her curls, I finished, "…the return."

She gently rubbed the back of my neck as I bared her completely to my view. I slid the panties to the floor and she stepped out of them.

Staring at her fully naked body, I trailed my fingers between her legs and murmured, "Me? I'm a *giver*."

CHAPTER 3:
Reflection

Every time I touched another person sexually, I couldn't help but feel intense satisfaction at the rage my actions would inspire in my mother if she knew.

I was a person who appeared to have all the right pieces in all the right order from the outside.

Years of practice, hard work to maintain perceptions, and a strong will to not let my past define every moment of my future…

Meant only *I* knew how damaged I was at the core.

For less than a second, I remembered the last beating I took before leaving home two months shy of my sixteenth birthday.

"Fornication is a sin! A sin!"

Blow after blow landed but I shut out the pain after the first one. I'd had *years* of practice. I refused to cry for her and it made her fury burn brighter.

"You're a *whore*! I know what you did!"

My biological mother went through my diary - something I thought I'd hidden well. Daily journaling was deeply ingrained in my habits.

This time, I'd been the architect of my destruction.

Paula knew I had sex with my best friend from high school. Campbell and I had been friends for almost two years and I offered to take his virginity.

He had *not* taken mine, unfortunately.

It was clumsy and awkward because we were nervous but it was also strangely beautiful. I *hated* that the creature who gave birth to me knew something so private.

Glancing up through the blur of blood in my eye, I saw my younger brothers in the backyard at my bedroom window.

They were *screaming* for me, banging on the glass. The sight of their terror went through me like an electric current. *Another fucking generation steeped in the sights and sounds of abuse.*

That was the *moment* I reached my limit.

Grabbing Paula by the shoulders, I pushed her through my louver closet doors with little effort. She crashed into the drywall at the back and cracked it.

There was an expression of utter shock on her face but I didn't care.

Picking up my always ready backpack, I put the diary she'd thrown at my forehead inside and took down several photos of my brothers on the wall.

No matter what she did to me, she never laid a hand on the boys. I knew they'd be safe - from beatings at least - when I left. There was no choice *but* to leave. Her beatings were escalating.

The woman would eventually kill me.

I could have physically stopped her at any time but that day was the first time I ever fought back.

Paula crawled out of the closet screaming. "I'll call the police! I'll have you locked up for attacking your mother! You disrespectful whore!"

I bent down to stare into her face. "Do it, Paula. I remember every hospital you've driven an hour to take me to for injuries you inflicted on my body. The broken bones, stitches, and concussions. Your cult leaders might protect you but the *law* won't. Stay away from me. We're done."

Crashing at Campbell's place, he fed me and patched me up as his mom sobbed over my condition and his father paced in rage on my behalf.

I was grateful for his body warmth while I slept. Having sex with each other didn't change the fact that the person I loved most was gay.

I was just happy to have a clean memory of sex with someone who actually cared about me as a person. It had not been part of my previous life experience.

Without it, there's no telling how I would have fared in the world.

The next day, we shared a look when I was called out of class. Campbell was already shaking with fear for me. I took my backpack and went to the office.

Practically vibrating with righteous anger, the vice principal told me, "Your mother *withdrew you* from school. She says you're moving two hours north and she'll reenroll you once you're settled."

"That's a lie, ma'am."

"She's tied our hands repeatedly - citing religious persecution - and her pending suit against the school board means I have to be cautious about how I proceed." There was a long pause and she added tearfully, "She beat you *again*."

I shrugged. "I survived it. Put her through a closet. To be honest, I'm shocked I'm not in jail."

Ms. Vania shook her head. "She knows *this* is a worse punishment for someone like you. Getting you out of school has been her goal for a long time."

She nodded to someone behind me and I turned. A pretty woman dressed in an expensive pantsuit sat in a chair behind the door.

Normally hyper aware of my surroundings, I was surprised I hadn't noticed her when I entered.

"Sarah, this is Monica Carter. She's a family law attorney. I asked her to talk to you."

Staring into the woman's eyes, I murmured, "Okay."

It took almost two months to get me back in school but Ms. Vania made sure I received all my work so I didn't fall too far behind.

Campbell's parents let me stay at their apartment, but I knew it wouldn't be long before Paula came to cause trouble for them. I didn't want his family wrapped up in my messy bullshit.

When I was legally emancipated, I found an apartment I could afford and walked or rode the bus until I saved enough for my motorcycle.

Taking on more hours at the grocery store job I'd been doing since I was fourteen, I started over with nothing. It wasn't perfect…but better than what came before. Juggling school and work was doable and Monica made sure I signed up for benefits to help me until I was old enough to work full-time.

Little by little, I figured out a rhythm to my life. I made a ton of mistakes but I kept going.

I earned everything I had.

It made me proud to think about it.

And once in a while, something awesome landed in front of me that relieved the residual numbness I felt most of the time.

Like a hot blonde who wanted me to crawl all over her until her legs didn't work.

I embraced those opportunities with both hands and didn't apologize for shit.

CHAPTER 4:
The Interview

I ran my hands up Vivienne's thighs to her abdomen and around to her ass. When I looked up, she watched me with interest.

"Are you wondering if I'll know what to do? If I'll be able to please you?" I kissed her belly button and edged her towards the chaise. "If I'll be able to make you come as badly as you want to?"

Vivienne's look was ravenous as I encouraged her to sit and pushed her upper body against copper throw pillows. Stroking over her hips and thighs again, I liked the image she presented.

A feast laid out to be devoured.

"I decide what I want and go after it single-mindedly. Let me know if you need me to dial it back, yeah?"

Something flickered in her eyes but was quickly gone. "Noted. You're different from many of the dominant women I've been with…and so young."

"Does my age bother you?"

"Does *mine* bother you, Sarah?"

"Not at all. My mouth waters for you. I don't give a fuck how many birthdays you've celebrated."

Her smile was slow and it somehow made her even more attractive. "Excellent answer." Stretching one arm over her head, she said, "I want to see all of you. Undress." Before I could stop it, a small chuckle escaped me. Viv winked. "I'm not dominant…just impatient."

"I'm happy to undress for you, Vivienne."

I stood and moved a couple of feet away. I toed off my running shoes and removed my ankle socks. Moving to unclasp my plain bra, I appreciated her smile when my breasts were revealed.

I slid my hands up my arms, along my collarbone, and down over my tits. Lightly tweaking my nipples, I slipped my palms over my stomach to the button of my jeans.

Spreading the fabric wide, I used one hand to caress my lower abdomen as it was bared. Using the flats of my hands, I slid the denim off and rubbed the triangle of my panties. Like my bra, simple white cotton, as I usually preferred.

When I removed them, Vivienne noted, "A natural redhead. I wasn't sure - haven't seen one in a while. Come closer." I did and she stroked her fingertips through the hair I kept trimmed.

I liked the way she smiled and wondered if this afternoon together would be the only time I'd see it.

"Turn around once for me, Sarah."

I pivoted slowly, showing her my back. My body was fit and strong - I'd always been an active person. I had scars scattered over my skin, several bones that never healed quite right, and residual pain I hid from others. I was flawed…but I *appreciated* the body I lived in and took care of it.

I wasn't a shy person. I faced forward again and waited for her eyes to return to my face.

When they did, I went to my knees in front of her. Vivienne held my face in her hands and kissed me deeply. I licked into her mouth, over her lips and teeth, wrapping my tongue around hers.

After a minute, I leaned back and let my eyes move lazily over her body. I caressed her breasts again, rolling her nipples between my fingers and thumbs.

I liked the way she felt.

Vivienne's body was slender but she wasn't hard bodied. We were so different physically. Where she was long and lean, I was thicker and harder.

She moved to hold one of my breasts in her palm. "They're heavy but firm." Bending, she licked back and forth across the nipple that responded instantly to her attentions. "Responsive."

I gently pulled her away and flattened my palm between her breasts to push her down to the pillows.

"It's not my turn right now. Stay there, Vivienne."

Lowering my face, I kissed and licked the inside of her thigh. A shiver traveled over her skin and it made me bite the silken flesh lightly.

I enjoyed the sounds she made in the throes of pleasure. I wondered how much noise she'd make when I made her come.

Draping her long leg over my shoulder, I separated the lips of her pussy and lowered my mouth to her most sensitive skin.

First, I made a gentle exploration to see where Vivienne wanted me to focus my attention.

"Fuck, I want to come…"

"Wait a while, Vivienne." I grinned. "I feast until I'm satisfied...you should pace yourself."

With a long lick from her pussy to her clit and tiny bites along her outer lips, I softly circled the entrance of her with my fingers.

She writhed against the cushions of the chaise.

Judging by her moans and hip movements, I focused on her clit at my own pace. Licking and sucking it while she ground her hips into my face.

Vivienne came five minutes in and settled back with a long exhale. I used my fingertips to smooth gently over her mound while her breathing slowed.

As her eyes drifted shut, I smiled to myself. She thought we were done.

How cute.

When her body settled and she regained her composure, I alternately tongue-fucked her and used my fingers when I moved back to sucking her clit.

The blonde spread her long legs and tried to get closer to my mouth. Moving my other hand up her body, I caressed her breasts and loved the way her nipples tightened further.

"Oh, yes! Just like that," she begged.

One of her hands clutched the chaise. She gripped the back of my head with the other - holding me against her.

When Vivienne hit a second climax, I pulled her tightly to my mouth. She arched off the chaise with a long moan.

I wanted every drop and didn't stop lapping at her until the orgasm faded to aftershocks. Leaving small kisses over her pussy, inner thighs, and lower belly, I rested my face there.

Vivienne ran her fingers through my hair and I lifted my head to stare at her. Her smile was one of pure satisfaction. She leaned forward to kiss me and sampled her own essence from my lips. My tongue worked slowly around hers.

She encouraged me to stand and we walked naked to the staircase that led to the second floor of the apartment.

As we climbed on her king-size bed to continue exploring each other, soft satin sheets of robin's egg blue whispered across my skin.

The brilliant Florida sky at sunset acted as the backdrop to our lovemaking.

Every sensation felt heightened.

Vivienne was the oldest lover I'd taken voluntarily and her experience was obvious. She took her time making me come - maintaining a single-minded devotion to my pleasure.

By the time the first explosive climax slammed through me, I acknowledged that she was the best oral sex I'd ever experienced – male or female.

Teasing was something she *intensely* enjoyed.

The blonde brought me to the edge of orgasm and slowed her ministrations to make me wait. Again and again, she took me to the brink…until I begged her to let me come.

I'd get payback the moment I was able.

Vivienne was beautiful and seemed honest in her responses to me as a lover. She was outstanding at wringing pleasure from my body.

After she made me come three times to the two I'd given her, I considered it a personal challenge to better the score.

We were slick with sweat when I hovered above her, my legs positioned to bring our pussies in direct contact. I began with a slow grind, rotating my hips, loving the warmth and wetness of her against me.

She clutched my thigh, her nails digging into my skin as I quickened my pace. Every muscle in my body was tight and focused as I worked our clits together.

When she came, her lower body tightened so hard that her pussy sucked against mine. I joined her - beads of sweat sliding between my breasts.

Over the rest of the night, she taught me many new tricks while complimenting my technique and attention to detail.

We bathed together before dawn in her tub filled with warm water and scented bubbles.

After drying off, we changed the sheets and got between them. Vivienne slept quickly and deeply.

I slept for an hour or so then spent what was left of the night trying to figure out how a normal day ended up so far from where it began.

Eventually, I wandered into her library downstairs to see what she had to offer. I could tell her books were primarily for display. There were various expensive sets with perfect spines – as if the titles had been assembled by a decorator.

My own collection was ragged from constant use. I made coffee and relaxed in her kitchen with a discovered edition of *Sense and Sensibility*.

It was mid-morning when she joined me, still looking soft and warm from sleep. She moved around the kitchen in her hip-length silk robe with nothing beneath it.

The visual turned me on.

With a cup of coffee in her hand, she noted, "I can't believe you're up already." She looked at the book in my hands. "Did you read all that this morning?"

"I'm a fast reader."

Tilting my head, I took in her body language. She seemed uncertain what to say. I understood her hesitation. Scenarios straight out of a Henry Miller novel just didn't happen to normal people.

Putting the book down, I smiled. "Vivienne, last night was amazing. I can't help feeling it was leading to something else. Am I right?"

"Sarah…I have a proposition for you."

With a wink, I replied, "I thought you might."

I drank some of my coffee and spread marmalade on toast Vivienne placed in front of me. I sat naked at her breakfast table and wasn't the least bit ashamed.

She joined me and brought her vibrant blue gaze to rest on my face. Her coffee steamed from the mug and she blew softly across the top to cool it.

It reminded me of the hot oil massage I'd received at two in the morning. I stopped mid-chew and smiled seductively.

Vivienne grinned. "Don't let those naughty thoughts get away, Sarah." She ran her hand over my bare thigh. "First, let's talk."

"Okay."

"First, no matter how you take what I'm going to say, you were an excellent lover last night. I wouldn't have missed it for the world."

"That sounds ominous," I quipped.

She set down the mug and sat up straight. "I'm a business woman. Quite a successful one actually." I could see her choosing her words carefully. "I'm a Madame. I run an escort service."

"Hmm. I thought it might be something like that."

"My clients are female - though some do have men in their lives. They book discreet *appointments* with the small group of young women I employ."

I tilted my head. "So last night was…an interview?"

"Sort of." She leaned forward. "I needed to see what you knew, how open you were to new situations, and how confident you were."

"How did I do?" I asked curiously.

"Brilliantly. Bottom line…I'd love to hire you."

She waited for my answer in a way that told me she'd gotten mixed responses in the past. She was practically holding her breath.

"One question…does Monica know what you do?"

There was a long pause before she said, "Yes."

"Don't tell her I asked. I won't tell her you answered."

"I…would appreciate that, Sarah."

"Well. It's different and that makes it interesting to me as a life experience. Let's do it."

Vivienne blinked. "That's it?"

I put down my toast, picked up the jar of marmalade, and nodded. "I'll clean you super well to prevent a urinary tract infection." She frowned in confusion at the topic change. "So…can I find out how your clit tastes with marmalade on it?"

* * *

After an hour of play and cleaning up, Vivienne drove me back to Monica's law office to get my ride.

She attempted to go over the standard procedures of her business on the way.

"Your first appointment will be the last weekend before Thanksgiving. The majority of our clients schedule their dates on the weekends - between Friday evening and Sunday night. There are exceptions sometimes but they're not the norm."

"Should I quit my other jobs? I'm not sure I should do that right away. I mean, you don't even know if I'll be *good* at this."

Vivienne smiled. "Let's say I have a good feeling. Wait on quitting - you need to try to maintain your usual schedule. Instead, consider narrowing your availability. Don't overlook days to rest."

I considered what she was saying and what she wasn't. "Because it's illegal, right? I need to look like I have a regular job or people will wonder where I'm getting my money."

She cleared her throat. "It will take a couple of weeks to get you fully set up and on the payroll of my front company."

"Front…?"

"Technically, you'll be working for the modeling and talent agency I've owned for almost fifteen years." She winked. "It's a legitimately functioning company. It provided the initial funds to start the escort service eight years ago. I wanted to diversify."

"Um, I'm not a model though," I reminded her.

"You weren't an escort yesterday either." Reaching out, she put her hand on my thigh. "Trust the process, Sarah. Let me do what I do best."

Arriving at the closed law office, I got out of her car and straddled my motorcycle.

She nearly fainted. "That's what you consider transportation? Are you *kidding*?"

"This is a Honda Nighthawk 650. Beautiful, fast, and almost zero maintenance." I lamely assured her, "I always wear a helmet…"

It did nothing to take the fearful look off her face so I tried another tack.

"Come on, Vivienne."

I extended my hand and she looked as if it was a snake that might bite her. It took almost thirty minutes and all my powers of persuasion to get her on the back for a quick ride around the block.

When she finally agreed, I gave her my helmet. Her hands shook as she pulled it over her head.

At first, she gripped me so hard I could barely breathe. Then she felt the vibrations between her thighs and fell in love. I turned the trip into a quick jaunt over to the beach and back.

When we got back to her car, she was wind-blown and laughing. Her face flushed and hair tousled - it reminded me of how she'd looked after hours of pleasure. Somehow, she was even lovelier.

She followed me in her car to my one-bedroom apartment in Lighthouse Point.

I wanted to see what she looked like on *my* sheets.

CHAPTER 5:
Reflection

In recent years, there'd been gathering validation behind the phenomena of *sex addiction.*

Looking back, that term never applied to me.

There wasn't an addictive element to having sex for me. I didn't act reckless or go through withdrawals without it but didn't shy from it either.

I know many of my unusual perceptions about sex were based in sexual abuse I sustained as a child.

Like my writing, it was a sort of therapy.

Much like I rewrote my trauma in my stories to cope with the experiences I'd endured, I touched lovers' naked bodies - and let them touch mine - to prove my abusers hadn't fully broken that part of me.

My mother knew my so-called *virginity* hadn't existed for almost a decade the day we fought.

Her invasion of my private journal would have given her a glimpse into the horrifying past I lived with her older sister and various step-uncles.

No adults protected me.

No one came to save me.

Instead of dealing with reality, she buried her head in the sand and called me a whore.

It was an easy solution that cost her nothing.

Still, I guess I *was* a whore if you subscribed to mainstream society's narrow views about sex and relationships. The majority of my recent partners were friends first whom I genuinely cared about.

Everyone gave consent - including me - which is more than my past abusers could claim.

I'd been with men, women, and a gentle soul who told me they believed they'd mistakenly received the body of a man.

People that were honest about who they were and what they needed didn't scare me. Liars and pretenders were the ones who filled me with fear.

Though I was young, I'd lived a life that trained me to read people. I learned to trust my instincts.

On the outside, I appeared to be a bubbly redhead - even a bit airheaded with my big smiles and tits.

On the inside, I possessed a dark core that understood the bright and shiny world was like that, too. I took my pleasures where I could get them.

An early morning run.

Driving my motorcycle up A1A at sunset.

Finding a new series at the library.

Trying a recipe and finding it delicious.

Writing a story that made me think.

Every so often, I found intense pleasure in touching another human. Watching their expressions change as I gave them little choice but to sweat, moan, and lose control for a brief moment in time.

It was the ultimate power and I took it seriously. I didn't abuse it. I didn't pretend that every connection would lead to a life-long romance. I didn't allow my emotions to slip out of my control.

If I was a whore, I was a conscientious one.

To balance the scales, I tried to give more than I received in every sexual exchange.

Vivienne and what she offered would be the latest representation of my life mantra. I doubted very much that she would have complaints.

Unsatisfied lovers were a blight on my reputation and a strike against the way I lived my life.

One couldn't have that.

CHAPTER 6:
My Campbell

Parking in front of my small apartment building, I suddenly felt a little self-conscious.

Only a handful of people had ever been inside and Vivienne was accustomed to luxury.

There was a palm tree by my front door and a cheerful welcome mat. Along the railing sat a tiny table and two chairs.

It overlooked the parking lot - not very exciting. I sat out there when I was restless in the small hours of the morning. Two miles from the ocean, I could enjoy a cool breeze and read by my porch light.

Entering my apartment, I kicked off my shoes and waited for her reaction. I could tell she'd been expecting a shitty dive and was pleasantly surprised.

Inside, my artwork was reprints and garage sale finds but they were pretty and arranged nicely.

I'd refinished several pieces of my furniture personally. My results weren't perfect but figuring out how to do basic things made me feel confident.

My living room contained oak tables and a plush camel-colored sleeper sofa - which doubled as my guest room. Above it was a framed poster of Van Gogh's *Almond Blossoms*.

Two large bookcases that went almost to the ceiling were filled to the brim with books of every kind. I'd collected them from garage sales, library sales, and thrift stores.

Reading was my passion. I kept my desk and computer in my bedroom so I wouldn't be tempted to read when I should be writing.

I didn't have a lot of decor, other than a few pictures of Campbell and me, the two family members I claimed, a couple of small statues, and candles.

More belongings meant more dusting and that was unnecessary in my mind.

I'd repainted my apartment a bright white when I moved in since it looked like it hadn't been painted in twenty years. I created a faux backsplash in the kitchen with peel-and-stick floor tiles I bought at a hardware store.

There wasn't much counter space but it was big enough to make a nice meal when the mood struck.

My dining area consisted of a table and two matching chairs. There was a vase of fresh flowers in the center that were beginning to wilt.

I'd gotten the three-piece set at a yard sale for ten dollars and sanded it smooth before applying the forest green paint. The change was significant.

There were eight vintage postcards of Italian cafés I found in a thrift store for cheap and put in oversized frames on the walls.

When Vivienne caught sight of the mahogany four-poster bed that dominated my bedroom, her jaw dropped.

It screamed, *"Have sex on me at once!"*

I'd draped the posts with deep burgundy swatches of faux velvet and a burgundy comforter on the bed. The overall effect was like something straight out of a medieval romance novel.

It was my favorite piece of furniture and the most expensive thing I owned. I'd purchased it for two hundred dollars in a dumpy local store and paid some guys with a truck to transport it.

I nearly killed poor Campbell having him hold the upper bars while I attached them with heavy bolts.

Vivienne stripped out of her clothes, climbed on the mattress, and spread her legs with a smile. "That ride left me aching…would you mind?"

Happy to oblige, I was out of my clothes in under a minute. As I climbed up beside her, I thought of the long silk scarves I kept in my nightstand.

Removing them, I stroked them through my palm. "Vivienne…?" She waited breathlessly. "May I tie you up?"

She hesitated - as I may have in her position. After all, she'd known me less than thirty-six hours.

"I…haven't done much of that."

"I'll be gentle."

"Alright."

Once Vivienne's wrists were loosely tied to the posts, I knelt beside her. "The bindings are loose. You can slip them if you need to." I could see the relief on her face. "Your safe word is *starfish*."

Removing a small but effective vibrator from the bedside drawer, it hummed when I turned it on.

Vivienne was not quiet as I fucked her with it while sucking her nipples to my satisfaction. I made her come three times and she was limp.

"I don't think…I can come anymore, Sarah."

Her pussy dripped on my sheets. I caressed her face and she licked her fluids from my fingers.

"How do you feel, Vivienne?"

"Boneless."

"Wonderful. Let's shower and figure out food. You need to get your energy back." After a slow kiss, I untied Vivienne and led her to my bathroom. She was exhausted. "Let me take care of you."

She kissed me and whispered, "I think…that's going to be your specialty, Sarah."

For some reason, I really liked the sound of that.

* * *

Once we were dry, I dropped one of my sleepshirts over Vivienne's head. I doubted she'd ever worn such a thing in her whole life.

She looked adorable.

"You relax on the couch and I'll go pick up something to eat. Do you like Middle Eastern food?" She nodded. "There's a great shawarma place around the corner. Garlic sauce to die for."

"We'll be lethal to each other after eating that but it makes my stomach growl."

I put on shorts, a t-shirt, and sneakers. Grabbing my helmet, I kissed her lightly and went to get the poor thing some nourishment.

Campbell's car was parked downstairs when I got back twenty minutes later. I internally groaned.

He would have *questions*.

I entered my apartment poised for awkwardness and found Camp chatting happily with Vivienne.

He stood up and kissed my lips. "Hey, babe! Don't feel like you need to feed me. I didn't give you any warning that I was coming."

"You know I always get extra. Grab napkins and drinks. We can sit around the coffee table."

My best friend was so fucking pretty. Six-one with silky brown hair, broad shoulders, and heterochromia - one brown eye, one blue-gray one. Smart, funny, and loyal to a fault, Campbell Lynch always had my back.

Once we were settled and shawarma was dripping through our fingers, I asked, "So. What, uh, did you guys talk about before I got here?"

Camp shot back, "Welp. She tried to tell me she was hiring you as a *model* at first. After I wiped my laughter-inspired tears, I suggested she try again. As if *your* goofy self is gonna pose for pictures all day, every day. I never heard such nonsense."

He wiggled his eyebrows at me and I waited. "You gonna be a ho, huh? About time you got paid. Your fine ass always out there in the streets for free…"

I snorted. "Stop it. You're ridiculous."

"I'm honest. It's why you love me best." Turning to look at Vivienne, he got serious. "Tell me you screen the clients?" Her eyes widened but she nodded. "They're all women? Sarah can beat the snot out of most folks but…I worry about some big dude."

"All women as clients. Uh, sometimes there are husbands or significant others…"

"Hmm." He said nothing else for almost a minute as he took a bite and chewed thoughtfully. "In those scenarios, are you strict on pregnancy prevention?"

I choked on my Dr. Pepper.

"What…? It's a valid question. You have young lady eggs and are the healthiest person I know. The wrong sperm gets all up in the business and…you know. You sure as hell don't need that."

Vivienne nodded. "We enforce even stricter policies if or when a male participates in an appointment."

Camp blotted his lips. "Okay then. I'm holding you personally responsible if anything happens to her." Smiling broadly, he added, "Love your eyebrows. Girl, who does them?"

Just like that, the mood lightened.

They chatted animatedly and I found myself happier than usual that he stopped by. He'd asked Vivienne questions I hadn't thought to ask and I realized that was foolish of me.

We cleaned up and put away the leftovers.

When Camp got ready to leave, he winked at Vivienne before kissing my lips. "Pee after sex. Those UTIs ain't no joke." I chuckled and he tipped up my chin. "Take care of yourself,

Sarah. I can't always be with you. Sometimes, you're a little too trusting. It would hurt me if anything happened."

"I will. Promise."

He hugged me and whispered in my ear, "Have fun, too. Earn that money. Come around when you need snuggles without bullshit."

"Thanks. Love you."

He straightened. "Love *you*. Thanks for feeding me. That garlic sauce means an extra half hour on the rowing machine tomorrow. Worth it."

With a wave, he was gone. It always gave me the tiniest ping of sadness.

Locking up, I returned to sit with Vivienne.

"The two of you are close," she noted.

"Yeah. Since we were freshmen in high school."

"You've been intimate." I turned my head to look at her in surprise. "It's obvious. I assume he's - let us call it - unavailable."

"Uh huh. He didn't think so at first." I shrugged. "It used to hurt but it's better these days. He's my best friend. Besides, it's not like I'm out here *lonely*."

"A lovely little orgasm, a quick chat about the week, and then I'm going to head home."

I really liked Vivienne's priorities.

After playtime, we showered together. Having company during the grooming process was strangely intimate. It made me realize I hadn't done it before.

A question on my mind all day had to be asked. While it was to satisfy my curiosity…it seemed fair.

"Do you have sex with men, Vivienne?"

We stepped from the shower onto fluffy bath mats and I toweled her dry.

"I enjoy being with both men and women. They each have their benefits." She towel-dried her hair. "Some of my clients are lesbians who want nothing to do with a dick. But…there are straight women who use my services also."

"Maybe not so straight," I quipped.

Vivienne laughed. "I started the business to cater specifically to women. Until recently, we were sorely overlooked by the majority of the sex industry."

I rolled my eyes. "Just look at porn."

"Exactly. What about fulfilling fantasy? Getting something extra your partner doesn't provide? Feeling at ease with a female lover in ways you maybe can't with male partners."

Thinking about men I knew who hired hookers, I murmured, "Easing basic loneliness."

"That's a big one, Sarah. Huge." She hung up her towel. "A lot of women know they want more of *something* - but they might not know what it is or how to get it. That's where you and the others come in."

Vivienne stroked her fingers over my cheek. "We have a lot to go over." *So true.* "I'm going to get dressed and wait for you in the living room."

I contemplated the last twenty-four hours of my life. I was excited and anxious to get started.

It would be a long time before I realized my initial naiveté about my new occupation.

Those first months, the only thing on my mind was the unique experience, endless pleasure, and imagining the stories I could write one day.

This vibration under my skin…

Since I was sixteen, I maintained a healthy appetite for carnal pleasure…but I didn't let it rule me. I couldn't start now.

Losing control was dangerous.

Like most people in my family, I had the tendency for addiction. I avoided excess in every area. I didn't drink, smoke, do recreational drugs, or date dangerous people because I didn't always trust myself to maintain my boundaries.

I was strong. I could handle being an escort…by taking what I needed and leaving the rest.

Looking back ten years later, I realize that I never once questioned the moral dilemma of being a sex worker. It never crossed my mind.

Then and now, I believe in the right of every person to make their own decisions – good or bad.

I didn't plan to hurt anyone and I hoped the people I crossed paths with would have similar methods of conducting their lives…so I wouldn't get hurt either.

Time would tell.

CHAPTER 7:
Devil in the Details

When I joined Vivienne in the living room fifteen minutes later, she was perusing my bookshelves. Music played softly from my stereo.

She held one of my favorite books - *Erotica: An Illustrated Anthology of Art and Literature* - and smiled when she heard my footsteps.

I was in shorts, a tank top, barefoot, and toweling my hair. She watched me turban the towel and I noticed a distinct sparkle in her eyes.

She'd asked me to be prepared to discuss business and I planned to exhibit my *mature* behavior.

Returning the book to the shelf, she joined me on the couch. We sat at opposite ends with glasses of fresh iced tea. She curled up in the corner with her long legs tucked beneath her, oblivious of her affect.

I resolved to ignore the stimuli.

She talked for a couple of hours about the business end of my new job while Fleetwood Mac and the Eagles played in the background.

"All your appointments will begin and end at my penthouse. I never have more than six escorts on staff at any one time to accommodate preparation, transportation, and space to recover."

"I like that there aren't like a dozen."

"We would all be overwhelmed. One of our drivers - Kylee or Max - will take you in either the Town Car or the limo to your appointments. I prefer that you *not* drive yourself. Someone needs to see you walk in and make sure you come back out."

"That makes sense," I agreed.

Some of my appointments would be overnights in which case a bag packed with my essentials would be transported to the appointment location.

Vivienne held up her fingers. "One, you are never to discuss your rates with a client. If they hand you cash or gifts, those are yours to keep above and beyond your fee. Two, keep your cell phone on you at all times, in case of emergency."

She hesitated and I tilted my head. "Three?"

"Sarah…don't fall in love."

I laughed. Vivienne didn't.

"You're serious…"

"Very. It's the riskiest part of this job."

"Uh…okay."

As far as etiquette, Vivienne thought I should go with what I knew. "You're good about sensing the needs of your lover. I think you'll be able to determine what the client wants and deliver it with satisfaction."

"I appreciate that."

She sipped her tea. "Some clients enjoy role-play, toys, and so forth - but most just want to have their world rocked by someone who knows how to eat pussy properly. You'll have no issue in that area."

I didn't doubt it.

"Now. About the participation of men during your appointments." Vivienne cleared her throat. "I *always* know beforehand. If I don't, there's a problem and you must leave immediately. You have the right to decline their involvement."

I couldn't hide my surprise. "Really?"

"Of course. Some of the women I employ are lesbians. Rolande and Ezbeth refuse to entertain men in any capacity." She paused before continuing. "However, there are situations where a client wants to fulfill her significant other's ultimate fantasy."

Snorting, I commented, "Ah, yes. The holy grail of jack-off material for straight men. Two women going at it and worshiping his *throbbing member* like the second coming."

She grinned. "They are *horribly* predictable, aren't they? I assure you, it isn't a common occurrence to have a man join. However, you can rest assured that we run a background check on all clients and their significant others. They must submit the results of a recent physical exam prior to any appointment."

"Got it. Anything else?"

"If you cancel an appointment, you'll service the client free of charge. This is really availing yourself as a love slave for two hours. Most clients pay anyway." She winked. "That brings me to the money…"

"Better than working in retail, I'd imagine."

"For a typical overnight - which the majority of long-term clients prefer - you'll earn seven-hundred-and-fifty after I take sixty-five percent off the top." She paused and asked, "Does that seem excessive?"

"I guess that depends on your overhead."

"Good answer…and accurate."

My eyes widened as she explained. Running a high-end escort agency had a lot of moving pieces behind the scenes…and they were not cheap.

Vivienne clothed and groomed her staff, arranged all the details, and booked hotels when necessary.

Her ladies were chauffeur-driven and encouraged to crash at Vivienne's condo to rest after an appointment. She covered medical expenses and even provided financial advice.

Then there was the risk.

She managed all the money. Everything funneled through her legitimate businesses and all of her escorts were paid as employees. Each appointment was listed as a gig.

In the studio, pictures of every escort hung on display. Clients were billed, on the books, as regular customers for the studio who purchased high-class boudoir images as discerning collectors of adult art.

We received paychecks every two weeks and paid taxes and all the rest on every cent we made.

Other than cash tips and gifts, of course. There were a *lot* of those.

Everything remained above-board and the IRS remained blissfully unaware.

Before I ever earned a dime for Vivienne's service, a lot of money was invested in me.

The day after I agreed to become a paid escort, I was scheduled for a complete physical with a doctor Vivienne kept on retainer - which explained why he'd see me on Sunday.

I'd consult with a wardrobe stylist regularly. That person would be responsible for dressing me from head to toe. They would decide on everything that went on my body - from panties to accessories.

To remove and shape my body hair, an esthetician was being brought in.

A professional makeup artist would take care of my hair, makeup, fingers, and toes before my appointments.

Having a personal trainer was expected and familiar. I didn't expect to be out of my element with them.

Over time, coaches might be brought in to teach me things like etiquette, dancing, or acting - depending on the needs of my clients or my own interests.

The honor system was a big part of the industry - with clients and escorts. If a client requested something unusual, they knew to get an updated total. Little *extras* were common practice.

Vivienne often received gifts intended for us to wear on our next appointment. Items like clothing, jewelry, or toys.

It was a strange and wonderful world.

When we were done going over the particulars, I walked Vivienne to her car, opened her door, and handed her inside.

She rolled down the window. "You're going to be really good at this, Sarah. See you tomorrow."

A few of my neighbors knew me but I had to wonder what some of them thought about me over the years I lived in that apartment.

Returning to the second floor balcony, I sat in one of the chairs and propped my feet in the other one.

I looked forward to the work with curiosity more than anything. I liked sex and found people interesting. I figured if things went sideways, I could blame it on my youth later.

Besides, who'd believe this shit anyway?

CHAPTER 8:
Staff & Stable

After a couple of hours of sleep, I went for a run, took another shower, and read a book I'd read a dozen times before.

At ten o'clock the next morning, I rode my motorcycle to Vivienne's. I took the long way down since I wasn't due there until eleven. A1A was the main two-lane road that ran along the ocean on the east coast of Florida and I loved the view.

Sunday morning, Miami was still asleep.

I wore my standard outfit: jeans, t-shirt, and running shoes. No makeup, no styling shit in my hair, no jewelry. I believed in the minimalist way of thinking…*way* before it was cool.

That characteristic separated me from most of the American population. If I didn't need it, or didn't have the cash to pay for it, I didn't buy it. Period.

When I pulled into Vivienne's parking garage, an attendant keyed me into her elevator. The older man talked to my chest - and only my chest - until the elevator doors opened and I stepped inside.

Men were so simple…I tell you what.

Unlike the day before, the penthouse was bustling with activity when I walked in. Several strangers openly stared at me.

I didn't doubt they were calculating what kind of effort it would take to turn me into some kind of sex kitten. Pretty sure I've established that I wasn't exactly into the glitz and glamor as a young woman.

I guess the pros in the room saw that right off.

Compared to the kind of women I imagined did this type of job, I would be a *roll up your sleeves and apply some elbow grease* kind of project.

Tucking my helmet under my arm, I smiled as two women approached and introduced themselves. They both wore tailored pants, dress shirts, and vests - their jackets were missing.

"I'm Kylee. One of the drivers." She was a few inches shorter than me and real pretty with pixie-cut strawberry blonde hair and big gray eyes. "Um, are you Sarah?"

"I am." I held out my hand and we shook. "Nice to meet you, Kylee." *There was something strangely sedate about her.*

Her smile was slow. "I like your vibe already."

The woman beside her reminded me of the original *Wonder Woman* comics. She was six-one, leanly muscular, with dark brown hair and green eyes.

"Max." She extended her hand and I took it. Her fingers held mine a beat longer than I expected. "I drive the limo. Welcome to the agency."

"Hi, Max. Thanks." *Intense and seriously hot.*

They sized me up, looking a bit doubtful. I didn't blame them. Hell, I wasn't convinced clients were going to pay actual money to fuck me.

Max murmured, "I'll let Viv know you're here."

I nodded and found a place to stand out of the way to watch what everyone was doing.

A photography area was set up in the living room, complete with lights and backdrops.

The den on the first floor had been converted into several smaller spaces separated by screens.

One was a full beauty salon. On the other side of the screen was a masseuse table and opposite that one was a reclining chair and what looked to be some sort of crockpot.

Max leaned around the door. "Vivienne is with the personal shopper. She says to come on back."

I followed her to Viv's office and stopped just inside the door. Max leaned against the wall beside me and crossed her arms.

It appeared the man brought an entire damn store with him. Everything from lingerie to formal gowns – each with accessories – was displayed on the furniture and hanging from rolling clothing racks around the room.

Vivienne looked great. Her hair was swept into a sleek chignon and small reading glasses sat perched on the end of her nose. She wore a knee-length suede skirt, matching heels, and an iridescent pearl blouse.

Hottest librarian ever.

I drank from the bottle of water Max offered and watched as Vivienne and the unidentified male coordinated my new look.

She turned when she heard me cap the water and gave me a warm smile. I received a demure peck on the cheek that made me laugh internally.

"Sarah, I'd like you to meet Walker Gibbons. He's going to be responsible for making you feel positively *radiant* when you walk out the door."

The man was stunning. He looked like *he* should be modeling for nude photos instead of dressing strangers in pretty clothes while fretting about the right shoes.

I held out my hand. "It's a plea-…"

Without a word, he grabbed my breasts in his palms. "These are heavy, Vivienne. You don't want to go with spaghetti straps that will press into her shoulders. We need to avoid anything strapless. She'll look like she's falling out and not in a good way."

I absolutely *hate it* when someone acts like you aren't standing there. He continued discussing what colors to *never* put me in - seeming to forget he still had possession of my tits.

Clearing my throat, he stopped mid-sentence and glared at me as if I'd interrupted the Pope's Mass.

"That's real interestin', Walker. Yellow is definitely *not* my color…*so* right. Anyway, how about releasin' my tits? And next time, consider shakin' hands first, you *fuckin'* caveman."

Max grunted beside me.

He released me after a firm squeeze and I decided he wasn't nearly as good-looking as I originally thought. In fact, within seconds I couldn't stand his ass.

"What an accent. Where exactly are you from…er, *Sarah*, is it? You sound like Daisy Duke."

His condescending tone made my blood boil.

I didn't give a damn that he was six inches taller than me and built like an NFL quarterback. "I'm from Texas. Want me to show you what we do to swingin' dicks with grabby hands where I come from?"

He bent and whispered, "Feisty."

I whispered back, "Fucker."

Vivienne interjected cautiously, "Walker. Refrain from getting your ass kicked by Sarah on day one. Please and thank you."

We practically growled at each other.

He rolled his eyes at me. "Lucky for *you*, I can even make *trailer trash* look good."

Max warned, "Dude…"

I smiled tightly. "Lucky for *you*, I haven't bashed your pretty face in with my helmet. *Yet*."

I'm fairly certain he saw something in my eyes that caused him to straighten and take a step back.

He held up his hands and gave me a placating smile. "We don't have to be friends to work together."

"Damn good thing, I guess." Quietly, I added, "Don't touch me without my consent again or I will rack your balls into your goddamn throat. I don't need *any* job bad enough to put up with that."

After a pause, he nodded. "Understood. My apologies, Sarah." He held out his hand. "Let's start over. I'm Walker. I'll be dressing you."

"Awesome." I shook his hand and dropped it instantly. "Tell me what you want."

"Kirkland?" he called. A slender black man bounced into the room with a huge smile. "This is Sarah. We need her measurements."

"Hi! I'm Kirkland. Lots of people call me Kirk. You can call me whatever." Grabbing my free hand in both of his, he shook it excitedly. "You're like sunshine! My grandmother would call you peaches and cream. You got meat on your bones. Girl, you're gonna be so damn pretty in our clothes."

"Thank you, Kirkland." The difference between this man and his boss was jarring. I took a deep breath. "It's really nice to meet you. Tell me what you need and I'll try not to be any trouble."

"Trouble? *You*? I don't see how. You're sweet as a sugar cookie! Come on, honey. I'm gonna ask you to strip to your panties but think of me like your big sister. I'm only looking for the sake of the clothes."

"That's fine. I'm not shy."

I followed Kirkland out of the room and heard Vivienne say, "I can't believe you managed to piss her off in less than five seconds. Jesus, Walker."

"You fucking know better," Max added. "Do *not* pull that shit again."

Later, I replayed the interaction in my mind and tried to figure out how the man got under my skin so fast.

It had taken me *years* to rein in my temper.

I decided to keep my interactions with him as minimal as possible going forward.

CHAPTER 9:
Photo Shoot

For the next hour, I did what had to be done. When Kirkland had everything he needed from me, we returned to the den.

I wore a properly fitted bra - which was apparently different from the size I'd been wearing - and matching bikini panties.

Keeping my gaze just past Walker's shoulder, I didn't speak. I allowed the two men to dress me and pin where alterations were needed.

More than once, I had to remove the bra entirely but I was careful not to make eye contact with the idiot.

Vivienne watched from a chair in the corner and made occasional suggestions. Max remained utterly silent in the position she'd originally taken.

After several outfit changes, I begrudgingly admitted that Walker's sense of color, texture, and style was extraordinary. He added the right touches to every outfit without seeming like he was trying.

I didn't like *him* but his skills commanded respect.

When they were finished, Kirkland appeared in front of me again. "Here's a robe, honey. I'll hold it while you take off the bra and panties. You gotta be naked as the day you were born for the next part."

Tying the robe, I turned to follow Vivienne. I paused at the door and looked back. "Thanks for the help. Y'all are good at what you do. I've never pretended to know anything or care about this stuff."

I moved on to a manicure - happy they kept the length short and blunt - and my first pedicure with a small woman who never said a word. She also cleaned my eyebrows but left them thick.

I'd always been careful with my grooming but never treated myself to things like this.

When the hair stylist got me in her chair, Vivienne delivered firm instructions. "Neaten it…do not fuck with it. It's unique from our other girls."

"Yes, ma'am." The girl looked about my age and laughed at me in the mirror. Lucia was from Puerto Rico and I found her adorable. "She's afraid I'll give you a straight bob or something? Tsk! As if I'd destroy this head of hair!"

She kept up a steady stream of chatter throughout the cut. I learned about her entire life in a matter of forty minutes. She kissed me on the cheek when I got up to leave.

Waxing was my next stop.

Wait…*waxing?*

I laid down on the table in the robe I'd been given earlier, interested in how they planned to make me hair-free without a razor.

When the robe was moved aside and warm wax was spread on my most sensitive flesh, it felt nice. She smoothed soft cotton fabric over the wax and that was fine, too.

However, *removal* of the wax must have been perfected by some Nazi bastard.

I actually threw myself off the table when the first of two strips came away with a horrible ripping sound.

"Miss Sarah, you must return to the table!" the small women ordered urgently.

"What? Oh, no, I'm sorry! I think we're done here."

I backed toward the screen. She was flustered and I wasn't sure she understood my babbling because she looked perplexed at my reaction.

No, thanks.

"Sarah?" Vivienne peeked around the screen. "What are you doing, darling?"

"I don't like this."

"I know. I'm sorry." Stroking her fingers into my hair, she kissed me deeply. "Beauty is pain, darling."

It was the perfect distraction for Ma-Ying to rip away the second strip.

I didn't hold back my scream.

Walker skidded into the space, took in the scene, and mumbled, "Natural redhead. Nice."

Then Max grabbed him by the back of his neck and yanked him from the room.

Vivienne patted my cheek, reminded me the doctor would arrive in twenty minutes, and followed Walker.

Ma-Ying intended to do my armpits, legs, and the crack of my ass. I accepted that I wouldn't escape nor did I want anyone else in the room.

I returned to the table with a whimper and submitted myself to the process. She even did the tops of my feet and toes.

People paid money for this shit?

In the end, I managed to thank her through my tears and admitted the new silkiness of my legs was hard to match with a razor.

Dr. Reinhardt was a kind man in his fifties. He didn't pretend I was a patient of non-gender but was professional otherwise. In a serious voice, he declared me fit and in need of an older man.

I politely declined.

He gave me a long sigh and an endearing chuckle. "It's always *no* but I can't help but ask. A pleasure to meet you, my dear. Please call if you feel under the weather or need advice on birth control, etcetera."

"I appreciate that, Dr. Reinhardt."

In the kitchen, I took another bottle of water from the fridge and waited to see what was next on the strangely *exhausting* agenda.

Vivienne walked into the room with Max beside her and poured a glass of wine. "How are you holding up? The first day is always the hardest since you don't know what to expect."

"Hanging in there," I told her honestly.

"He bothered you." The words were said quietly and I didn't misunderstand what she meant.

"It was…the *arrogance* of touching me intimately combined with the *dismissiveness* of me as a human. Like I was nothing more than a *thing*." I shook my head. "I've dealt with situations like that before. It hit me wrong. I'm fine now."

"I understand." She reached out to hold my hand. "I'd never have someone in my circle who would hurt my girls. Still, I'm sorry, Sarah."

With a bright smile, I said, "It's in the past. What do you need me to do next?"

Vivienne maintained eye contact for a long moment. "We're taking your boudoir photos."

"Uh, my skin is still red from the torture session."

"No worries at all. They'll even your skin tone in editing. So, about the photo shoot…"

Her voice trailed away and I narrowed my eyes with my hand on my hip. "Let me guess…the asshole *hot guy* is a regular *prop* in those things, right?"

"Walker is *normally* a sweetheart. You two blended like oil and water. As in…not at all." She lifted one side of her mouth. "We use his back or chest to frame the man-woman shots and Kylee or Max for the all-female shots. The only face seen is yours. Can you try for me?"

"Walker is here a lot…that means his presence is something I'll need to get used to. It's important to you that we get along. Right?" Vivienne hesitated before she nodded. "Then I'll work on it."

"He's the best at what he does in South Florida, Sarah. Trust me and work with him. He promised to be civil."

I hummed an affirmative as the man himself entered the room.

"Thank you. I have to meet a vendor offsite for about an hour. Will you be okay if I'm not here?"

"Of course." *Beating his ass probably wouldn't even wind me.*

She kissed my cheek and turned to leave.

Walker caught me staring at her figure as she walked away and asked, "Are you only into pussy?"

Max leaned against the counter but said nothing.

"If *you* possessed the last cock on Earth, I'd definitely opt for straight pussy until death." Max muffled a snort. "Otherwise, I'm not particular. I was appreciating the vintage seam in her stockings. Not a common look so I was going to ask if that was *your* touch."

Grabbing another water, I headed for the living room. "Never-fucking-mind though, dude. Let me get through today like an adult."

Kirkland waited with the first bra and panty ensemble and I dropped the robe to put it on.

The photographer introduced himself as Blaine and gestured to the green chaise where I'd played with Viv the day before. "Do you have any hard stops I need to know about, Sarah?"

"I've never done this so I'm not sure."

"Don't worry about anything." He gently nudged me against the back of the chaise and adjusted the pillows. "That's an excellent backdrop for you. Stretch one leg out. Arms over your head. Just like that. Glance up and to the side. Perfect. Next outfit."

I did dozens of sensual poses alone and even more with Max and Kylee. They started in their suits but Max ended up in rolled shirtsleeves and slacks while I was naked.

In one, I reclined between Max's long legs with my cheek on her abs. As I sat up, I glanced at her groin and back to her face. It was hard to hide my curiosity and she winked.

For the next set, I was chest to chest with Kylee's naked upper body while I stared into the camera and kissed her shoulder.

No matter my dislike of the man, Walker chose ideal pieces to complement my coloring and figure.

We did a casual series on Viv's balcony where I wore my own worn jeans, a soft tank top, a pair of boots, and a straw cowboy hat over my loose curls.

I was surprised at the choice of attire. "Didn't expect boots and a hat after your *Daisy Duke* comment."

The man shrugged. "She was hot."

"Uh, okay then."

There was a formal series with me on the main staircase. Walker dressed me in a gold sequined gown, high heels, and delicate accessories. Lucia quickly created a loose chignon at my nape.

I looked older and sophisticated - neither of which I could usually pull off convincingly. As I started to descend the stairs, I gratefully took Max's hand to keep from falling.

"Thanks. I'd be mortified if I tripped. I never wear long gowns like this."

"You're doing great." She gave my fingers a squeeze and walked away.

Walker appeared in nothing but black leather pants and stretched out on the leather sofa in Vivienne's staged library.

I understood why they used him in these sessions. His body was phenomenal.

He was about six-two, lean, and chiseled like he spent hours at the gym every day. His shaggy black hair was swept off his stupidly gorgeous face and his blue eyes glowed from his tanned skin.

Pretty as hell with a shit personality.

Kirkland held out my next outfit and I groaned. A see-through emerald green top that spread into an upside down V just under my breasts and matching thong. I was *basically* naked.

"You can do it, Sarah," Max murmured.

I crossed the room like I was going to my execution. My eyes widened when Walker held out his hand.

"It's alright, Sarah. Just hit the poses Blaine wants and it will be over quickly."

The photographer finished setting up the lights. "Just like with Kylee and Max, your body is going to block the view of Walker's face. First, I want you to sit on his abdomen and cross your legs."

"You're *kidding*. I'm way heavier than I look…"

Max laughed. "It's fine. He can take it. Up you go."

She lifted me to sit on Walker's belly. It was firm and hot. I'd never felt so self-conscious in my life.

I tried to figure out how to suspend all my weight from the man under me.

Blaine murmured, "Relax, Sarah. Let's tilt your torso a bit. Put your elbow on the back of the sofa - hand in your hair. Cross your legs - top knee touching his side - give me a bored expression."

I was neither comfortable nor bored so it took a while to get the effect Blaine wanted.

"Now straddle Walker's belly, bend a bit, and look over your shoulder back here at me."

"Let me get down and start over."

"No need." Walker lifted me and gave me time to put my knees on either side of his body.

"Great. Hand on his shoulder to hold yourself up, Sarah. Excellent side slope of the breast. Your hair will block his face. Walker, hold her knee…now her hip. Yeah, I like that one better. Excellent. Sarah, get on the floor between his knees."

"What…?"

"Let's remove the top so we get a clean line of her back with all that hair."

The barely-there fabric was taken from me by Kirkland and Lucia came to drop my hair down my back.

"That's it. Hands on his knees, Sarah. Look back at me. Love that. Walker, stretch both arms along the back of the couch and drop your head back so all I get is your jawline. Lift a bit and lean over his lap, Sarah. Exactly. That should do it. Good job today!"

Walker straightened his head to look at me as I instantly moved away from his crotch.

His gaze flicked to my chest and I figured he could see the flush that gave away my nervousness.

Our eyes locked for a moment and I didn't like that he got *any* physical reaction from me…or that he knew about it.

Max helped me stand and Kirkland dropped a robe around my shoulders. The tension-filled moment evaporated and I was glad.

Blaine ran the photo studio and would select the images to hang on display as well as those to go into my portfolio.

He seemed like the perfect gentleman. I found out later that he'd attended the same college in Connecticut as Vivienne and Monica.

Calling me over, he said, "Take a look, Sarah." Standing beside him, I watched as my photo session images started showing up one by one on the monitor. "Good stuff. Vivienne will love them."

"I-I'm glad. That was nerve wracking."

I was unbelievably relieved it was over.

CHAPTER 10:
My New Coworkers

I was exhausted and sore. All the running I did didn't wipe me out like this. I attained a new respect for models and actresses.

Just as we finished the photo shoot, a couple of the other escorts arrived to prepare for their evening appointments. They seemed like a *couple*.

They smiled warmly and welcomed me to the company. As they rushed off to get ready, one called, "We'll be seeing a lot of each other!"

Then they disappeared into hair and makeup.

I padded down the hall and the masseuse sent me into the steam room for ten minutes where I almost fell asleep.

Finally, it was time for my first massage. It was glorious. I could have stayed on that table all day.

Georgette's fingers pulled every ache and pain from each area of my body…replacing it with pure warmth. She removed stiffness I didn't even know I had until I stood up and felt about as substantial as a toasted marshmallow.

Afterwards, I took a quick shower and was about to put my daily wear back on when Walker asked me to try one last dress, chosen for my first client.

I grumbled and whined about it the whole time I was in the wardrobe room.

I returned to the living room, in a pair of four-inch heels. The photographer and his equipment were gone, leaving no trace of their presence behind.

In the long mirror at the elevator, I studied my appearance. The emerald green dress came mid-thigh on me, with an empire waist and cap sleeves, flowing loosely along the bottom. The neck scooped low enough to be seductive, without looking cheap. There was even matching jewelry to complete the ensemble.

Elegant and beautiful.

"I have to admit Vivienne was right about your wardrobe skills. This outfit is perfect."

He stood behind me, gathering my hair in an upswept style. "This is how you need to wear this mane of hair with this dress or it will appear bigger than the clothing and overwhelm it."

The smile he gave was warm over my shoulder. He had a look in his eyes I'd seen a thousand times.

He was still taller than me, even in heels. A dark god of sensuality who was muscular in all the right places.

The dress wasn't the only thing that was perfect.

Walker's problem was *conceit*. He knew his effect on women and exploited it. He figured he'd have a little sample of the newbie.

I saw from the beginning that he expected me to fall all over myself to impress him. That wasn't me. That would *never* be me.

I didn't chase people.

Particularly men.

Walker worked his charm on me, but honestly, I preferred sex partners who weren't narcissists.

"Thank you for your styling expertise. I'm going to change and take a nap. When Vivienne gets back, I'll take her for a ride on my bike, get something to eat, and hopefully fuck her until she passes out."

From the living room, Max laughed.

"You get one chance to make a first impression…and I was not impressed. Your pretty face and hot bod won't change my mind."

Walking to the guest room, I changed into my own clothes. When I emerged, he was gone. The only sounds in the condo came from the salon as women talked and laughed.

My predictions for the evening proved accurate. Sometimes, it was fun to be me.

***

Over my first week with the agency, I met the other escorts and the rest of Vivienne's key staff. She chose women who were unique in some way, sometimes only in a way she could sense.

I guess the *small town girl* quality was my thing. I'd been that girl most of my life so I didn't mind.

She had some interviews over the years that had gone badly, a few girls who didn't work out, but her overall success rate was uncanny.

Viv knew people. She knew which girls to match with which clients and always kept them coming back for more.

Ezbeth Burgess was from the United Kingdom. She'd been with Vivienne about three years. She vowed to never return to the cold and damp she'd been raised in outside of London but swore prettily if you dared to disparage her homeland.

She was a dainty lily, pale and blonde. She was one of those people who could discuss any topic intelligently and I envied her grasp of the world at large. She also had the flexibility of Stretch Armstrong. It was quite the party trick.

Rolande Benjamin was from Kingston, Jamaica. She'd grown up during a time when her country was experiencing political unrest and violence. Her adult self oozed relaxation and primal body heat.

Her hair was usually done in tiny plaits down her back and her skin shimmered like amber. She wanted to change the world. Her laugh was infectious and her passion unrestrained.

Paige Wilkinson was Connecticut born and raised. She couldn't help her charm, good breeding, and sophistication. It was like the air she breathed.

She was beautiful in an Audrey Hepburn way with shiny dark hair and alabaster skin. She knew everything there was to know about art and would be happy to go on and on about it all damn night if you let her. She came from money but worked for Vivienne as a sort of life experience. The wealthy could be strange like that.

Sonja Grant hailed from California and the term *blonde bombshell* was made to suit a woman like her. Sonja's mom had been a top supermodel and saw nothing wrong with her little girl living the same life she did for the most part.

There was not an outfit created that could conceal her ample curves. Sonja was never without cherry red lipstick, perfectly applied. She planned to be a physical therapist - which was good since her clients probably needed it when she got through with them.

Lyra Bell was born and raised in Chicago. She was a huge environmental activist like her parents. She'd been raised by happy hippies. She did her thing but wasn't pretentious or condescending about it.

When she wasn't working, Lyra's style was Bohemian chic. She wore clothes made of natural fibers, sandals for the most part, and volunteered at the local animal shelter. She had extremely curly black hair, blue eyes, and sported a perpetual tan from one community project to the next.

There were college girls who only worked over summer break and models who picked up dates between shoots to help ends meet.

Kylee drove the Town Car and was positively adorable. Short strawberry blonde hair and gray eyes gave her a younger appearance than her actual twenty-seven years.

Both of her parents were dead and she'd been raised by an older sister who went to school with Vivienne. Kylee wasn't a working girl…but I had the feeling she possessed a fascinating past.

Max - short for Maxine - drove the limo. She topped six feet and owned it, maintained an unbelievable air of sexuality that felt ambiguous, and seemed to regularly sport a fake cock…or something equally interesting.

She had straight mink brown hair to the middle of her back, but it was always wrapped in a complicated knot at the base of her neck.

Since some appointments actually took place *inside* the limo, Max was the assigned driver. If there was ever trouble, she was prepared to handle it.

The imagery was pretty hot.

Both drivers were trained in hand-to-hand combat and had licenses to carry concealed weapons. They never left home without them.

Mrs. Quincy was the housekeeper and personal assistant to Vivienne. She was a widow with no children who looked on Vivienne as the daughter she'd never had.

Vivienne cooked up her *business plan* while still in college. Mrs. Quincy was an overworked, underpaid administrator in the registrar's office at the time. She jumped at the chance to start a new life.

Her smaller apartment was on the third floor of the same building. Her duties included scheduling their appointments and keeping the books. Everyone reported to her.

Over the years I worked with Viv, I learned a lot about the backgrounds of her people.

Ma-Ying's daughter was once one of Vivienne's girls – which supplied the money she needed to bring her parents from Vietnam.

She'd been discovered through her photos at the studio and now modeled around the world. Ma-Ying stayed on to help with beautifying the rest of the girls and lived in a nearby condo paid for by her devoted daughter.

Dr. Reinhardt was Vivienne's doctor when she was a young girl. She trusted him completely and used the caregiver to keep her girls safe and healthy.

He enjoyed seeing some of the most beautiful young women he'd ever laid eyes on. He happily fulfilled his naughty fantasies with the widows who lived in his 55-plus community.

So he said. I suspected he had a secret thing going with Mrs. Quincy - who was still a hot ticket at fifty-six.

Lucia had skill with any type or texture of hair. She also did the escorts' makeup. Her husband brought her to the States and promptly abandoned her for greener pastures. Instead of returning home to her family, she took cosmetology courses at night and was grateful to Vivienne for her dream job.

Blaine worked in a club as a flash bartender. He'd been disowned by his family when they found out about his sexual orientation but never lost his positive attitude.

He was skilled behind a camera and made a sizable living on the side doing weddings and bar mitzvahs. Women tended to fall for him despite his being gay. He was always a good sport about it.

There were never more than six escorts at a time. Vivienne believed in keeping things simple and not getting greedy. The system worked well for her and kept her pretty ass out of trouble.

When other madams were indicted, Vivienne's business thrived and survived.

It wasn't an easy business but Viv made it look that way. In the end, it was hard for her to know when it was past time for her to quit.

That story comes later.

CHAPTER 11:
The Attorney

November 2009

Before I knew it, Friday arrived…as well as my first appointment as a paid escort.

I could barely contain my nervousness.

When I started thinking about the luxury I was being exposed to for the first time - worrying about getting accustomed to it - doing my laundry in the coin machines at my apartment building delivered a welcome dose of reality.

I'd come from nothing and too much had already been taken from me at eighteen. Staying grounded, true to myself, was vital to my future happiness.

No matter how tempting some aspects might be as I dove into a glittering new world.

I showed up at Vivienne's place Friday evening earlier than scheduled. It was a habit born of anxiety that I might be late.

The nerves were really beginning to kick in. I figured it was normal under the circumstances. Lyra admitted to almost puking on her first client.

Someone would have to stop me from disappearing and changing my name if that happened to me.

To relax and prepare me for my first outing, I had a facial, massage, manicure, and pedicure.

After my shower, Lucia gave me an upsweep that added necessary years to my appearance. Then she applied makeup artfully to enhance my full lips and the shape of my eyes. She was outstanding at following my less-is-more request.

I was grateful. Looking into the mirror and not recognizing the person staring back at me would probably shake me in ways I wasn't ready to handle.

After donning an emerald green bra and panties set, I stepped into a gorgeous pair of heels.

Max paused at the open door and said, "Wow." I blushed lightly. "Nervous?" I nodded. "You look beautiful. Don't try to be anyone but yourself. That will have the biggest impact."

"Thanks, Max."

"See you later."

She walked away and Vivienne joined me looking as nervous as I felt.

Pondering the shoes, I asked, "Do you think the shoes are too much? With the height and all?"

She looked me over from head to toe. "No, Sarah. They're perfect. You aren't used to wearing such things but you will be soon. Are they comfortable?"

"Not sure I could *dance* in them but they're fine. I want to learn how to pull off elegant. It's new for me. I'll, uh, talk to Walker about it for future dates." I chose my words carefully. "Is my client tall?"

I *wanted* details about my appointment but was honestly kind of scared to ask.

She moved behind me and smoothed her palms over my upper arms. "She'll be close to your height in heels. Are you nervous?"

With a small shrug, I admitted, "Not really. I guess…I don't want to make an ass of myself." About that, I was deadly serious. "Also, what if I'm not what this person is expecting?"

Vivienne laughed in disbelief. "No worries there, Sarah. You'd be a pleasant surprise to anyone. Can I get you anything? I can pour you a glass of wine or give you a valium to settle your nerves."

How easily she offered made me frown internally but I schooled my expression.

"No thanks. I can barely handle Tylenol." I turned from the mirror. "I'm fine. At least, I will be. Rookie nerves. I'll see you in the morning."

Vivienne immediately relaxed. With a nod, she kissed me softly and left the room.

I pulled on the flowing mini-dress Walker picked and added the understated emeralds at my ears and throat. It really was a pretty outfit.

One last glance and I went to the living room. It seemed there was always a gathering of one kind or another at Vivienne's.

Since all the escorts began their evenings at her condominium, there were periods of a lot of activity. The dates were spaced so Kylee and Max could get everyone where they needed to be.

Vivienne's place featured five luxurious bedrooms for preparations and morning-after recovery.

There was a *do not disturb* rule when she was interviewing a new girl - as there had been with me the prior weekend. When that happened, all preparations occurred at the studio, which was similarly well equipped.

Learning information like that reinforced the importance that I not get emotionally attached to Viv. She maintained sexual relationships with multiple people. I knew falling for her new teenage escort wasn't in her plans.

I was an investment.

Understanding that basic fact - and watching for it with my clients as well - saved misunderstandings and hurt feelings during the time I worked for her.

Glancing up, I watched as Rolande descended the stairs in a panther-like strut. I was jealous of how smoothly she manipulated the marble steps in black four-inch stilettos. She wore a black faux fur coat that came to mid-calf.

I didn't understand the fashion choice. We were in Florida. It was hot as hell and *rarely* cool enough for a coat.

She stopped in front of me when she reached the bottom of the stairs and opened the coat. Beneath, she wore a black thong and shimmering pasties on her nipples.

Her body was curvy, tight, and inviting. It was impossible not to respond to the image she presented.

She smiled, fully aware of the reaction she caused, and closed the coat. "I have an anxious client waiting, pet. Perhaps we will talk another time about the shine I see in your eyes, yes? Have fun while you work…it makes all the difference."

Leaning forward, Rolande kissed my cheek. Then she sighed softly at my ear before pulling back and walking into the open elevator.

Both hands spread to her sides on the railing, her head dropped back, and the coat fell open in the soft light. A breathtaking creature to watch…and she was well aware of that fact.

Walker stepped out of the salon and stared at me appreciatively. I waited for sarcastic comments but he remained silent. Bending to adjust my hem, Walker subtly smelled the delicate perfume I'd applied.

He stepped back. "You look remarkable."

"Thank you." I avoided looking him in the eye.

Vivienne nodded at my finished appearance and hustled me into the elevator when it returned. She wrung her hands as the doors closed. I found it charming, almost maternal.

I would *rarely* think of her in such a way.

Rolande's appointment would take place entirely in the limo driven by Max so Kylee drove me in the Town Car. The windows were dark and I was glad for the privacy to settle my racing thoughts.

I'd learned from Vivienne I was going to the Broward Center for the Performing Arts. I would be attending my first opera.

It wasn't something I enjoyed personally and silently hoped my client wouldn't quiz me about it.

Kylee pulled to the curb at the valet stand and I forced myself to wait, as instructed, for her to come around and open my door.

Stepping from the back, I was thankful I didn't fall on my face. She quietly reminded me where she'd pick me up the following morning. "Take a deep breath. You've got this, Sarah."

"Thank you, Kylee."

Clearing my throat softly, I didn't look back as I walked through the doors alone.

I felt people staring. Part of me wanted to run back to the car. Instead, I straightened my shoulders, lifted my chin, and pretended I belonged.

Receiving more scrutiny as I crossed the lobby, I realized people weren't focusing on me because I seemed out of place.

I wore thousands of dollars in clothes and jewels and honestly looked fantastic. The realization settled my panic a bit.

My ticket was in the clutch bag I carried and an usher showed me to the private box of my client. I walked through the small door, then a curtained partition, and waited for my eyes to adjust.

In the dim lighting, a woman stood and turned.

Monica Carter - my *attorney* and recent *boss* - was apparently my first *client*.

I gasped softly, lost for words. Shame slammed into me as if I'd been caught stealing.

She was appealing. It wasn't the first time I'd thought so. With her black hair, gray eyes, and glowing olive skin, she was a vision. The burgundy brushed silk sheath she wore looked divine on her figure.

After a few tense moments, I collected myself and somehow managed to lower myself to a chair without falling. She sat beside me and took my hand.

"I don't understand," I whispered.

"I know it's a bit of a shock, Sarah." She rubbed my hand between hers. My mind raced frantically. "I've known Vivienne since college. I knew you'd be perfect for her…and for me." She spoke in soothing tones meant to calm and reassure me.

I managed to meet her gaze. "You're a…*scout* for her or something?"

"Not usually. Not in the way you're thinking. Your situation has always been unique. I thought you'd be a good fit." She continued to gently rub the inside of my wrist with her thumb. "I apologize for the sin of omission."

Though I'd always found her attractive, there were reasons I *never* entertained having a relationship with her - even one that was casual.

Monica had a long-time lover. They'd been together for fifteen years and lived in a house they purchased together. I met Jade when I was invited to their house for a barbecue.

"I-I'm not sure what to say." I didn't want to offend her. "Aren't I crossing a *line* here?"

With a smile, she answered, "I told Viv your moral compass would definitely balk. We agreed that I'd be a good test for that reason. Though you know *me* personally - as well as my *partner* - you won't always know if your client is involved, married, has kids at home, etcetera. You have to compartmentalize certain aspects of this job."

Glancing at the polished wood railing along the balcony, I considered what she was saying. She gave me silence and stillness to do that.

Either I could show up and *be an escort* - no matter the client's circumstances I may or may not know - or I couldn't. That was the real test.

For someone like me, it wasn't an easy task. I *liked* Monica's significant other. I knew if I went through with this appointment, I could never look Jade in the eye again.

There would be *no way* to hide my guilt.

Lying had never come easily to me and I wasn't about to start trying to do it well now.

Without looking at her, I said quietly, "You can never invite me to your house again. I can't interact with you outside of *this* going forward. I won't go to your office if we need to meet. That's your *real* life. Not this." I met her eyes. "Do you understand?"

Monica nodded. "I do. I'll keep you on the payroll for a while as my clerk. You need the cover." She sighed heavily. "I know it's difficult to separate the two areas but…I'm aching to touch you, Sarah. I have been for a-a while now. Having you as a *client* and then an *employee* almost drove me mad."

Reaching out, I slid my palm along her neck. "You're *that* attracted to me?"

She leaned into my touch. "You've been the image in my mind for over a year every time I touch myself."

"*Monica…*"

"Even if you're disappointed in me, even if you hate me after - and you *might* - I need this. I need you."

"There's no doubt I find you attractive." I smiled gently. "I won't hate you. I might have to give myself a stern talking to about my carnality."

"Your vocabulary is so fucking *satisfying*."

Leaning closer, I nuzzled my cheek along hers. "I'm here for you, Monica." *In whatever way you need…you've earned that from me.*

Her perfume drifted across my senses. "You smell delicious." I licked the skin beneath her ear with the tip of my tongue. "I'm enthralled."

A shiver coursed over her skin.

Sitting back, I smiled. "It's too bright in here to explore you as I'd like." Crossing my legs demurely, I sat back but kept hold of her hand. "Let's talk until the lights go down. Rushing is the last thing I want to do. I want to savor every moment we have together."

"That sounds...perfect." With a smile, she ordered a glass of wine and sparkling water for me. We sipped them while we talked.

In the back of my mind, I allowed my thoughts to turn over this new development and examine it from all sides. It was complicated and radically different from anything I'd considered in the past.

I never lied to myself and the truth was…

I *wanted* to sate my curiosity about what sort of lover Monica was. I wanted to know what she looked like naked, how she tasted from head to toe, and what sounds she made in the throes of passion.

For the woman who'd always seemed so powerful to be gasping and shaking from my touch.

Half an hour later, the house lights went down and plunged us into near darkness.

I took this opportunity to put so many questions to rest about a woman I'd known for almost three years. Placing my clutch on the seat beside me, I cupped her face in my hands and kissed her softly.

It was critical to figure out what my client liked so I could provide it to their satisfaction - something I'd always taken seriously with my sexual partners.

It was shocking to discover what Monica *liked* was having sex in public places.

Preferably with an audience.

CHAPTER 12:
Monica

The music had barely begun before Monica had my dress and bra pulled low enough to expose my nipple. She groped beneath my dress, trying to touch me through my panties.

While I liked the way she touched me, her vibe seemed *desperate* in a way that felt off.

I pulled her face to mine and held her gaze in the near darkness. "I want to savor you."

She exhaled roughly and nodded. "Sorry. I-I've wanted this for so long."

For a couple of minutes, I held her, stroked my fingers through her hair, and kissed the sense out of her head. Taking my time, I gave her my complete attention. Her reactions made me wonder what she was missing in her personal life.

Every person had a story.

Few ever read all the pages.

Her breathing sped up against my cheek and she released a moan that gave me goosebumps. The way she held me to her seemed like she worried I'd get up and leave at any moment.

Gently massaging the back of her neck, I kissed my way along her jaw and whispered in her ear, "You deserve everything you want. Let me please you, Monica."

Moving to the deeper darkness of the floor beneath the balcony railing, I knelt at her feet. Beside her was a diaphanous wrap that I put across her shoulders. She could pull it around her if necessary.

I found the side zipper of her dress and slowly lowered it. Tugging the straps off her arms, I slid it down her body and she lifted so I could take it off. I laid it carefully on the seat so it didn't wrinkle.

As she sat partially naked in front of me, I wondered if anyone beyond the box could see her. She didn't seem concerned and that made me bold.

I examined her legs with my hands. They were tight from hours spent every week on her stair-climber. I fondled her clit through the thong she wore.

My eyes steadily adjusted to the dark and I was certain I could see more of her than she could see of me. That didn't stop her from staring at me with an intense expression of need.

Moving Monica's panties aside, I traced a finger between her folds before sliding two fingers into her pussy. It clenched - hot and wet - around me. She pumped her hips against my hand.

I was glad I hadn't bolted like a scared rabbit.

A faint rustling sound behind the seats of the box made me glance past her shoulder toward the exit.

Two of the parking valets had snuck into the box and were hiding on either side of the door behind the heavy curtains.

One was a young Hispanic man with beautiful features and a trim build. The other was an older white guy with a buzz cut and thickly muscled arms.

They rubbed their crotches through their pants while they watched what was happening.

I observed them for a few moments from my position between Monica's legs as I rubbed her clit.

I'd always loved watching men masturbate. There was something fascinating about strong hands stroking an engorged cock.

Not to say I don't enjoy watching women as well. I wasn't picky when it came to gender.

There was something primal about witnessing someone find their *own* pleasure. It provided insight into the person they were at the core.

The overall sexual experience was heightened when you had that knowledge.

Monica's *preferences* were clearly known in a place she frequented. She wiggled in her seat and moaned softly as I touched her.

No one had a clear view of what I was doing to her, but *noise* would definitely draw attention.

I lifted enough to cover her mouth with mine. Then I moved to her ear and asked, "Do you mind if two valets watch? They're hiding in the curtains behind us, fondling themselves, and waiting for a show."

I knew what her answer would be before I asked the question, but never took consent for granted.

She glanced at them over her shoulder, pulled the cup of her bra down to tweak her nipple, and nodded at me.

The valets retreated into deeper shadow when she turned but emerged again at her permission. They planned to watch me work and I didn't mind getting a performance of my own.

I went back to what I was doing.

The older of the two unzipped the front of his pants, pulling a thick cock through the opening and gripping it tightly.

His partner spread his waistband wide, reached lower to cup his balls, and stroked his cock swiftly with his other hand.

"I want to see you eat her pussy," the older one whispered. "Dear god, that will make my *year*."

No one would have been unaffected by the words in that situation and I couldn't believe how wet it made me. Sex in public had never seemed sexy before.

Monica unsnapped the front clasp of her bra and released her breasts. Cupping one, she squeezed her nipple between her finger and thumb. I took a moment to suck the pert tip and she gasped.

Her pussy clenched around my fingers stroking in and out of her body, she rolled her hips chasing her climax, and I smiled against her flesh.

Not yet, sweetheart.

Giving her another kiss, I said, "Don't come, Monica. Let it build."

She blinked twice. "I…"

My kiss was aggressive and I thrust faster into hot, wet velvet. Lifting slightly, I repeated, "Hold it back. Take what you deserve." Tugging her lower lip between her teeth, she nodded. I winked. "Good."

Settling back on my heels, I used my other hand to remove her thong and nudged one of her legs to the arm of her seat. Removing my fingers from her body, I rubbed the slickness over her clit.

Spreading her folds with my fingers, I pushed my tongue into her sheath as far as I could. I wasn't able to hold back a moan at the way she tried to keep me there. I thrust several times as her body began to tremble. Then I dragged my tongue up to her clit and swirled around the bundle of nerves.

Her lower body lifted from the chair and she gasped loud enough that it would have been heard if the music hadn't swelled at that moment.

While I ate her, I returned my fingers to fucking her as deeply as possible, rubbing my thumb over the delicate skin that separated her pussy from her ass. I used my other hand to massage her inner thigh.

Practically sobbing, Monica murmured, "Right there…oh, god. Don't stop. Please let me come."

I enjoyed making a lover beg.

Her fingers pinched her nipples so hard it must have hurt. I filed the information away for future play.

The entire time, I'd idly watched and listened to the men behind her play with themselves. The experience was exhilarating on a level that was new to me.

After a few minutes of stimulating her entire groin with my hands and mouth, I slowed down and whispered, "Monica? Ready to come for me?"

She answered a little too loudly, "I *need* it. I need to come…it's even better than I imagined."

Then her head dropped to the back of the chair and her hips rolled to meet me as I sucked her clit like a miniature cock.

The older valet moaned, "How's her pussy taste? Must taste so good. Watching you eat it…" He tensed up hard and started coming with a look of pleasure-pain on his face. "*Fuck*."

I watched him pump himself into a Kleenex as he gasped for air. It made me so hot, I felt like I could almost come, too.

The other guy cupped his balls with one hand and stroked the hell out of his dick with the other.

When he came, he said in Spanish, "*Oh, my sweet god.*"

The poor thing looked like he was on the verge of a heart attack. He almost missed the bar napkin he held to catch his release.

I never stopped fucking Monica with my fingers. When she came for me, I *knew* we would have been busted if the music at the end of the first act hadn't been so loud.

"Yes, Sarah, *yes*. Feels so good. Oh god, *yes*."

After a few moments, her breathing returned to normal. I lapped at her fluids and worked her thong up her legs. Pressing my palm against the fabric, it was quickly saturated with her wetness. Smiling smugly, I managed to get her dress back up her body.

She sat up, fastened her bra, and adjusted her breasts before taking my face in her hands. "I'll make that up to you, Sarah. Right now, I think we should go…what do you think?"

I nodded and we stood. We took our time straightening our clothes and smoothing our hair before turning for the exit of the box.

The valets hadn't moved but had managed to put themselves back together. The younger one was still panting softly.

I paused to meet their eyes.

Closer to me, I grabbed the older guy's dick through his refastened pants. It wasn't fully soft and I found myself quietly impressed. "Think about us later. Too bad your come went to waste."

I licked my lips.

Monica stroked her hand down the younger valet's chest. "How pretty you are. I hope you enjoyed the opera. I know I *always* do."

The men made strangled sounds in the back of their throats as we left them standing there.

The venue lobby was quiet since it was a while before intermission. We walked through the building, nodded at a few members of the staff, and got in Monica's black BMW when another valet retrieved it.

She headed out on Broward Boulevard and I started laughing. "That was fucking insane!"

Monica grinned. "I knew you'd be adventurous enough to play my little game." Stopping at a light, she looked at me. "I wasn't kidding. I'll make it up to you later."

"So much of the pleasure is in the giving. I love that part the most. Don't worry about me."

She was quiet for a long moment. Lifting her hand, she cupped my face. "That. That's what makes you perfect for this line of work. I feel so relieved."

I winked. "I'm happy to provide more…relief."

It felt good to laugh after such an experience. Monica was one of the few people who knew my past. That she wanted me *anyway* was a soothing balm to a broken place inside myself.

"Food…then more pleasure. Sound good?"

"Perfect," I answered.

I felt good and that seemed strange. I'd just performed my first act as a paid escort.

All I wanted was *more*.

CHAPTER 13:
Big Thoughts

Monica drove to a Japanese steakhouse for dinner and we talked for an hour while the chef chopped and grilled at lightning speed.

"Why are you using a service?" I wanted to know the answer even if it wasn't my business. "What about Jade? I *know* you love each other. You talk about her - and your relationship - all the time."

"The situation with Jade is difficult to explain. She's beautiful, intelligent, and fun to be with…as long as sex doesn't come into the picture." She sipped her wine and her expression turned thoughtful. "I *know* she loves me. I love her. That's the truth."

Our first plate appeared and I gave Monica time to think about what she wanted to say. I wasn't a therapist but…people seemed to be comfortable talking to me. The Monica I knew didn't seem like one to risk a relationship she valued.

Clearing her throat, she said softly, "I'm a little *outgoing* when it comes to my sexual tastes."

"Yeah, I noticed when I was eating you at the opera." I whispered. We laughed. "Seriously though, have you talked to her about what you like?"

"Oh, yes. I'm met with a blank stare. She's into *romance* and I do what I can to make her happy because I love her."

With a shrug, she added, "I was married before." My eyes widened. "I was young and didn't love him but sometimes I miss the craziness we shared. I mean, *making love* is nice but sometimes a person just wants to be *fucked*. Do you understand what I mean?"

I *did* understand.

Monica excused herself to make a quick call. I let the server know we'd be right back, followed, and watched her have a short conversation in the narrow hallway leading to the bathrooms.

She ended the call with a frown. I walked up and guided her into the bathroom. I kept going to an empty stall at the end. Pressing her against the wall, I exposed her breasts and suckled a nipple as I raised the hem of her dress to her hips.

Putting my thigh between her legs, Monica responded immediately by grinding against it. Someone entered the bathroom but I didn't stop.

Even when they took the stall next to ours.

My finger traced lazy circles on her clit beneath her panties as I whispered dirty thoughts in her ear.

"You love getting off in this filthy bathroom. If I asked, you'd straddle the toilet and happily eat my pussy. Especially if someone heard us. You love the *doing* and people *knowing* you're doing it." Her body coiled and I licked the shell of her ear. "I'll fuck you. However you want it. Come for me."

She did.

We returned to the table a few moments later after washing up. Monica kept touching me. I didn't mind.

Back then, I didn't give a damn what anyone thought about my lifestyle. I was still stupidly naïve about what other people endured just trying to live their lives with the people they loved.

When we finished dinner, she asked nonchalantly, "Do you like the beach?"

"Of course. Especially at night."

We drove north then east into Palm Beach County. I played with her from the passenger seat.

Working her up, making her crazy.

We arrived at Boca Inlet and parked. There were only a couple of cars in the lot. It would close soon and the cops didn't play about handing out tickets - especially to people getting it on.

Monica rolled the windows down a bit so we could hear the ocean. Then she removed her seat belt and shoes before coming across the console into my lap. I settled her on my thighs and kissed her violently while rubbing my hands roughly over her ass.

The moon was full and gave the sand beyond the car a dreamlike glow. The waves crashing onto the shore were rhythmic.

Water always called to a primal part of me.

"I've wanted to be with you like this for so long, Sarah. A sexual relationship would have been *incredibly* inappropriate before you were legal."

I laughed. "That didn't stop several people from fucking me before I was."

Warm hands cupped my cheeks as she sat up. "That's the thing. They *shouldn't* have, Sarah. I'm crossing a very real line with you as an attorney. I can't seem to help myself but that's a poor excuse."

"Monica…I want to be here with you. You aren't *taking* anything I'm not *giving* willingly."

She traced her finger along the upper slope of my breast. It sparked warmth in my belly.

She smiled sadly. "You positively *blossomed* once you were away from your mother. I'd catch myself watching you and remember you were a client, an employee, and half my age. It's been difficult to remain distant."

"You don't have to be distant now. Get as close to me as you want." Resting my face on her chest, I soaked up the warmth between her breasts. "No matter what happens, I'm glad you were my first, Monica. I would have been scared with anyone else."

Her fingers smoothed the hair at my temple. "As you've done your entire life, you'd have *hidden* that fear. No matter the client, you would have been spectacular and blown them away, Sarah. Believe that."

"Thanks."

"Let's stay like this and listen to the waves for a while. Be still together. You've made me come hard and repeatedly." She laughed. "I'm exhausted. Our age difference has *never* been more apparent."

I snorted and held her close. "You relax. I'll wake you up if you fall asleep."

Within a couple of minutes, her breathing went deeper and I knew she'd drifted off.

I watched the moon sparkle on the water, listened to the waves, and thought about many things. In my life, I'd had few moments of stillness. I kept moving forward no matter what.

Always reaching goals…rarely finding peace.

Holding another person *just because* wasn't a common thing for me. Particularly a person who'd seen some of the ugliest parts of my life.

I didn't *love* Monica or plan on *falling* in love with her. However, I thought maybe I could get used to sharing little moments like this with someone one day. Happily ever after, romantic love, always felt painfully out of reach after the things I'd been through.

Though I was only eighteen, it felt like I'd lived for a long damn time. Still, there was a lot of life *left* to live and that felt odd to me sometimes.

I hoped the rest was better than the start.

Not for the first time, I wondered what other epiphanies would be revealed during my time as an escort.

If they would shake my entire foundation for the better or worse.

* * *

Monica woke after an hour and lifted her head. "Oh, god. You must be in pain. I can't believe I fell asleep."

Smoothing her hair away from her face, I smiled. "I'm fine. You work a lot. It's okay to be tired."

"You also delivered like half a dozen orgasms so…" Her expression was almost shy. "Sarah. Will you let me book you again?"

"If that's what you want."

"I'm sorry I'm not as good a person as you thought I was."

I cupped her cheek in my hand. "Hey. You're a *great* person. This and that are separate." I kissed her lightly. "I'm sure relationships are hard. I don't know what you're going through and I won't judge you for your choices. I'll be here for whatever you need as long as you need it."

"Thank you." She sighed heavily as she raked a hand through her hair. "I have to be in court early or I'd book a hotel. Next time, alright?" I nodded and her eyes went wide. "I didn't do *anything* for you…"

"That's okay. Did you get enough? It's my first time so I'm not sure."

"I've used the service before. This is the first time I feel calm at the end. Usually, I'm kind of manic. You gave me more than you realize."

"I'm glad. I'll text Kylee. Drop me anywhere."

She laughed. "Absolutely not. I'll take you to the condo before I head home." I started to object and she kissed me deeply. "Let me see you back."

I nodded and she kissed me again before climbing back in her seat. I texted Kylee to let her know I wouldn't need to be picked up.

At Vivienne's building, I kissed Monica again before getting out.

She murmured, "See you next time."

Upstairs, Max waited for the elevator when it arrived. Her green eyes went wide when she saw me.

"A moment." I held the doors in place in case I needed to leave immediately.

Just past her, I made eye contact with Vivienne. She was replying to a text - I assumed from Monica. Her expression was hard to read but I thought she looked worried.

"Don't keep secrets. Not about Monica," I told her. "You don't know or understand our history, Vivienne. I could have ruined everything."

The madame tugged her lower lip between her teeth. "No more secrets, Sarah. You have my word."

I let the silence draw out for a moment before I nodded, released the doors, and said, "Sorry for the delay, Max."

Viv gave me a careful smile as I stepped into the living room. "She was pleased. Sent a fat tip, gave a glowing review, and booked another appointment."

I held her gaze for a long moment. "I guess I'm going to be good at this." Then I walked to an empty guest room, showered, and crashed.

There were many clients waiting in my future. Monica was my first and most memorable.

The reasons were complicated.

CHAPTER 14:
The Mystery Client

November 2009

My appointment the next day was with a woman who was something of an enigma to Vivienne and her staff.

Wrapped in a robe after my preparations, I found Walker and Max talking quietly when I returned to the guest room to dress.

I was genuinely surprised by the outfit chosen for me to wear. Glancing at the clothes, I frowned.

Walker chose his words carefully. "This client has been through six girls over the last couple of years. Even Vivienne has tried to please her. She keeps trying to find someone who *suits* but we can't figure out what that means."

At that moment, Vivienne walked into the room. "You'll be paid whether this appointment is a success or not. However, if you're not the right fit, I'll have to remove her as a client. I can't handle the stress of repeatedly failing."

Confused and a little concerned, I asked, "What's her feedback after appointments?"

Vivienne shook her head. "Just didn't feel it. Not a good match. This won't work. You don't get me at all…that sort of thing."

Staring at the brand new designer jeans, t-shirt, crisp flannel overshirt, and hiking boots, I wondered, "Where is the date supposed to take place?"

Walker cleared his throat. "Same place as always. Her cabin in the middle of nowhere off highway 27. She wants *rugged*…or something."

I couldn't help myself…I laughed. "Clearly, you don't know how *rugged* works. Let me help you out."

Walking into the closet where each of us left a few of our own things, I removed the boots I'd been kicking around in for years from Texas to Florida, worn jeans that had been washed a hundred times, plain white cotton panties, and matching sports bra.

I grinned when I found a t-shirt I went running in with a faded Dr. Pepper logo on the front.

Hanging my towel, I put on my underthings, dragged my hair into a messy bun, and finished getting dressed in my own clothes.

I gestured at the clothes on the bed. "Get rid of all that. It's too new. She knows none of y'all have a clue about her life. Those boots alone tell her she has *nothing* in common with the wearer. I bet that makes her feel weird - maybe even feel bad about herself."

Walker didn't understand and stood to the side with his arms crossed. I could tell he was annoyed and frustrated that he'd missed the mark on a client.

Max simply watched me in silence.

Vivienne shrugged. "We've tried everything else. Maybe something different will change things for her. If you're wrong, no big deal."

"I'll drive myself and you shouldn't charge her."

"Sarah…" Max said quietly.

"All the escorts came back in one piece. She's not *dangerous*…just *unsatisfied*. It's not right to charge her if she's unhappy. She doesn't want some sparkling fluff piece dropped off by a driver. Give me the location and I'll take my bike. I'll be fine."

"What if you're wrong, Sarah?"

"Viv. I'll be *fine*."

Finally, she nodded.

Max handed me detailed directions she'd received from Kylee since the other driver had dropped off most of the escorts in the Town Car. "You *sure* about this, Sarah?"

"You were going to take the *limo*?"

"No. I was going to drive you in Walker's SUV. Kylee had back-to-back drop offs today and she said the last road to her house is shit."

"Well, don't worry about me. I'll be fine. You know where to start looking if I go missing." Her eyes went wide and I winked. "I'm kidding. Seriously."

My prep done, I got on my bike and headed west. An hour later, I turned off Highway 27 and carefully took a pitted gravel road for about a mile.

The client's mailbox was cemented inside a heavy pot which held no plants at the moment. The name on the side was *Robineaux*.

I turned and headed through a tree canopy that opened up about two hundred yards later to a clearing. In the center sat a simple cabin. Beside it was a large workshop. A newer model truck and a fishing boat on a trailer were on the other side.

I parked my bike, got off, and removed my helmet. Taking down my hair, I returned it to a *neater* messy bun as a big dog came skidding around the side of the house.

Going to one knee, I grinned as the shepherd mix practically knocked me over. "Hey, boy! You're so pretty. What's your name?"

A voice answered, "That's Felix. I'm Ilene. Who might you be?"

The woman was about my height and a little thicker. She had a no nonsense expression on her gently lined face and an intense perusal happening behind her slate blue eyes.

As I expected, we were dressed similarly. I imagined I might look like her one day.

"I'm Sarah. Viv sent me." I tried to stand but Felix wasn't done rubbing his entire body on me. "One second and I'll say hello properly. Dogs insist on bein' first. Don't you, sweetheart? Yeah, that's alright."

"Where you from?"

"A little town in Northeast Texas. Been here a couple years and schoolin' out the accent isn't always successful." I wasn't making an effort this time. It kind of felt good to relax without worrying about sounding too *country*. Felix licked my face and I scratched him behind the ears. "Alright, ya big baby. Lemme say hey to your mama."

I stood and Felix circled my legs in happy bounces as I made my way to Ilene. I wiped my palm on my jeans and held out my hand. "Puppy slobber. My apologies. Good to meet you."

She shook firmly and I returned it. Her hands were strong and calloused. "They mention I'm difficult?"

As if sensing a change in mood, Felix sat regally between us looking up.

"Nope. I was told you've been unsatisfied with the girls sent out. I asked about your feedback and guessed why you might be."

I shrugged. "Figured we'd at least have a good conversation. I waived my fee. Thought we should meet and see if we mesh before you invest any more money in things that ain't workin' for you."

"You drive all the way out here by yourself?"

I nodded. "I take road trips back to Texas on my bike. Gettin' to your place was a piece of cake. When I was a kid, I used to ride my horse to a campsite along the Talimena Trail. This trip was easy."

"Southern Oklahoma?" I shrugged. Ilene was quiet for a long moment. "Can I get you something to drink?"

"Sweet tea, water, soda…anything really."

"Come inside. Let's talk in the kitchen."

Entering a minimalist space that smelled like fresh basil and mint, she gestured to a chair at the four-top table and I sat. She poured us glasses of tea while Felix rested his head on my knee for more scratches.

She took the chair caddy-cornered from mine and placed my glass in front of me. "Felix…he's particular. Could tell right off those other girls were scared of him. Kept his distance."

"I've always loved animals. I'm not shy about lettin' them know it either." I took a sip of the sweet tea and smiled. "Subtle flavor of mint. Perfect. Thanks."

We sat in silence for a couple of minutes and I didn't try to fill it. I could see her mind working on something.

"You remind me of myself a long, long time ago. You got people?" After a short hesitation, I shook my head. "I can tell that's a sad topic so I won't pry."

Clearing her throat, she said, "I got people. Too damn many of them some days. I was married for over thirty years to a minister."

"Wow."

"You're the first one I've told from your place. I'd appreciate it if we kept it between us."

"Of course. You have my word."

"Had three kids back to back. Two boys and a girl. Did my duty every time it was expected of me…but never once in thirty damn years did I enjoy a single moment."

My heart hurt for her. "I'm sorry, Ilene."

"Thank you. I am, too. A few years ago, he took over a church in Seattle. We had a couple grandkids by then - our daughter was living with us after her marriage fell apart. I started to panic a bit. Life was passing me by day by day. Still, I would have stayed."

Her expression turned to one of fatigue. "We got divorced when I realized he was enjoying his *moments* with somebody else. A good looking young man he picked up on the street. Seems we both had our secrets."

"Holy *shit*. What a plot twist."

Ilene laughed and I could imagine her laughing all the time. "It was certainly that. I got half our money, loaded up my dog, got on the road, and ended up as far from him as I could get. I don't know who I am. Fifty-two and haven't figured my shit out. Not sure how to do it."

I tilted my head. "You know how *not* to do it though."

She tapped her finger against her glass. "Those girls were real pretty. Delicate and refined in ways I've never been and never could be. They showed up in fancy cars and a driver let them out on gravel they couldn't walk on because of their shoes. My dog scared the bejeezus out of them. I think I did, too."

With a heavy sigh, she added, "I fed them and sent them on their way. No regrets about that. We weren't the same and it never would have worked." Ilene lifted her face. "You come from dirt roads and know pain. You're pretty but sturdy." She glanced down and asked, "Those *your* clothes?"

"They are." I lifted my foot. "Had these boots for four years. Leather worn down soft just how I like it. About time to replace the heel but I worry they won't feel the same."

"You like fishin'?"

"Love the water. Not scared to bait my own hook. I've been told I talk too much and scare off the fish. Suffice it to say, I'm not *good* at fishin'. Never catch a thing."

"How old are you, Sarah?"

"In years or life experience? Because they don't match even a little but the former might put you off and I don't want that."

"That young, huh? How'd you get into this kind of thing?" I told her the story and explained I'd only officially started the day before. "Well...*fuck*." I chuckled and drank the last of my tea. "Keep me company for a little. There's a dock out back."

I nodded, stood, and went to the sink to wash my empty glass. Setting it upside down on the dish drainer, I turned to follow her.

Ilene stared at the glass with a strange intensity.

Finally, she murmured, "It's funny. The manners we take for granted until we either see them or don't. The others, I could tell they grew up easy - maybe even fancy. Put my back up, how different we were."

"I didn't go to prep school. Even my high school experience wasn't what I wanted. I don't know etiquette or fashion. Those ladies run circles around me in all that and I don't mind."

I rested my palms on the sink edge behind me. "I can bale hay, can tomatoes, and clean a house until it's sterile enough to operate in. Different lives, that's all. Makes things interestin'. Don't you think?"

"Yeah." She added with a smile, "I don't have my back up with you."

"Good. Let's go fishin'."

CHAPTER 15:
Ilene

From the backdoor, we walked a gravel trail to the edge of a canal. A dock with chairs was built over the water. The lowering sun was gradually giving it shade.

Once we dropped poles in the water and settled, Ilene filled a bucket with cool water and set it between us.

I sighed. "It's real pretty here. Reminds me of my uncle's place as a kid."

"You spent a lot of time there?"

"Every summer and winter holiday. Loved the land and all the animals."

"I guess y'all don't speak?"

"My granny has Alzheimer's. She doesn't know me but I go back to see her a couple times a year to make sure the facility is takin' care of her. Lost my grandad when I was ten and still miss him. He was sick a long time though so…it was a blessin' when he went."

I frowned at the water. "As for the rest…they can't forgive me for involvin' the law. I can't forgive them for makin' it necessary. Nothin' to go diggin' for at this point. Too much insanity, violence, and dirty laundry." Trailing off, I glanced at Ilene. "You spent a lot of years gettin' folks to talk, huh?"

The sun's reflection on the water rippled light over her face. Her expression was gentle and I imagined she'd made a lot of people feel reassured with it.

"Twice weekly Bible study, women's group, baptisms, crazy hormones, weddin's, funerals, regular old temptations…somebody always needed help in one way or another. Most didn't know how to ask for it."

"Do you miss it?"

"Some things but mostly…no. I knew *everything* about those women - their traumas, marriages, and kids - but they didn't know *anything* about me. I kept pourin' from an empty cup. You should be careful in this new job, Sarah. You could find yourself in that situation real easy."

The silence stretched out and we stared at the water. Finally, I asked, "What made you use the service?"

Inhaling deeply, she shook her head. "I was curious. I use a fake name on social media where I join groups who talk about things I want to know."

"Smart."

"Mm hmm. Got talkin' to this woman from Louisiana in messages. Lila mentioned going on vacation to Florida. Finding out about the escort service from a friend of a friend. Said it answered a lot of questions for her she didn't even know to ask."

"Yet all it did was make you anxious…"

"I don't know why I kept callin'. I really don't. I should have given up a year ago. Every few months, I start wonderin' again." With a frown, she added, "Not sure what to do about you."

"I'm relatable - like you are to me. Maybe you can get those answers if I'm the one takin' the questions."

"You know, the water is too damn cold right now for decent fishin'…"

"Yup. You wanted to see if I'd really bait my own hook." Without looking at her, I asked, "Did I pass?"

"You did. Figured you would the second I saw those boots." Quiet for a minute, she cleared her throat. "Will you come back?"

"I will."

"Alright then. I need to get more…comfortable. Might take a couple appointments."

"We go at your speed. You make the rules."

Nodding, Ilene stood and reeled in her line. "Let's make some food and keep talkin'."

"I like the sound of that."

We made grilled salmon and roasted potatoes with a salad and bread, took our time eating, and talked about all kinds of things.

It felt like I'd known her a long time. I wasn't lying when I said she was relatable. She felt…familiar.

The sun went down and she worried about me getting back on my bike.

"I'll be alright."

"Next time, let's meet durin' the day. Safer for you to take these roads in daylight."

She walked me out and turned on the yard lights. Beside my bike, I turned to her and gave her a strong hug. She returned it almost painfully.

Leaning back, we were eye to eye. I raked my fingers through her shaggy ash-blonde hair and found it was softer than I expected. Her expression was anxious.

"Whatever you need to know, whatever you want to learn, I'm okay with it, Ilene. I'm not gonna judge you or make you feel weird."

"I want…" She took a deep breath and started again. "I barely kissed my husband in thirty years. I've never kissed a woman." My eyes widened in surprise and she reminded me, "They made me nervous."

Gently cupping the back of her head, I smiled. "Then allow me the honor of bein' the first."

I took it slow, kept it gentle, as my mouth met hers. I didn't grope her or rush the experience.

No matter what happened, I never wanted her to forget her first kiss with the gender she preferred.

Leaving soft kisses over her lips, I traced the tip of my tongue over the crease and she opened for me. I accepted her invitation with an internal smile.

My tongue coiled with hers and she tasted like the peach cobbler she served after dinner with a hint of whipped topping.

Stepping slightly closer, I tightened my hold and deepened the kiss. Strong hands explored my back, waist, and the top of my ass.

Ilene moaned into my mouth and I wanted to push her, to hear her make more sounds of pleasure. I thought about leading her inside and showing her everything she'd been missing.

I wanted her.

I couldn't have her yet.

Breaking the kiss, I rested my forehead against hers. "If I *don't* leave, I *won't* leave. Let's slow the pace so you have no regrets."

"You…want me?" I nodded and a tear slipped from the corner of her eye. "No one has *ever* wanted me."

Straightening, I maintained eye contact and pulled one of her hands from behind me. I rubbed her palm over my breast so she could feel how tight my nipple was furled. Her lips parted in surprise.

Guiding her hand down my stomach and between my legs, I pressed her fingers flat over my mound.

"Can you feel how hot I am through my jeans?" She nodded. "I want you, Ilene." I kissed her again as her fingers stroked between my legs. Kissing along her jaw, I admitted, "I want to make you come."

"We-we're outside…"

"No one can see you from the road."

Lifting the bottom of her t-shirt, I unfastened her jeans and slipped my palm flat beneath them and her panties. Her pubic hair was trimmed but present.

Sliding between plump lips, I circled the pad of my finger over her clit and she nearly buckled. I tightened my arm around her back for support.

"Stay with me, Ilene. Let me give you a sample of what pleasure should be." Her head rested on my shoulder and I whispered in her ear, "You're wet for me. Hot and slick."

I suckled her earlobe and was pleased at the shiver that worked its way through her body. "Your clit is hard, throbbin'. You like bein' touched here."

"Feels…so good. Better than when I do it myself."

"Later, when you touch yourself, imagine me between your legs." She gasped sharply. "Lickin' your sweet little clit until you come on my face."

"Gracious…" Her hands tightened on me as the climax hit her hard. "S-Sarah…" I left kisses along the side of her face as she rode the pleasure. "I've never come with somebody else."

The words broke my heart. I murmured, "That's your past. Your future will be different."

When her tremors slowed, I pulled my hand from her clothes and put her back together. As she watched me, I sucked the tips of my fingers.

"I like the way you taste. Here."

Gripping the back of her head, I delivered a deep kiss that quickly had her moaning again as we shared her flavor.

Against her lips, I suggested, "Maybe one day, you'll let me taste it from the source." One more kiss and I slowly let her go. "Think of me when you're alone and let me know when you want me to come back." I firmed my voice. "I *will* be back, Ilene."

She nodded and watched as I climbed on my bike, put on my jacket, and reached down to pet Felix.

"Take care of your mom." He released a puppy huff. "Good boy."

Reaching out, I pulled her closer and kissed her once more. "See you later, Ilene."

Then I put on my helmet, started the bike, and went in a careful circle around the woman and dog toward the drive leading to the road.

I thought more than once about turning back.

* * *

Back at Viv's, I took off my boots at the front door. I wasn't surprised to find her in her living room watching television in nothing but a loose gown.

I dropped my helmet on the carpet and shrugged off my jacket. Yanking my shirt over my head, I unfastened my jeans.

She started to speak and I kissed her roughly. "Talk later. Right now, I need to come."

"Sarah…"

"Later. Orgasms first."

I stripped us and positioned our pussies against each other, grinding us rapidly to mutual release. The entire time, I claimed her mouth almost violently to keep her from saying a word.

Beneath me, her breathing was ragged, her body limp. "H-hello. The appointment went okay?"

"She'll make another one. Got her off. Needed some relief from workin' her up then spendin' an hour on the bike." I grinned. "Thanks."

"Uh huh. You're so *welcome*. Sarah…don't freak out."

As she said it, I knew what I'd missed. Glancing over my shoulder at the big chair hidden from the main door's line of sight, I stared into Walker's eyes.

"I had no clue how to make a graceful exit…" he said breathlessly, "then I didn't want to. That was *incredible*." He sprawled in basketball shorts, legs spread, the t-shirt he'd been wearing in his lap.

Leaning down, I kissed Viv deeply before I stood and took in her post-coital appearance. I bent and dragged my tongue through her folds and she moaned my name.

"I like seeing our come on your creamy thighs."

Crossing the room to Walker, I bent to move the shirt he used as he stroked off watching us. "Nice cock, even softened." I cupped his balls and his eyes rolled back in his head. "Wow. You came *hard*."

Standing up, I smiled. "Don't plan to dress me for my appointments with Ilene. I'll handle it." I grabbed my clothes and helmet before turning naked toward the guest room with a wave. "Have a great night."

Closing the door, I leaned against it with my hand over my mouth. I could feel a fit of giggles trying to break out but stomped them down.

Relieving my very real pressure on Viv had been spectacular.

Knowing it drove the narcissistic fashion expert to fist his own cock made it so much better.

"Looks like I'm winning our bizarre little war."

I took a long shower, got myself off, and read a book on my phone. Eventually, I crashed for a few hours.

When I opened my eyes just before dawn, Max was stretched out beside me on top of the bedding.

She was fully dressed other than her jacket, tie, and shoes. Hands folded on her flat stomach, her breathing was deep and even.

She had a *killer* profile.

CHAPTER 16:
Reflection

Blinking at the ceiling, Max turned to look at me. "The other rooms were taken. I needed to crash. The weekends can get nuts."

"It's no problem at all," I assured her. Going up on my elbow, I gestured at her clothes. "You could have gotten comfortable."

"Not without consent. You were sleeping." She rubbed her hand over her face. "I'm better now…though starving."

"Same. I'll make us something." I left the bed in boxers and a tank top, padding to the kitchen as I pulled up my mass of tangled hair.

By the time she joined me, I'd pulled eggs, spinach, and two different kinds of cheese from the refrigerator. There were a few decent spices as well.

"Anything you don't like?" She shook her head and I washed my hands. "Then I'll improvise something edible." I cleaned as I went to avoid making a big mess in someone else's kitchen.

Ten minutes later, I plated omelets and we sat at the small table where Viv confessed her line of work after our first night together.

"This is damn good." Max ate quickly and efficiently.

"Are you former military?" She nodded. "For *years*, I planned to join." The driver looked up in surprise. "Wanted to be part of the journalism corp. Things went sideways and I ended up on a different track."

"You could have joined anyway…"

"Yeah. There was a time I wanted to be the next Stone Phillips. Figured I'd get experience as a war correspondent. Being thousands of miles from my younger brothers or best friend if they ended up needing me felt…wrong."

It was a change to my life goals I hadn't thought about in a couple of years. Somehow, it felt fresh.

I plastered a smile on my face. "Anyway, I can do shit without the credentials."

Max ate her last bite and sat back. "How the fuck did you end up *here*?" I shrugged because it was kind of hard to explain. "What do you want to be now?"

"The goal has always been to make a living as a writer. I'll do this for a while, save my cash, live simply, and write books until my hands fall off."

"You're a writer?" I nodded. "What do you write?"

"I started with cringey poetry. Lots of short stories that I enjoy. A few novels about people from shit origins who make good and find love."

"When you're ready for someone to read your stuff, I'll give you honest feedback."

"Wow. Um, thank you. No one has ever read my writing before…or even offered." Tilting my head, I asked, "How did *you* end up here?"

"My dad is career Air Force. I attended military academy since I started school - joined the Marines the second I could and planned to go career. I took shrapnel on my second tour - received a medical discharge against my will. I got into private security once I was back on my feet and met Viv at an event in Miami."

"You were an escort first?"

"Hmm. It didn't feel like that to me. I had two clients for a little over a year. They enjoyed my…let's call it a skill set. Because it's a specialty, my rate was higher."

Clasping my fingers under my chin, I whispered dramatically, "Did you spank their naughty asses?"

Max grinned. "Among other things. One got too attached and I lost interest in the other. Viv suggested I use my training to protect her girls."

Elbow on the table, I rested my chin in my hand. "That's fascinating. I've never done anything like that. A guy I briefly dated wanted to tie me up but I didn't trust him. Figured I'd end up beating his ass in the end."

She laughed and I liked the sound of it. "Glad you didn't cave to pressure. Domination is *impossible* without the complete trust of a submissive."

Glancing out at the balcony, I murmured, "I…doubt I'd *ever* trust a man that much."

"You've dated more men or women?"

"About the same but more sexual relationships with women. I prefer how they think and react to things. I can also…" I didn't finish the thought.

Max was silent for a few seconds as she held my gaze. "You can *take* them - beat them in a physical confrontation if it comes to that. That gives you peace of mind. You've obviously been through some personal hell. Why not just date women exclusively?"

"Uh, well…n-not sure." I couldn't believe she had me off balance. "Want the rest of my omelet?"

She took it, ate the last few bites, and stacked our plates. "Thank you for making food."

"Sure."

"And you shouldn't be embarrassed about wanting or needing to be filled and fucked hard. It's nothing more than a physiological need - our weird human bodies at work."

Standing, she walked to the sink and washed the dishes we'd used as I stared at her back with my jaw dropped.

Drying her hands, she glanced at me and I closed my mouth with a light blush. People rarely made me blush and I was not prepared.

"Men aren't the only ones who can deliver a deep and dirty fuck. Not to mention, *their* dicks always go soft eventually. Something to keep in mind." With a wink, she turned for the hall. "See you next weekend, Sarah."

Part of me wanted to chase after her for more information…and maybe a sample of what she meant. It was a bizarre sensation.

The rest of me was in awe. "She has *dude* confidence," I whispered to the room. "That's different and crazy hot."

I'd always maintained a position of dominant sexual energy with my partners…but no one had ever really pulled it off with me.

A few men got close while others thought they did but really were just being assholes.

Shaking my head to clear it, I murmured, "I need to go home and be normal for a few days before I fall down some rabbit hole of sexual excess. Holy shit."

I got my ass together and did just that.

CHAPTER 17:
Bad Penny

The following day, Vivienne called to let me know Ilene sent payment anyway for our appointment as well as a hefty tip.

She thanked Viv for getting it right at last.

My boss laughed over the phone. "Look at you…racking up satisfied customers. She wants to see you again next weekend."

I refused to be falsely humble…it felt amazing.

* * *

Living the kind of surreal life I had for a long while, I usually blocked out the fact that I came from a lot of messed up people.

Some of them liked to make trouble for me. One lived in Florida - fifteen minutes from my apartment.

Too close.

I received a reminder when my biological mother, whom I hadn't seen in two years, caught me shopping in the grocery store where I'd worked before I left home.

It was bad luck but my own fault.

The store was the only place she *could* have found me since she had no idea where I lived and there was a standing restraining order - regularly renewed - to keep her away from me.

Paula had a flair for the dramatic.

I'd met her when I turned ten. For most of my childhood, I'd been raised by her older sister Julie. A psychopath who *hated* Paula…and me by association.

In the beginning, I pitied the woman who gave birth and lost custody of me when I was an infant. I made a real effort to love someone I didn't know existed until I was dropped at her door from Texas.

Within days of meeting, I realized being abused provided Paula with an excuse - in her own mind - to abuse me. There's some sick shit in my family unit.

I had two much younger brothers I'd found out about when I was shipped to Florida. They were forbidden to see me after I was emancipated by the court and permanently freed from the insane adults who'd controlled my life up to that point.

We couldn't talk but I tried to keep an eye on them from a distance to make sure they were okay.

They were *not* okay. From what I'd heard from their friends' parents, the boys were skipping school and their grades steadily declined after I moved out.

I carried a lot of guilt over it.

They'd grown dependent on me to take care of them since Paula was always too *sick* or *depressed* to be a parent. She didn't make sure they were fed or clean, much less that they went to school or did their work.

I stayed in contact with their social worker as well but the overworked woman with way too many horrible cases couldn't check on them often.

The day Paula showed up to stir shit in my new life, I could tell she'd been saving it up.

Her temper was legendary. She was the queen of causing a scene guaranteed to make people I didn't even know cast sympathetic glances my way.

It didn't matter where she was or who was around. She screamed, cried, and even became physical when she lost all control.

She used to look like me and I probably would end up looking like her…if I decided to become an alcoholic, chain smoker, who stayed with abusive bastards who constantly rearranged my face.

Paula was one of those women who stayed with a man no matter what. She wasn't stupid and possessed considerable artistic talent. Somehow, it always came back to needing a man to care for her.

I was never going to be *that* woman.

Our final confrontation before I moved out was the last time I'd dealt with her face to face outside of a courtroom.

I don't break easily…*that* is what my childhood taught me.

Now here stood the woman who brought me into the world hell-bent on jeopardizing the peace of mind I'd worked so hard to attain.

I had no reason to fear her. I was younger, stronger, and indignant at her nerve when she had no business being within fifty feet of my person.

"I found you, ungrateful little shit! You thought you could run from me and ruin my reputation!"

"Your reputation? You gotta be kiddin'."

Removing my phone, I took several photos of Paula and texted Monica. My *attorney* would know what to do from a legal standpoint. When they were sent, I started an audio recording.

"Don't take photos of me! You don't have my permission!" She tried to grab my phone and I evaded her, slipping it into my jeans. "You bitch…"

"Paula, leave. You're violatin' the restrainin' order."

Her volume climbed. "I haven't seen you in *years*. You had me *served* like some criminal…"

"You *are* a criminal."

"You think you can just disappear and make a new life after what you did to me?"

"Paula, don't do this." I said quietly.

There was no avoiding her, no calming the situation, no behaving like an adult. She came to fight. That was the way it always was, always had been, between my mother and me.

She grabbed me by the front of my t-shirt and yanked me to her. "You don't tell me what to do. *Don't do this*," She mimicked shrilly. She laughed at her own cleverness. "Running off acting like little miss high-and-mighty. You make me sick!"

She shook me hard which I'd grown out of the habit of expecting. I felt red creeping into my brain - still calm but not for much longer.

I told her coldly, "Take your hands off me. You have no right to touch me."

"That's funny, Sarah. You think you're better than me? You're not! You're nothing but a whore! Look how skinny you are! You're probably a drug addict or something…not that it would surprise me."

I'd been on my own for almost three years - safe from this bullshit. No way was I letting her drag me back into her crazy.

I didn't have to put up with her anymore. The longer she kept her hands on me, the more violent I felt on the inside.

"Sarah, I know you've been *stalking* your brothers. Did you forget about the restraining order?"

"Never within fifty feet, you sociopath. I've never once violated the court order. I bet they're doin' *awesome* in your care. I'll contact the case worker for a wellness check."

Her eyes widened. "You wouldn't dare…"

"I would." Going very still, I lowered my voice. "Get your fuckin' hands off me, Paula. You don't know me. You never did." No matter what, I had to avoid a physical showdown with this woman.

I would probably kill her.

Playing out her little drama in front of people I used to work with and some I still considered casual friends also wasn't an option.

Paula grabbed me harder. "You and your smart mouth…"

My old store manager approached and he wasn't happy. Mitch Bledsoe bodily pushed his way between us, forcing Paula to release me. He was a big man in his late fifties with a barrel chest and gray hair cut in a high-and-tight.

"Get out of this store and don't come back. I see your face again and I'm calling the cops." He glanced to the side. "Never mind. They're already here."

"None of you see it! How horrible she is to her own mother." Paula rarely engaged in confrontation with adult men. Other women and vulnerable children were fair game to her physical aggression but she used *tears* on men. "Sarah doesn't care if I live or die…"

"Lady, I've known this young woman since she was fourteen. I'm the one who hired her. I saw the bruises, scratches, and broken bones from the constant beatings you gave her. I *know* what you did. So does the law. People like you make me sick. You shouldn't be allowed to have kids."

Mitch looked like he wanted to spit on her.

One of the officers approached and said, "Ma'am, you need to leave the premises. You're in violation of a court-mandated restraining order."

Paula left yelling, cursing at me, and continued arguing and crying at the cops outside. She lit a cigarette the moment she cleared the doors.

A few minutes later, I watched as she stormed to her car and threw herself inside. I hadn't realized my brothers were with her but saw them through the windows as Paula sped away.

The cops left without taking a statement. Paula should have been arrested and charged for violating a court order.

Once again, she faced no consequences for her actions. That's why she kept acting like she did.

I needed to call Monica about my brothers. It also might be time to file a hefty civil suit against Paula. If jail didn't scare her, I'd hit her in the wallet.

Thanking Mitch, I accepted his hug, and left without my groceries. I was emotionally exhausted and couldn't even remember what I'd meant to buy.

For the hundredth time in my life, Paula caused a public scene and drew negative attention to both of us. I struggled to put her out of my mind.

She wasn't *worth* the very real anxiety she caused.

It was strange - and frustrating - that such things took a toll on me anyway.

I desperately wanted to be numb to it.

CHAPTER 18:
Another Birthday

December 2009

The following weekend, Ilene had to cancel our appointment when she returned to Washington at the request of her oldest son.

She sent a personal note of apology with a promise to make it up to me when she returned.

Monica went out of town for two weeks with Jade for their anniversary. It was a surprise trip her partner sprung on her.

For the next three weekends, I was booked with several new clients. Most were one-offs with tourists visiting South Florida.

Two bookings would be regulars I thought were a better fit for Ezbeth or Rolande.

With each date, I felt more confident about what I was doing.

The morning after my birthday - which fell on Christmas - there was a knock on my door. I opened it to Campbell on the other side.

He shouted, "Hey, hoe! I mean that *literally* now." I snorted. He shoved his way inside and grabbed me in a hard hug. "Happy birthday and Christmas. Sorry I didn't come by yesterday. Mom was sick as a dog."

"Thanks." I closed the door. "You're the only one who knows or remembers. I have presents for you and your folks. I hope she feels better."

"Don't worry. A nasty little stomach bug that came, saw, and made her ass raw."

"Lord, Camp…"

He took hold of my shoulders and stared deep into my eyes. "You made it to nineteen. Congrats, Sarah."

"It was…touch and go there for a while, huh?"

Camp shook his head. "You're no quitter. You get knocked down, get up with your face bloodied, and tell the universe to try harder." He hugged me tight. "Enough morose bullshit. Let's have good food and binge the entire *Lord of the Rings* trilogy."

"You're such a nerd…I can't wait."

My best friend spent the next thirty-six hours at my house and it was kind of magical. He had presents for me - books, posters, and funny t-shirts.

The gifts from his parents were cash and beautiful journals I'd keep forever but probably *never* write in.

We ate good food we cooked together as well as garbage we picked up from the convenience store. After all three movies, we crashed in my bed.

Campbell was a world-class snuggler and it was nice to experience it every once in a while.

We repeated our silliness the next day until the sun started to set. When he got ready to leave, he hugged me hard enough to hurt.

I heard the tears in his voice when he told me, "I'm sorry I'm not straight."

"I'm sorry I'm not a man."

His arms tightened. "I love you. I really do, Sarah."

"I know, Camp. I love you, too."

There had only ever been truth between us. He never lied to me - even when it hurt - and I respected him for it more than anyone I knew.

It was good to have one person who knew where all the bodies were buried in my past but still showed up to binge eat chips and scream at *Die Hard* with me for the hundredth time.

"Happy birthday, babe."

"Merry Christmas, Camp. Give my love to your folks."

"Stop avoiding them. They miss your face." I nodded but he knew I didn't mean it. "They love you too. You know that, right?"

I held his pretty, beloved face in my hands and whispered, "I can only handle so much normal before I bleed all over it. Take my love to them. Bring yours to me once in a while." Lightly kissing his lips, I added, "Thank you for being with me."

He held my face to his chest and kissed the top of my head. Then he grabbed the bags I gave him and left without looking back.

I closed the door and didn't watch him leave.

* * *

An hour later, I received a text from Viv to be dressed and ready by nine o'clock. Frowning, I asked what I should wear.

"Whatever you go dancing in," was the response.

I laughed out loud. "This bitch is *not* ready for me on a club crawl for dancing. No way she can keep up. What is going on?"

At nine on the dot, I was stunned to see the limo pull into my parking lot. I walked downstairs in confusion and Max held the door for me. She wore a three-piece suit and highly polished black shoes, her dark hair was coiled tightly at the base of her neck. I could barely see the gun under her jacket.

"Sarah." Her gaze rolled down my entire body and came back to my eyes. "Happy birthday."

"How…?"

Viv reached out and pulled me inside. I looked around at two of the escorts and Walker as I landed on the supple leather. Even Kylee waved from the passenger seat up front.

The door closed behind me.

"Your friend Campbell texted me, the darling." Viv held my hand in both of hers. Max slid behind the wheel. "He said you never make a big deal of your birthday but you work hard to get to each one." Leaning close, she purred. "This is what you *dance* in?"

"Um, I didn't know it was a whole thing."

The other women were dressed in delicate skirts, dresses, and heels that highlighted their femininity.

When it came to moving to music, I went for comfort over style. A strategically ripped body suit - with a bullet-proof bra underneath - stayed where it needed to but still gave me air. Jeans hung low on my hips and well-worn Doc Martens protected my feet from other dancers.

My hair was in high pigtails that would probably end up in space buns by the end of the night because of the very real sweat that would be pouring off my body. I always applied two layers of deodorant.

No makeup because, honestly, what was the point?

Suddenly feeling out of everyone else's league, I murmured, "I don't drink when I go out. Or-or really talk. I just…dance for hours."

"We shall do the drinking! You just have fun and we'll get you home safely."

Ezbeth gestured to my outfit. "I *really* like this. Walker, you need to kit us out like this sometimes. It has a youthful exuberance to it."

"Noted."

Viv asked, "What is your favorite place, Sarah?"

I gave Max the address of a club where I sometimes danced four nights a week and she smiled in the rearview mirror as she pulled out of my parking lot.

I had my phone and a fat wad of small bills in my pocket as well as a slim wallet with my cards, license, and house key.

Pulling up to the club, the pounding music from inside spilled onto the sidewalk. The bouncer's eyes were huge as Max opened the door and I got out. He'd been manning the front door since the place opened. I estimated he was in his forties and still looked damn good.

"Hey, Jack. These are a few of my friends. Think we can skip the line?"

"Sarah…looking fine as ever and you brought eye candy for days." Removing the rope, he gestured to the entrance.

I pointed at Max and Kylee. "They're going to park and join us. Make sure they get in, yeah?"

"Sure thing, sugar. Give old Jack a kiss." I offered him my cheek and he bent to kiss it. "You little heartbreaker. Good to see you."

"Thanks."

"Go shake your ass for six hours and I'll see your soaking wet self when you leave."

We high-fived and I led the way through the dim hallway toward the main room. I was anxious to get out on the dance floor but felt conflicted leaving my group behind in a new place.

In Viv's ear, I said, "I know they have VIP rooms if you'd feel more comfortable there. I never bother."

"You do your thing. We'll be fine."

Without a word, I made my way to the center of the floor and allowed the music to take over.

The scent of sweat, musk, various perfumes, and more drifted to me as other dancers brushed against my body. Some contact was due to close quarters but some of the touches I received were intentional.

A man's hand moved from my waist to cup my breast and I casually grabbed his hand in a grip that would break bones if he didn't remove it.

It wouldn't be the last silent confrontation of my night but I never let it mess with my pleasure at being able to dance uninhibited.

After an hour, I coiled my pigtails into knots and secured them with elastic bands from my pocket. One of the servers appeared in the crush with a cold bottle of water and I gave her a ten for the much-needed fluids and a tip.

"Lookin' good, girl!"

"Thanks, Brit!" I drank the water but never stopped moving.

Once in a while, I glimpsed a member of my party on the outskirts of the floor - dancing with each other or strangers.

The club played high-energy hip-hop, metal, and techno beats that never slowed. It was loud enough for the rhythm to feel like it pulsed through the blood in my veins.

Writing, sex, fighting, and dancing were the only activities that unplugged my brain completely. I didn't think about the past, the present, or the future...it was all about moment by moment.

I loved every chance to disconnect.

After another hour, Brit brought another bottle of water and took the empty that I'd shoved in my back pocket. We didn't talk. I was past the ability. I handed her another ten and she saluted as she walked away.

I'd been dancing, jumping, and screaming along to music for almost three hours when Walker appeared in front of me. He didn't speak or try to touch me and I appreciated his restraint.

Not long after, I caught a woman who'd had way too much to drink as her heel gave out beneath her.

Practically carrying her, I took her to the edge of the dance floor, set her on a stool, and gestured to one of the servers. Tony appeared in seconds.

"She might have twisted her ankle. She needs water. Don't let anyone take her off, alright?" Lifting the woman's face, I asked, "What's your name?"

"K-Kathy…"

"Did you come with friends?" She nodded. "Stay right here. Let Tony help you, alright?" Dazed, she managed to nod again. "Cool down and sober up."

I used the bathroom, declined an offer of drugs from one of the stalls, and washed my hands. After I got a fresh bottle of water from the bar, Mama Celia leaned over the bar to kiss my cheek.

"It's weird not to see you here every night."

"New job…"

The older woman grinned. "Have something to do with that pretty group you showed up with?" I shrugged. "Be safe out there, kitten."

"Yes, ma'am."

Back out on the floor, I let the pounding beat wipe away everything that snuck into my psyche between my self-described *therapy* sessions.

Being around someone like Campbell was wonderful and I appreciated his presence, his attention, and the love he was capable of giving me.

I always felt off-balance when he left and my heart ached. It was my own problem…one I'd never burden him with.

Coming out to dance had lessened the pain this time and I made a mental note to thank my new coworkers for their well-timed intervention.

But first…*dancing*.

A few hours and bottles of water later, I went in search of my colleagues. I found them in a VIP room I'd never entered.

There was an orgy in progress and I laughed. "As long as you guys are having fun." I gestured to the door. "I'm going back out...'kay?"

"If you change your mind, come play, Sarah." Viv sucked Ezbeth's nipples while Paige ate their boss lazily. "This is an *excellent* evening out."

"Good to know. Enjoy yourselves."

Turning, I made eye contact with Max at the wide window overlooking the dance floor below. Kylee was stationed just inside the door.

"You guys are *working*? Tell them to lock the door and go relax..."

Max said, "You have *incredible* stamina."

Realizing she'd probably seen me out on the floor when I had my guard down completely, I felt myself blush. "I...like to dance."

"I can tell. Everyone knows you here." I nodded. "It must have taken time to find a place where you felt comfortable."

"Who also let underage people in...yeah. I have to watch the older guys. They're handsy."

"You make a delectable offering."

Hand on my hip, I gave her a slow smile. "You like testing me. Seeing what makes me tick."

From behind me, Viv's voice was a little slurred. "Max has *insanely* high standards."

I walked closer and stared down at the first floor of the club. "It's hard to tell how many people are out there when you're in the thick of it." She was several inches taller than me. "I like feeling invisible."

"You could *never* be invisible…but you're able to shutter yourself to seem merely unapproachable. It's a good skill."

Quietly, I said, "I genuinely like people. I just don't always trust them." With a small laugh, I added, "Makes this an *odd* career choice, I guess."

"Or the *best* for this stage of your life." Lowering her voice, she told me, "Be picky, Sarah. Don't let Viv dictate your number of clients and don't let her make you a catch-all. It's not healthy for you."

"There were a lot of different, um, people this month." I rubbed my temple before I realized what I was doing. It was a physical sign of weakness that I regretted. "I don't think…I liked that."

Until I said the words, I didn't know how much I meant them.

Cycling random strangers through my bed - most of whom I'd never see again - felt off in a way I hadn't really known how to verbalize.

"Set your boundaries, Sarah. Do not budge from them. I'll back you up."

Meeting her startling green eyes, I whispered, "Thanks. Really."

"Anytime. Go dance. I'll keep an eye out."

Exhaling roughly, I admitted, "Sometimes, I need the therapy of it."

Placing one finger beneath my chin, she raised my face. "Therapy comes in many forms. Should your usual methods ever fall short, come talk to me." Max held my gaze without blinking.

"I will. I promise."

There was...something that flickered in the green and then it was gone. "Good girl." The words sent a shiver down my spine. "Enjoy yourself."

We ended up closing the place. Max settled the VIP tab and Kylee gently herded Viv and the girls to the exit.

Jack grinned as I stepped outside. "Looks like you outlasted everyone else yet again, Sarah. Don't stay away too long. Give us a kiss." Again, I gave him my cheek and he left a smacking kiss on it. "If I were twenty years younger…"

I winked. "I just turned nineteen."

"Saints preserve us!" he gasped in a fake Irish accent. "Uh, *thirty* years younger then. You're surely the Devil sent to tempt us geezers."

"As if you need tempting. See you next time, Jack."

I supported a giggling Ezbeth as she got in the limo and smirked as Paige insisted on a quick make-out session with me before joining her inside.

Viv pouted. "I didn't get kisses." Dramatically puckering, she dropped a kiss on me. "Happy birthday, Sarah. I hope you celebrate many with us."

"May they all be as entertaining."

Walker appeared between two vivacious older women and announced he had plans elsewhere. "I'll see you guys at the condo tomorrow."

"Have fun. Use protection, ya slut."

"Those in glass houses, Sarah…"

"Still use protection, ho."

He laughed. "Touché." With a wave, the women led him away as if they'd just won the lottery.

Kylee mumbled, "The man has no sense of danger when he's drunk. Hope he doesn't end up rolled in an alley."

Max snorted. "When he wakes up and realizes they're both in their late forties, he'll have *many* regrets. He's a walking stereotype sometimes."

I clapped my hands together and said, "Not our circus, not our monkeys. I'll take a cab. You guys have enough on your hands with these three."

From behind me, Jack offered, "I'll take you home, Sarah. It would be my *pleasure*."

"Absolutely not, you lecher."

"Ouch."

Max bodily put me in the limo. "I picked you up. I'll drop you off. That's the way it works."

I started to argue and she closed the door.

At my building, the enigmatic driver let me out and closed the door. "If you're tired, sleep before you get on that motorcycle. Understood?" I nodded. "See you later." Bending slightly, she dropped a kiss at the corner of my mouth. "Happy birthday, Sarah."

When I unlocked my apartment, I glanced over my shoulder. Only then did Max open the driver side door and get in. The limo didn't pull away until I was safely inside.

I showered, cleaned my entire place, and slept for four hours before I drove to Miami.

In the back of my mind, it kind of felt like I was following an order.

CHAPTER 19:
Drawing Boundaries

January 2010

When Monica returned from her vacation, she booked appointments with me on three consecutive weekends.

Dates with her were wild in ways that often went beyond exciting to *desperate* and I hoped we didn't end up getting arrested playing out her favorite fantasies.

We'd gotten dirty at a concert, the movie theater, and a gas station bathroom. The latter was so gross, I told her I'd *never* do such a thing again.

She was apologetic and tipped me stupidly well for the night.

Ilene was still in Washington but let me know she'd return in mid-February.

Vivienne *again* tried to book me with every *single-use* client that came across her desk and I knew it was time to sit her down for a conversation.

In the third week of January, I showed up on a Monday morning and found her going over the bookings with Walker and Max.

"Sarah! Hi! We were about to break for food. I'd rather eat something you made…"

"I'm happy to make you guys food. Then, we need to talk." I gestured at the calendar. "Preferably before you book me on another appointment."

"Um, okay. I think I know what you're going to say." Viv sighed heavily. "It's just…you're so good with the single bookings. They rave about you."

"I appreciate that." Leaning against the door frame, I crossed my arms. "However, you're burning me out. I need time to form a connection with these people. Otherwise, it's just fucking strangers for money. No different than standing on a corner…and that's not what I'm looking for."

"I didn't…"

"The one yesterday kept calling me Shauna. She couldn't get my fucking *name* right, Viv. I need a few regulars. I'll occasionally do a single booking…but I've done *nine* in a month. I'm worried I'm going to end up with a disease from these tourists."

Max murmured, "Viv, you booked her with *nine* singles? What the hell were you *thinking*?"

"So many came in…you know, with the holidays and all. I even upped the rates for you, Sarah."

I said firmly, "I'm not here because of money."

You could have heard a pin drop.

Viv appeared genuinely distressed.

Max kept her expression neutral.

Walker's expression showed his obvious confusion. "Not here for money…?"

"No. There are *many* ways to make money or the equivalent to live. Ways I've kept myself alive since leaving home before I was sixteen. You didn't ask me a lot of questions when you hired me and that's okay. I worked at a grocery store and took home expiring stuff every night so I had fresh food."

"Sarah…"

"I bought a fake ID back then that made me eighteen. The strip joint near my house does an amateur dance night every month. I take in three grand in cash for less than thirty minutes of work, wear a mask to conceal my identity, and no one is allowed to touch me."

"I didn't know…"

"These days, I take a hundred dollars of that money and play poker and blackjack at the casino. I learned it from a homeless vet I met at the beach where I run. I buy him a meal, give him cash for a bottle, and he shows me strategy. I go there ready to lose that hundred. Most nights, I leave with many times that."

"Seriously?" Walker whispered.

"Every few weeks, there are sports bars that do girl-fight nights. It's meant to showcase tits and ass, get the boys drinking and spending. While everyone else is there to flash the crowd, I knock my opponents the fuck out. Last pot was four grand."

Tilting my head, I continued, "I'm an anonymous cam girl. Campbell set up my gear and pings my signal all over the globe. I bring in about two grand a month and only make two new videos."

Taking a deep breath, I continued, "I took a leap of faith because all of those things - every single one of them - are solitary. I have no family in my life. Camp is my only real friend. I struggle with rage and PTSD. I need controlled *connections* with other humans, Viv. If I can't get that here, I'll figure out another place to get it. I'm not risking my health or safety for a thousand a night."

Straightening from the door, I said, "I'll make you guys some food while you talk. It appears y'all each have a stake in this thing or manage it together. Take your time." Before I turned, I added, "If I'm not the right fit, that's okay. I won't have any hard feelings."

I walked into Viv's kitchen and took stock of her ingredients. I doubted she knew it but most of what I needed to make a dumbed down version of Mongolian beef was sitting in her fridge and pantry. She even had rice noodles.

What I was missing, I could improvise.

Pulling the necessary pans and utensils from her cabinets, I put up my hair, washed my hands, and got to work. I made a pot of rice just in case.

By the time they appeared on the other side of the bar, the beef - a more expensive cut than I usually bought - was sliced and marinating in a bastardized sauce that smelled almost right.

I didn't look up from thinly slicing carrots and pushing them beside the onions I'd already cut.

"Food will be ready in ten. Get yourselves something to drink."

Sautéing the vegetables in a super-hot pan, I added the beef, the sauce I'd set aside, and the rice noodles in the last two minutes.

I quickly divided the mixture over four plates and spooned rice into small bowls. I couldn't find chopsticks so I added forks to the side.

"Enjoy." Viv looked at the food with wide eyes and I laughed. "All of this was in your kitchen. I took the liberty of using it."

They sat on the barstools so I ate standing on the other side. I was glad they seemed to enjoy it.

Max said seriously, "You're a *great* cook."

"Thanks. I've done it since I was big enough to reach the counter with a step stool. I didn't used to like it but appreciated the skill once I was on my own."

Taking a deep breath, Vivienne said, "No more tourists, Sarah. I'll actively look for a few regulars for you. Monica and Ilene are insistent that you're booked with them once or twice a month. There's a local jazz singer who's looking for something specific. I thought Max might train you on a few things."

Quirking a brow, I asked, "*Really*...? That sounds fascinating. She wants me to spank her?"

With a grin, Max said, "Work her over with a fake cock. I've seen you dance. You have the necessary hip movements to be convincing."

Tugging my lower lip between my teeth, I considered. "You're gonna teach me *dude* confidence."

"You'll be a natural."

"Thanks." Glancing at Viv, I wanted to clear the air. "I don't mind what I'm doing. I just don't want to feel gross. Do you know what I mean?"

"To be honest, I didn't realize the number until you said it. I'm truly sorry, Sarah."

"I'm glad we cleared it up."

I ate as much of my food as I could and offered the rest to Max. She took it with a smile.

Walker gasped, "Why did *she* get it?"

"I like her *way* more than you." Nothing more than the truth.

"Max is my cousin by marriage."

"She clearly got *all* the charm in your family." The topic of discussion snorted.

He was quiet for a long moment. "We need to start over. I don't like that you don't like me. You like everybody. I feel left out."

"First of all, I do *not* like everybody. A lot of people straight up suck. Second, I got a bad first impression of you because you touched me intimately without my consent and then had the audacity to be surprised I objected rather than roll over on all fours for you. If you want people to like you, maybe be less of a misogynistic ass," I advised.

Viv and Max snickered.

Walker pouted. "I'll do better."

"Do it for humankind." Taking their empty plates and silverware, I washed them before cleaning up the kitchen.

Max came around the counter and held out her hand. "Shall we?"

I didn't hesitate to put mine in it.

From behind us, Walker begged, "Can I *watch*?"

"No, cretin." I shook my head. "What did we just discuss?"

Max didn't let go of my hand as she walked to the guest room and closed the door. Leaning against it, she grinned. "He uses the cousin thing generously. My aunt was his uncle's mistress for like a decade."

"Hope she got *paid*."

Laughing loudly, she nodded. "Okay. I've seen you interact with Viv and Kylee. You have a natural dominant streak with women. You like being in control. This new client…she *wants* you in control. She figures it's not cheating on her long-time asshole boyfriend if the cock is silicone."

"Got it."

"I think you're good with the basic skills of a gentleman - opening doors, assisting from cars, offering your coat, that kind of thing." I internally agreed. "You were great with that woman at the bar who fell off her shoes."

"I tend to watch out for women alone. There are fucking predators *everywhere*."

"I know that's right." She pushed off the door. "The trick with conveying masculine energy is *slowing down*. When they're in hunt mode, they can be single minded like the world works on their schedule."

One arm folded at her back, Max extended the other to me. I placed mine in it.

She made intense eye contact, there was a pregnant pause, and then she said, "Hello, Sarah."

Holy shit.

I blinked once and took a deep breath. "Hello, Max."

Bowing slightly, she brought my hand to her lips and didn't look away as she kissed the back. When she straightened, she used the light hold to pull me closer. I went without hesitation.

It was effortless.

Maintaining her hold, she used her other hand to smooth a stray tendril of hair off my face. "You'll have about the same height differential with Tricia. You'll be in a suit with your breasts bound."

My heart slammed against my sternum.

"Take off the jacket but stay in the rest of your clothes. Remove your cock through the zipper and fuck her stupid. She'll be one of the most *selfish* clients you'll ever have…but she also needs the attention desperately. It's unlikely you'll get the chance to come. I don't think it crosses her mind."

"Who was her last escort?" I asked breathlessly.

"Me." My eyes widened. "Over the year she was my client, she became emotionally attached. Be on guard for it." I managed to nod. "Physically controlling her makes her wet."

Max put my back to the door and pinned me there. Raising my hands above my head, she held my wrists in place. "You have to *remove* her ability to participate. She wants to be taken, forced to feel pleasure, and worshiped."

"Treated like a queen who only bows for a king."

Her smile was slow. "Exactly right, Sarah." Bending, she nuzzled my ear. "Doing everything slowly, drawing it out, is important for *you*. She likes to come half a dozen times and if you aren't teasing her between…you'll be physically wiped out."

I ground my hips against the cock I felt behind Max's zipper. "She tries to rush…"

"Inherently greedy, if you lose control, you'll be buried in Tricia's pussy within minutes. Maintaining that pace gets harder after four hours." She used her hips to pin mine. "Make her wait. Make her beg. Force her to match your rhythm and be arrogant about it." Max took several slow, deep breaths at my ear while her thumb smoothed my inner wrist. "Heighten every sensation until she's on edge."

"Mm hmm. On edge."

My nipples were hard, I was wet, and needed more. No lover had ever pushed me so easily or thoroughly to such a point without a single kiss.

She licked the outer shell of my ear. "Sarah?" I hummed something. "Change your clothes into what Walker left for you. We're leaving."

Taking a full step back, she put her hands on her narrow hips. I stayed against the door for a moment before I realized I still had my hands above me and she'd given me an order.

Staring into her eyes, I said, "Sweet lord. You're *good*." She smiled but didn't speak.

I walked to the closet and found a simple black cocktail dress and heels. Underthings were with them. Back in the bedroom, Max sat in a chair, her legs slightly spread, feet flat on the floor.

It was a silent demand to change in front of her. I stripped slowly, removing every item before casually turning to hold the black dress against my body to inspect it in the full length mirror.

"Temptress," she murmured.

"Sexy demon," I shot back.

I pulled on one item at a time and made sure to check how it laid on my skin before adding the next piece. It ended up being as much a tease for myself as Max.

By the time I dropped the diaphanous layers of black chiffon over my head, I was more turned on than I'd ever been. The bodice cupped my breasts but left the upper swells exposed to the bra line.

Depending on how I turned, you could see glimpses of my bra and panties beneath the dress.

Stepping into the shoes, I stood in front of the mirror and unbraided my hair. I finger-combed it out and it sprung into wildness. Using two sparkling black clips from a tray of accessories, I pulled it away from my face.

Walking across the room, I crawled into Max's lap and straddled her thighs in the chair.

"How was that?"

Her palms smoothed up my legs and beneath the hem to hold my ass. She guided me forward and worked my center over the ridge of her cock.

"I would have your legs spread taking me by now…but age has taught me incredible patience." She stood and placed me carefully on my feet. In my ear, she whispered, "Tasks to complete before I sample all you have to offer, Sarah."

"Go for the full menu…a sample will never satisfy."

A strong hand slid up to cup the column of my throat. "I think…you might be right."

Max escorted me rapidly from the high-rise condominium without a glance or word to anyone.

I followed her lead.

She took me to dinner, took me dancing at a members only club for all sorts of alternative lifestyles, and then took me to a luxury hotel where she displayed the stunning range of skills she'd attained since deciding to become a connoisseur of women.

Some of what she taught me - and brought out in me - would go on to make me even more popular with Vivienne's clients.

Most of it, I kept to myself.

It was too private, too personal, to use with people who would never have the ability to make me *weep with pleasure* as Max did during our night together.

Those beautiful and vulnerable memories were between us…and that was where I wanted to keep them.

CHAPTER 20:
The Singer

February 2010

Tricia Draper was my newest client. She was belting *Son of a Preacher Man* when I walked into the high-end jazz bar. The place was owned by her uncle and she performed there when she wasn't on the road or in the studio with her band.

A shimmering red dress hugged her ample curves beautifully and a tiny rhinestone chain draped her full hips. Delicate red-strapped sandals crisscrossed at her ankles as she glided slowly but confidently across the stage, microphone in hand.

It was our second appointment. She'd demanded the booking after our first one went well two weekends before. It was only possible because Monica had to cancel at the last minute to prepare for an emergency court appearance for one of her young clients.

Being honest, I *almost* turned her down. She'd wanted me the next day or the following weekend but I couldn't do it.

Impressed with the hip movements I'd learned from the master, Tricia wanted more and more.

I was unprepared to *maintain* the motion for two solid hours.

When you had a *biological* dick, *nature* ensured you got breaks.

When your cock was *manufactured*, you were expected to keep going.

That night, Kylee picked me up and I was limping by the time she let me out in the parking garage of Viv's place. My lower body was locked up and I was in agony.

Max took one look at me when I left the elevator, mumbled *fuck*, and scooped me into her arms. She carried me through the first floor to the massage room.

I held myself up with the edge of the table while she removed my clothing, strap-on equipment, and unbound my breasts. She lifted me to the surface and helped me lower to my stomach as I groaned.

"You warned me. I drastically underestimated her begging, Max." She put slight pressure on my lower back and I screamed. "Sorry. My fault. Sorry."

"One appointment a month. Always on a Sunday so you have a few days to recover."

I think I murmured agreement.

The tingling heat of the ointment she gently massaged into my back, hips, and thighs coupled with my exhaustion shoved me to sleep.

It was late morning when I opened my eyes. I was on my stomach with a heating pad on my lower back. Turning my face on the pillow, Max sat beside the bed with her elbows on her knees.

"She's greedy, Sarah. Starved for attention, trapped in a situation she dislikes, Tricia takes and takes until you can't breathe. Her talent, her beauty, her gentle heart won't make up for the way she sucks every ounce of energy from you the moment she's within touching distance."

"It's hard not to give in. It hurts…the way she is."

Max raked her fingers roughly through my hair. "You can't give at the expense of yourself, Sarah. You can't take her pain."

Leaving her palm on the back of my head, she firmed her voice. "Her situation isn't great. She's unhappy. Those facts are due to *choices* she made for her own reasons at the time. I'm not saying it's right."

"It's…hard to hear her talk about it."

"You aren't her therapist or her priest. She sold her soul to the devil. Shockingly, he held up his end of the bargain. She's mad *now*, but she *knew* what she was doing when she did it. She weighed her peace of mind and self-respect against fame and fortune…and chose the latter. Many people do."

"She was so young and he took advantage…"

"She has a *good* family - a *strong* one - who recommended that she take the slower path, the safer path. Tricia wanted it fast and she got it. It had a higher price."

Max bent and whispered in my ear, "You're looking for a victim to save, Sarah. Her situation isn't like yours. If you keep moving at her pace, she will *take from you* until you have nothing left."

"Will you help me, Max?"

"Of course. When your back is better, we'll role play your date with her. You give me the overview of how she behaved and I'll show you how to shut it down."

With a gentle kiss on my temple, she murmured, "I'm proud you asked for help." The simple words filled me with joy I didn't understand. "Rest, Sarah."

The second time I woke up, Max was again stretched out beside me on the guest bed. She wasn't sleeping and turned her head on the pillow to look at me. My entire body vibrated with a need that made me anxious.

"You know…" I was embarrassed.

"I told you she was greedy. She thinks *nothing* of your pleasure in pursuit of her own."

"Max…" I felt off-balance, greedy myself.

"I'll ease you. Don't strain your back more than it is."

Then she rolled toward me and slipped her hand beneath my naked body. Gently playing over my clit, my first climax was embarrassingly fast. She smiled, kissed me, then spent two hours giving me relief that sank to the bone.

Unlike Tricia, I definitely thought of her pleasure in tandem with my own.

Here I was, two weeks later - determined that *this* date would be different from the first one.

Max's words before I left echoed in my mind. "You are in control. At every moment, she must *bend* to your stronger will. It's what she *wants* - even when she pretends otherwise. Train her to your hand."

Now, I watched Tricia with a smile. She was short and curvy with a husky voice that could melt chocolate. Holding her microphone lightly, singing with her eyes closed, she was in her own world.

After her set, she exited the stage to applause - beaming at the room. I waited three minutes before ducking through a door and down a hall to her dressing room in the back of the club.

She was on her phone when I knocked but motioned me in with a smile. Sitting at her vanity, a white cotton robe tied loosely at her waist, she removed her makeup while listening to music I liked but didn't recognize.

Her hair was cut in a fade on the sides and curly on top. I liked the symmetry of it, the way it showed the delicacy of her skull and framed her face.

Apparently, her boyfriend and manager threw a fit when she cut it from just past her shoulders.

I'd wanted to touch it during our first appointment but didn't. A stripper I met once told me it wasn't appropriate and I never forgot.

For our first date, I wore a suit. This time, I went for comfort and mobility. I wasn't as physically strong as Max and was lacking her experience. I had to work this client somewhat differently to protect my body.

I wore skin-tight suede pants and a flowing linen tunic that brushed my upper thighs. The riding boots completed a look that made me feel a little like a pirate - in a good way. The top was cream but the pants and boots were dark brown.

Beneath the shirt, my breasts were bound snugly against my body and covered by a wicking tank top.

My hair hung down my back but a few micro braids were scattered throughout and connected to keep it off my face.

Under the pants…well, *that* little extra took some getting used to.

Max went with me to have a fake cock custom designed and fitted - a specialty I didn't know existed. She taught me how to wear it beneath my clothing and move in a way that didn't make it obvious.

Knowing Max *always* wore something similar - and how she used it - made my eyes unintentionally drift to her crotch whenever she was around.

A perusal she'd caught me making more than once.

Bringing my thoughts back to the present, I watched Tricia check her voicemails. She put down her phone and turned to me.

"Sarah! I saw you when I was on stage. Did you like the song?" Her tone attested to how self-conscious she was about her talent.

Every opinion mattered to her - in ways I'd never seen in anyone else. She could be crushed or made to feel incredible happiness with a few words.

"I loved it, Tricia. It was spectacular."

I crossed the room, cupped her face, and lifted it so she looked into my eyes. Stroking my thumb along her jaw, I allowed the silence to draw out.

Then I bent, dropped a light kiss on her full lips, and held her gaze again. "How have you been?"

"I-I spoke to him earlier. He told me he's with the studio people. A woman laughed in the background…"

"Ssh." The simple command caught her off guard. "I'm not here to please him. My time is for you."

"It's just…he's so cruel."

"That has nothing to do with us. He gets *none* of my time, Tricia. Do you understand?"

"Yes."

"Finish taking off your makeup. Enjoy a nice long shower. I'll wait."

I stepped back, sat in the club chair beside her vanity, and watched her as she went through her routine. I kept my body open, my legs slightly spread, so she could see what I had between them. The cock was clearly outlined beneath the snug fabric of my pants.

I didn't talk to her.

Building the tension and drawing this out was critical. She'd overwhelmed me during the first appointment.

I couldn't allow it to happen again.

The man who had her twisted up was Tricia's boyfriend of seven years. Jerrod Ross didn't realize - or care - how good he had it.

She was sixteen when he approached her after a performance at a local fair. Jerrod was almost thirty. He groomed her intensely - and secretly - for *months* before her family found out about him.

A predator who took advantage of a susceptible young woman.

Max was right though. She'd given me more background so I knew what I was dealing with - and what walls I'd hit if I tried to help.

Tricia's family adored her, supported her completely, and wanted her to be happy. They were solid and kind, a stable and loving support system.

They fought like hell to keep her away from the much older man who saw dollar signs the moment he heard her sing.

The ridiculous contract he talked her into the *day* she turned eighteen would keep her in the cage he constructed for another five years.

In desperation, her family convinced her to hire a trusted cousin as an assistant to keep an eye on her - and call for help if Tricia needed it.

They found shark-like accountants and attorneys to protect her money and assets as she acquired them.

Gently, lovingly, they did everything they could to keep her safe as she devoted her life to a man who neither loved nor respected her.

For all his faults, Jerrod made good on his promises.

Tricia made millions a year - booked at venues and events it would have been impossible to break into for a newcomer without his connections.

The band he hired to back her up were some of the best in the business. He fiercely guarded her image and privacy.

He'd trained her for *years* to take his orders, to put up with his behavior, and question nothing. That's why nothing would change until *she* changed it.

I knew that now.

I understood her better.

Tricia was fully under Jerrod's control. She *genuinely* loved him. There was nothing anyone could say or do to convince her otherwise.

Leave the bastard and take your talent with you.

It didn't work when Tricia heard it from her family, friends, or colleagues who'd known her far longer.

I wasn't any of those things. I wasn't her therapist. I wasn't her priest.

I was a paid escort meant to help her disconnect from her reality for a while and feel pleasure she needed like a drug fix.

After making her dependent on him in every area of her life, Jerrod quickly got bored with Tricia sexually.

He seduced her a few times a year to keep her hooked, to keep her docile, and got his kicks elsewhere the rest of the time. It was sad. She was obviously lonely.

It was none of my business.

Once she'd removed her makeup and jewelry, Tricia stood and came to crawl in my lap.

I stared into her face above me and gave her a slow smile. "You don't get rewards until you're ready. You have a normal routine after your show." I trailed my palm from her throat, between her breasts, and over the soft skin of her stomach - moving her robe aside as I went. "Do your work and then we'll play."

"I want…"

"Ssh." She tugged her pillowy lower lip between her bright white teeth. "I'll inspect you when you're done…so be thorough."

If it were up to Tricia, she'd ride my fake cock the entire night. However, if she skipped a shower and heavily moisturizing her skin, it would cause her an anxiety attack the following day.

Something I hadn't known when we met.

Slowing things down was key. Since the singer was also conscientious about her cleanliness - particularly after performing for hours - telling her of my plan to eat her forced her to stay on track.

Max was a wealth of fascinating information where this woman was concerned.

Tricia cupped my face and kissed me deeply. She whispered, "You-you want to inspect me…down there?" I nodded. "Okay. I'll be right back."

"Good girl. I'll be waiting with my mouth watering."

Climbing off my lap, she went to the bathroom and closed the door. I didn't move while I waited.

Twenty minutes later, she appeared in another robe - silk this time. She glowed head to toe from an expensive lotion with a delicate scent of wildflowers.

I patted the arms of the chair. "Take that off. Climb up here and let me have a closer look at my treat."

A shiver worked its way over her body but Tricia didn't hesitate to follow my instructions.

This time, I felt my power.

This time, I was fully in control.

It was heady stuff.

CHAPTER 21:
Tricia

Tricia climbed over me, her knees on the wide leather arms of the chair as she held my shoulder for balance.

Lifting my hands, I held her ass in my palms, bringing her forward to inhale deeply of her various scents. Body wash, lotion, and the natural musk she couldn't entirely remove.

I would have her dripping with her flavor before I was done.

Against her most sensitive flesh, I told her, "During our first appointment, you were so anxious to be fucked that you rushed my enjoyment of you." I planted a kiss above her clit. "You won't deny me this time, Tricia."

Swirling the tip of my tongue around the tight bundle of nerves, I smiled at the desperate sounds she made. "Do you want to come?"

"So badly…please."

Her voice was beautiful…even when she begged.

Massaging her ass, I held her still as I feasted on her plump folds in warm brown tones. She was hairless but I wondered what it would have looked like, how it would have felt against my lips.

Warm, wet pussy tried to pull my tongue deeper as I pushed it inside.

"Please, oh, please…"

"This is where you'll take my cock as deep as I can get it." I thrust the tip inside again and again. "But not until I'm ready. I want you wet, hot, aching for me first. So when I take you, you coat me in your slick come."

Returning to her clit, I suckled it firmly and she tumbled into climax with a long moan as I moved one hand to support her back.

I lapped at her lazily, pushing her through the first and into a second.

"Such a good girl." I planted open-mouthed kisses on her skin - wet and throbbing from my attention. "I'll feed your body something delicious since I know you haven't eaten. Then I'll feed this pretty pussy every inch of my dick and watch you take it."

"More…"

"Food first." I carefully moved her into my lap. "Then you can have more."

Tricia held my face in her hands as she made out with me almost violently. "Just…a little?" she asked breathlessly.

"Greedy darling." Turning her, I reclined her on my torso and spread her legs to either side of mine. "Play with your nipples." She instantly cupped her breasts and I nuzzled the side of her head. "That's it, let me watch while I fuck you with my fingers. One more, Tricia. Then food."

"I promise…"

Her third climax was harder to achieve because she couldn't touch me, couldn't see me. I thrust my fingers inside her but offered no other touch.

It was by design, courtesy of Max. "If you manipulate Tricia's clit too much in the beginning…she'll go numb. Alternate things to keep it from happening. She's highly sensitive to vaginal stimulation - more than any lover I've ever met. Use that to your advantage."

"Your nipples are so pretty," I said in her ear. "Little brown berries. When I fuck you full later, I want to suck them."

"Fill me up…"

By this point in our last appointment, I'd already pounded her through two orgasms with the toy between my legs.

Admittedly, I felt a little smug about it.

This time, I wouldn't give her what she really wanted until our final hour together. I would conserve my energy, protect my lower back, and drive her through the bed when it would leave the greatest impact.

Every part of the fantasy mattered.

"You'll get my cock when I say you can have it. I'm throbbing for you, Tricia. Hard and ready to sink balls deep into your dripping hole…but it isn't time."

I nipped her earlobe. "Be a good girl. Earn your reward." Pulling my fingers from her pussy, I rubbed the flats of them over her folds before returning to pushing as deep as I could. "I can't wait to feel you clench around me."

"I-I'm coming…!"

Her body tightened, her back arched off my torso, and she exhaled on a moan as the orgasm claimed her. I didn't slow my attention until she relaxed in my arms.

Leaving a kiss beneath her ear, I whispered, "You delectable woman. I can't wait to have you completely." I let her catch her breath for a couple of minutes and then sat up, taking her with me. "Dress so I can feed your belly…then I'll feed your pussy the meal it wants most."

Resting her face on my chest, she closed her eyes and took several deep breaths. Her hand stroked up and down the length of my fake cock.

"You're hard for me…I *love* that you're hard for me."

"Of course. Everything about you makes me hard."

It surprised me that Tricia didn't want women who presented as more masculine given her preferences.

Despite our clothing and silicone appendage, neither Max nor I could pass as male without considerable effort. Yet, Tricia enjoyed touching our hair, faces, and bodies while we took her.

Tricia murmured, "I want to suck you later…until you can't take another second without coming. Then you can do anything you want to me. As hard as you want."

The first time I saw myself in the mirror with my fake cock and flesh-tone fabric holding it in place, I was shocked.

Max stood behind me fully dressed - close enough that I could feel her body heat on my naked skin in the boutique dressing room.

"What are you thinking, Sarah?"

"How…insignificant it seems. It's no different than a nipple or a clit. Women possess so many ways to feel pleasure but it's men who chase it like animals." I gripped it in my fist. "For *this*? This is the *grand organ* they're always trying to satisfy? That dictates so many of their choices? It's…anticlimactic."

"You feel no desire to dominate?"

I laughed. "No. There are a couple of *men* I'd love to top though. Teach them a few valuable lessons about *taking* cock when they can't *deliver* it for shit."

Her eyes met mine in the mirror. "I like the way you think."

"Yours is the best." I said it softly but she heard me. Warm hands settled on my shoulders, massaging my muscles gently. "What are *you* thinking?"

She was quiet for so long, I didn't think she'd answer. "Biological dicks aren't nearly good enough for you."

Those words felt true for Tricia as well.

I cleaned up, watched her dress, and took her to dinner. We enjoyed some dancing at another club she liked.

I let the tension build and build. Then I used her key to open the hotel room she stayed in when she was in town. Since she traveled two hundred days a year, the thought of maintaining a place of her own seemed overwhelming to her.

Guiding her into the bedroom, I pushed her down at the edge of the bed and took my time unwrapping the sparkling packaging that concealed her from me.

Only when she was fully naked, leaning back on her hands, and spread for my viewing pleasure did I sit back to take her in.

"Stay like this. Open to me. Served up like a decadent feast."

Bracing one hand on the bed beside her, I bent to suckle at her breast. When the nipple was tight and dark from my attention, I paid homage to the other.

Every inch of her was soft, warm, and glowing. I took my time stroking my hands over her flesh, kneading and exploring, kissing as I went. I settled between her thighs and lapped at her pussy, filling her with my fingers, letting my moans vibrate against her slick skin.

She trembled for me and I wanted more from her. I wanted her weak, begging, aching for fulfillment.

I pushed Tricia there, second by second, lick by devastating lick.

I drove her through a first, second, and third orgasm as she collapsed against the bed and pleaded with me.

"Sarah! Please! I need it! Give me your cock…put it inside…take me."

Smiling to myself, I rose over her and bent her legs until her shins were flat to my torso. I let the back of my hand brush against hypersensitive folds as I slowly unzipped my pants and pulled the fake cock through the opening. I coated it with a small pack of lube from my pocket.

"This what you want, sweetheart?" I rubbed the tip over her clit, trailing it down to circle over the entrance of her pussy. "Is this what you need?"

She nodded, practically delirious with pleasure. "Fill me…do it."

Still, I took my time. Gave her an inch and pulled back. Gave her two more and pulled back.

Then I pushed deep until our bodies were sealed to one another and paused.

"Look at me, Tricia." Eyes glazed with passion and need met mine. "You were a *very* good girl."

I set a rhythm that made her incoherent as she gripped the bedding and panted frantically. Conserving *my* energy while sapping *hers* one climax at a time worked in my favor.

Another orgasm…and another. As a woman, I was impressed by her vaginal response.

Lowering a bit, I kissed her face that was drenched in sweat. "You are beautiful, powerful, and passionate. You make me hard and fucking *desperate* to come." *Absolutely true.* "Thank you for the opportunity to be inside your stunning body…to fill your pretty pussy and do my best to please you."

"Sarah…" she murmured weakly.

"It's okay. I know you're tired, sweetheart. Come all over my cock one more time, Tricia. Then I'm going to clean you up and tuck you in for a nice, long sleep. One more time for me."

Not long after, she did. I carefully pulled from her and lowered her legs. Gathering her in my arms, I hugged her tightly against me.

"It was an honor to be here with you." I kissed her entire face and laid her back on the bed. "Stay here while I get a towel to wipe you down. You can shower in the morning." I stroked my palm up her quivering calf. "Your legs would never hold you now."

Tricia was past the ability to respond. I kissed her and walked to the bathroom. I cleaned the cock and tucked it away before wetting a towel and taking it - with another dry one - back to the bed.

I wiped her from head to toe and dried her skin. Then I picked her up and carried her to the side of the bed that wasn't soaked with her sweat and come. It was the side she normally slept on because her phone charger was there with a carafe of water and a glass.

Holding her in a sitting position, I gave her two ibuprofen and held the water so she could drink. Settling her against the pillows, I found her robe and laid it over the end of the bed.

Then I leaned over her, kissed her once more, and told her I'd see her next time.

"Sarah?" I paused before straightening. "You fuck like you love the person you're with. I want you to know that I notice…and appreciate it."

"I'm glad. Goodnight, Tricia. I'll see you in a few weeks. Be safe out there and remember you're the most important person in your life. Your life doesn't happen without you. Treat yourself gently."

I pulled up her blankets, turned down the air conditioning, and let myself out.

Texting Kylee in the elevator, I took a seat in the hotel lobby to wait.

It was *Max* who came for me.

CHAPTER 22:
Reflection

Smiling, I stood to greet her. She looked incredible - as usual - in a tailored three-piece suit.

Max grinned. "You look *much* better this time."

"Our role play helped. Thanks for that. I might have died or been partially paralyzed without you."

"Don't even joke. You hungry?"

"Starving like I haven't eaten in a week." I tilted my head. "Don't you have to pick up the other girls?"

"Everyone is present and accounted for tonight. You're the last one out. I offered to retrieve you myself."

"Awesome. What are your thoughts on pancakes?"

She winked. "The closest Denny's is still open."

"Let's do it." I was surprised to see her personal car idling at the valet stand. "Yay! I don't have to feel weird in the back by myself!"

Chuckling, she opened my door and I slid into the passenger seat of her Audi sports car. It was as pristine as the cars she drove for Vivienne.

Behind the wheel, Max turned to look at me with her brow arched. "Don't take this the wrong way but…you smell like come."

"Unfortunately, not mine." She laughed and it made some weird little place in my chest happy. "I shall pay to detail your pretty car."

"Hmm. Tempting. Instead, let me rinse that scent off and cover you with ours. What's your opinion on that plan of action? After pancakes, of course."

Nodding, I whispered, "Uh huh. I am *here* for that itinerary. Please pencil me into your calendar."

"Excellent. I'll take you to my place after eating." She shifted the car into gear. Her smile in profile was gorgeous. "Then I'll eat what I *really* want."

"You sexy demon."

"I consider that the highest of compliments."

Our conversation never stopped as I asked her questions about her routines when she wasn't working, in military school, and in the service.

I avoided questions about her family in case that was too personal. I could tell she was careful about the questions she asked me in return.

For the next hour, I didn't touch Max getting in and out of her car, at the diner, or as I stripped in the bathroom of her oceanside condo.

Showering thoroughly, I let the hot water beat on my muscles. Doing it like a dude then deadlifting a grown woman was hell on the back.

After towel drying my hair, I found her blow dryer to handle the rest.

Max entered the bathroom in her pants and dress shirt with the sleeves rolled up. The jacket, vest, and tie were gone and she was barefoot. She took the dryer from me and worked it through my hair.

"Thanks. My arms were getting tired."

After a few minutes, she said with a smile, "You have a *lot* of hair."

"Hmm." Tired, I didn't think before I spoke. "When I was six, my aunt shaved my head because I couldn't get the tangles out before we made it to school."

Why the fuck did I say that?

Her eyes lifted to mine and I couldn't read her expression. I'd accidentally made things depressing. She turned off the blow dryer and put it down.

Assuming a playful tone, I added, "It was *blonde* then, down to my butt. Grew back *Little Annie* red. I was glad it darkened as I got older."

I stared at the bathroom counter. "I decided if - when - I became an adult, I'd let it get as long and ridiculous as Rapunzel's. I don't, obviously."

Her fingers fisted in my hair and she tilted my head back for a kiss.

It was destructive.

Against my mouth, she said, "You don't have to censor yourself. I don't mind darkness, Sarah. I can tell you've experienced a lot of it."

Turning around, I whispered, "Light is better. I try to find it where I can."

"Allow me."

Then Max picked me up and carried me to her bed with my arms and legs wrapped around her body. As the sun rose, it filled her bedroom with light from floor-to-ceiling windows facing the Atlantic.

The image of her moving rhythmically above me - a look of intense sexual power on her face - rivaled it.

Max provided magnificent pleasure but there came a point when my body couldn't keep going no matter how badly I wanted it to.

*** * ***

When I opened my eyes, I didn't know where I was. Confused and groggy, I sat up as panic climbed in my chest.

"Sarah." Max's voice came from behind me. I glanced over my shoulder and exhaled in relief. "You didn't recognize your surroundings." After a pause, I shook my head. "I'll keep bringing you here so it becomes familiar. I never want you to be afraid."

Taking a slow, deep breath, I murmured, "Thanks."

"Sleep more. You need it. I'll take you to get your bike later." She put her arm behind her head and I liked the way it looked.

Max was fit, strong, and beautifully confident. She didn't pretend to be otherwise. I hoped I could be like that one day.

Lowering to the pillows, I crossed my hands over my stomach and stared at the tray ceiling above the bed. My thoughts were still chaotic.

"I don't sleep much. My brain fights my body."

"There are ways to calm panic when it's happening. Find a point on the ceiling. Focus on it. Count slowly to thirty…then reverse to one."

The first part was easy, the second required greater focus and my brain gradually settled. Eyes wide, I looked at Max and she smiled.

"I had panic attacks for a while after the explosion. PTSD is common in military people. We used to pass tricks on to each other. If this one stops working, I know others."

"Thank you."

"You're welcome, Sarah. Have you ever tried meditation?" I shook my head. "I think it might help you relax before sleep. There are many methods. I can show you some after coffee."

"I'd like that." Turning back to the ceiling, I told her, "I'm like a little kid with nightmares…"

"You know you're not. I won't push. One day, maybe you'll talk to me about it. I might have a fresh perspective."

I thought about that for a long time. Max was older than me by over a decade. Every person experienced pain. No matter how happy her childhood was, she'd served as a Marine and been through war.

She'd even been wounded there. She had a long scar on the lower left quadrant of her back - and several smaller puckered ones - that must have been agonizing when it happened.

"I'd rather talk about you."

"We can do that."

"I like…how simple you make things."

Max lifted a strand of my hair and played it through her fingers. "Life is *complex* but it doesn't have to be *complicated*. Recognizing the difference can prevent a lot of unnecessary pain."

Being with her was easy. Easier than everyone else in my life - including Campbell. She demanded nothing from me but gave me pleasure and insight without conditions or judgment.

I wasn't sure what she saw in me as a woman or as a friend. We didn't have anything in common on the surface other than the agency. Still. I liked how I was when I was with her. As she said…

Complex but not complicated.

CHAPTER 23:
Ilene

March 2010

I got off my motorcycle at Ilene's place and barely secured my helmet before Felix greeted me with genuine puppy enthusiasm. I knelt to give him scratches behind the ears and he licked my jaw.

His joy was infectious and I couldn't stop smiling.

"You remember me? What a good and smart boy you are." Glancing up, I grinned at Ilene. "Hey. Welcome back. How was your trip?"

"Exhausting. Sorry I was gone longer than I said. I made food. I, uh, don't have anyone I can talk to about my family drama but I think you might understand."

Standing, I walked over and gave her a hug. I was surprised when she clutched me back tightly.

"It's okay. If you're upset but haven't talked about it, focusin' on our time together will be hard. I'm here for whatever you need, Ilene."

Ten minutes later, we sat at her table with bowls of food and ate the homemade chicken and dumplings without diving into heavy topics.

Pushing her plate away, Ilene took a deep breath and started to talk. "Todd - my ex-husband - met someone. A man. They're in love."

"That's good, isn't it?"

She nodded. "It is…but not accordin' to our kids. They're embarrassed and ashamed. The two oldest - their entire lives are wrapped up in that church. Their friends, friends of their kids, business connections. They want him to stay in the closet so it doesn't upset their lives." Meeting my eyes, she said through gritted teeth, "They wanted me to convince him to do the *right* thing."

"Wow." I tapped the table, trying to remain calm. "So, *they* get to live whatever lives they want but *their parents* have to do what they're told?" I shook my head. "Ilene, I might be the worst person to talk to about this. I don't have a dog in the fight and it's real easy for me to cut off blood."

Looking out her window, she said softly, "I've never been so angry. I thought…this is how they'll act when it's *me*. I knew if I didn't back Todd up, I'd be the biggest hypocrite of them all."

"You stayed to help him. That's what took so long."

"He retired from the church. We sold the house and found him a nice place near his boyfriend. There were a lot of tears. We realized how much time we wasted that we can't get back."

I placed my hand over hers on the table. "Imagine the rest of them though. Livin' a full and happy life that makes the sadness of what came before fade a little more every day."

Considering, I added, "If your kids come around, try again. If they don't, it shouldn't change your own path. We get one life - come in and go out alone - so maybe think about how you want that last moment to be. Filled with regrets or joy? I hope…when my end comes…I remember more beauty than pain."

A sad expression crossed her face and she turned her hand over in mine, squeezing me firmly. "It's unnatural for someone your age to speak of death so calmly unless they've dealt with a life of sickness. It breaks my heart."

"I'm okay." I smiled. "Death doesn't scare me but livin' sometimes did. I'm better now. Don't worry." Leaning closer, I asked, "Done with painful stuff?"

"Sarah…"

"I'm here for *you*. Don't forget."

"I don't, uh, want to be naked. I want to touch you and learn things." Her voice shook and she cleared her throat. "I've never even seen my own body up close."

"Decide where you want me and I'll wash what we used." She started to get up. "Uh uh. You cooked. I'll clean up."

I asked her random questions about her trip while I washed a few things and covered the rest of the food. When I was done, I stood in front of her.

"I present myself for exploration."

Ilene led me through the house to her bedroom. When we were inside, she told Felix to stay in the hall and closed the door.

"I have the best light in here this time of day."

"You can turn on more if you need it," I suggested as I took off my boots and socks. "I don't mind."

"You're not shy…"

I pulled my t-shirt over my head and shrugged. "It's just a body. My outer shell. Everyone has one and most of the parts work the same. Colors and shapes are different…that kind of thing. Mine is healthy and I'm grateful."

Ilene watched my movements intently with her hands folded in front of her. I shimmied my jeans down my legs and dropped them with my shirt on the bench at the end of her bed.

Standing in front of her in my white cotton bra and panties, I could see she was nervous…maybe even fearful. I removed both and she was not unaffected by the image of a naked woman in her bedroom.

"Things look different standin', sittin', and layin' down. Just let me know what you want me to do."

"Don't move…not yet. I-I need a moment."

I kept myself still with my arms relaxed at my sides. I didn't speak. I simply let her look at me.

"Will you take down your hair?"

I did and it fell around me in a wild tangle.

Approaching me like a skittish stray, Ilene reached out to run her fingers through it. The back of her fingers brushed over my nipple and she pulled back like the contact burned her.

Her eyes widened as it tightened. Reaching out, I took her hand and cupped it around my breast. Her breath stuttered from her lips. I held it there so she could feel the weight, the texture in her palm. I squeezed it using my hand over hers.

I lifted her other hand to duplicate the touch. When she began to plump them on her own, I lowered mine to my sides again.

"It feels good to touch them." Her eyes lifted. "Does it feel good to you?" I nodded. "Whenever Todd touched me here, it felt no different than nursin' my children."

"When I suck your nipples…you *won't* think about nursin' your children." Her fingers tightened around me. "That image affected you." I pushed my hair over my shoulders and asked, "Would you like to taste them?"

Ilene sat on the edge of her bed and pulled me between her knees. I braced my hands on her shoulders. She wrapped an arm around my back and sucked a nipple between her lips.

Her eyes drifted closed as she fell into the experience in a way I'd *never* seen. Her hands roamed my back and ass as she *intensely* suckled me, moving back and forth between them while her moans of hunger sent tiny vibrations over my skin.

After several minutes, she licked over the tip and said in a rough voice, "I'd love to recline in my chair and have you in my lap. Leaning over so your tits are in my face. Then I could suck your nipples for hours."

Definitely a breast woman.

It was strange but also highly erotic to have her so focused on one area of my body.

"I want to explore the rest of you." She gave my breasts another squeeze. "I'll come back to these." With a final lick, she sat back. "I want you to spread your legs for me. So I…can see your pussy."

Stepping back, I sat beside her on the bed and laid back. Resting my heels on the edge of the mattress, I dropped my knees wide.

"Oh, Sarah." She went to her knees next to the bed and stared at me. "You're wet."

"Mm hmm." I kept my eyes on the chain pull of the ceiling fan above her bed.

"It's prettier than I expected it to be. All different shades of pink."

"Every woman is unique. Some are shades of brown, beige, red, black…some have hair and others don't. Pussy lips might be thin or plump - just like the mouth. Some women have more folds, others have looser skin. The basic biology is the same but what brings us pleasure might be different."

A finger trailed over the outer lips and I gasped.

"Tell me what you mean."

"Some women can't come vaginally. A lot more than most people realize. Others experience horrific pain during anal and no amount of preparation seems to help. A lot of women can come explosively by manipulatin' the clit and the place just behind it in the pussy. Sprayin' like a man."

"Can you do that?"

"No," I lied smoothly. Max had made it happen and I didn't particularly want another lover to attempt it. "But I've seen it."

"What should I know about fingering you?"

My heart raced at her seemingly innocent questions. "I produce enough natural lubrication but a lot of women don't. You shouldn't rub the clit when it's dry. It's delicate. You always need it wet. From the pussy, your tongue, lickin' your fingers, or from a bottle. Even Walmart sells lube."

A finger circled my pussy and my lower body clenched. "Get it wet first." The light touch of her fingertip on my clit almost made me come. "It got hard and tight. Like a tiny dick."

"Ahh…"

"You're sensitive here."

Then she licked me and I couldn't believe a virgin to lesbian sex affected me so strongly. I wondered if it had to do with being a recipient…unable to return the attention.

"When you masturbate, do you focus on your clit?" Her questions were killing me.

"Yes, mostly. It's harder for me vaginally."

She lightly sucked the bundle of nerves and I gasped. Her tongue licked around the entrance of my pussy and I fought against closing my legs.

The curious exploration had been going on for a long time. My body was coiled for a climax.

"I like the way you taste. Clean, a little salty, a musk that's unlike anything I've ever tasted." She lapped at me like an ice cream cone and I started to tremble. "Does everyone taste different?"

"Y-yes…" I managed.

Ilene pushed a finger inside me and stroked several times. "You're really slick and hot. I didn't know it was ridged on the inside." She pulled her finger out of me. I didn't look but I could hear her sucking my fluids off her skin. "I want more."

Two fingers thrust into me and she used them to rub my slickness on my folds.

"I finally understand why it's called *eating* pussy. I want to spend hours with my mouth between your legs. Licking, sucking, drinking you down."

She pursed her lips around my clit again. "I want to make you come. Tell me what to do. Should I suck you here?"

"There…right there." My voice was hoarse. I could feel the climax just out of reach and worried it would become a strange cycle of almost getting there but not quite. "Suck it harder."

Ilene listened, followed my instructions exactly, and my body tightened as the orgasm broke loose.

The relief was exquisite.

Glancing at the clock, I realized she'd been exploring my body and asking her questions for almost an hour.

I went limp against the bed and she sat back, her fingers rubbing around my pussy. I could hear how wet I was as she touched me.

"Look at that. I didn't know that's how our bodies worked. It feels *crazy* to learn that so late in my life."

As my body settled, I took a deep breath and lifted to my elbows. Ilene's eyes met mine up the length of my body and she gave me a half-smile.

"Thank you, Sarah. Was this weird for you?"

I shook my head. "Different but not weird."

She stood and helped me to my feet. Wrapping a light cotton robe around my body, she said, "Let's have a snack. I made cherry pie." I snorted. "Right? It's like I *knew*." Her fingers stroked my hair back from my face. "After…can we do the other thing I mentioned? In my chair?"

My heart raced. "Sure."

For the next three appointments I had with Ilene, half of our time was spent eating and talking.

The rest was spent with her learning how to please another woman in bed…each and every time.

She took the lessons seriously.

* * *

The last day I went to Ilene's house, I knew our time together was over. In fact, I'd known all along that our relationship would be a short one.

For two years, she'd been developing a close friendship with a woman in Louisiana. Someone she met online and had spoken with on the phone and through video on the computer.

Lila was around the same age as Ilene, also divorced but didn't have kids.

They'd talked about sex but it was a topic my unique client always shied away from since she felt she had no working knowledge.

Her discomfort with the previous escorts sent to her hadn't helped Ilene overcome her lack of confidence and experience.

"Then *you* showed up, Sarah. I knew you could help me learn what I wanted to know so I didn't feel awkward and afraid when I was in front of someone I've been attracted to for a long time."

Reaching out, I hugged Ilene close. "I'm glad I was able to help. Thank you for spendin' time with me and lettin' me into your life for a little while. You reminded me of the good parts of home."

Her hands held my face and she stared deeply into my eyes. "Live a full and happy life, Sarah. When you get the opportunity to experience love, trust, happiness…grab them with both hands. Even if it doesn't last. Even if there's pain to deal with after. Grab it and enjoy every second. Your life slips by so much faster than you think."

Ilene kissed me softly and rested her forehead against mine. "Thank you for being kind, being patient, and letting me touch you. L-letting me learn how to touch another woman. I don't think I ever would have had the courage to take a step otherwise."

"You're welcome." I kissed her once and stepped out of her arms. Bending, I gave Felix scratches. "Take care of your mama, sweet boy."

Then I got on my bike, put on my helmet, waved, and drove away.

There was a small ache in my heart.

CHAPTER 24:
The Model

April 2010

I had a little more downtime after my dates with Ilene stopped. I managed to get my initial melancholy under control, thank goodness.

I couldn't explain why I felt it but kept it to myself.

Vivienne told me a new client would be joining my calendar. The day of my first appointment with Nadia, I was instructed to eat light. I was a little offended because I didn't eat a lot most days.

"Max, um…do I look like I'm gaining weight or getting flabby?"

For a long moment, she stared at me in a bra and panties where I stood in front of the guest room mirror at Viv's.

"Did someone say that to you?"

"No. No, it was my brain, I guess."

"Your body is exactly right." I laughed shyly but Max didn't even crack a smile. "You could gain fifty pounds…a hundred. Lose a limb. Shave your head. It wouldn't change the fact that you are exactly right."

She walked across the room to me. "But the answer to your question is no. If anything, you're lighter and leaner than you were six months ago." Holding me still with nothing more than her intense gaze, she added, "I recommend more cake."

"I-I do like cake."

"I like that you like cake." Lifting her hand to hold the side of my face, she asked, "Do you still run?"

"Three or four days a week."

"Doing amateur nights? Fighting and stripping?"

"S-sometimes."

Max stared at me - silently, barely blinking - for almost a minute. "I'll pick you up after your appointment. We'll have pancakes."

"Okay."

Max dropped her hand as Walker entered the room with clothes in his arms. It felt like…something had happened but I wasn't sure what.

"Time to dress, you little urchin."

"Uh huh." When I turned, Max's back was disappearing through the door.

An hour later, I was delivered to Ruth's Chris Steakhouse in Ft. Lauderdale.

I wasn't sure what to expect and felt a little off-balance. Vivienne had been strangely vague about my new client. I even wondered if she avoided me on purpose.

I'd been dressed in a DKNY black wrap dress that hadn't been introduced to the market yet and vintage Manolo Blahniks

Vivienne bought for me during her last trip to New York. My hair was tamed into a smooth twist at the base of my skull.

I *looked* chic even if I didn't *feel* it.

Kylee came around to open my door and I stepped from the car. She held out a hand to help me negotiate the curb.

"Max will pick you up at midnight, Sarah." With a wink, she got back into the car and drove away.

I turned for the entrance and noticed a woman watching me. She held a thin cigar in her hand. To me, she seemed unrealistically beautiful - like she was being photoshopped as she stood on the street.

Most of her height was in her legs and the dangerously high heels she wore made her six inches taller than me.

She headed in my direction before I had the chance to move. I received two kisses - one on each cheek - and a heavily accented, "You must be Sarah. What a pleasure, darling."

"Hi. Yes, I'm Sarah. Are you Nadia?" I asked politely.

"I am Nadia." She tucked my arm in hers and I was pulled gracefully inside.

When we were seated, she ordered two Vodkas on the rocks and asked what I drank. I ordered an iced tea with orange.

"I hope you are hungry. You do not drink alcohol?"

I liked the way her mouth moved and the sound of her voice. Something in the back of my mind whispered: *she's the epitome of a sexy villain.*

"I didn't eat lunch so I'm starving. I don't drink. I don't like the taste or how it makes me feel."

"I will drink for both of us, Sarah."

She removed a cigarette case from her tiny purse and lit one before remembering she couldn't smoke inside. Mumbling something in Russian, she dropped it in her water glass.

Snapping at a server, the girl practically bowed as she brought a fresh glass and removed the one with the tobacco in it.

There was no doubt Nadia was spoiled and a little awful but I took the opportunity to study her.

Her hair was a shade between brown and blonde. It was impossible to tell the length because it was arranged in a complicated knot at the back of her head. Her eyes were enormous, bright blue, and surrounded by thick lashes.

"Sarah. You like to look at me, yes?" Her eyes bored into mine.

"I do. Does it bother you?"

"Not at all. I like you to look. It is the only talent I have…being beautiful. It is how I earn my living."

"I guess I earn my living with similar talents." She laughed and it made me smile. Many patrons blatantly stared at the woman across from me. "You're a model, right?"

"Hmm. It is a way for women to get out of poverty in my country. My journey has also included selling myself. Stops on the way to somewhere else. Do *you* travel somewhere else?"

Had I become an escort to get somewhere else as she'd done?

"This isn't a *stop* for me. More like…one of those exhibits you visit by driving through."

"You say…your clients are animals."

"No. More like driving through to see Christmas lights on display - each more breathtaking than the last. But…if you were an animal, you'd be a jaguar or a cheetah."

Another server set down our drinks and Nadia waved him away impatiently. He seemed grateful she acknowledged him, even rudely.

"I'm not ashamed of being an escort. I have plans but…it's a good fit for me right now." I tilted my head. "Will you ask if I enjoy what I do?"

Her eyes widened and her nipples pebbled against the thin drape dress she wore. It was clear she wore nothing beneath it. "This is a question I do not need to ask. You have hunger in your eyes."

"Yes." In many ways.

"You will eat and we will talk. May I order for you?"

It was an odd request but I nodded. We were in a steakhouse so I'd eat anything on the menu.

Our waiter stood nearby. Nadia glanced up and said sharply, "You. Come now."

He practically tripped over himself to appear at her side. Order pad in hand, he hung on her every word.

I was so fascinated by the display that it took me a moment to realize how much food she'd ordered for me. Appetizer, house salad with extra dressing, rare steak, loaded baked potato, bread, dessert.

Did I look like I ate that much?

Nadia ordered herself a salad with no dressing.

When he left, I laughed nervously. "Please tell me you plan on sharing all that food with me."

Nadia did not laugh. "No. I will watch you enjoy the things I cannot."

"Huh," I managed.

"Perhaps you cannot eat every bite. Enjoy what you can. Allow me to live that experience through you."

I was stunned. "You won't eat anything but the salad? Honestly? *Why?*"

Her expression held weariness and seemed much older than her twenty-six years. "Because beauty truly is my *only* talent, darling. Without it, I wander loose in the world with nothing to support myself. I must not gain a single ounce before my photo shoot on Sunday." My sadness for her must have shown itself on my face. "Do not be sad for me, pet. I walk this path freely. To somewhere else, yes?"

"Where are you going? What's your final destination?"

She shrugged. "Someone wealthy enough to keep me satisfied as long as I live. They must have money and not be ugly."

I blinked. Absorbing such a mercenary statement took me a moment. I wasn't naive. I knew people thought like Nadia and had similar goals. I'd just never heard it said so plainly.

"If I must, I will give them a child. The contracts will be inches thick and take lawyers much time to create."

"What about love…?"

"Such a thing does not exist. I want to be *safe*. I wish to be *protected*. Money will give me what I desire most."

Confused, I asked, "Don't you make a lot as a model?"

She leaned forward, her eyes wide. "I could *never* make enough to be satisfied. The time I can use my beauty…the clock ticks even now. My face and body will bring a mega-millionaire, perhaps even a billionaire, to the palm of my hand. Even if it does not last, I will be set for life."

"That sounds lonely."

Shrugging, she sipped her vodka. "I care little for emotions or even sex. I prefer cash."

I was not a therapist.

I was not a priest.

I was an escort meant to supply pleasure…and this woman required something *specific* from me.

"Why hire someone like me?"

"Hmm. I met Vivienne when I made my debut at twelve. She knows the pleasure I need. It is a kink I have had for a long time. She thought you might be able to withstand it."

"Tell me about the kink."

"I am asexual. I prefer not to be touched at all. Being with men has been a necessary evil and I learned to act when I am with them. Watching you eat will make me wet, make me ache. At the hotel, you will eat more and I will masturbate."

Yeah, that was specific.

I kind of got why Viv thought I could handle this client. I'd seen the other escorts eat. I had a good appetite so I could probably eat more than all of them if I paced myself.

I avoided drinking my tea to keep from making my stomach fuller, faster.

The appetizer of shrimp cocktail was placed in front of me. I took my time peeling three of the six massive shrimps and ate them slowly…dipping them in cocktail sauce, licking a bit from the end, and taking small bites.

The effect on Nadia was instantaneous. Her eyes glazed, her lips parted, and her body relaxed against the chair.

I'd never eaten so slowly.

When my house salad arrived, I slathered it in the dressing. Avoiding the croutons and cheese - which would fill me up - I ate the tomatoes and cucumbers as well as a bit of the lettuce.

A loaf of warm bread and a ramekin of butter were next. I cut a thin slice and covered it heavily in butter before nibbling it with a deep sigh.

"A-another," Nadia whispered when I finished it.

I repeated the process and my steak and baked potato were set in front of me by the time I was done.

Leaving the skin, I ate some of the potato that was practically drowned in butter, sour cream, fresh bacon crumbles, and chives. I cut small bites of the steak and moaned while I chewed.

The entire time, Nadia didn't look away from my mouth. Her breathing was rapid and her pulse pounded in her neck.

"Eat more…"

I did and felt when my stomach was full. There was so much food still on the table. She hadn't touched her salad but finished both vodkas.

In the end, she begged until I'd finished the loaf of bread, the inside of the potato, and the majority of the biggest steak I'd ever had. My stomach hurt.

There was no more room. Nadia demanded the six-layer chocolate cake be boxed to go with a side of whipped cream.

"We leave now." Standing, she added. "I will not come in this place."

I'd been eating for over an hour while she drank and watched me chew and swallow every bite. I felt bloated and a little nauseous.

Outside, a driver held the door as we climbed in the back of a Mercedes SUV.

Her hand instantly moved under the hem of her dress. I watched as she played with herself beneath the fabric and made herself come, while the driver pretended to notice nothing from his position in the front seat.

It was bizarre.

I didn't understand it.

I thought I should talk her through a fantasy involving food - the idea made my stomach clench.

At her hotel, she held the bag from the restaurant and led the way to the bank of elevators.

Inside the room, she placed it on the coffee table, stripped her dress over her head, and reclined naked on the couch.

"Sit here in front of me. Eat the cake."

I lowered to the table and removed the cake, opening the box and dreading what came next.

When I picked up the fork, she shook her head. "No. With your fingers."

Please don't let me throw up.

Taking a deep breath, I picked it up and took a tiny bite. She settled her fingers over her folds and started to circle her clit. I could barely get the rich chocolate down but Nadia didn't seem to notice.

By the time I'd eaten half of the huge slice of cake, she'd made herself come twice.

"Give me the whipped cream." I opened the small cup and held it out to her. "Hold it to my mouth." I did and she stuck out her tongue to lick a dollop from the top.

It made her come.

I didn't know what to do so I sat still holding the cup, filled with confusion.

Nadia stood. "Take the cake and cream with you. I will see you next time." I got up and headed for the door. At the last moment, she called, "You are good, Sarah. Thank you."

"You're welcome…have a good night."

In the lobby, I paused and held my abdomen. I crossed the lobby with my head up and shoulders back.

Max met me at the door and murmured, "You okay?"

"Too much food. Way too much. Need to throw up…won't do it here." She opened the passenger door of her car. "I need a gas station or the side of the road. Something." I held the bag with the cake in it. When she slid behind the wheel, I said, "I won't throw up in your car…"

"Understand this…it's just a fucking car, Sarah."

"I'm sorry. I'll feel better once I get it out."

She tore from the parking lot to a boat launch a block away on the Intercoastal Waterway. Whipping into a spot, she came around to help me out.

"Stay here…"

"Like hell. Come here."

Max led me to a trashcan and tipped off the lid. The second the smell of random garbage hit me, I lost everything in my stomach. It took a long time to get it all up and the dry heaves were vicious.

I stood there, shaking and gripping the edge of a public trash can, spit and vomit on my lower face and coming out of my nose. I was exhausted and humiliated.

"Don't move." Max walked to the car and I heard her trunk open. Moments later, she wiped my face of the absolutely disgusting mess. Standing me up, she held fabric over my nose and said, "Blow." I did and it burned. "Rinse and drink."

A bottle of water pressed against my hand and I opened it. I had to spit, rinse, and get the gross out of my sinuses. I couldn't believe I was doing it all in front of Max. She made me blow several more times.

"These are alcohol wipes from the first aid kit. They'll do alright to wipe your hands." She threw something in the trash and I realized it was a t-shirt. Before I could say anything, she explained, "From my gym bag. No loss."

I straightened and she removed a handkerchief from her pocket. Wetting it with some of the water, she wiped the tears I'd shed while vomiting and the rest of my face.

Holding my shoulders, she asked, "Better?" I nodded. I was too embarrassed to speak. "I'm going to be pissed if you develop an eating disorder from this fucking client." She squeezed me gently. "Right now, you need tea and honey to soothe your throat and calm your stomach."

Half an hour later, I was showered, dressed in one of Max's shirts, and sitting cross-legged on her couch with a mug in my hands. She sat on the coffee table in front of me and I answered her questions about Nadia and our date.

"Viv didn't warn you?"

"She told me to eat light. I thought…she meant I was gaining weight or something." My voice was a bit hoarse. I'd thrown up *hard*. "Thanks for helping. You always see me at my worst."

"Untrue." Max wore sweat shorts and a tank top. The way the simple clothes highlighted her fitness kept distracting me. "What are you thinking?"

"How you always look so fucking good in suits but you're somehow even more gorgeous dressed like this." Considering, I added, "I bet you were hot in fatigues."

Max was quiet for a long time before she got up and walked to her office. She came back with a photo album and held it out to me, taking my tea. Lowering into the big chair beside the couch, she watched me.

I ran my fingers over the cover that was embossed with *Maxine "Max" Huxley, United States Marine Corps.*

"My mom made this for me."

The first photo was her official picture taken after she became a Marine. The serious look on her face sent a chill up my spine.

I took my time going through each page. There were photos of Max in training, with her unit, and some while she was deployed overseas. Two of her were in full military dress but the rest were her in her everyday uniform and fatigues between missions.

"You're only truly smiling in a few." I tapped the image of a pretty woman close to Max's height with blonde hair and brown eyes. "She made you smile?"

"In the beginning."

"Where is she now?"

"Married with a kid. Her husband was my C.O."

The last few pages were dedicated to Max's recovery after leaving the Corps - mostly pictures of her in physical therapy.

"You could have died. I'm so fucking glad you didn't." I closed the album and set it on the coffee table. "You were hot as a soldier. No doubt. I think you're hotter right now though." I crawled into her lap and laid my head on her shoulder. "I like when you smile, Max."

I like it right here...so much.

Strong arms went around me and I didn't realize when I fell asleep. I trusted Max enough to let down my guard in every situation - no matter how vulnerable.

It said more about her than me.

CHAPTER 25:
Making Lemonade

May 2010

A year before I became an escort, an elderly woman swerved into my lane to make a turn and braked suddenly less than three feet in front of me.

I was travelling at forty miles per hour - the posted speed. There was no time to stop, nowhere for me to go, no way to avoid the impact. I hit the rear of her Cadillac then flipped over her trunk, roof, and hood.

While I laid on the pavement trying to get my bearings, the woman got out of her car, and walked around the front to look at me.

"I almost missed my turn," she said kindly. "Oh, thank *goodness* you were wearing a helmet. So many young people don't think about their safety."

The lenses of her glasses were as thick as my pinkie. To say I was thankful the poor thing didn't gas it and run my ass over is an understatement.

A little piece of me was angry and kind of wanted to throttle her. Another piece whispered that she looked like my grandmother.

She was clearly confused and I was getting pretty fuzzy myself. Everything hurt as I got myself into a sitting position and removed my helmet for air. It felt like it weighed about three hundred pounds. I left it sitting on the street.

The fact that I could move at all told me I probably hadn't broken anything in my neck or spine.

"You're so pretty, dear."

"Th-thanks."

My jeans were torn from my left ankle to my knee and my shirt was filthy. Using the front of the woman's car to brace myself, I managed to work myself off the ground and put my weight on my right leg. I sweated heavily from the effort.

The initial shock of the impact was fading and pain was beginning to set in. I limped slowly around her car to take a look at the damage to my bike.

Other cars were beginning to stop and pedestrians watched from the sidewalk. A man called out, "Are you okay?" but I was on the verge of screaming or throwing up so I didn't answer.

My front fender was cracked in half, partially blocking the tire. I popped my storage compartment, pulled a small socket tool from its sleeve, and managed to remove the broken piece. I put it and the tool back.

There was serious paint damage along the entire left side from sliding on the street once I was no longer in control.

The woman stood next to her Cadillac with her hands folded. I tried to give her my name and information several times but was starting to forget what the hell I needed to tell her.

"Is this the shopping center where TJ Maxx is?"

"I-I don't know, ma'am."

I needed to get to the hospital.

Managing to get my left leg over the body, I straddled my bike and tried to start it. It didn't cooperate the first few times, but eventually kicked over. My pride and joy sounded like it had the flu.

I settled on the seat and pressed my palms against my temples. A raging headache was already starting.

Walking it back carefully to the intersection I'd just crossed, the light turned green and I rode down Sample Road toward the nearest hospital.

I couldn't wait for the police or an ambulance. I wasn't letting myself pass out on a public street where I was completely vulnerable to strangers.

How I made it to North Broward Medical Center two miles away, I didn't know. I apparently passed out the moment I staggered inside.

I woke up an hour later with a broken ankle, three broken ribs, a fractured wrist, and a concussion. I was relieved there were no internal injuries.

After they patched me up and I waited to be transported to a regular room, a Broward Sheriff's deputy entered the screened area to talk to me.

"My name is Jake Johnson." *What an awesome porn star name.* "I was on my lunch break at the diner across the street when you had your accident. I saw the whole thing." He set my helmet beside my clothes.

"I followed you to the hospital. Didn't want other cars too close since you were only doing about fifteen. Not sure how the hell you made it."

He'd gotten the old woman's plate information and another patrol car intercepted her as she pulled into a parking spot in front of the ever-popular TJ Maxx.

"You were lucky, ma'am. Why didn't you wait for an ambulance?"

The light meds the nurse gave me were beginning to kick in and the pain was fading to a dull roar.

"I don't remember what went through my head except getting out of the street before I passed out."

He laughed and I thought he was cute. Dark blonde hair cut close and light green eyes. Nice physique. Not an overly tall man - about five-nine - but solid in the upper body. He took my statement and we chatted for a while.

"Will you have dinner with me, Miss Kent?"

"Ask again when I can think straight, officer."

He smiled his dimples at me and gave me his number on the back of a business card.

Campbell arrived hours later from Orlando with another rant about the *death machine* I insisted on using for transportation.

When he was done, he slapped a stuffed panda and a book on the tray table and threw himself into a chair.

"I'm staying here. I already told your nurse and she's bringing me a blanket." He sounded furious but I knew it was how he coped with genuine fear. "I'll take you home when they release you."

"Thanks, Camp. Love you."

"Yeah, I fucking love you, too. Shut up."

I smiled and opened a Dean Koontz novel I hadn't read yet. I was lucky to have such an amazing friend.

They kept me for two days for observation. I was bruised from head to toe but my pain tolerance was off the charts.

After I was released, I hobbled around for weeks waiting for my bones to heal. My motorcycle made it to the hospital and refused to start again. It was towed to my apartment.

Monica handled things with the insurance company of the woman who caused the accident and arranged to have my bike towed to a shop that would repair and repaint it.

Otherwise, I was stuck in the house. Camp dropped off my grocery list each week and spent Friday nights eating ice cream and bingeing comedy shows.

I always saved money for bills ahead and it was a relief because I wasn't working anywhere in my condition. I had my savings but never liked to touch that if I could avoid it.

On a Sunday four weeks after my accident, I found Jake's business card on my desk and called him on a whim. He came over after his shift and brought movies.

When he asked me to go on a real date the following weekend, I said yes. I didn't intend to date him seriously but I needed some outside stimulation.

It had been almost a year since I dated a man. I took my time getting dressed in a pretty sundress so I wouldn't have to fight my casts and put a sandal on one foot. I left my hair loose because I honestly couldn't be bothered.

Jake picked me up for dinner just as the sun was beginning to set and drove to JW's on Deerfield Beach. He asked me to wait while he jogged around the back of his Expedition and opened my door.

He guided me slowly up the walkway, held the restaurant door, helped me into my chair before he sat - all the chivalrous things I did for women myself.

Dinner was relaxed and easy. He never asked me what I did for a living and I didn't pry into police business. It was strange but comfortable.

He knew I was seventeen and I knew he was twenty-six. I assumed he'd done a background check on me and probably discovered I was an emancipated minor. It was splitting hairs but...

In the eyes of the *law*, I was a legal adult.

Jake ordered iced teas and oysters which we enjoyed while people watching the tourists on the beach. He had a sarcastic sense of humor that showcased his intelligence - which honestly surprised me at first.

When we got back to my apartment, he walked me to my door and lightly brushed my cheek with his lips. Then he returned to his vehicle.

I saw him every few days after that.

We watched a bunch of movies and ordered take-out. We talked a *lot* which was new for me with a man who wasn't Camp.

Eventually, we got around to a sexual relationship but he didn't push for it and I was glad. When the time came to take our friendship to a friendship with benefits, he let me call the shots.

He was easy to please sexually, mild compared to past boyfriends, and didn't give me a bunch of meaningless promises he didn't intend to keep. We were well matched with zero long-term expectations.

Jake had an ex-wife he remained madly in love with - a fact he'd been honest about from our first date. We talked in-depth about their relationship and where he thought things went wrong.

Dating him casually for almost two months, I figured out what the problem was. He treated his ex-wife like she was made of spun sugar.

I bet it drove her nuts.

"Jake, you're masculine but super gentle with women. Not that we don't appreciate it. Um, but you're gentle and too careful in *every* area. If you know what I mean…?"

He did not.

"Maybe let your *rugged* side show." Men can be a little thick. I sighed. "Dude, did you ever *fuck* her?"

"Of course, we made love…"

"Nope. That's not what I mean."

With nothing more than a soft cast on my ankle, I pushed and pushed him until he snapped and drove me to the bed like an animal taking down prey.

Candy, flowers, and sweet romance are nice. But at the end of the day, humans are primal. That part of our nature wants to come out once in a while, one way or another.

In the end, Jake fucked me dirty before finally collapsing in a gasping, sweating pile of male flesh beside me. I was pleasantly sore.

He was quiet for a long time. "That's what you meant about me being too nice…isn't it?"

"Yup. Sometimes, a good fucking is in order." I propped my head in my hand. "Have you talked to Tracy since the divorce?"

He shook his head. "At first, I was furious. Then it hurt to think about seeing her, maybe finding out she was with someone new. Eventually, I settled into my routine and tried not to think about it."

"You love her, right?" He nodded. "Give her a call. See where it goes. You owe it to both of you to make one last effort to get her back. If it doesn't work out, at least you'll know you tried."

He texted her the next day and asked to talk. She replied immediately and invited him to stop by for a few minutes after his shift.

As it turned out, she'd been missing him too. They ended up talking on the porch of their old house for over an hour before he kissed her. Once he did, they *both* knew he was staying.

We found pleasure in each other during our time together and I would always consider him a friend from a distance.

That's why I was *floored* to receive an invitation to their second wedding in the mail six months after becoming an escort.

Which was illegal.

At the bottom was a note in a woman's handwriting that said, "Please come, Sarah." It was signed by Jake and Tracy.

The police officer and his lady.

Fuck.

CHAPTER 26:
Plus One

June 2010

"You're gonna go to jail…" Camp whispered in a sing-song voice as we entered the wedding reception arm-in-arm. "You're gonna have to fight Big Aggie for her spot at the top of the pecking order."

"Shut *up*, Camp. I'm nervous enough as it is."

I'd insisted on sitting in the back row as far from the aisle as possible and we were the first to leave the chapel where the ceremony was held.

I also planned our arrival at the reception after the initial introductions. I hoped to avoid being in any sort of receiving line or something that would make meeting Jake's wife inevitable.

"Orange is *not* your color. With *that* hair? I'll smuggle paper in because you'll lose your whole ass mind if you're not able to write."

He stopped, turned to me, and held my shoulders. "I'm kidding. I'm done now. Though…you have to admit this is nuts. No, no, seriously I'm done now." Glancing at my body, he said, "You look good."

"Thanks. So do you."

I'd texted Kirkland and Lucia for help dressing me and doing my beauty prep. I also had Kirkland measure Camp for a tailored suit.

I bought the goods, paid them double what they quoted me for their services, and got them gift cards for full-treatment spa days.

"How are we *this* hot and not taken, Sarah?"

"One of life's *many* mysteries…"

From nearby, I heard, "*Sarah…?*"

Turning, I couldn't hide my shock at seeing Max and Walker - both turned out in immaculate suits - standing side by side.

"Whoa." Eyes huge, I asked, "How are you *here?*"

Max tilted her head. Then she gave me one of her slow, devastating smiles. "Holy shit, I *cannot* believe it. You're *Cupid*."

"Wh-what?"

"I served with Jake for a couple of years," Max explained. "He only did one tour - got out when he met his wife. We met again at a military mixer a couple of years ago."

"You…know Jake? Oh." I reached out to touch Camp's arm and missed twice. "Th-this is my best friend, Campbell Lynch. Camp, this is Max Huxley and Walker Gibbons. We work together."

Closer to Walker, Camp shook his hand first. "Heard a lot about you. Almost pissed myself at the titty grabbing story…you're *so* lucky she didn't kill you. You might think I'm kidding but I am *not*."

"I'm *haunted* by my past self," Walker groaned.

Camp winked and turned to Max, shaking her hand firmly. "It's a *pleasure* to meet you." His gaze strolled down her body and back to her face. They stood eye-to-eye. "As stunning as my girl described." I murmured softly beside him. "I *am* behaving, Sarah. Always, love."

"I'm Max's plus-one." Walker asked, "How do *you* know the couple?"

Camp released a nervous laugh. Our eyes met and I could see he was hellishly attracted to Walker.

Lord, Camp…anyone but him.

Clearing his throat, he answered, "The nice policeman followed her to the hospital after an accident on her demon cycle. They were FWBs for a couple months."

Max continued, "She got him to reach back out to his ex-wife, they fixed things, and here we are."

Her electric green eyes landed on me and I felt like a butterfly pinned to a mat.

"After a few drinks at one of our get-togethers, he talked about you. Refused to give any of us your number or even your name." Pausing, she didn't blink as she added, "And, believe me, we *asked*. We dubbed you Cupid. What a *small* world."

"You must be Sarah!" a heavily accented voice almost shouted beside me.

I startled badly an instant before I was grabbed in a tight hug and didn't know what to do.

Leaning back, I stared into the golden eyes of the bride. "I'm *Tracy*. I have *you* to thank for today." She hugged me again. "Girl, without you, we woulda kept limpin' along like pure idiots."

"No. Y'all would have figured it out. I know it." My voice felt shaky and I firmed it with effort. "It's real nice to meet you, Tracy. You are breathtakin'."

Camp snorted. "There it is. Any time she's around someone with an accent, hers pops up like she never trained it out."

"This is my best friend, Campbell Lynch."

"Hi, Campbell. I think you've met Jake…?" Tracy gestured to my side and I followed the movement. My former *sex partner* stood a foot away in a tux.

The men shook before Jake turned to me, bent, and kissed my cheek. "How have you been, Sarah?"

"Good. Congrats, Jake." My nervousness was hard to hide. "I'm so, so happy for y'all."

"I appreciate that, Sarah."

The couple had clearly already spoken with Max and Walker who watched the interaction in fascination.

Camp sang softly, "The warden threw a party in the county jail…" I elbowed him in the side and he gasped. "Pull your *hits*, vixen."

Tracy laughed and it was lovely. "You two are a *riot*. I can't believe you're so *young*. You're so dang *elegant*."

"Oh…no, we're not," I assured her. "It took *professionals* to make us look like this. We didn't want to show up in something from the Gap."

"Worse, Forever 21," Camp mumbled.

"Bite your tongue," I grumbled.

"I hope y'all have a *blast* today. Eat and drink…dance when the DJ starts up. Don't be strangers." Hugging me close, Tracy whispered, "I mean it. I owe you, honey. Thanks."

"Congratulations, Mrs. Johnson. I hope you share many decades of love and happiness together. Hard times can show you so clearly what you want most."

"You're like a *poet*." Fanning her face, the bride said, "You're gonna make me *cry*. Lord, honey."

Jake slipped his palm along his wife's waist and tugged her close. "I'm glad you came, Sarah. I wanted you to see the result of your influence. Thank you for everything. I mean that."

I nodded, he left another kiss on my cheek, and the couple moved away to circulate with Tracy waving over her shoulder.

When they disappeared in the crowd, I exhaled roughly.

Camp said, "See? I *told you* it wasn't a trap."

"Uh, no you didn't. You said it would be a pig blood reenactment of *Carrie* and then they'd haul me off to jail for selling my lady bits."

Walker laughed and Camp glared at him. "Straight men shouldn't be allowed to look or sound like you. Stop it at once!"

"Oh," Walker said seriously, "I'm not straight." His eyes flicked to mine. "Can I arrange a playdate?"

"Sweet baby Jesus…they will *never* find your body, Walker." Closing my eyes, I added softly, "Camp, raise your standards! Damn it."

"Uh, look at him. How high could my standards be? We come to the amusement park and you don't want me to ride the rides? Stop cock-blocking me."

Walker grinned. "Sarah has a…"

"I will *destroy* you." My voice was low and dangerous. "I'm talkin' lime sprinkled over your naked corpse in a deep hole. Keep talkin'."

"You are positively *terrifying*."

"You have no idea. Don't toy with him. I don't care if you guys fuck. He's a grown ass man. However, if you play him emotionally…I'll rip your internal organs out through your mouth."

"Uh…"

My terms clearly stated, I leaned up to kiss Camp on the lips. "He's definitely *pretty*. Guard your heart because I'm not sure he *has* one. I'm gonna get something to drink. I hope they have some of that tasty wedding punch I've seen in movies."

I started to turn and Camp swung me back into a hard hug. "Nobody looks after me like you. Thanks, you little psychopath."

With a heavy sigh, I replied, "You're welcome."

He released me and Max's arm instantly went around me. "Let's take a look outside first."

She guided me through the ballroom to balcony doors overlooking a garden. She kept walking until she found a nook hidden from the guests inside.

Her thumb traced my lower lip. "Is this a stain?" I nodded in confusion. "Excellent."

Holding me tightly, my arms trapped against her chest, Max kissed me until I couldn't stop my moans from escaping. Gradually gentling her attention, her tongue stroking against mine, she lifted her head.

"When I saw you, it was surreal. Like two different worlds colliding." *An excellent way to put it.* "You look incredible."

"You do, too."

I wore a dark green sheath in a lightweight faux velvet and matching platform heels. My hair was in a half up, half down style and Lucia did a classic makeup treatment that made my eyes pop.

"If Walker hurts your friend, I'll help carry his body."

For the first time in hours, my smile felt real. I took a deep breath. "Thanks."

"Think you'll dance with me today?"

I frowned. "Why wouldn't I?"

"Question withdrawn." She kissed me again before leading me back inside. "Food and dancing."

"Oh, my god…cake. I hope they went traditional white. I bet it will be amazing."

"Have you never been to a wedding?"

I chuckled. "How would I have been? Camp is my only friend."

She stroked the back of her fingers along my cheek. "I see. If it's not everything you imagine, we'll stop at a diner when we leave and get slices of whatever you want." It took me a minute to realize what she said. "We'll make sure the boys get where they need to go. Naturally."

"Okay."

We ate, drank, and danced for hours. I ended up begrudgingly dancing with Walker - who was better than I thought he'd be.

Then Campbell swept me around the floor like he'd done at our prom.

I shook my ass on the regular but Camp was a *classical moves* bitch who'd spent years imitating dancing he saw in old movies.

Every time I found myself in Max's arms, I felt calm. She affected me like a sedative, wiping away my chaotic thoughts about being at an ex's wedding or worrying for my friend.

It felt good and helped me enjoy a day I'd stressed about for weeks.

We ate *far* too much cake - during and after the wedding.

CHAPTER 27:
The Housewife

July 2010

The following weeks were more of the same.

I only saw Nadia once more while she was scheduled for work in Miami...with the same outcome that made Max livid on my behalf.

The model married a Greek oil tycoon the following winter and moved overseas. A few months after their marriage, it was announced she was pregnant with twins. The news made me sad since she didn't believe in love or physical touch. I wondered how that would turn out for her...and her children.

Three clients weren't a good fit, a couple of others became regulars. They were into basic stuff that didn't require much from me mentally or physically and it was a nice break.

One gentle woman in her thirties who owned a pet boutique wanted me to bring her a bouquet of flowers, take her to dinner, go dancing, and walk her to her door with a goodnight kiss.

She paid my usual rate for *romance*.

The CEO for a major company visited their Miami offices once a quarter and she was a standing appointment for hours of oral from yours truly.

The lower half of my face was numb and my jaw ached by the time I left her. She always tipped me ten thousand dollars and a piece of diamond jewelry.

Occasionally, I saw her in the news. Stephanie Brockwell was married to another powerful tech giant. They lived in a fifteen-thousand square foot mansion in California. The private lives of the uber rich were both fascinating and bizarre.

The days passed quickly and my client list expanded and contracted like the other escorts. Monica saw me twice a month and I allowed Viv to book me on one or two single appointments when they came up.

Some clients gave me the wrong vibe.

Others seemed meant to be.

I paced myself during appointments with Tricia for seven months. In the early fall, she went on tour for her new album so I didn't see her for a while.

Being honest, I enjoyed the break for two reasons.

First, she became more emotionally attached after each appointment we spent together and I thought the distance might be good for her.

Second, I'd taken on another client who required my hip movements with a fake cock.

The first time I met Deirdre Dorn, I was surprised she requested an appointment with me.

She was married, had a couple of teenagers, and was president of the PTA. Active in her church and community, she was apparently the *queen* when it came to fundraisers for anything and everything.

Deirdre had a great body in her mid-forties but looked like she'd given up on her outer appearance. She was barely five feet tall.

She had no clue how to dress - choosing loose outfits that made her look twenty pounds heavier. She wore her hair in styles that made her appear much older. Too much of the wrong makeup did nothing to highlight her natural beauty.

I hated how sad she seemed.

After two appointments, I asked Vivienne to arrange for our crew to make her over.

Lucia did her hair. The shag style made her look years younger and the brightened up mahogany brought out the light green of her eyes.

Walker brought casual and professional clothes suited to her petite frame. There would be no more sweat suits hiding her from the world. He also put her in a properly sized bra.

Deirdre was truly lovely under the den mother getup. The makeover did wonders for her self-esteem. She carried herself straighter almost at once.

Walker made a huge deal of her natural grace and lingered over her hand when he kissed it goodbye. As attractive as he was, showing the older woman attention did wonders.

It was a charming touch and I told him so later. He blushed but didn't say much.

Deirdre had been married almost twenty years. Miles Dorn was a bank executive who worked about ninety hours a week. She suspected he was fucking his assistant for about twenty of those hours.

He was good-looking, brilliant, and emotionally absent from their marriage - she loved him completely.

We always met at one of the beautiful hotels along Manalapan. I wore a specific brand of cologne and a suit - complete with wingtip shoes - as instructed.

Walker *loved* the days I met with either Deirdre or Tricia and went out of his way to find men's clothes that rocked my figure.

My hair at the start of our sessions was pulled snugly in a chignon at the base of my neck and smoothed.

Before our first appointment, Deirdre requested I wear a strap-on that was custom made to her husband's measurements.

Max took me to be fitted for the toy when it was ready. I liked having her input.

At that point, I'd been seeing Tricia for months. My ability to act and fuck like a man had been refined.

Each time I entered Deirdre's body and began to thrust, she closed her eyes. I knew she imagined Miles inside her.

She always came *hard*. Her obvious gratitude made me want to kick her husband's ass.

Deirdre *needed* romance in her life and I delivered.

I arrived at the suite early, checked on the flowers, battery-operated candles, strawberries and cream…

All the trappings people surrounded themselves with for window dressing when there was another issue going on they wanted to avoid.

She listened to the Neville Brothers, Linda Ronstadt, and Foreigner while we were together. Her voice was pretty and clear. Occasionally she broke into song while we were in the shower.

In the early nineties, she was a backup singer. Then she met Miles and he swept her off her feet to a life of raising children and cleaning their big house.

I kept my opinions to myself, gave her what she seemed to need from me, and sent her home happy.

A month after her makeover, Deirdre asked me if she should involve her husband in one of our appointments. He'd been in London for six weeks.

I'd been expecting the request for a while.

"It could go one of three ways and you should know that up front," I explained as I held up my hand. "One, he might be pissed that you've been seeing someone like me and blow up your life. Two, he might see your time with me as his permission to see and fuck whomever he likes. Three, best case, he sees you - and your marriage - in a whole new light."

Including him was a gamble. They'd been married for two decades. I didn't want the sudden kink to throw their entire marriage into turmoil.

"How would *you* feel about it, Sarah? I don't want you to be uncomfortable."

We faced each other on our sides, having just *made love,* as Deirdre liked to call it. She played with my hair and didn't see the danger of adding a woman like me to her marriage bed.

"Deirdre, I'm bisexual. I date men and women - and have sex with both. You have to ask yourself if you can handle watching someone else fuck your husband. You'd be giving him *permission* to be naked with someone else who isn't you."

I wanted to be clear and open with her - preferably *before* her husband's naked body was in the same room with me. Brutal honesty up front was necessary.

Deirdre smiled. "You've brought so many new things into my life, Sarah. I'm hot all the time now and that's different from how I used to be." She caressed her nipple with one hand, mine with her other.

"I love your body and what you do with it. I'd enjoy seeing how your presence…makes him feel. Maybe it will bring me closer to him." Her eyes lifted to mine. "Can we try?"

"We can. There will need to be additional terms. Your husband might not like them."

"Whatever it takes." I could see her excitement - even after I outlined what I wanted to do.

A few days later, it was confirmed: my next appointment with Deirdre would include her husband.

I'd been assured by Vivienne that Miles' recent physical with his private physician was clean - always my number one concern.

I'd opted for a French Maid outfit since the room would already have a man in a suit.

My hair was piled on top of my head and curls fell around my face and shoulders. I wore four-inch platform heels and the hem of my costume fell just below my panty line - then it was all legs encased in fishnet.

I checked myself in the mirror while Max and Walker watched in silence. Kirkland appeared beside me and handed me a trench coat.

"Do you have the bag? Oh, I think the button is caught…" He fixed the coat, belted it carefully, and grabbed the bag from beside the couch. "Thanks for all your help and insider tips."

"Oh, *anytime*, honey. This is *definitely* going to be a first. I can't wait to hear what happens."

Max straightened, "Wait…*what* first?"

I winked. "I'll tell you all about it when I get back."

"Sarah…"

Pausing in front of her, I held her gaze. "Trust me?" Exhaling roughly, she nodded. "I'll tell you when I get back. Promise."

Placing her fingertip under my chin, she murmured, "There's going to be a dick in the room. Be careful."

"Max…*his* won't be the only one." I took her hand and slipped it under my clothes. Her eyes widened and I blew her a kiss. "See you later."

I arrived early at the hotel and prepared everything as I usually did…with a few extras. Placing everything where I wanted it, I waited for my clients.

I'd be serving the Dorns as if I was hired by the hotel - if the hotel was owned by *Hustler*.

I planned to observe and act accordingly.

When they entered the luxury suite, Miles couldn't keep his eyes off his wife. He stared at her as if he hadn't seen her in years.

Encouraging.

He sat sealed to her side while I served oysters and shrimp cocktails. He even fed her an oyster and licked the juice from her lips.

The Escort: In the Service of Women

To be clear, he threw plenty of appreciative attention at me - *dirty boy* - but he was respectful about it. I knew what kind of image I presented so his restraint was impressive.

Beef tips were the entrée and they talked throughout. Things between them looked good and I thought maybe Deirdre didn't need me after all.

When I went into the suite kitchen, she followed me. "Shall I make a graceful exit?"

"Don't leave, Sarah!" she begged. "I'm *so* nervous. I need you here. When he got back yesterday and saw my new look, it-it made him hard but he didn't *do* anything. Let's not stop now, okay?"

I hugged her. "I'm doing this for *you*, not your husband. If things make you feel uncomfortable, give me the word and it stops. Do we have a deal?"

She nodded.

"Alright. Let's prepare dessert."

When we reentered the main room, Deirdre wore nothing but high heels. She walked to the couch I'd covered with a sheet before they arrived, stretched out, and smiled up at me.

I lifted one of her legs to the back of the couch and moved her arms above her head.

"Leave them there."

Then I used a can of whipped topping to cover her nipples and freshly waxed pussy.

"Sir. Dessert is served." I guided Miles across the room and removed his jacket, tie, and vest. "Let's roll up your sleeves." His hands trembled softly. "I highly recommend starting with Deirdre's responsive little nipples. They're delicious."

He turned and stared into my eyes. His expression seemed *frightened*. At that moment, I wondered if more was going on with him than Deirdre realized.

Quietly, I told him, "Deirdre misses you desperately. She's terrified of losing you."

"What…?" he murmured.

"She hired me three months ago. She has me dress in the same style clothing you wear, the same cologne, and fuck her with a cock designed from yours. She thought this might spark something in your marriage and convince you to stay."

Kneeling beside the couch, he took his time kissing Deirdre. "I'd *never* leave you. I'm sorry you were scared." She blinked away tears. "I've been having, uh, trouble and I was embarrassed. You're the only person I love, the only one I've been with since I made you mine."

Leaning back, he looked at her body. "This looks fantastic. It makes my mouth water." He licked all the cream from her breasts, sucked them thoroughly, and leaned over Deirdre again. "During the appointments with Sarah - does she eat your pussy?" Deirdre nodded. "Can I…watch her do that?"

With a grin, I knelt between her legs and licked away the whipped cream. Then I spread her lips and tongued her clit until she came on my face.

"I-I'm hard. All the way." Miles rubbed his temple and gave his wife a half-smile. "That's been the issue, you see. I get hard but not completely. I didn't want you to know."

"We work through things together, Miles. That's always been the rule."

"It's not easy to talk about. I haven't been able to come more than a little in months. The doctor said my diet changes helped but some of it might be psychological."

Deirdre moved to kiss him deeply. "Then we try something new to shake the stress loose."

Sitting back on my heels, I tilted my head. "Oh, Miles. Our plans for today are going to blow the top of your head off. I hope you're fully open to them."

Standing, I helped them to their feet and led them to the bathroom, which featured a group shower. It was the primary reason we booked this particular suite.

Turning on the multiple jets in the shower, I told Deirdre to straddle the bench. She didn't hesitate. "I'm going to get you squeaky clean and ready to play."

I glanced at Miles. "Sit in front of her. I bet she'd love to touch you while I prepare her."

"Prepare her for what…?"

"For us to fuck her, of course. Double penetration. Filling her completely with our cocks." I stripped away the maid uniform and his eyes widened at the equipment between my legs. "Don't be nervous, Miles. This one is exactly like yours."

I used a lubed condom over my fingers to spread Deirdre's ass so I could gently insert the narrow wand I'd added to the faucet. I could tell she'd prepared ahead of time. I cleaned the attachment with soap and put it aside.

Deirdre would call the shots and I'd do whatever she wanted. Miles seemed to be on the same page. He held his breath as she moved forward and took his cock in her hand.

"I've missed you…and I've missed my favorite toy." She licked and sucked him - clearly familiar with what made her husband tick. "Miles, I need you to trust me. Let Sarah prepare you, too."

"Wh-what?"

"Let her get you ready for anal play. If you're having trouble staying hard…a prostate massage might help." She sucked him to the back of her throat and his eyes rolled back in his head. "If you don't like it, we won't do it again." She dragged her tongue along the underside. "I think you're going to like it though, darling."

"You won't think it's weird…?" Deirdre shook her head but didn't release his dick from the depths of her mouth. "The doctor suggested it but I was terrified."

"I'll be gentle," I promised him. "Your safe phrase is *fuck this*." He laughed. "Seriously though, if you don't like it or can't handle it, everything stops. I'll pay close attention."

The light steam felt fantastic as the shower warmed.

"What do you need me to do?"

"Stand up and let Deirdre keep sucking you. Put one foot on the bench beside her. Try to relax. You won't like the first part but the rest will be worth it."

He was completely frazzled at first. Halfway through preparing him, he excused himself to use the toilet closet. I'd been told to expect it from Kirkland.

When he returned, I cleaned him thoroughly while he blushed crimson. Once I was done, I inserted a lubed plug that stimulated his prostate.

Turning it on to the lowest vibration, he came instantly - all over Deirdre's face and chest - as he moaned like an animal caught in a trap.

There was so much more than I'd ever seen a man release and it was insanely thick. Most of what he mumbled was incoherent but Deirdre was thrilled.

"You look so *relieved*, darling. I'm glad. I want you to feel as much pleasure as you can handle."

I turned off the toy but didn't remove it. Then I rinsed Deirdre before leading them from the shower. We dried a dazed Miles and she held his hand as we walked to the bed.

For the next half an hour, I ate Deirdre through two orgasms while her husband watched, panting softly and stroking himself.

It took him a while to get hard again but once he did, he practically vibrated with need. Deirdre spread her legs and invited him between them. Miles accepted the invitation as sweat beaded on his skin.

I was happy at how quickly she climaxed but not surprised. After all, Miles' cock had always been the one she fantasized about having between her legs.

Pushing at his shoulder, she got him to roll to his back while she rode him. "Fuck me, Sarah. Like we talked about."

Rolling on a condom and lubing up, I placed the head of my cock at her ass and pressed inside. She came before I was fully seated and Miles groaned beneath her.

"I can feel it…rubbing on mine," he whispered.

"Does it feel good?" she asked her husband.

"I didn't think about something like this. It's not as intimidating with another woman. You feel so good around my dick, sweetheart."

Deirdre spent a full minute making out with him as we thrust in tandem into her body.

When she came again, she lifted her mouth from his and said, "You have to feel this, Miles. Let Sarah fuck you while you're inside me."

"Um, I-I'm nervous…"

"I can't let you fuck Sarah. Your dick belongs to me and I can't bear sharing it. She'll take *good* care of you. If you don't like it, we can stop. I want you to know. Can you try it once?" He nodded.

I pulled from Deirdre's body and removed the condom before replacing it with a new one. They rolled so Deirdre was on her back and were heavily making out.

Removing the plug I'd left in Miles' ass to stretch him, I lubed myself and gently moved his knee into a wider position. It made Deirdre spread her legs as well and she moaned.

One foot flat on the bed beside them, I balanced on my other knee and placed the head at the pucker of his ass. It flared from the stimulation of the plug.

Holding his shoulders, I massaged him firmly to help him relax. He was a good-looking man and I stroked my palm over his spine to his hip.

Then I pressed forward, filling his ass inch by inch, until my body was sealed to his. His breathing was ragged and he trembled between us.

Deirdre wrapped her arms around his neck. "How does it feel to have her filling you while you fill me?"

"So-so different. She's touching something inside. It makes my entire body shiver."

"I hope you come hard, Miles."

Taking that as my cue, I started to thrust. Within seconds, he was groaning. I could tell he wanted to stroke forward and push back at the same time so I synced my rhythm to what he needed.

It lasted less than three minutes. Deirdre hoarsely whispered his name several times, Miles shouted hers, and they came gasping.

They collapsed together as I carefully removed the cock and cleaned them up.

The couple was sound asleep when I returned from the bathroom dressed in my street clothes. Everything of mine was in my pack and I quickly straightened the room.

Leaning over the bed, I kissed Deirdre and her eyes fluttered open. "I left the toy and lube in the bathroom. It's clean if you want to use it again later. There are snacks in the kitchen and water beside the bed. Rest and reconnect."

She lifted her hand and held the side of my face. "Thank you, Sarah."

"You're welcome, sweetheart. We'll talk soon."

They held each other tighter and were asleep by the time I left the suite.

I felt fucking *incredible*.

* * *

Max paced at the condo when Kylee dropped me off. I was earlier than usual but she looked stressed.

"Hi. Looking for me?"

Grabbing my shoulders, she asked sharply, "Are you alright?"

"I am. I did the fucking - to *both* members of the fabulous couple - but I didn't get a *single* orgasm for myself. Think you could help me out?"

She blinked once. "You…used your cock on *both* of them?" I wiggled my brows. "He didn't fuck you?"

"Absolutely not. That was my condition for letting him participate in our appointment. Deirdre had to be possessive and mean it. I didn't want her to have a memory of her husband's penis in another woman's body and to be honest…" I grinned. "You've spoiled me when it comes to cock."

Max's expression turned predatory. "That a fact?"

"It is." I ran my hands around her waist. "Any chance I can get some of that?"

Without a word, she turned for the guest room and practically dragged me there.

I couldn't contain my smile.

* * *

Overall, the time I spent with the Dorns seemed to strengthen a marriage built on a solid foundation of love and mutual respect. They'd been searching to find their way back to each other.

I was glad to be part of it.

We continued our dates bi-weekly until Miles was transferred to a branch in New York City - where their youngest child attended college.

Before they left, Max and I took Deirdre for an appointment to be fitted with her own cock. She blushed the entire time but I could see her excitement.

Walking her to her car, I kissed her gently. "Good luck, Deirdre. I'm so happy for you. For Miles, too."

She hugged me hard. "Thanks for reminding me that I was a woman as well as a wife, mom, and manager of the universe. Let us bring you up for visits now and then. Will you?"

"See how things go with just the two of you first."

With a nod, she hugged me again and drove away.

No matter what the future might hold, they'd be a hard appointment to forget.

CHAPTER 28:
New Subscriber

August 2010

In my apartment, I kept my desk in one corner of my bedroom so I could do my live shows twice a month. Camp was the one who set up my feed, my equipment, and showed me how to use it.

Behind me, there were thick floor-length drapes over my window, an oversized chair shaped to the corner - draped in a heavy satin sheet, and a gallery wall of abstract art and posters.

I wore a mask, fake green contacts, and scattered black extensions in my straightened hair to throw off my usual look. I always started the night in gloves, a corset, jacket, and leather skirt - which I slowly removed as my live viewers increased. Most of the time, they requested I leave the thigh-high boots on.

Few people had ever been in my bedroom - my circle of friends was hella small - so I didn't have to worry about anyone recognizing the space or me.

Typically, I pulled in a couple grand for a fresh video the day I recorded it and got donations on older ones consistently.

It was a steady source of income that was deposited into another of my many savings accounts.

Two years prior, Monica connected me with an accountant who made sure I claimed what needed claiming and protected myself within LLCs and DBAs. I made the money, Joe put it where it was safest while still earning a little something extra on the regular.

Every other Wednesday, I recorded a new video live and uploaded it to my profile.

I was halfway through my usual performance, answering viewer questions, stripping as donations went up, when I received a notification that I had a new subscriber to my channel. They made an instant donation of a thousand dollars.

Maximum Overdrive.

My heart raced a bit. I pitched my voice lower and focused on not revealing my accent. "Welcome to the show. It's *always* nice to have a new viewer. Do you have any special requests?"

So many...

Other viewers voted for me to remove my skirt and I slowly unzipped it and let it drop on the floor.

Turn for me...

I did so slowly, pausing to look over my shoulder. I knew the image I made in the corset and thong. Straightened, my hair brushed the top of my ass.

Stunning...

Facing the camera again, I lowered to the edge of the chair and used the remote to change the angle. Once it was set, I moved to the back of the deep chair and relaxed against the pillows.

Your skin looks soft...

Stroking my fingers from my shoulder, across my chest, and along the swells of my breasts, I answered, "It feels familiar but I hope it's as soft as it looks."

Several votes came in for me to untie the corset and I took my time. Little by little, I removed the cording I'd have to restring later. I held it together with one hand as if I was shy and they begged for a peek.

Opening one side, then the other, I let them glimpse my nipples before hiding them away again. Donations came in faster.

> *Going to need more of those gorgeous tits…*

I tugged my lower lip between my teeth as the new viewer sent me another thousand.

"Whatever it takes to please you."

I opened the corset and pulled it from behind me. My nipples were hard and I was genuinely turned on for the first time in a long time doing a show.

"I hope you like them."

> *They make my mouth water…*

> *I want to cup them, play with them…*

I slipped my palms around them and squeezed them lightly. Donations spiked yet again. Taking my nipples between my fingers and thumbs, I rolled them, pulled them, pinched them.

> *Watching you do that makes me hard…*

I wasn't *certain* my new viewer was Max but my instincts told me it was. I wanted to perform exclusively for her. Staring into the camera, I pretended there was no one but the two of us.

"Tell me what you want."

Comments flew along the side of the screen but I ignored all of them except hers.

I want to suck those hard little nipples...

I'll satisfy myself by making you come for me...

"I'd love to come for you." I pulled my nipples out from my breasts. "They ache."

Are you wet for me...?

Instead of answering, I slipped a hand down my belly and pressed my panties against my folds. The silk darkened instantly with my slickness.

I'm going to need to see your wet pussy...

Another thousand dollar donation flashed in my notifications and I gasped.

Without thinking, I murmured, "You don't have to pay me to touch me."

Money doesn't matter...

It's worth every penny to show you that...

I blinked rapidly behind my mask, almost on the verge of tears. This was Max. I was sure.

Take off the boots...

One at a time, I slowly unzipped the boots and kicked them off my feet. I wore only the mask and panties and felt more exposed than I had in a long time.

Untie your panties for me...

Touching the bow on my hip, I pulled the tie loose. Moving to my other hip, I untied the other as well. Lifting my ass, I removed the scrap of fabric from under me and dropped it on the floor.

Look at that delectable pink pussy...

Show me more of it...

I lifted my feet and put them on the edge of the chair, spreading my legs. Trailing my palms from my knees to my inner thighs, I waited.

Spread those plump lips, let me see your clit...

I didn't hesitate and my notifications went nuts.

You follow instructions beautifully...

Such a good girl...

"Pleasing you is important to me. Tell me what to do next. Whatever you want."

How wet is your pussy...?

I slid two fingers inside and stroked twice. "I'm soaking wet. If you were closer, you could hear how wet I am."

Taste yourself...

I imagine you're delicious...

Placing the fingers on my tongue, I sucked the fluids from them with a low moan. "I wish you could taste me. I hope you like the way I taste."

Probably the best delicacy on the planet...

I left a bit of moisture on my lip as I pulled my fingers away. People went crazy over details like that in my videos.

Get your fingers wet again to play with your clit...

It's hard like a little cock - it's probably throbbing...

I returned them to my pussy and thrust several times. "I'd love your cock right here. I'm aching to be filled. I want to come so bad." Staring into the camera, I asked, "Will you let me come?"

As much as you want...

Play with yourself but go slow...

Draw it out until you're desperate...

"That sounds amazing."

I dropped my head against the pillows and circled my fingers over the bundle of nerves. I thought about every time Max played with my clit, lapped at me hungrily, or sucked it between her lips.

Several times, I almost came and barely stopped myself. Each time, she praised me as I paused my movements and caught my breath.

That's right, let it build...

You listen so well...

"It's right *there*...I really, really want to come. I won't do it until you let me. I want you to get *exactly* what you want. Do I have permission?"

You deserve to come...

Do it...

I returned my attention to my clit and it didn't take long to fall over the edge. Donations flooded in but I ached - unsatisfied with my own touch.

That was fucking stunning...

Until next time, beautiful...

"Thank you for being with me tonight. I need a nap but I'll see you again in a couple of weeks. Sleep deeply and dream dirty."

As I signed off, there was a knock on my door. I ran through the apartment and opened it without checking to see who was there.

Insane since I was completely naked.

Max stepped inside, slammed the door, engaged the locks, and lifted me fully against her body. She carried me to my room without a word.

She drove me down to the bed, pushed my legs wide, and pulled her cock from her pants. I held her as hard as I could as she tried to fuck me through the mattress. We didn't use words but I felt as if we had hours of conversation.

I lost count of how many times she made me come with her hands, mouth, and cock but I eventually passed out.

The next morning, I made her breakfast. It was the least I could do after the pleasure she delivered right to my door.

Max spent the day and another night with me. It was the first time she'd been inside my place and it felt amazing - and different - having her there.

It became a standing date every other week…her talking me slowly through climax live on the internet and then fucking me unconscious in the privacy of my apartment.

My videos had never been so popular.

I'd never been so satisfied making them.

CHAPTER 29:
The Pilot

September 2010

Whenever Vivienne traveled, she booked a charter service. She never knew what clients or escorts with her might get into and couldn't afford an issue with the FAA if they did something considered illegal on a public flight.

Her regular pilot was a pretty brunette with a bright smile named Priscilla Auger.

I'd met her the first time when Tricia offered triple my rate to meet her in Chicago. I agreed because of how lonely she sounded on the road.

Priscilla screamed professionalism and class in her crisp uniform and oh-so-serious high-heeled pumps.

Her co-pilot was a man named Roan who - though openly and spectacularly gay - flirted from the moment he saw me.

After a weekend with Deirdre and Miles Dorn at their gorgeous Manhattan loft, Vivienne called me in the car on the way to the airport where the charter waited to take me back to Florida.

"Hi, Sarah. Priss wants an appointment with you."

"Who?" The name didn't sound familiar.

"The *pilot*. You've met her several times now."

"Ah. Captain."

Vivienne giggled. "That's what you *call* her?"

"Hell, yeah. She *earned* that shit."

"That explains so much."

Considering, I mentioned, "Are you sure she meant me? She's never shown the slightest interest…"

"I'm sure. Have a good flight."

"Uh huh."

Disconnecting, I spent a few minutes texting Campbell. He'd just started his sophomore year at the University of Florida as a business major with a technology minor.

Mr. Smarty Pants.

He liked to give me the breakdown on his professors and any interesting potentials for sex. Our chats were filled with memes, gifs, and links to crazy shit.

I think I'm about to fuck a pilot…

> *No shit? Those are seriously friendly skies!*

You're ridiculous, Camp. I'll buzz you when I'm back. You up for Universal this weekend? I can meet you there.

> *Sign me up unless a supermodel top throws me against the wall and demands access to my adorable ass. I mean…*

Understood. Never pass that up on my account.

We made tentative plans before he took off for an afternoon class. Taking a selfie, I sent it to Max.

On my way back. The Captain scheduled a date…?

Whoa. Didn't peg her for the type.

That was my thought. I asked Viv if she was sure I was the escort she wanted.

Haha when will you understand…?

Lord. I hope never. I have enough issues without becoming a vain bitch.

It's not vanity, sweetheart. Call me after you get some sleep. Let's catch a movie and dinner.

Always up for both. See you soon. XO

The moment I sent the text, I cringed. I added *hugs and kisses* to the end. *What the hell was that?* Covering my mouth with my hand, I wished I could call it back but it was already read and Max was typing.

Right back at you, Sarah.

Sitting back, I marveled at how *nervous* the exchange made me feel. Then I realized Max was probably humoring the silly ass *teenager* she occasionally had sex with and calmed myself down.

Meeting me on my level, so to speak.

Half an hour later, I climbed the stairs to the passenger door of the small luxury jet. Priscilla and Roan waited to greet me.

"Captain. Roan. Nice to see you again."

"Welcome aboard, Sarah. You know the drill. Roan tries to get our licenses suspended by beating the three-hour standard for this flight in our model."

"Go nuts. If you'll hand me a bottle of water, I'll let you work. You know I'm low maintenance."

Roan sucked his teeth. "Sonja and her older couple wit' us yesterday. De nonsense and foolishness d'ose t'ree get up to…"

Born and raised in Jamaica, I *loved* his accent. It was thicker than Rolande's and he slipped into Patois more than she did.

I nodded sagely. "Believe me. I know. They're obsessed with her. She tries to act cool but I can tell she adores them."

With a wink, I took the water from the co-pilot and went down the aisle. I sank happily into a plush leather seat and buckled up.

Taking the opportunity before we got underway, I checked my emails and quickly reviewed some documents from my accountant.

Monica emailed me the scanned response from Paula's attorney about the civil suit. I'd keep making her throw money she didn't have at legal fees until she got the message to stay the fuck out of my life.

Roan appeared to give the required emergency drill and I gave him my full attention. It was performance art that would make him viral if a video ever got out. He sported a trim figure and applied eyeliner better than I did.

"And dat be dat," he said at the end.

We chatted for a few minutes and he told me about his new boyfriend - Marcus - who liked to fuck him while singing rap music the *entire* time.

"Imagine, yeah? Ya gettin' it hard and deep when somebody busts out with Snoop Dogg. Ya no know what to do. I love dat dick but his *voice*…mm. Nowhere near as pretty." Shaking his head, he blew me a kiss and headed for the cockpit.

The Escort: In the Service of Women

I was practically hysterical.

We'd been in the air for ten minutes when the *fasten your seatbelt* sign clicked off.

I got up and walked to the front, knocking lightly on the door that separated the flight crew from the passenger area. Roan opened it.

"Captain, may I have a few minutes of your time?"

Priscilla looked at Roan and he said, "We cruisin' right along. Go'n now. I got dis."

Clearly flustered, she joined me and closed the cockpit door behind her.

"I heard you'd like to spend some up close and personal time together. Is that true, Captain?"

She blushed and couldn't seem to form actual words with her lips. I had to help her.

Bracing my hand on the wall beside her, I whispered, "I'm glad." I trailed my finger along the lapel of her uniform. "Seeing you in this makes me wet, Captain."

"No one else calls me that…"

I met her warm brown eyes. "Really? It's a title you worked hard for, right?" She nodded. "You want more people to acknowledge your efforts. I like that about you." Nuzzling her cheek, I said in her ear, "Tell me what I can do to please you, Captain."

"I-I don't even *know*."

It was hard for her to say and I knew I'd need to lead her while leaving her in complete control.

Our time together would be about balance.

Page | 245

Taking her face in my palms, I left little kisses across her lips until she opened for me. I licked inside and kissed her deeply.

I could tell she didn't kiss much - if at all - and slowly showed her the motions until she learned them. I didn't stop until she was gripping my arm and my waist, trying to press closer to me.

"You want me naked," I murmured against her mouth. She nodded. "I'd love to be naked for you."

I took my time letting her go, went back for a few more kisses, and finally backed away from her.

In the main cabin, I stripped my t-shirt over my head and took off my running shoes and socks. Pushing my capri leggings off, I took down my ponytail and put it back up in a messy bun.

I chose simple styles for underthings when I wasn't working. After my shower, I'd put on pale pink cotton panties and a matching sports bra. I removed them.

Unbuttoning her uniform jacket, I slid it off her shoulders. Laying it neatly on the seat beside me, I removed her skirt and blouse, but left the heels.

Underneath, she wore an *expensive* blue lace bra, panties, and garter belt. Her thigh high silk stockings were topped in the same lace.

"The Captain enjoys wearing fancy lingerie under her serious uniform." Going to my knees, I looked up the length of her snug body and smiled. "Your naughty little secret?" She nodded. "I'll keep it."

Lips slightly parted, Priscilla panted softly. There was a pink flush on her lightly tanned skin. Sitting back on my heels, I took her hand and guided her forward. Her pussy was at face level.

The Escort: In the Service of Women

I held her gaze as I rubbed the flats of my fingers over her folds through the panties. "You're hot and wet. I'd love to taste you, Captain. Do you mind?"

"I-I don't mind."

Tugging the fabric to the side, I dragged my tongue between her lips and moaned. "Oh, yes."

I pulled them down her legs, glad they were over her garters and stockings. She stepped from them as her blush deepened. Beside me, I laid my t-shirt on the leather seat and guided her to sit on it.

"I'm going to need more of you."

Resting the back of her thigh on my shoulder, I settled in to lick and suck her neatly trimmed pussy. Licking around the entrance made her insane and I focused my attention there.

"Y-your tongue," her voice was barely audible, "inside…push it inside."

"Mm hmm, Captain."

I fucked her shallowly with my tongue as I used my fingers to play with her clit. Her first orgasm was so intense, she almost fell out of the seat. I'd never seen someone clench so hard.

Licking her through it, I thrust two fingers as deep as I could and stroked them in and out while she writhed under me.

"Take off your bra, Captain. Let me see your nipples and find out what you like."

She managed to get it off with shaking hands and I played with her pussy using my fingers as I raised myself high enough to take a nipple between my lips.

They were large for how small her breasts were, poking up like little traffic cones.

It was clear how much Priscilla liked them to be sucked and I took my time giving them attention.

Slickness dripped into my palm from where I thrust into her with my fingers.

"You're soaked, Captain. Play with these while I lap up your come. I don't want to waste a drop."

Delicate hands settled around her breasts and she tugged her nipples away from her body *hard* while I returned to her pussy.

"Fucking *dripping* for me…"

It was the last thing I said because I was so caught up in the taste of her, the smell of her, the texture of her, I couldn't think of anything that needed saying.

She bucked, moaned, and clutched me between her soft thighs as I feasted on her. It was *raunchy* but strangely *innocent* at the same time.

I ate her pussy like it was my last sexual experience and I was damn well going to make it a good one.

When she was about to come, I could actually see her pussy tighten up and it spurred me to new heights. I couldn't lick enough of her at once, fuck her deep enough with my fingers, or swallow enough of her pleasure. She came so hard…she fainted.

I was finally appeased.

A minute later, she blinked in confusion, met my eyes, and started to cry.

The Escort: In the Service of Women

Completely lost, I panicked. "Did I hurt you, Captain?" She shook her head. "Tell me."

Eventually, she smiled and pulled my face to hers. She licked my lips, tasting her own essence. She smoothed my hair away from my face.

"Oh, my God, Sarah. What the hell *was* that?"

I wasn't sure how to respond.

"I've never been made to feel like that. What you did, how you made me feel, it was magic. I don't have any experience – but I'd like to try and give you some of what you gave me."

Dropping her leg, she sat forward and ate at my mouth. "The floors are sterilized. I could lay down and you could ride my mouth."

It was so shocking to hear such a thing from a woman who could barely kiss me at first that it made my body spasm.

There was also no way she could handle that.

"We're running out of time, Captain." I pushed her back on the seat. "You want to see me come?"

She nodded and I stood. Putting my foot on the arm of the seat spread my legs wide and bared my pussy inches from her face.

Priscilla reached up to touch me, rubbing the entrance of my pussy before pressing inside.

Licking two fingers, I put them over my clit and circled it rapidly. Her eyes glazed as she watched me. Her thrusts into my body weren't coordinated but her focus made up for the lack of skill.

"Can I taste it…when you come?"

"Anything you want, Captain."

Letting my eyes drift closed, I recalled another scenario when I really *didn't* have control. When I found myself at the mercy of someone who wielded power and pleasure in equal measure.

Who never failed to make me come screaming.

The climax flooded my body and I gasped, barely remembering where I was and who I was with.

"That's so sexy…" A soft tongue licked me and it sent a shiver over my skin. "It tastes like mine but also different."

Catching my breath, I put my leg down and bent to kiss her. Leaning back a bit, I reminded her, "We're going to land soon. Let me help you clean up and dress." We both smelled like sex.

Fifteen minutes later, we were put back together. I had to get a fresh t-shirt from my bag.

Priscilla kissed me. "I haven't had much experience. My upbringing was extremely religious. I think it was Roan who called Vivienne and I'm glad. I never would have found the courage to do it myself. Thank you for being amazing, Sarah."

I gave her a slow smile. "You're welcome, Captain."

"I've never felt so…sexy before."

"Go with that feeling. Make it bigger. Get everything you want and don't apologize for a fucking thing."

After one more kiss, she turned and walked to the cockpit. I gathered my stuff and leaned my head against the seat. I felt intense relief when we taxied into Ft. Lauderdale.

I was exhausted.

Kylee parked on the tarmac of the private plane area and smiled as I walked toward her with my duffle and backpack. "Nice flight?"

I waved at Priscilla and Roan standing at the top of the stairs. "Yeah. Nice flight."

CHAPTER 30:
Reflection

Closing me into the back, Kylee walked around and got behind the wheel. I was surprised when she started up a real conversation.

"How are you feeling, Sarah?"

"I'm good, thanks for asking." I thought she was just being polite.

"I ask because you have more appointments and clients than the other girls. I wanted to check on your health and well-being."

"That's good of you, Kylee." I considered her concerns seriously. "Some clients are more draining than others. I still get nervous the first time. It's been ten months so I thought that would get easier."

"Max and I...we keep an eye on the escorts more than just driving you from point A to point B. Watch for signs that someone might need help."

"Do I show signs of needing help?"

Watching her in the rearview mirror, I could tell she chose her words carefully.

"There are times I see painful weariness in your eyes - more than just as an escort." *Astute of her.* "You put the needs of your clients before your own, Sarah. You cater to them like a true lover and they respond intensely to it."

"I try to keep them at a distance." I'd seen signs of emotional attachment from most of my clients and blatantly ignored it. "I respond to their neediness."

"The curse of the giver." She smiled as she changed highways. "You seem most relaxed around your friend Campbell…and Max."

Tugging my lower lip between my teeth, I smiled and murmured, "Are you fishing?"

"No. Max is a good person and incredibly protective of you. I think you guys are good together."

"It's not…like that. She looks out for me."

"Hmm. You think Max sees you like a younger sister or a student? Like a teenager?" I shrugged but the words hit home. "How do *you* feel about Max?"

I met her eyes briefly before she returned them to the road. It was a question Campbell asked me more than once.

"I'll keep your confidence, Sarah. From every person on this planet. You probably don't know but I planned to be a nun once upon a time."

Nothing could have shocked me more.

"Falling in love with another postulant flipped my world upside down. I left the Church, joined the Air Force, and here we are."

"That is…fascinating."

"Right?" Lifting her gaze to mine again, Kylee smiled. "I have no designs on you - unlike Walker. I'm not too close to the situation - unlike Campbell. You can trust me to keep your secrets."

How I felt about Max was wrapped up in how I viewed myself - which wasn't always in the best light emotionally or mentally. I knew that, understood it, but didn't know how to alter my perception.

"Uh, I'm really...messed up."

"Do you think so? I don't get that impression from you at all. You're one of the most put-together people I know, Sarah."

"No. I-I don't know how things work. I feel different from everyone around me. Outside how normal people live and understand. I can't even trust people."

"Untrue. You're trusting me right now to keep your confidence. You trust your clients at your most vulnerable - something I couldn't do. You trust Campbell with your entire life."

Getting off the freeway, she stopped at a light. "Do you trust Max?" I nodded because there was no hesitation in my mind. "In the years I've known her, Max hasn't had a long-term partner. She's never been interested in the escorts or clients - even when she had some of her own."

As the light changed, Kylee smiled. "In fact, she spends more time with *you* than I've seen her spend with any other person. I've rarely glimpsed her at the condo outside of meetings or heard a peep from her on days off. You have her acting positively *social*."

The piece of my heart that I kept hidden from everyone in my life throbbed painfully. I didn't want to think about this because I knew too well what wanting and hoping led to.

Leaning my head against the seat, I felt wiped out. "She's not meant for me. I'd add nothing but drama to her life. Like a rock thrown into a still pond. Nobody needs that shit."

Watching the scenery flow by in the tropical paradise so many people flocked to, I got lost in thought for several minutes. I longed for something different but didn't know what.

We pulled into my apartment lot and Kylee let me out. I was surprised to hear my name called from above and behind me.

Glancing up, I muttered, "Fuck."

Reagan Olson stood next to my front door. Arms crossed, she had a pissed expression on her face.

Kylee asked, "Friend of yours?"

"An ex-girlfriend who doesn't understand the word *over*. It's been two years, damn it. Can you hang for a minute so I can pretend I have somewhere to be?" Kylee nodded. "Thanks."

With a sigh, I went up the stairs to deal with a woman who kept showing up no matter how clear I made things.

When we dated, I felt like a trained monkey around her. She got pissed, I fucked her out of her mad, and we got on with our day.

She was happy, I was perpetually bored.

"Where have you been, Sarah?"

"Working. Why are you here?"

"You didn't answer my calls or reply to my texts."

"That's because I have nothing to *say*, Reagan. We've been through this. I'm out of patience. I need to be back in the car in five minutes and have to get ready." I shooed her away from my door. "Do you mind?"

"Sarah! Don't be like this. I-I know I cheated on you with that guy but…"

I cut her off. "If you think that's the only reason we're not together, you're deluded. You're *incapable* of listening. You being here now is a perfect example. You're so self-absorbed that other people are unnecessary for anything more than flattering you."

Walking around her, I unlocked my door. "I'm not doing this with you, Reagan. Don't come here again. I have to get ready."

She grabbed my arm. "Give me another chance…!"

"No. We dated. It didn't work." I gently pried her fingers off my arm. "I feel no emotion for you. I'm not sexually attracted to you. We're incompatible."

"You used to *love* fucking me! Let me remind…"

"What the hell *is* this? Why the hard press? You need somewhere to stay or something?"

Her eyes flickered.

"Ah. I see. Of course. You cheated again and lost the dick owner paying for your life. Now you're here." Removing my wallet from my pack, I took out two hundreds. "This should give you a couple days in a motel to figure shit out. Don't come back here."

"Sarah…I *know* I messed up."

"Good. No hard feelings then."

"You treated me the best…of all of them."

I sighed and rubbed my temple. "Reagan. Take the money and go. We're done. Get your shit together. Apologize to your parents. They'll help you. Don't come to me to save you from your stupid choices."

"Are you seeing anyone?"

"Yes. Go home to your folks and ask for forgiveness for all the bullshit you put them through. Do *not* come back here, Reagan. I'm serious. You'll make me call the cops."

"You really would?" I nodded. "Th-thanks for the cash. Think about what I said…"

"Already did. The answer is no."

I entered my apartment and closed the door. I heard her leave a minute later. Peeking through the living room window, I saw her car turn onto Federal Highway a block away. I walked back out to Kylee.

"Thanks."

"No problem." She smiled. "You were kind but firm. Think she'll be back?"

"Depends on how soon she can find another cock to finance her living expenses. I'm wiped. Gonna shower and crash. Forgive the ridiculousness."

"See you later, Sarah."

Upstairs, I made it through a hot shower and fell on my bed in the towel. I slept for nine hours and woke up with a cold.

As many bodily fluids as I swapped with other people, I guess I was lucky I didn't get sick more often. The knowledge didn't help my melancholy.

Neither did missing my separate plans with Campbell and Max - who both stopped by at different times with soup and meds.

CHAPTER 31:
Masquerade

October 2010

When Vivienne threw a party, she didn't mess around. She supplied gallons of champagne, tons of delicious food, and a wait staff that was efficient as well as beautiful.

Every year, she hosted a costume party for Halloween. She invited employees, clients, and various business partners.

I had no idea what costume to wear to such a thing and was relieved when Kirkland came to the rescue.

A huge fan of DC comics, he turned me out as Harley Quinn and Max rocked her getup as a sexier version of the Joker.

When we were fully dressed, she mumbled, "I'll keep my comments about their highly toxic fucking relationship to myself."

"Right...? It's *not* just me." We laughed and went to join the festivities.

Vivienne paired with Walker as the Wonder Twins. They wore jumpsuits and ground their pelvises together shouting, "Wonder Twin powers - activate!"

The other escorts pulled out all the stops. Paige dressed as Sailor Moon. Sonja was a perfect Dallas Cowboys cheerleader

- a choice close to my heart. Rolande made herself into a sexy puppy that kind of made me understand the Furry kink a bit more. Lyra dressed as a wood nymph and it totally suited her.

Ezbeth showed up in body paint - a walking canvas done by a friend - that made her look like a bird complete with long feathers braided into her hair.

Lucia was a belly dancer, Blaine the main character from *Saturday Night Fever*, and Mrs. Quincy came as Alice from *The Brady Bunch*. Dr. Reinhardt wasn't exactly in costume but walked around in his lab coat asking guests if they wanted to play doctor.

It was a chance to mingle and get to know people you never had a chance to meet. Apparently, some escorts traded clients as different sexual switches were flipped over the course of the night.

Two people requested to be added to my roster and I declined gracefully. I wanted to *reduce* my number of clients, not add more.

My dance card was full with Monica, Tricia when she begged, sporadic trips to see Deirdre and Miles, and a few other clients I saw regularly for run-of-the-mill servicing. Then there were the one-off dates…who occasionally reappeared and became regulars.

Vivienne knew how to throw a sensual bash and made sure there were plenty of beds, showers, and private nooks for her guests' pleasure.

Sometimes several guests gathered in one room. People like watching beautiful people fuck each other…though few would actually admit it.

By midnight, most of the attendees were drunk, high, or both. The mood changed drastically.

Rolande and Lyra ate each other on the drop cloth covered sectional in the living room. Around them were multiple couples in various stages of undress fondling each other or outright fucking.

Vivienne, Paige, Ezbeth, and Walker were in her massive bedroom. Earlier, she had floor cushions and two futon mattresses moved into the space. She'd clearly been expecting an orgy.

She got it.

I watched with Max as the gorgeous foursome crawled all over each other on the bed with an audience. The mattress was covered with a heavy sheet. The rest of the linens were folded at the foot.

Paige rode Ezbeth's mouth almost *violently* as she gripped the headboard in front of her. Ezbeth held her back in a way that communicated her own enjoyment of the act.

Vivienne looked up from her position between Ezbeth's painted thighs. "Wanna play with us?"

Walker never slowed his thrusts into his boss's pussy from behind. He stood on the floor beside the bed. A man I'd never seen before stood next to him and reached out to stroke his hand over Viv's ass.

I shook my head. "You have a good vibe going already. Don't let us interrupt."

"If you're sure…" She licked Ezbeth from her pussy to her clit. "There's plenty of pleasure to go around." Her eyes rolled back in her head. "Harder, Walker. Oh, *fuck*…right there."

He slammed into her pussy brutally and turned his head to accept a kiss from the other man.

Max pulled me into the corner, partially concealing us beside the drapes that hung on either side of the balcony doors. The other people in the room were too loaded to notice us.

I didn't want to *participate*...

I definitely wanted to *watch*.

There were couples and threesomes of mixed gender all around the room writhing on furniture and even the floor. The sights and sounds of so many people sucking, fucking, and moaning - flesh slapping against flesh - had a definite effect on me.

A strong hand slipped across my stomach and into the spandex shorts I wore as part of my costume.

Max whispered, "Your pussy is so wet that your panties are *drenched*." Her teeth closed on my earlobe. "Don't come yet, Sarah."

"Max..." I groaned softly.

"There's more cock in this room than usual. Does it turn you on?"

"Watching men fuck each other is a sexual stimulant for me but..." I struggled for calm.

"What an interesting tidbit of information. There's something else?" I nodded. "Tell me."

"Just...imagining us doing some of those things in their place."

"Ohh, *which* things, I wonder?" Her fingers played with my clit. "Taking you hard from behind? Being watched by a roomful of people? Or is it…riding my mouth like your own personal fuck toy until you come on my face?"

Inhaling sharply, I couldn't stop the climax. It doubled me over but Max held me up, curled herself around me, and kept fingering my slick folds.

"You *dirty* girl…you want to sit on my face." I breathed raggedly through the pleasure as she licked the side of my neck. "I bet your come would *soak* me." She kissed the skin beneath my ear. "Then I could fuck you until you couldn't stand up."

Barely audible, I begged, "Fill me up, Max. I *need* it. Please, Max. Please…"

I was wet, aching, and trembling by the time Max led me from the second floor. At the base of the stairs, I stumbled and she picked me up, carrying me to the guest room and attached bath we often used.

The door was locked all night to keep others out but wasn't now. She turned the lock once we were inside.

Stripping us, she guided me into the shower and we washed off the costume makeup. She scrubbed the blue and pink sprays out of my hair and conditioned it heavily.

We were barely dry when she stretched out on the bed and lifted me over her, my knees on either side of her head. Her green eyes practically glowed.

"Be rough - I can take it. Come until you're satiated, Sarah. Then I'm going to have my way with you in every position until dawn." She lifted my hands to the headboard. "Hold on, sweetheart. Take what you want, as much as you want."

And holy fuck…I did.

I'd never been so selfish in my life but I didn't hold back. I *used* Max's mouth to make myself come three times before I collapsed beside her, my entire body rocked by aftershocks.

Her lips were swollen and red, the lower half of her face slick with my release. She placed her palm over my quaking womb with a grin.

"That was incredible. Anytime you wanna ride my mouth, you let me know. I'll happily assume the position and drink you down."

I was incapable of speech.

Standing, she went to the bathroom. When she came back, she wiped my inner thighs with a damp towel and said firmly, "Let's keep going."

She reached into the bedside table for a cock I'd never seen before. It didn't have a strap to keep it in place. My heart raced.

"These aren't comfortable if you have to walk around. However, I think you'll like the way it feels."

She inserted the smaller, strangely curved end into her pussy and positioned a silicone extension over her clit. Moving between my legs, she rested my thighs on top of hers. Setting the head against my pussy, she pressed forward and I caught my breath.

"Feel that, Sarah?" I processed the different shapes rubbing along my inner walls. "Not something to use every day. The overstimulation would cause desensitization. I'd never let that happen to you."

"M-Max…?" Then she turned on a low vibration and I arched from the bed with a small scream.

"You relax. I'll do *all* the work."

The Escort: In the Service of Women

The woman was the hardest worker I'd ever met.

* * *

We didn't stop fucking until the room was bright with morning sunlight, then crashed until noon.

It was impossible to know how many orgasms Max gave me or herself. I quickly lost count in my sensual delirium.

Each time, she gritted her teeth against the pleasure and kept going - the expression on her face filled with raw hunger.

It made me shiver remembering.

I was curled into Max, my head under her chin. Her arms held me firmly to the front of her body. I didn't want to wake her up. She'd done a lot more than I did during our marathon.

She dished out the ecstasy…I just took it.

Kissing the skin over her heart, I inhaled deeply. I loved the way her skin and hair smelled first thing in the morning. I knew I was being weirdly emotional and blamed it on what felt like a sex hangover.

"Good morning, Sarah."

"Oh, hi. You don't have to get up…"

"I'm *not* up," she noted accurately.

I sighed. "I'm going to have to be. I need to pee and I'm stupidly thirsty."

Loosening her hold, she tilted up my chin. Our eyes met and the sun lit the green of her eyes like emeralds. I lost myself in them for a moment and felt a blush climb over my skin.

"Why the blush?" she asked softly.

"If Keanu in his late twenties was morphed into a woman, he'd look like you. But he wouldn't have your fucking gorgeous green eyes." Mine went wide. "I-I mean…"

"Considering how much I know you adore literally *everything* about Keanu…that's incredibly flattering, Sarah."

"I could have just said you're beautiful and have eyes that sparkle like emeralds in sunlight."

Max smiled and it stole my breath. "You just did." She cupped the side of my face. "Thank you. I find you equally stunning."

Pressing a soft kiss to my lips, she said, "I'm only letting you out of this bed because I know you need the bathroom and both of us are starving."

"I'll hurry." I hugged her before realizing I was going to and got out of bed without looking at her again. "Think about what you want me to make."

Leaving the door cracked in case she needed to come in, I used the toilet and started the shower. I washed quickly and conditioned my hair again.

I blow-dried it and piled it on top of my head.

Max wasn't around when I left the bathroom. I dressed in leggings and a tank top. My nipples were sore from her focused attention before dawn so I decided against a bra.

Padding down the hall to the kitchen in my bare feet, I was suddenly grabbed in a tight hug from behind.

As I determined the level of force required to remove myself from male hands roughly groping my tits, I realized it was the husband of one of our clients. I could still smell the alcohol on him.

"Let go of me. Right now. I don't want to hurt you."

He squeezed me harder and I flinched at the pain in my breasts. "I'm glad my wife found you guys…"

Louder the second time, I warned. "Let me go or you're going to suffer."

"Oh, yeah…*punish* me." He took a deep breath at my neck and pressed his dick against my ass. He was hard. "You smell great. I'll pay…"

Gripping his wrist, I twisted his hand hard, spun his body using his own forward momentum, and slammed his face against the wall.

Max and Walker appeared beside us. I didn't look at them as I pinned his arm to his back.

"Ow…"

"I *told you* twice to let me the fuck go. You don't *touch* me without my consent."

He laughed. "Honey, it was a misunderstanding. I get it…money up front."

I released him and stepped back. He turned with a smile and I slapped him across the face.

"What the *fuck*?"

"You think *this*," I grabbed his groin, "can handle *me*?" I leaned into him, rubbed his unimpressive cock through his pants, and he groaned.

Making my voice low and seductive, I asked, "You want to sweat over a naked nineteen-year-old? Touch every inch of my tight body? Watch my tits bounce while you thrust your cock in my hot holes? Maybe coat my pussy with your come? My ass…?"

He shuddered and came on a gasp.

I hummed in disappointment. "You couldn't handle my attention for twenty *seconds*." Pushing his chest, he fell against the wall and I held him there. "I got all the hard cock I wanted for three hours this morning. You have *nothing* I want at any price. Sober up. You're welcome for the free hand job."

I walked to the kitchen and washed my hands. I removed ingredients I'd requested Mrs. Quincy stock for me from the pantry and started mixing batter for several types of pancakes.

Max entered the kitchen. "Sarah, are you alright?"

"Yeah."

"He's gone. His wife is pissed."

"Good."

Behind me, Max gently removed the whisk from my hand and rested it against the bowl. Turning my body to her, she hugged me hard.

Her palm cupping the back of my head, she told me quietly, "There are at least a dozen people here I don't recognize. They slept over like it's normal. That can't happen. They all should have been gone and the apartment locked up. I'm sorry, Sarah."

I pressed my face to her shirt. "He grabbed me. I tried to stay calm. I shouldn't have jerked him off."

"Are you kidding? I'm smug as *fuck* right now. I love the way your brain works."

With a watery laugh, I asked, "Hungry?"

"Starving. I didn't want to rush you so I used the other shower down here. I was also worried about tackling your ass back to bed because I'm sure your precious pussy needs rest."

"Please don't ever call it precious again…but you're not wrong." I took a deep breath. "Thanks, Max."

"I didn't do shit…"

"Having my back. Never judging the crazy shit I do." I leaned back to stare into her eyes. "Thanks."

Her fingers tightened in my hair and the kiss she gave me made my toes curl against the tile. When she broke it, she replied, "You're welcome."

I made dozens of pancakes and kept them in the warming oven Viv probably didn't know she had.

People ate and mumbled appreciation as they appeared from around the condo looking a little worse for wear. All of them still had their costumes and makeup on from the night before.

Max and I sat on the balcony and soaked up some sunshine while we ate. When we were done, we cleaned up and left together. My motorcycle was at her place and she talked me into staying.

After a long soak together in her deep tub, I announced that my *precious pussy* was fully recovered and hopeful for round two.

Saying yes to time with Max *wasn't* hard.

On the other hand, she was *always* hard.

CHAPTER 32:
Daily Life

November 2010

I'd officially been an escort for one year.

From the first day, I wrote in my journal every morning. I kept a spreadsheet of my clients and experiences - with alternate names to protect them if Vivienne or her staff were ever investigated.

The day Vivienne approached me, I'd been with seven sexual partners voluntarily.

That number climbed to thirty-one in my first year.

I was grateful my clients were women. I had zero pregnancy risk. Every client was required to submit frequent bloodwork and mine was done every thirty days for their protection as well.

Still, the mental and physical exhaustion I was beginning to feel was something I hid from everyone in my life.

To counter the effects on my mind and body, I returned to running every morning, took up yoga, and carefully monitored my nutritional intake.

Max taught me several types of meditation that I used every morning and night.

No matter my precautions, I knew I couldn't maintain what I was doing forever.

I called Joe to discuss my financial portfolio and asked him to place fifteen percent of my cash assets into slightly higher risk-higher yield stocks.

My personal goals were important to me and I was reaching them faster as an escort than I might have in other ways - saving roughly eighty-percent of everything I earned.

However, it wasn't a long-term solution.

On a random Tuesday, I worked on a glass-fronted cabinet I'd found on someone's trash pile.

My living room was a wreck, with painting tarps over everything. The cabinet sat in the center of the room as I sanded it back to bare wood.

It would be fantastic when it was done.

Every window was open and I sang along - for better or worse - to Matchbox Twenty while I worked.

My bedroom was mostly closed to limit the dust and a tarp hung across the entrance to my dining nook and kitchen for the same reason.

I was surprised when someone knocked on my door but turned down the music to answer it. My face broke into a big smile at Max standing on the other side.

"Hi." I looked behind me. "Uh, you can come in but there's *nowhere* to sit."

She stepped inside and removed her sunglasses, taking in my trashed living room with wide eyes.

The basketball shorts, t-shirt, and sneakers she wore looked damn good on her leanly muscular frame. Her sleek ponytail hung through the back of a Nike baseball cap.

Taking off the hat, she dropped her shades and keys inside it. "You're doing all the refinishing?" I nodded. "It's going to be pretty."

"I think so, too." I confided, "Found it in the trash."

"You what?" I grinned. "How the hell did you get it here? You ride a motorcycle."

"I paid a landscaping guy forty bucks to haul it home for me in his truck. It was fucking *heavy*. We barely got it up the stairs." I reached out and traced the fine engraving along the trim. "People throw everything away. It's crazy."

Max looked floored. "You've done this before?"

"Uh huh. When I first moved here, I didn't have any money. I found the dining set, both bookcases, and my coffee table in the trash. The rest of my stuff came from thrift stores and garage sales. Took me a long time to refinish everything with work and school but I got it done."

"That's awesome."

I waved my hand. "I didn't even offer you anything to drink. I have all kinds of stuff."

"I'll grab something later. Can I help?"

"It's...probably boring. Don't feel like you have to."

"I don't. I came to see if you were up for some tacos. Why don't we eat first and finish it up when we get back? It'll go faster with two people."

I glanced down at my cutoffs and old t-shirt. "I probably have stuff in my hair…"

"You look great. Take it down, shake it out, and you're good to go."

"Are you sure?"

"I *know* you're hungry…" I nodded and she dropped a kiss on my lips. "Let's go get *tacos*."

Removing my shirt, I used it to wipe away the light coating of grit I could feel on my skin. Then I shook out my hair and threw it in a messy bun. In my room, I quickly exchanged my flip-flops for sneakers and chose a clean shirt.

Moving part of the tarp in the living room, I grabbed my wallet, phone, and keys from the bookshelf.

There were two missed calls and three texts from Max. I looked up sheepishly. "Sorry. I…didn't hear my phone."

"I figured when I got here and heard the sander going and music blasting." After I closed the front windows, she draped her arm around my shoulders and guided me to the door. "The woman you are is endlessly fascinating, Sarah."

"Hardly."

We ate our fill of street tacos then picked up some fruit smoothies and walked along the beach. I was energized from good food and better company.

It took two hours to finish the sanding, clean the piece, and vacuum the entire area so dust didn't get into the first coat of stain.

Turning on two cheap box fans I used during my projects, the ventilation was pretty good. I applied the light stain - happy to have all the tarps gone but the one on the floor.

While it dried, we left to pick up a set of small battery-operated lights that would illuminate the inside of the cabinet.

Naturally, we stopped for ice cream cones and sat talking while we ate them.

The wood was ready for a second coat by the time we got back. After it was applied, I stared at it intently. "We have to kill an hour before we can apply the top coat. I'm gross but…I have a flat sheet I can throw over my bed if you're interested."

Max walked me backwards into my bedroom while she kissed me stupid. Against my lips, she murmured, "Always interested."

We ended up showering, spending the rest of the night in bed together, and applying the top coat the next morning.

I'd never enjoyed a project as much.

* * *

The week before Thanksgiving, Lyra gave her official notice to Vivienne.

Her acceptance and assignment with the Peace Corps had finally come in. By the end of November, she'd be embarking on a new life. Her clients would be distributed among us.

Taking me aside, Lyra said, "Sarah, I asked Viv to assign *you* to Juliana because I think you'd be the best choice. She needs some finesse because she isn't like most of our clients."

"I hope I'm a good fit."

"You will be. You're kind. Gentle in ways the others aren't. She'll like you."

Vivienne informed us she'd be looking for two new escorts - one to replace Lyra and another to fill in for Sonja who was rarely around due to the couple who booked her exclusively.

The expressions of dread on everyone's face when she said it made me wonder what they thought when she hired me.

As if reading my mind, Max murmured, "Vivienne normally has decent instincts but her level of partying dulls her judgment. Fingers crossed."

Vivienne started looking for new girls and we held a going away party for Lyra two days before her flight left for South Africa. Then she'd take a train north to her assigned location.

We danced until dawn and dropped her at a duplex on Hallandale Beach. A 50cc scooter sat in the driveway with a sticker that read *Sea Turtles Dig the Dark* on the luggage pod.

Vivienne gave Lyra a leather book filled with her studio portraits. We all had gifts for her. There was hugging, a few tears, then we watched her wave from her doorway and disappear inside.

The others chatted about losing one of their numbers as we drove away. The basic consensus was that Lyra was a good person who'd always been an outlier in the agency.

Everyone *liked* her but no one was truly *close* to her.

My eyes met Max's in the rearview mirror. The same assessment could be made of me…and probably would be one day in the not-so-distant future.

The next day, I called Vivienne to ask her about setting up appointments with Juliana.

We'd meet at her restaurant – a Brazilian bakery and cafe – the following Friday.

CHAPTER 33:
The Chef

December 2010

For my first date with Juliana, I toned down the glamor as Lyra suggested.

I kept my hair pulled back from my face in a clip, a bit of gloss on my lips, and wore a hippy-style skirt that came to my ankles with a soft cotton wrap top. The boots I wore under it were flat, plain, and comfortable.

Walker cringed at the ensemble but I insisted.

When Kylee dropped me off in front of Juliana's restaurant, the place was *packed*.

There were only a few tables inside, a couple on the sidewalk, and no parking. It was on a prime stretch of Ft. Lauderdale beach with tourists strolling along the waterfront in light jackets for the cooler weather.

The older building had a lot of charm and I fell in love with the décor done in warm tones and amber glass pieces on the shelves running near the ceiling.

The front was open to the water and a cool breeze blew in, ruffling the white linen tablecloths. The smell of garlic and fresh bread hung in the air.

My mouth watered as the hostess approached me. "Hi. I'm here to meet Juliana. She's expecting me."

"Certainly. Follow me." I was led into a spotless kitchen with state-of-the-art equipment.

My first impression of my new client was of a woman who absolutely *filled up* the space she occupied.

She was neither skinny nor overweight. *Sturdy* - that's how my grandfather described me when I was a kid.

Her thick black hair was in a French braid and pulled into a snug bun. She wore chef whites and there were beads of sweat on her forehead.

The hostess walked to her and I waited by the door. Juliana leaned in to listen to the lowered voice of her employee and her dark eyes came up to meet mine. The girl passed me returning to the dining area.

Juliana appeared flustered.

She wiped her hands as she came my way. "You must be Sarah?" I nodded and gave her a calm smile. "Forgive me. My second-in-command broke his wrist - playing tennis, if you can believe it."

The way she said it held complete disgust - as if playing tennis was beyond ridiculous.

"The girl who preps for me is who-knows-where. I have no staff to cover. I, uh, suppose I must cancel our appointment."

I understood the situation she was in.

When another order was delivered to the kitchen, she actually jumped.

"I can help." My voice was calm, my body still. Julianna's eyes widened. "No strings attached. You need a couple of extra hands and I'm useful in the kitchen. I'll wash dishes if you need it. What can I do?"

Speechless at my offer, I watched the *business owner* inside her battle with the *woman* who had needs.

"This is not something I should accept. You did not come here for work. I mean! Oh my. I am sorry."

I placed my hand on her forearm. "Please let me help. I'm good at lending a hand and you seem to be in a situation that could use the skill."

She backed into the heart of her kitchen. "Yes, okay. This might work. I have an apron on the hook for you there."

I saw it and stepped into a small alcove to gather my hair into a tight twist. I managed to get it clipped in place at the base of my neck.

Washing my hands, I pulled the apron over my neck and walked to what I assumed was the prep station.

Juliana gestured to several baskets. "Just, uh, begin dicing until I tell you to stop." She turned to go back to her station and paused. "Thank you for this."

With a nod, I got to work. I don't know how much I diced but no one said *stop* so I kept going until there was nothing left in the baskets and the containers set out to hold them were full.

I'd never worked in a restaurant so I didn't know the protocols. Using common sense, I tried to navigate the chaotic space without getting in anyone's way or contaminating food.

Cleaning up the station, I saw a pot of water on a gas burner that I assumed should be boiling - so I turned it on. At the sinks, I washed what I'd used and a few other things sitting nearby.

Throughout my unique experience, I watched Juliana shout orders to her staff in Portuguese. Every so often, she glanced at me but I let her work and tried to be helpful.

I swept carefully, sautéed onions, restocked missing supplies, washed more dishes, stirred a cream sauce that seemed to need it, washed even more dishes, and removed a tray of bread when a timer went off no one seemed to hear but me.

Overall, I loved it. I liked cooking and performed well under pressure.

The hours ticked by and before I realized, it was one in the morning. I was sweaty, probably red from the heat, and no one would have believed I was a paid escort hired for sex.

Juliana removed her apron and stood in front of me. I wiped down the counters and hummed to myself. A bit of a song I didn't know from earlier was stuck in my head.

She placed a hand on my shoulder and gave me a sincere smile. "Thank you. I am grateful. I know it is late. You must be exhausted. I will understand if you need to go…"

My laughter clearly took her off-guard. "I've been smelling this incredible food all night. Feed me and we'll call it even."

"Food - you are kidding? This is not enough…"

"I *never* joke about food. Besides, I'd like the chance to actually *talk* to you."

She nodded enthusiastically. "Of course! We must eat. Do you mind if I send the staff home? Some have been here as long as I have. I do not like that."

An hour later, the place was clean, restocked, and empty of everyone but the two of us. The front was closed up and locked with privacy shades drawn.

It was strange to see it so still and quiet after the noise and chaos from earlier.

She warmed two bowls of black bean stew - I learned it was called *feijoada* - and my mouth watered. Using a pasta dish, she added a scoop of rice and spooned chicken thighs that practically fell off the bone in a rich orange sauce beside it.

Cheese bread that I'd been eyeing for hours came out of the warmer and into a basket.

She set everything down and said, "Sit. I will get the rest." A minute later, she returned with glasses of a fresh fruit drink and two servings of coconut cake.

"It's so pretty here. I love the location, the building, the atmosphere, and the smells. Thank you for not canceling our appointment."

She inclined her head in response and we sat in silence, enjoying the food.

"Tell me about yourself, Sarah. What is it that makes me want to *keep* you when I barely *know* you?"

I didn't know how to reply. "Working together for an evening might have helped."

"You are not afraid of hard work. I like that." She gestured to the room around us. "I opened this cafe when I came here from Brazil. My parents own a similar restaurant where I grew up."

"You run a tight ship," I told her.

"Ah. I have employed many and watched them run screaming when they could not handle the pressure. You behave as if you have been working in restaurants your whole life. I am impressed."

"Thanks." I placed my hand on her thigh. "You have a system you want everyone to follow. Once you see the rhythm, it isn't hard to match the beat."

She leaned in to kiss me and I tasted fruit and spice on her lips. My hand massaged her neck as I deepened the contact and drank her in.

Resting her forehead against mine, she said, "I live above the restaurant. We should go up, I think."

With a nod of agreement, I gathered our dishes and washed them while she shut down the restaurant and armed the security system.

There were doors at the front and back of the building beside the main exits from the restaurant. They opened on narrow flights of stairs leading to her living space above the cafe.

The decor in her home mimicked what she'd chosen for her business. Warm tones, jeweled accents, plush rugs over teak flooring. The lighting was soft and gave the room an amber glow.

Placing her keys in a hand-made bowl on the foyer table, Juliana took me in a firm embrace as if she was a lover I'd had for years.

For a moment, I was internally startled.

Concealing my strange reaction, I returned the hug and dropped kisses along her jaw and neck. She smoothed loose tendrils of my hair, and I started removing the pins holding hers.

"I shower after working. Will you join me?"

"Of course."

She led the way through double French doors to her bedroom and master bath. Against one wall was a king-sized bed covered with linens ranging from cream to espresso.

The bath was a masterpiece of design done in cream tile shot through with cocoa brown and plants hanging from alternating heights in front of the wide window. It felt as if we stepped into a spa.

She clicked on one light from a panel featuring several switches and the room filled with a gentle glow.

Juliana reached into the custom shower without a door and turned on the water to heat. Within seconds, the room filled with steam.

I undressed, watching as she did the same. As she unbraided her hair, it fell heavily to her waist. It immediately began to curl from the moist air and I knew she tried to tame out her curls as I did.

Naked in front of her, I watched her take me in from head to toe. "You are fit, strong. I like that."

I stepped closer and slid my hand over her bare shoulder and down her arm to take her hand. Her body was also strong. Heavier than what might be popular, she carried it well with full breasts and hips, muscular legs, and a gently rounded belly.

Walking into the shower, I tugged her with me. We were practical, washing our bodies and masses of hair. It felt good to wash away my sweat and the scent of food that gradually clung to me from the hot kitchen over the night.

When she reached for a razor, I offered to shave her. She laughed and it echoed. "It is a lot but you may if you wish."

Kneeling on the floor, I spread gel over the skin of her legs before whisking it away with the razor. Her calves were thick and hard from many hours spent on her feet. I gently touched up her bikini area and then shaved her armpits as well.

Most of my body was hair-free by design. For once, I wished it wasn't. I wondered how it would feel to have Max shaving me like this. It was erotic to shave someone else.

Thoroughly rinsing, we held each other and kissed deeply. I thought I had a read on this new client.

Juliana spent every day serving others. Having someone's attention fully on her needs was a gift she not only appreciated but needed in her life.

Holding her close, I kissed her while lightly massaging her breast in my hand, tweaking a brown nipple that was tight and distended. When her head tipped to the side, I nibbled her neck and shoulder.

"You are a beautiful, sensual woman. Thank you for allowing me to be here with you."

"I search for artifice in you but find none."

"Search all you want, Juliana. I don't say things I don't mean."

I tugged her from the shower and we dried off. Walking backwards to her bedroom, pulling her with me, she laid down on the bed.

Both windows were cracked and faced the ocean less than fifty feet away. The sound of the waves was low and hypnotic.

"Let me take care of you." I patted the bed. "Roll over on your stomach."

When she did, I straddled her thighs and started a deep tissue massage at her shoulders. She released a moan that was filled with pleasure.

"Tell me about your childhood, Sarah."

I obliged - leaving out the unpleasant parts as usual - and wasn't surprised when she fell asleep within minutes. I stopped talking but continued rubbing forcefully into the muscles of her legs and feet.

When I was finished, I texted Kylee about the evening and explained I would take a cab in the morning. Then I laid down beside her and pulled the blankets over us.

Surprisingly, I fell asleep myself.

Two hours later, I woke to the sensation of Juliana eating my pussy. Disoriented for a moment, I stayed calm using one of Max's tricks and landed back in my surroundings.

Juliana knelt between my legs, licking me as if it was the most natural thing on Earth. She was in no hurry and seemed truly relaxed.

I gripped the sheet under me, amazed at her attention to detail. Her fingers held my lips apart as she sucked each part of me separately, licking the entire area before beginning again.

In a whisper, I told her, "Turn around so I can taste you, too."

She uncoiled and changed position, one leg bent to make her pussy accessible to me. I assumed the same position and duplicated her movements. My fingers stroked lazily into her wet heat as her thighs flexed.

When she came, she shouted, "Oh, god! Yes! I must come for you. Do not stop."

I wouldn't have dreamt of stopping.

As her lower body went limp, she fell on my pussy like a woman possessed. "The pleasure you give me, I must give you. To have you come for me, feel you tighten and climax from my fingers inside you, my tongue licking you. I must have it."

She followed this with a string of Portuguese whispered in her soft and sensual voice.

When I came, I hugged her, my face against her hip as the last remnants of her own orgasm coursed through her.

It was unusual for me not to service my clients repeatedly during our sessions but I enjoyed the change of pace. She was gentle, easy.

Juliana ended up being the last new client I took on as an escort and became one of my favorites. All these years after leaving the industry, we contact each other several times a year to catch up.

There was no artifice in *her* either.

CHAPTER 34:
Rookies

January 2011

Escort life was *chaotic* during the holidays.

Lyra had been gone for several weeks. The rest of us assumed her clients and maintained our own.

People didn't want to be alone during the festivities. Since we couldn't - and wouldn't - increase our days of *intimate* work to a dangerous degree, we offered *zero intimacy* packages. These could happen any night of the week between Thanksgiving and Christmas.

Many of these dates were with male friends or relatives of our existing clients. Often, they were closeted by necessity and required the appearance of a female significant other on their arm.

This was a particular strength of mine and I became the unspoken number one for such requests.

Over the two weeks leading up to Christmas, I escorted a dozen gentlemen to office parties, joined them during the boat parade, and even showed up as their plus-one for mandatory family dinners.

I dressed beautifully, smiled brightly, flirted shamelessly, and eased interactions with their coworkers, neighbors, and relatives.

Vivienne made a killing on the bookings.

I made even more in tips and gifts.

By Christmas Eve, I was completely burnt out.

Campbell appeared at my door with food, presents, and a massage therapist carrying her portable table. Max stood behind them.

In the doorway, Camp gasped in gay shock when he saw me. "Tomorrow, you turn twenty…not sixty. You look *ratched*."

"Thank you," I muttered in my oversized pajamas and ratty bunny slippers. I hadn't brushed my hair or my teeth. "I haven't had a day off in three weeks, didn't get home until four hours ago, and couldn't eat last night. My date accidentally stepped on my foot and I took a nasty tumble. Don't be mean."

Max moved between them and took me in her arms. I leaned heavily on her with my face buried in her sweater. She smelled amazing.

"Set up your table. Campbell, get Sarah something to nibble until we can feed her properly. Let me help her for a few minutes." Max bent and picked me up.

She didn't talk as she set me on my bathroom counter and brushed out my hair. Leaving me there, she went to get my white robe from my closet.

Stripping me for my massage, she inspected the ugly bruise on the side of my foot and the scrapes around my knee that was also bruised. Sighing, she wrapped me in the robe and quickly put my hair in a loose braid.

With a gentle kiss on my temple, she said, "Brush your teeth, pee if you need to, then get the massage you clearly need."

She started to leave but I grabbed a piece of her sweater. Gathering me close, she gave me a tight hug that made me instantly emotional. Warm hands held my face and she stared into my eyes.

"I'm not going anywhere. We're going to take care of you tonight and tomorrow. You should have called me." I shook my head. "Why not?"

"You're busy. Working as many hours as I am."

"Most of which is spent sitting in the limo reading a book. Not performing like a circus bear."

My eyes filled with tears. "They're so majestic. They shouldn't be used in the circus. It's not right."

The hug she gave me was almost painful and I never wanted it to stop. "You're so *tired*, Sarah."

She kissed my forehead and turned me to the sink. I watched as she put toothpaste on my toothbrush for me and took it. While I brushed, she rubbed my back.

"Do you need to pee?"

"I just finished when I heard the door."

"Good."

She picked me up and carried me back to the living room. The curtains were pulled, soft music played on the stereo, and the lighting was dim. Camp held an apple slice with peanut butter to my lips and I ate it - as well as the six that followed.

Setting me on my feet beside the massage table, Max stepped back as the massage therapist smiled gently.

"I'm Constance."

"Hi. I'm Sarah."

She held up the sheet and turned her head. "You get comfortable and tell me when you're ready."

Removing the robe, I put it over the end of the sofa and stretched out. Constance lowered the sheet and laid her hand in the center of my back.

I jerked sharply.

"I'm sorry, dear. Typically, I do an interview with my clients before a session. I'm going to rest my hand here and let you get accustomed to a stranger touching you before we start. If you need me to stop at any point, let me know."

I closed my eyes. Constance massaged me from head to toe, front and back, and delivered deep tissue stimulation that had to border on pain for it to truly benefit me.

Afterward, I showered, dressed in comfortable clothes, and let Camp put braids in my hair while we watched movies. I fell asleep several times between them. Each time I woke up, they were there with a hand on my head or my foot.

They were the most important people in my life. A fact Kylee pointed out months ago.

I'd woken up before their arrival sad, hurting, and dangerously on edge. It was like that sometimes.

Max and Camp fed me, laughed with me, and gave me genuine affection that helped get me level.

Having their presence helped.

Not for the first time, I hoped I never lost them.

***

The week leading up to New Year's was insane. All of us were exhausted and noticeably cranky.

When Max updated me on a couple of potential escorts Viv interviewed, I was floored.

The first two were cousins from Michigan who apparently looked like they arrived in Florida for Spring Break and never left. Bad tans, bad bleach jobs, and attitude to spare.

"Viv threw them out in the middle of the night when they asked her where they could score some coke." Max took a bite of her burger, shaking her head.

"I don't understand. How did they make it into her house to begin with? Where did she *find* them?"

Grinning, Max popped a fry in her mouth. "Hooters."

"You're lying…"

"I assure you…I'm not."

The next possibility ticked all the boxes. She was pretty, smart, personable, and supposedly intelligent.

The staff was assembled as they had been my first day and I was getting ready to participate in her photo spread.

From across the condo, I heard a commotion and went running down the hall in lingerie and a robe.

The pot used to heat wax was overturned just outside the skincare room and wax was all over the floor.

"I'm not letting you touch me! Who knows what weird shit you've been touching?"

Lucia stood in the doorway of her mini-studio. Vivienne, Max, and Kylee came from the direction of the kitchen. Kirkland and Walker frowned in confusion as they joined the gathering.

Viv asked carefully, "What's going on, Cara?"

She yelled, "I need someone *else* to wax me. I don't trust Asians. Slant-eyes fucking eat dogs and shit."

Everyone started talking at once but I didn't have the patience for words. I walked over and slapped her in the mouth. She held her face with an expression of shock that told me *no one* had ever hit her before.

That was probably part of the problem.

"Get the fuck out and don't come back. Our clients are every body type, race, age, and walk of life. We don't need a racist piece of shit like you fucking up our groove."

"I'll *sue* you."

"Go ahead, Cara." I stepped close and she whimpered. "If I'm willing to slap the fuck out of you for saying something disgusting about someone else, *imagine* what I'll do if you try anything with me."

"You can't…"

"Oh, I can and I will. By the end of the day, I'll know *everything* about you. Where you live, who you hang out with, how much money you have."

I leaned in and whispered, "My uncle is part of the Irish mafia. He likes to dismember people who make him upset, Cara. Get your shit and get out before I lose my temper."

Following her through the house as she got dressed and grabbed her stuff, I escorted her to the elevator.

As the doors closed, I murmured, "Be careful out there, honey." Her eyes widened in genuine fear and then she was gone.

I turned around and walked to Ma-Ying. Gently taking the plastic spatula used to stir the wax from her hand, I went to my knees and started scraping the cooled wax off the floor.

A moment later, Max joined me with a utensil from the kitchen and a trash bag.

After a few minutes of silence, she said quietly, "I don't think I've ever wanted to fuck you into a coma as much as I do right now."

I smiled but it felt weird on my face. "Put it on the calendar. I could use a break."

In mid-January, Viv found a woman named Summer Mooreville. Originally from Des Moines, she had pixie-cut blonde hair and pale blue eyes. She was nice, attractive, and seemed normal.

We were all relieved when she made it through all the initial preparation and her first two appointments without a hitch.

After Summer had a date with her third client, she talked about the woman as if they were deeply in love. Apparently, she'd done a lot of talking to Kylee, too. The rest of us didn't see the situation ending well but hoped for the best.

Then Vivienne found Delta Osborn at a jewelry counter in the mall.

She raved about the latest addition. "She's from New Orleans. Has a killer body and an incredible sense of humor. You're going to love her as much as I do."

I did *not*.

The Escort: In the Service of Women

In fact, I could barely tolerate her.

On the surface, Delta was awesome. Flawless skin, ash blonde hair, and legs about a mile long - she carried herself well and spoke intelligently.

She loved anything to do with the sea, was a master diver, and found out through Vivienne that Max knew people who ran a charter boat in the Keys.

I relaxed on the sectional in the living room after making Monday morning brunch and cleaning the kitchen. I had my bare feet under Max's thigh while I read a book on my phone. She reviewed her emails and caught up on the news.

Delta entered the room and sat against Max's other side despite there being plenty of other places to sit.

"Viv just told me about your friends in the Keys! We should plan a group trip. Make a day of it and enjoy the fresh air, sunshine, and water." Gripping Max's forearm, she said in a low voice, "I bet you know a *lot* of interesting people."

Something about her grated on every damn nerve I had.

Without looking away from my phone, I said, "Max has led a fascinating life. She's a beautiful, intelligent, retired Marine in her early thirties. It would be weird if she *didn't* know a lot of interesting people."

"That's true." There was a long pause. "You're like two peas in a pod. I always see you together."

"Yeah. That's how it is with peas." I closed my book and stretched. "There are waffles left in the kitchen if you're hungry, Delta."

"Ohh, thanks…but no. I don't eat that crap. I work hard to keep my body right and tight."

"Cool. I love food. I down carbs and sweets like somebody will take them from me."

"You must spend your life at the gym…"

"Not since high school track. I run for mental health and go dancing sometimes."

"Really. Wow." She seemed annoyed and it made me happy. "We should go dancing…"

"Maybe." I stood. "I'm gonna head out. See you next week." I *wanted* to irritate her and didn't know why.

Max showed up at my place a few minutes behind me. She didn't call me on my juvenile bullshit.

However, she did make me come until I passed out.

* * *

Delta settled in and had a full roster of clients within weeks - taking several all of us had struggled to fit into our schedules.

She took one-off appointments without hesitation and worked four nights a week rather than our standard three.

It was a good thing because Summer ended up vomiting emotion all over the client she fell in love with and scared the *hell* out of the poor woman.

Viv put her on a plane to Des Moines with advice to get an education and avoid escort work in the future.

Delta was a good addition…but I still didn't like her.

CHAPTER 35:
Unwanted Attention

March 2011

I didn't strip often because I liked to maintain an air of mystery on the scene - the money was better that way.

Every few months, I signed up for a nearby club's amateur night and pulled out all the stops. A friend of Campbell's made my costumes and one of the regular girls did my makeup and hair.

The club was well known in Florida and beyond. People came from all over to participate in a night of fresh faces.

They also spent *buckets* of cash.

I decided to dance on a rare Friday when I didn't have any client appointments. It had been four months since I last appeared. I texted Campbell and he promised to be there.

That night, there were whispers in the dressing room about several big names in the crowd that included a rapper, comedian, and two football stars.

As I prepared for my set, I spotted Campbell at a front table. He sat with several of my coworkers - including Walker and Max.

The traitor.

My costume this time was a sexy schoolgirl. It wasn't something I'd done before due to my own trauma but everyone in the club was grown and so was I.

I knew I could pull it off.

I went with more of an anime high school girl style with thigh-high socks, pleated skirt, tied up dress shirt, tie, and pigtails. My makeup was colorful like the plaid in my skirt.

Walking out to *My Love Is Like Woah*, I didn't go straight to the pole. I'd worked out a routine the night before that got gradually sexier as my song played.

As I always did, I let my eyes blur so I didn't see the crowd watching me for most of my four-minute set.

During the last minute, I found the people I knew up front and smiled as I went to my knees. Crawling to the edge of the stage, Campbell held out a lollipop and I took it in exchange for a kiss on his lips.

Winking, I sucked it and crooked my finger at Max. She smiled as she appeared in front of me and tucked a hundred in my bright pink thong that opened when I spread my legs.

I took the sucker from my mouth. "Kiss me, Max."

She slipped her palm along the back of my neck and slid me closer to the edge. It was no small kiss. She went hard and deep. I was breathless by the time she broke it.

Naturally, the crowd went wild.

Her hands around my waist, she lifted me to my platform heels and I bent to kiss her again. Walker and the other escorts tucked money in my thong while Viv threw several large bills at me like she was making it rain.

Laughing, I grabbed my stuff, bowed, and left the stage covered in cash. The guys would gather it.

In the back, I quickly changed into jeans and a tank top. Removing most of the makeup, I coiled my hair to the base of my neck, put on a baseball cap, and stepped into my boots.

Folding everything into my pack, I slung it over my shoulder and went to see the stage manager. He handed me a fat envelope. I removed nine fifties and told him to tip the servers and bar staff. I tucked a hundred in his chest pocket.

"And here's another one for the DJ."

"None of these dancers tip like you, sugar."

I winked. "I like them to look out for me when I'm here. See you next time, Tank."

"Sure thing. Don't be away too long."

Leaving through the back, I got on my motorcycle and went to an IHOP several miles away.

It was my usual routine after a show. I lived less than a mile from the club. I didn't want some asshole following me home. Campbell would tell the others.

I secured a huge table and ordered three glasses of water with orange slices from a server who knew me well enough to ask if my friend was joining me.

"A *few* friends this time. Be patient and know I'll tip heavily for putting up with us," I told her as everyone walked through the front door.

"You got it, hon."

Campbell dropped into a chair on one side, Max on the other. I handed him the envelope and he was giddy to count my take.

"Girl. You made just over four this time." He tilted his head. "You already tipped the whole staff?" I nodded. "So that was another six hundred plus. Wow. Nice job shaking your ass."

"Thanks." I counted out a thousand and handed it to him. "For your trouble. Take Bobby to a nice ass dinner on me. Tell him I said thanks for the outfit."

"Bitch, stop giving me money…"

"I will not. You run all my tech." Turning to Max, I smiled. "Thank you for being part of my finale."

"My pleasure. I don't need to tell you but I will. You looked damn good up there." She tipped up my chin and kissed my lips. "Glad you sneak out. There were quite a few admirers looking for you at the dancers' exit. You went through the kitchen?"

I nodded. "I'm starving…"

"So am I." Her eyes held mine.

Leaning close, I whispered, "Eating…then eating?"

"Such a brilliant woman."

"I'll shower off the body glitter first."

"Hm." Her gaze flicked to my chest. "Maybe…leave it for a while."

"Done." After another pause, I whispered, "I have the entire outfit in my bag."

"Oh. That's excellent information."

Walker stared at us from across the table quizzically. "How much do you two hang out?"

"I'm pretty much taking her perfect cock in my various orifices every chance I get. Why?"

"Must you *repeatedly* break my heart? Haven't I paid for my asshole behavior? I try so hard."

Crossing my arms on the table, I laughed. "You're right. Fresh start from today. I will *never* fuck you so make a note."

"But…why?"

"Because your dick was in my best friend and I have rules." He choked on his own spit and it made me grin. "Besides, he gave me a play by play against my will so I feel like I was *there* anyway."

"Jesus…"

Campbell studied the menu with a relaxed and uncaring expression.

"I heard Camp called for our Lord and Savior *many* times that night." I winked. "I'm messing with you. You were passable at best. Time for noms."

"How dare you." Walker rested his elbow on the table. "I am *never* merely passable…"

Opening the menu, I whistled. "One who disappears the morning after without a word of thanks for the orgasms must take the grade they're given since the assignment was left incomplete. Oh, maybe crepes." I turned the page. "Since I know how Campbell fucks - both men *and* women - he gets top scores."

The table went silent and my best friend groaned. "You stole it…you *stole* my virginity."

"Lies."

"Fine. I auctioned it off for free-ninety-nine…but I wasn't the one who suggested the threesome."

Chuckling, I reminded him, "That was all Evan. It's your fault for being so pretty." I turned my face and he kissed my lips.

"That idiot still calls me randomly when he's drunk."

"Campbell. In the name of all things holy, don't answer…the man is *addicted* to your ass." We rolled our eyes and said at the same time, "Literally."

The entire table cracked up.

We placed our food orders and conversation flew fast and furious around the table.

At some point, I'd taken Max's hand and held it on my thigh. I glanced at my lap and wondered if it was a strange thing to do under the circumstances. As the thought passed through my mind, she tightened her fingers around mine.

I decided they were fine where they were.

* * *

Exhausted from a late appointment with Juliana two days later, I was groggy when I woke up at the condo Monday morning.

Max's arm was thrown over my torso and her knee was over my thigh. I stretched and she pulled me closer. Raising my face, I kissed her jaw.

"I'm gonna pee and make breakfast. You stay here and sleep more." Another kiss and I climbed from the bed. After using the bathroom, I took my phone from my bag and carried it with me to the kitchen.

The moment I took it off *do not disturb*, my notifications went nuts.

Frowning, I saw that most of them were from Campbell but several were from Monica as well.

Both instructed me to call the moment I was up.

Max walked into the room as my call to Campbell connected on speaker.

"Sarah. Don't freak out. Alright? It's fixable. I went in with your passwords and made all your social media top-level private…"

Confused, I asked, "What social media?"

"Those random profiles you set up when we were in high school to play games. Remember?" *Vaguely*. He paused and I braced myself. "Your mom…she tagged you in something."

Everything inside me stilled. "What the fuck are you talking about?"

"She outed you, Sarah. Named us both in a post from the other night…"

"Send me screenshots. You back at school?"

"Yeah. My mom's been duking it out with yours on fucking Facebook since five this morning. Don't go home. People from the club know your name. It's too easy to learn your address."

"I'll call you back."

The screenshots came moments later. The original post was from a Miami rapper I hadn't heard of - it was flattering.

"Wish I had video of this hottie shakin' her ass but here are two prime shots from her finish. She'd be great for the next vid, yeah? Anyone got digits?"

There was a censored image of me kissing Campbell and another of me kissing Max.

I couldn't believe the number of comments. I received screenshots from the ones my mother made.

> *Her name is Sarah Kent from Lighthouse Point. She's my daughter, unfortunately. A whore who sleeps with anything that moves. That's her so-called gay boyfriend Campbell Lynch and some other whore who dresses like a man. No telling what deviant behavior Sarah is involved in. That's why I threw her out of my house. Disgusting piece of trash.*

Monica picked up on the first ring. "Sarah. Don't engage her. It's what Paula wants. Everyone is on your side. She's being *dragged* in the comments. This is going to give greater weight to the civil suit."

The silence drew out.

"Sarah? She can't do shit to you but you can't stay in that apartment. It has zero security. Camp's mom is going to organize everything. She found you an adorable place with everything you need by the beach. You run near there. You know how much they love you…"

I stood in Viv's kitchen, staring at nothing, as I vibrated with white-hot fury.

Distantly, I registered Max taking my phone.

"Monica…"

"Max? Oh, thank Christ she isn't by herself. Keep Sarah away from her place and especially her biological mother. Even if you have to tie her up."

"Understood."

"Paula is a lunatic. Don't underestimate her. She comes off as nothing more than a religious nut but she's violent and unpredictable, Max. I'll call back when I have more information."

I wanted to scream and destroy shit.

Yet, I stood in Vivienne's kitchen, unable to do anything at all. Powerless to protect the people I cared about most from the viral being that was the internet.

My *mother* put them at risk.

She didn't care how dangerous it was for Campbell and Max to gain the attention of crazy people. She didn't care who she hurt.

"Sarah…"

"She won again. I can't go back to the apartment that I love - that I've worked so hard to make into a home. I can never go back to the club. She outed Campbell and put you both at risk from fanatics. P-people know my fucking *name*."

"It's going to be okay. I swear it, Sarah."

It was Max…she had to say that.

CHAPTER 36:
Rage

For days, I paced Max's apartment like an animal trapped in a cage while everyone handled problems that shouldn't have been on their shoulders.

Campbell's parents had my entire apartment moved by the following weekend to a secured building on Deerfield Beach. They took care of everything - with Monica's help - and wouldn't tell me the cost so I estimated for myself and transferred them cash.

Susan Lynch personally packed my belongings to protect my privacy and her husband Ray watched the movers hired to load and unload the truck like a hawk.

People no one recognized were there every day trying to meet me, talk to me, or get my contact information.

Some left business cards.

Others freaked Susan out.

I was surprised to learn that Jake drove by several times a day - in uniform and out - to run off anyone who didn't live in my building and check on Camp's parents.

Max must have called him.

He happened to be there in street clothes the day my mother showed up and tried to get into my place.

Susan refused to let her inside and Paula physically attacked her. Jake pulled her off but she didn't know who he was or that he was a cop.

Once she realized, Paula turned on the tears. None of them were moved by them in the slightest.

Unlike so many other law enforcement people in my past, Jake filed an official report. Monica requested and received an emergency appearance in court on my behalf to explain my mother's rampant disregard for the lawful restraining order.

Paula was ordered to pay fines and serve community service. The restraining order was renewed with stronger repercussions from the judge who'd listened to my case since I showed up in his court battered and broken at fifteen.

Filing several motions, Monica also ramped up the civil suit. She cited repeated harassment - including outing me on the internet - to explain why it was being placed in the court's hands.

She expected us to win.

If we did, Paula would spend the rest of her life paying me - even if we had to garnish her wages.

I personally filed yet another complaint with child services about her. My letter expressed concern for my brothers given Paula's erratic and dangerous behavior.

A day after the post, a random asshole was busted spraying a homophobic slur on Campbell's car by campus security and arrested.

For the most part, Camp was out as a gay man to those closest to him but hadn't planned for *everyone* to know until he was done with college.

He assured me he was fine but I was terrified for his safety.

There was a misconception that backwards ass rednecks only lived in the southern states…but they were scattered all over the country in every state, every city. No matter how accepting you thought your stomping grounds were, there was a pocket of folks near you who lived to hate anyone different.

That's a lesson I've learned over and over again.

Max took me to the new apartment and watched in silence as I checked it out. It was beautiful. The building and parking garage were accessed with a badge or a keyed code so it was definitely safer.

Bigger than my other place, it had a second bedroom for my office and recording equipment.

There were elevators. The rooftop had been converted into outdoor living space that featured grills, dining areas, and landscaping.

My appliances were new, the view was spectacular, and I could simply walk downstairs to go running anytime I wanted.

It didn't feel like my *home.*

I knew I wasn't being fair, that it would take time to settle in and make it mine. I saw the potential and felt gratitude to Campbell's parents and Monica for everything they'd done.

It was hard to embrace the change.

I'd lived in my small apartment for four years and planned to stay there another two while I worked and saved. It was cheap and close to everything I needed. I was familiar with the area and my neighbors.

I resented having my plans derailed by a woman who clearly despised everything about me…but *refused* to stay the fuck out of my life.

Max stayed with me for three days - cooking meals together, moving furniture around, and helping me unpack so I could settle in.

At night, she gave me endless pleasure and her presence in the morning helped anchor where I was before I panicked.

She tried so hard to help and I was desperate to snap out of whatever was going on in my brain. I didn't want to disappoint her but I felt out of control.

My life felt so fucking *messy*.

When she got a call from her building super that there was a pipe break in the apartment above hers, she debated whether or not to leave me.

"I'll be okay," I assured her. "Make sure your stuff is good."

"Fine. I'll be back tomorrow." She held my face. "Call me if you need anything."

Nodding, I kissed her again. "I will."

But I knew I wouldn't.

Rage with nowhere else to go had slowly filled me up for six days…and I finally *drowned* in it.

There was a sports club in Ft. Lauderdale that hosted amateur fight nights and I planned to fight the fuck out of some people.

I texted Campbell my plans so someone knew where I was but I kept things light.

Fight night! Gonna make some cash.

Uh, who do you think you're talking to right now?

It's fine! I haven't done one in a while…

Lying isn't a good look for you, hooker.

I'm not lying. I had to take all of last weekend off and you know I stress out when I don't earn money for an entire week.

Sure. Okay. It's about money. I'll buy it. You better be safe or I'll be the next one squaring up to fight you.

I would destroy you…

And then you'd cry so…who really wins here?

Fair. Love you.

I love you back, Sarah.

Changing into a cropped workout tank and body-hugging shorts, I pulled jeans and a t-shirt over them and stepped into sneakers. Tugging my hair into a snug ponytail, I coiled it into a bun.

There were hair-pulling bitches at these things and I *never* gave them an opening.

Packing my bag with a change of clothes, first aid kit, hand tape, towels, and bottles of water, I left my pretty new apartment and went to fuck some shit up.

* * *

They put me in a cell alone but my brain and emotions weren't calming down. I tried to think clearly but everything was loud and red.

I was still in the workout gear and sneakers that I'd left the ring wearing. I'd planned to change in the bathroom but got dragged into the alley behind the club before I could.

Blood was splattered on my clothes and skin. Some of it was mine - most of it wasn't.

"Kent. Your attorney is here."

The words didn't make sense. I hadn't called anyone. I stood and followed the officer from the holding area and he walked to the main room where I'd entered the satellite police station as the victim who became an assailant.

The instant I cleared the hall door, the bitches who jumped me started yelling and carrying on.

"Your ass got what it deserved," one of them called.

"You mighta won the money…but we got the last laugh."

"Keep your bitch ass out the ring…"

I was so fucking tired of bullies.

Hands cuffed in front of me, I jumped two chairs and launched myself off a third as I went for the ringleader. She released a blood curdling scream at the same moment I was snatched out of midair.

Holding me around the waist, Max's voice said in my ear, "Count. Count, Sarah."

I tried. I tried as hard as I could.

"That your dyke girlfriend? Fucking figures…"

There was so much rage…

"Come closer and call her that again, you fucking cum rag." I tried to get loose but Max held me tight to her torso.

She was strong but careful not to hurt me. Even now. I didn't want to hurt her either.

"Yeah, she better hold you back. We whipped your ass once and we'll do it again."

I was confused when Campbell said from somewhere behind me, "She beat you in the ring. When your little gang jumped her, she beat all your asses *again*. I suggest you shut the fuck up."

"No one asked you, fag…"

Vibrating with negative energy, I stared at the woman a few years older than me and smiled. "Keep. Talking. I dare you. Run your mouth some more with nothing to back it up. Even your friends are weak and useless."

I laughed and wanted blood spilled - someone else's or my own. "Keep fucking talking and digging yourself a little deeper."

"You talk all bad but…"

"I'm right here. What do you say? I'll even give you a head start…free shots. Just know this: it'll end with you consuming your meals with a straw until your new teeth come in." I held up my bloody fist. "Already got one, yeah?"

"You're a *psycho*."

"Maybe." My voice was quiet. "Come over here…let's find out together."

Campbell murmured, "Girl, *shut up*. Somebody needs to snatch those cheap plastic extensions out of your head and slap you with them. Can't you see you don't stand a chance against her? She fights survival style - full streetfighter mode. Read the *room*."

My attacker shifted her weight from one foot to the other, jittery like she suddenly understood she'd fucked with the wrong person.

"I don't care what you say about me," I told her through gritted teeth. "You won't say shit about them. I'd do hard time to make my point."

Her eyes were enormous in her face. "W-what…?"

"You heard me. I'm so fucking pissed my teeth are throbbing to draw blood. Apologize for your hate speech…right now."

"Your…teeth? What?" She tried to cloak herself in bravado but failed. "W-whatever. Sorry."

"Stay out of the ring if you see me. I might lose my temper in front of all those dicks you're so anxious to impress." I glanced at the officer closest to me. He was a young guy who looked like he was watching pay-per-view. "What are my charges?"

"Uh, we didn't have any against you. You were pretty enraged when we got there. I only put you in cuffs and a cell to calm you down."

The other officer nodded. "It was self-defense on your part. Clear assault and battery for those three. We have witnesses to what went down and their other friend was *nice* enough to record the whole thing for evidence."

Camp murmured, "I *want* that video…"

"Drop the charges," I said. "Keep the paperwork on ice for thirty days in case they try some shit."

Bending, I spit blood in the trash can.

Monica objected firmly. "Sarah, they *attacked* you. Jumped you from behind, three on one."

"I won't press charges unless they do something else. They got their shots in. I got more. They'll be hurting pretty bad in the morning. I chose my defensive strikes carefully. I'm tired. Campbell has classes tomorrow. No sense dragging this out."

"Are you sure?"

I nodded. "I am. Sorry you got called out for this."

After signing some paperwork, I was given my bag and we filed out of the station.

Beside Max's car, Monica took a deep breath. "Sarah, I need you to *talk* to someone when those old feelings surface. To Campbell, Max, me…you can't keep it bottled up until you explode."

She reached out to hold my face and I felt the bruising under my eye from the first sucker punch I took in the alley.

"Taking pain, letting people hurt you, those are things you don't have to do anymore. Don't let her drag you back to that place. You're going to get yourself killed." Monica leaned forward and lightly kissed my temple. "Call me tomorrow."

Getting in her car, she waved and drove away.

Campbell pulled me into a hug that hurt but I didn't make a sound. "I knew you were lying, bitch. You *never* do these fights spur of the moment. There are safer ways to deal with the anger you keep trying to crush down. Pick one of those."

Leaning back, he held my shoulders. "I'm staying in your swanky digs tonight and driving back first thing but I'll be here on Thursday. Take your punishment like a grownup." Then he kissed me and left in his SUV.

"I-I need to get my bike."

"Kylee dropped Walker at the club and he rode it to my place. They left the keys." He had a motorcycle so I knew Walker was fine on mine but I was annoyed that his groin touched my seat. "I'll have it detailed to avoid cross-contamination."

Despite the shit show of a night, I laughed. I risked a glance at her face for the first time and stilled.

Max was *furious*.

CHAPTER 37:
Terms & Conditions

Leaning around me, Max opened the passenger door of her car. "Get in, Sarah."

I did and buckled up with shaking hands. When she got behind the wheel, I told her softly, "I'm sorry."

"We're going to postpone this conversation until I get you to my place and you have a chance to shower. Then I'm going to patch you up because you took a beating. After that, we'll talk."

An hour later, I sat at her dining table while she treated my cuts and scrapes. Holding the skin together on my knuckle, she brushed wound adhesive over it and held it closed until the glue set.

My hair was wet and I wore one of her t-shirts. She hadn't joined me in the bathroom…just left towels and clothes for me. I felt vulnerable and more than a little afraid of what was about to happen.

Cleaning everything up with efficient movements, she put away the kit and returned to stand beside me. Max held out her hand. I put mine in it.

Tugging me to my feet, she led me into the living room and nudged me down on the sofa. She took a seat on the coffee table in front of me.

For almost a minute, she held my gaze in utter silence. Shaking, I didn't fill it.

"When you are out in the world, living your life as a strong and beautiful young woman, I have certain expectations as someone who cares for you."

There were tears in my eyes but I held them back.

"I expect you to *return to me* in the condition I *leave* you in. When I left you this morning, you were flawless despite three days of hard fucking. You placed yourself in my hands and I drove you to the brink of what I thought you could endure without leaving so much as a scratch on your body."

I twisted my fingers together in my lap but didn't interrupt her. She was right.

"It's been twelve hours since I left your house. Ten since I received a terrified message from Campbell. Eight since I watched you step into a ring to fight strangers and take punishment you *don't* deserve but *think* you do. Six since you dragged your exhausted body out of that ring and were jumped by the last woman you beat and two of her friends. Four since receiving assurance that you would *not* be charged for defending yourself. Two since I witnessed you walking out of a jail cell - battered and in handcuffs."

My heart ached in my chest.

"I won't beat you. I won't yell at you. I will not lay my hands on you in anger. I will never give you reason to fear me. However, if you require *pain* to purge the darkness that's coiled inside you…I can deliver it. Without bruises, tearing your skin, or breaking your bones."

The tears slipped past my control.

"You will *not* leave my presence and allow others to hurt you like this *ever* again. Do I make myself clear, Sarah?"

"Yes." It was hard to talk around the lump in my throat.

"You need rest and your body needs time to recover. When you're ready to continue talking about this…we will."

Standing, Max picked me up and carried me to her bed. She was gentle as she laid me down and pulled up the blankets.

I watched her walk to the bathroom, close the door, and turn on the shower.

I cried myself to sleep waiting for her to come back.

* * *

In the middle of the night, I opened my eyes to the darkness of Max's bedroom.

Spooning my back, her arms were wrapped firmly around me. The warmth and safety she made me feel brought tears to my eyes yet again.

I didn't want to wake her so I cried silently - gripping her forearms like a lifeline - needing what she offered so much more than I dared to admit.

"Everything is okay, Sarah. I'm not angry at you. I'm angry I didn't notice how desperate you felt. Furious you were hurt tonight. Worried because I want nothing more than to keep you safe. I didn't know *you* could be the threat to yourself."

"I-I'm sorry, Max."

She hugged me harder and I didn't care that my torso ached from the hits I'd taken. "Why didn't you tell me you needed help?"

"I already take so much…"

"Do you think there's a finite amount of care someone can give you? That one day it suddenly runs out?"

"Yes," I whispered honestly.

"If something happened to Campbell and he needed you to take care of him for the rest of his life, would you do it? Even if it meant you had to feed him, change his diapers, wash his body, take him everywhere he needed to go, support his living expenses - could you do whatever it took?"

"Yes. Even if he ended up hating me for seeing the ugly sides and he resented being dependent on me."

Max kissed the back of my head. "And yet...if the roles were reversed, I imagine you'd request to be put into a care facility so you weren't a bother, so you didn't cause a single fucking ripple in his life. You wouldn't give him the chance to take care of his best friend."

Rolling me over, Max stared at me in the dim light from the bathroom. "You are not a *bother*, Sarah. You have the *right* to take up space as a human being. You matter to so many and *we* have the right to make you a priority, to take care of you, to worry."

Tears slipped into my hair. "I miss my apartment..."

"I know. I'm sorry you had to leave it."

"I-I'm frightened something will happen to you or Campbell..."

"I'm fine and I hired a friend to keep an eye on Campbell when he isn't with us."

"My n-name, my life, is *out there* now. I don't want people to get too *close* to me, to act like they *know* who I am because of two sexy photos and a nasty paragraph from that bitch who gave birth to me."

"Change your name. Create a new life."

"What…?" I whispered.

"You don't have to be Sarah Kent - related to that woman. You can be whomever you choose. You're only twenty. Start over. Make life what you want it to be."

I frowned. "But…*you* call me Sarah."

Max's hands went into my hair and she held the side of my head as she kissed me delicately. Something about it made tears well in my eyes again.

Resting her forehead to mine, she placed her palm over my heart. "The spaces between your words - the silences symbolizing the things you can't say - humble me."

Trembling, I moved her hand to cup my breast. "Max…"

"You are one of the strongest and bravest people I've ever met. If touch is how you need to communicate for the time being, then I'll touch you until you hear me, Sarah."

Gathering me in her arms, she whispered in my ear, "It isn't your name or your body that enthralls me. Changes to either will never matter to me."

Then Max devoted herself to touching me until I couldn't think, couldn't speak, could only endure wave after wave of pleasure until I lost consciousness.

* * *

I *loved* Max.

Part of me had known it since the first day she touched me and every day since.

If I said the words, they would coil through her and bind her to me forever. She was someone who would never falter, never hesitate, never leave me.

That was why I held them back.

Intellectually, I *knew* and *believed* that what I'd endured as a child was not my fault.

That didn't prevent me from feeling *tainted* by it. Ugly, used, and worthless.

Infected…like something I could pass to her like a virus.

Max was easy to understand…even easier to love. She had a core of honor and a desire to protect those weaker than herself.

Few were weaker than me.

She didn't think about hunting down and torturing people. Caging them and watching them starve. Raping them with foreign objects until they begged for mercy. Beating them until they were nothing but sacks of bloody meat.

I had detailed dreams of doing all of those things to men from my childhood. I always woke from those dreams feeling peaceful and content.

We were not the same *species*, Max and me.

I had never loved or wanted anyone more - not even my precious Campbell.

For years, I'd limited my presence in Camp's life and the lives of his parents. Even if my brothers ended up in foster care, I wouldn't try to raise them myself. I planned to never bring children of my own into the world.

After all…

The solution to a virus was *quarantine*.

CHAPTER 38:
First & Last

April 2011

Three days later, Monica scheduled an appointment with me during the week. The timing was unusual for her.

My torso was mottled with bruises but my face was almost entirely healed.

Max was amazed. "I've never seen *anyone* heal so fast from injury."

I smiled. "My brothers called me Wolverine." We'd made dinner and were relaxing on her couch. She'd insisted I recover under her watch and I didn't hate it. "I need your input, Max. I'm thinking in circles."

"Let's talk it out." She held my hand.

"Monica isn't in love with me but if she lost Jade, she'd cling to me and *pretend* it was love to keep from losing everything."

"That's insightful. You care for her."

"Of course." Clearing my throat, I knew it was time to explain the foundation of my unusual relationship with my attorney. "Monica saved me. If she hadn't taken my case pro bono and fought to get me free of my mother's control, I wouldn't be alive."

Max stilled. "What…?"

"Either Paula would have killed me or I would have ended things myself. I already had plans in place."

"It was that bad?" Her voice was a whisper.

"Yeah. I ended up in hospitals all over the state for broken bones, concussions, internal ruptures…I didn't fight back. I *let* Paula beat me for years because that was better than the life I'd lived with her older sister for a decade. I didn't want to be sent back."

"That was *better*…?"

"I don't…want to talk about that."

"…Alright."

"I was prepared to die. Monica made sure I didn't have to. My feelings for her were almost *maternal* - though I wasn't immune to her looks or sex appeal. Being with her as an escort mixes up a lot of things in my head. It's why I was furious with Viv for not warning me that she was my first client."

I lifted my gaze and stared into Max's green eyes. "I need to end it and still be able to keep her in my life. Do you think that's possible?"

Max lifted me fully into her lap and held my head against the front of her shoulder. "I do, Sarah."

We talked for a long time and Max helped me lay the groundwork for my conversation with Monica - someone I didn't want to lose but couldn't keep having sex with.

For two days, I'd been slowly severing ties with my clients. I owed it to all of them - as much as we'd shared - to talk to them first.

Then I would have a conversation with Vivienne.

My time as an escort had to end.

* * *

During most of our appointments, Monica used me as a sort of sounding board about her long-term relationship with Jade.

Her lover was an avid reader and a fantastic cook. Once in a while, I brought gifts for Monica to give her that spoke closely to the person Jade was.

I made sure to explain *why* she'd love it.

The initial little presents were so successful that we shopped as a team for all their special occasions.

Monica couldn't wait to gush about how much Jade loved what we picked. She was one of the smartest women I knew…but remained strangely ignorant about the woman she loved.

I'd struggled for over a year to understand how she could be so blind.

When we were settled across from each other at one of her favorite restaurants, I said, "How are things going with Jade?"

Monica sighed. "I *want* to be the woman she thinks I am but…I *always* fall short."

"There *have* been improvements," I reminded her.

"Our sex life expectations are still miles apart. She likes it safe. I like anything but." Monica took a sip of her wine. "Jade is a free spirit in most things. I wish she could apply that to our sex life instead of scheduling time for us to fuck."

Our server brought fresh drinks and bread.

Monica released a deep sigh. "Sarah, I *love* our time together. I hope you know how important you are to me." I smiled gently. "You think it's just sex, don't you? It isn't. You have a fresh way of looking at the world. You make me feel hopeful. As if happiness is waiting just beyond my line of sight."

"Simply being on the planet doesn't entitle us to happiness. We have to *work* for it every day - look for it in all the little pieces of being human. I've known that all my life."

Meeting my eyes, she said seriously, "With your past, it's a fucking *miracle* you think like that."

It was rare for Monica to bring up our other relationship - that of attorney and client - during one of our dates. Her eyes held mine and I could tell I wasn't the only one thinking deep thoughts recently.

"I'm selfish, Sarah. I don't ask enough about how you're doing personally."

"And yet, you keep watch over all the things." Her eyes widened. "I pay attention. I saw my brothers on Tuesday. My visits are supervised but at least I can make sure they're alright. Thanks for fighting the restraining order so hard."

"It's the least I could do. I know how worried you've been for them. How did they seem?"

"Too thin. I'm worried about their teeth. Joshua wore clothes too small, David wore clothes too big." I stared at the table and tried to silence the anxiety I always felt for them. "Let's...change the subject."

Over our plates of shrimp scampi, I wondered aloud if Jade would be amenable to some sort of *protected* sex in the open.

Monica looked at me quizzically. "I'm not sure what you mean. Those two things are the opposite of each other, aren't they?"

"You love sex in public. Jade is against it because of all the rules society enforces about private matters." I paused to sip my water. "What about starting slow? Like sex on the balcony of your room at a crowded hotel. *Compromise.* You get what you want and she still has a sense of safety."

Monica thought about it for a long time. The waitress removed our plates and returned with dessert. She ate tiny spoonfuls of chocolate mousse and seemed to have an epiphany.

"I've never considered *compromise*. I've never tried to *understand* her reservations. I wanted something, she wouldn't let me have it, and I got pissy. Like a child." She sat back. "How did you know?"

"Jade loves you. Naturally, she *wants* to please you. It's hard to toss away a lifetime of behaviors overnight. Introduce her slowly. Let her see what you like and what she's willing to do."

"Test her boundaries?"

"Not wanting to fuck in the middle of an opera house surrounded by three thousand people might not mean she's *closed* to the entire concept. Maybe that's just too big an ask on day one."

She murmured, "It wasn't for *you*."

"That's the issue, isn't it? Our relationship is setting a standard your lover - the person you live with every day - can never hope to meet. That's not fair to her. I'm a fantasy, Monica. She's the reality."

I laid my hand over hers on the table. "Meet Jade *where she is* and go from there. There was a time she was enough for you. You either love her or want to change her. It can't be both."

"I *do* love her."

"I know you do."

"You don't want to see me anymore."

I wanted to put her at ease. I also wanted her to face reality before she blew up a life - and love - she truly needed.

"You can't live two separate lives forever, Monica. You've known that from the start." I smiled. "You're important to me for so *many* reasons…but losing Jade would hurt you far more than losing me."

I sat back as the server refilled our drinks. "Stop fucking an *escort* and experiment with the *woman* you love and sleep beside. If you give her a chance, maybe you can find a happy medium."

Monica gave me a sad smile and nodded. "You're right. I can't keep both of you indefinitely. I-I wanted to wean myself from my addiction to what we share. I know it sounds cowardly."

"No. Just honest."

"I'm in love with Jade and have been for a long time. Still, you're a powerful presence in my life. I don't want to lose everything we have."

"Then let's make sure we don't. We'll figure out what works without putting your relationship at further risk than we already have."

"Alright." She took a deep breath. "I can do that."

"Let's get out of here and talk more."

Max had driven me to meet Monica in the limo. After dinner, we exited the restaurant and the attorney grinned when she saw Max standing beside the luxury vehicle looking gorgeous.

"This is new. Hi, Max."

"Ms. Carter. You are *lovely* as always. Allow me." She held the door and Monica got in. As I bent to join her, Max winked.

The moment I settled on the seat, Monica kissed me lightly. I heard Max slide behind the wheel and felt us pull away from the restaurant.

She whispered in my ear, "Have you ever been with a client in front of Max?" I shook my head and she smoothed my hair. "She's your main lover outside of work."

"My *only* lover outside work," I admitted.

Pulling back, she held my face. "Truly?" I nodded. "Hmm. I didn't know that." Her voice shook.

"You sound upset…"

She put her fingers over my lips. "You wanted to talk more and I agree that we should."

"Okay."

"I want to ask you questions and for you to answer them. Even if they make you uncomfortable. Will you do that for me?"

"Of course." I smiled gently. "Asking questions is kind of your forte."

Glancing over her shoulder, she said, "Max, I know you don't get involved with clients and I wouldn't ask you to. However, can you find somewhere safe to park so you can come back here?"

Glancing in the mirror with a small frown, Max replied, "Of course, ma'am."

"Monica, what are you doing?"

Without answering, she kissed me deeply. It felt contrived to keep me off balance.

The limo stopped and Max opened the door. Climbing inside, she locked the doors. "How can I be of service?"

"Get comfortable. I'd like you to hold Sarah while I chat with her. You have a calming effect on her that I've never seen anyone or anything have before."

Max shrugged off her jacket, loosened her tie, and rolled up her sleeves. Then she scooted beside me and lifted me to sit between her legs.

"Every appointment, you're generous to a fault while I take and take, Sarah."

"I'd say it's the nature of the business but I also like seeing you happy."

Monica held my hand and kissed the back with her eyes closed. "That's a core aspect of your personality - making other people happy." Lifting her face, she stared into my eyes. "You'll make me happy by playing along with me tonight."

"Then I will."

She trailed her palms from the backs of my calves to my knees over my fitted black pants. "The first time we met, you were *covered* in bruises. Some were so deep, I didn't know how you survived getting them." *Don't talk about that.* "Right now, I imagine you're covered in bruises again. The other night reminded me of the day we got you out of Paula's."

"Her bullshit and all the recent changes I wasn't expecting triggered my fight or flight. I'm better - level again." I could see she was filled with stress. "What's wrong, Monica?"

"I don't want you to think too deeply about your answers. Say the first thing that pops into your mind. Alright?"

"Okay."

"What word surfaces when you think about me?"

"Savior." My eyes widened as I said something out loud I never intended her to know. "I…"

"Yes. I was the first adult in your *entire* life to be kind to you, to treat you with respect, to help you. It makes sense you'd put me on a pedestal - even if I didn't deserve it."

"You did deserve it." *It was the truth.*

"You're wrong, darling." She held my gaze. "Don't think too hard, remember?" I nodded. "When you met Vivienne, why did you agree to go with her?"

"She was your friend. I figured I'd be safe enough and you would know where I was if I wasn't."

Monica blinked against tears and I didn't like the change in her demeanor.

"That's what I thought. I hoped I was wrong." She swallowed hard. "I began viewing you sexually after a *year*." *That surprised me.* "You weren't even seventeen yet and had been horrifically abused for the majority of your life by every person who should have protected you."

"Monica…I'm *fine* now."

"Are you, Sarah? I'm not so sure."

"What do you mean?"

"For two years, I exerted unbelievable control over your life. I influenced everything from where you lived to what you did with your money."

"That's over-simplifying…"

Rising, she held my face in her palms. "Then, when you were legal - working for me, I brought my old friend to meet you.

Someone you'd automatically trust because of her association with me."

"Monica…"

"Knowing if you became one of Vivienne's *escorts*, I'd gain more access to you through another door. I would *finally* be able to touch you without all those pesky morals in the way. No matter how you look at it - subconsciously or not - I *groomed* you to become my sex partner."

Max exhaled roughly and placed her hands on my hips.

I frowned. "No…"

"Yes, Sarah. I'm only seeing it now and I've *never* been more ashamed of myself. You see me as your savior but I was actually another predator."

"Don't say that," I whispered. *Stop it.*

I was suddenly cold, covered in goosebumps, and she draped Max's jacket over the front of my body.

"Despite your childhood filled with nothing but pain, you remain the gentlest, most loving person I've ever known. To satisfy my own desire for you, I allowed you to expose yourself in ways you never would have chosen for yourself."

"That's not true." *Stop…please stop.*

"It is, Sarah. It is. You strip, make your videos, and fight - all things that show your body but don't allow people close enough to really know you. If I hadn't placed the path in front of you, you wouldn't have considered exchanging sex for money."

I don't want to talk about any of this.

"I was sexually active before…"

"Six or seven partners around your age is not the same as fucking a *madame* or following along with your *attorney* who crossed ethical lines while exposing you to situations that crossed legal ones as well. Not the same as getting naked with two dozen strangers when I know how hard it is for you to trust others."

What's happening? "You're making everything black and white…"

"There's less gray than you think. You put your health and safety at risk to meet people you don't know and give us pleasure - making Vivienne a fortune in the process. How do *you* feel about this life, Sarah?"

"I like it well enough." *Parts of it.*

"I've made a career out of knowing when someone is lying. You, sweet girl, are *lying.*"

I didn't realize I was digging my fingers into Max's thighs beneath the jacket. I tried to loosen them.

"You want out. You're worried about losing my presence in your life if you stop providing sex…and I let you keep going because I was so very greedy."

"I'm getting out of the agency…"

"After last week, I knew you would. There are too many people who know you now. If Vivienne wasn't a friend of mine, you wouldn't have stayed through the photo shoot. If I hadn't been your first client, you would have dropped it in less than a week."

All true.

Instead, I said noncommittally, "Maybe not…"

"Sarah. You were bartered by your aunt so she could live in luxury. She married three wealthy pedophiles and looked the other way while they stole every ounce of hope and innocence from you."

No, no, no…

Behind me, Max gasped softly. Strong arms went around my waist and held me painfully hard.

I didn't want her to know.

Monica held my face and tears spilled over her cheeks. "Max doesn't know about your past. She doesn't know how *truly* vulnerable you are with people you care about. That you'll sacrifice yourself - every time - to make them happy."

A sob broke from Monica's chest. "Even now, you don't see that I did the same thing. I let you *sell yourself* to all those other people so I could *excuse* buying you myself."

Tears flowed over my cheeks and dripped off my jaw. "Why are you doing this? I don't want this…"

I don't want to see this, think this, know this.

"I'm so fucking sorry, Sarah. I didn't see it clearly until you told me Max is the only lover you've had other than your clients in all this time."

Don't tell her…don't trap her.

Max's arms tightened and she pressed her face against my hair. "Sarah…"

Monica laid her head on my lap and sobbed. "I didn't mean to push you into a life like this. You trusted me and I took advantage of that trust for selfish reasons. Please forgive me."

I sat staring at a small light in the back of the limo for a long time. My mind spun and my heart hurt but I knew one thing for certain…

"Monica." My voice sounded strange to me. "I've lived a lot more than most people my age." She lifted her tear-streaked face. "I'm not a *child*. I could have said no. At any point, I could have walked away. By taking all the blame, you're saying I had no will, no choice of my own, that I didn't know better."

If you want the truth…

I shook my head. "I *did* know better, Monica. Yes, I went with Vivienne because she was your friend…but I fucked her because it made me feel *powerful*." I paused. "*That* is why I stayed."

Monica blinked slowly but didn't speak.

"I've always been powerless - that's true - but I could make my clients *beg me* for pleasure. No matter their age, education, or money…I had all the power. For the first time, I didn't feel like a little girl being raped by grown men at a hunting party."

Max's tears fell on my shoulder.

Leaning closer, I whispered, "You will *not* take that from me. You will *not* make me regret using all of you as much as you used me. I knew this was temporary. I knew it from the moment Viv confessed why I was at her house."

"You did?"

"I decided to take every second and see what happened because I'm young enough to put it behind me when I walk away. I am not *stupid*. I've saved eighty percent of my earnings. I'll take my cash and prizes, experiences, memories, and friendships…and start over when it's done."

The Escort: In the Service of Women

I stroked my fingers through her hair. "You're older, richer, and smarter...but you will *never* be stronger than me, Monica. You're incapable of making me do anything I don't want to do. Until you see that, I'll *always* be that beaten fifteen year old girl in your mind...and I laid her to rest a long time ago."

I leaned closer to her. "Do you think I can't spot a *predator*? Do you think I let anyone touch me now - after all I've been through - without being aware of every aspect of what they want from me?"

My voice was stronger than I felt. "Not a fucking chance. Every moment we spent together was *consensual*. Don't let misplaced guilt or worry about my trauma convince you differently."

I held her gaze. "I came tonight to encourage you to mend your relationship with Jade and stop gambling what you have with *her* to get off with *me*. I've been worried about losing you, Monica. As a friend and someone I've counted on for years."

With a shrug, I added, "I won't lose you though. Not ever. I'm on your *level* - even at twenty - and few people in your life can say that. Be my friend. Be my attorney. Stay in my life."

Leaving a gentle kiss on her lips, I told her, "I will never touch you sexually again...but I don't regret a single time I did. Know that."

Stripping away Max's jacket, I could practically *hear* their racing thoughts.

She nodded as she wept into her hands. I pulled them away and touched her chin, raising her face so I could wipe her cheeks.

"I'm okay. Thank you for everything. Including putting Vivienne in my way. Without taking that path, I wouldn't have met so many incredible people. I wouldn't have…"

I caught myself before giving away too much. Monica didn't blink. She knew what I would have said.

Instead of focusing on it, she said, "I *do* love you, Sarah."

I laughed softly. "Love me like a sister from now on."

"Okay."

"Do me a favor?" She nodded. "Don't pay me for today's appointment. I'm done taking money from you. You aren't my client anymore."

And just like that…my first client's last appointment was done.

* * *

Max and I didn't say a word to each other but she held me hard enough throughout the night that it was difficult to breathe.

She now knew things I never wanted her to find out…ugly, dirty parts of my past I tried so hard to hide so she didn't look at me with pity.

The last thing I wanted was Max feeling sorry for me - to stick around out of a misplaced obligation to protect me from all the big bads in the world.

Besides, when I left the agency, we'd have nothing linking our daily lives. I knew I wouldn't - couldn't - stay in Florida forever.

I loved Max.

I'd take the joy of being *able* to feel that love with me when I left.

Thinking about leaving her made my stomach hurt.

CHAPTER 39:
Endings

April 2011

The morning after my heart-wrenching talk with Monica, I rushed out of Max's apartment with mumbled excuses.

I found it difficult to look her in the eye.

A few miles away, I sat down with Vivienne at her place for a long overdue conversation. I made her a cup of coffee and toast for the hangover I could see she had.

She'd clearly been warned to expect my resignation. Her eyes were puffy from recent crying and I admitted that the display of emotion surprised me.

"Stay with us in another position, Sarah."

I laughed. "As what? I don't have any skills other than writing and fucking."

Reaching across the small table where our arrangement started, she held my hands tightly. "That's a goddamn lie."

The vehemence of the statement caught me off guard. "Uh, Viv. I have a high school diploma, experience as a cashier, and clerking at a law office. None of those skills will help y…"

"Shut up." She swiped at the fresh tears on her face. "All of that is bullshit. You don't even *know* it's bullshit and that makes me angry."

I stared at her with wide-eyed confusion.

"Sarah, you're so fucking smart. If your idiot mother hadn't messed up all your plans, you'd be in college right now."

"Monica told you…"

"That Paula fucked up your scholarships and sent letters to every college in Florida you might have applied to? Yeah, she told me. She wanted me to understand how lucky I was to get someone like you - even temporarily."

"I changed tactics. I'll be fine."

"Sweetie, you need therapy. Maybe that will help you see yourself the way everyone else sees you."

"Harsh."

Vivienne leaned closer. "I'm an alcoholic and sex addict, Sarah." I couldn't hide my surprise that she stated what I'd noticed so plainly. "I have daddy issues, am compulsive about cleanliness, and have been arrested six times for shoplifting."

"Are you kidding?" I asked softly.

"All of that…despite coming from a rich family where there was little affection but zero abuse. My younger brother was one of your dates over Christmas - you took him to a work event."

I thought back. "Um, do you mean Kendall?"

I'd actually thought at the time that he was like the male version of my boss.

She nodded. "He raved about how you impressed his coworkers - who are not easily impressed - with your personality and ability to facilitate conversation. First time I've ever heard him compliment a woman in such a way. Probably because you weren't trying to make him straight."

"Huh…"

"You've got a grasp on money like few people I've known. You'll be a millionaire the way you save and invest. Yet, you started with nothing when you left home. You didn't even have a bank account."

"I'm not sure how comfortable I am with you knowing all these things about me, Vivienne."

She smiled. "You're a vault about yourself, Sarah. I respect that about you. Most people can't wait to gush about their accomplishments. You hide yours."

Taking a deep breath, she told me, "Think about staying with the agency. Mrs. Quincy will retire in the next year or two. I could use someone like you running things in the background."

"I appreciate the offer but…"

"Don't say no now. Give it some real thought. Take time off, get your feet under you, settle into your new apartment…then let me know what you think."

Part of me wanted to cut all ties.

Another part wanted to stay near Max.

"I'll think about it. Give me a few months to get my balance."

"Done." She got up and hugged me tight.

When she released me, Max stood in the doorway, leaning on the frame with her arms crossed.

"Hi," I said quietly.

"Hello, Sarah. You rushed out like there was a fire. Thought I'd check on you."

She hadn't moved from her position.

Viv said, "All the girls are stirring for our meeting in a few minutes…"

"Want me to make some food?" I asked.

The blonde stepped close and stared intently into my eyes. "Tell me you'll still stop by and cook for us sometimes."

"If you want me to."

She stroked her fingers through my hair. "Oh, Sarah. What *will* we do with you?"

Max said softly, "I have ideas."

"I'm sure you do. I cannot *wait* to witness the fireworks." Turning, she walked out of the kitchen.

Twisting my fingers together, I tried to explain. "I figured Monica would talk to Viv and she did. I thought it was wrong not to tell her face to face."

Max straightened and dropped her arms. She crossed the space between us like a panther hunting prey.

"We're going to endure the meeting and then settle in for a nice, long talk. Plan to spend an undetermined length of time at my place, Sarah."

"A-alright."

"Good girl." She dropped a hard kiss on my mouth and left.

The woman never failed to affect me powerfully. Whether sex was involved or not…she was a force to be reckoned with.

Shaking myself, I made an assortment of snacks, diced a bowl of fruit, and prepared myself for everyone to find out I was leaving.

I should have known I'd end up annoyed. After all, my unspoken nemesis would be in the same room.

* * *

Within moments of appearing downstairs - having obviously spent the night with Vivienne - Delta seemed determined to piss me off.

"This dip is so *fatty*…" she complained.

I smiled despite wanting to smack her. "It's Ezbeth and Paige's favorite. You can eat the fruit."

"Well…what did you put on these wings?"

"The blend Rolande likes best." *Give me strength.*

"They're too spicy…"

"I didn't make them for you. Eat the fruit. There's also hummus and tabbouleh from our favorite deli. They delivered it with warm pita slices."

Delta sighed heavily. "Ugh. Never mind, I guess."

Bitch, then starve.

"Why don't you make a list of what you *do* eat since what you *don't* eat appears to number in the thousands? That would be helpful to people who do shit for you without being asked."

"No need to get catty."

I inhaled deeply and counted forward to thirty and back again. "I don't get *catty*, Delta. I get *angry* like an adult with a brain."

Lucia snickered as she slathered hummus on a piece of pita. "You *really* wouldn't like her when she's angry. She's fearless and takes no shit."

Delta flipped her hair and it landed on Max's shoulder. Naturally, she'd chosen to sit *right* beside Max rather than choosing any of the *many* seats in the room while I was bringing out food.

"Sounds like toxic *male* behavior to me."

Coldly, I asked, "Does it?"

Vivienne entered the room with her iPad and I shifted my attention to her.

"It breaks my heart to announce that Sarah is leaving us as an escort." Delta snorted and Vivienne frowned in her direction. "She'll still be around for a while but she's already informed her clients."

"So, we're taking on her people?" Delta asked with obvious excitement.

"No one is getting her clients."

Delta whined, "What? *Why?*"

"Because all of them have expressed that if it isn't Sarah, they have no interest in continuing to hire escorts."

Paige nodded. "I get that. Sarah has a real niche group of clients."

"Agreed. None of us have the same style." Ezbeth smiled at me. "You're an original, Sarah."

Rolande said, "We haven't had Sonja with us in forever. She's been exclusively with the Bettencourts for over a year. Lyra had a collection of wounded doves that took time to integrate."

Her warm amber eyes met mine. "Like them, your people need something only you can provide. Settling for someone else would probably feel like betraying you."

"You act like they're in *love* with her or something. It's just *fucking*." Delta shrugged. "I'm sure if they spent time with me…"

Vivienne's voice interrupted her and I could tell she was getting irritated. *Join the club.* "That won't be happening. They were quite clear. Moving on…"

Flipping through her iPad, she said, "We've received a request from a long-time client to perform a sort of BDSM cabaret for a select inner circle during an event. No sex will be involved."

Delta's look turned smug. "I'll do it with Sarah. It can be her last hoorah as an escort." I was stunned into silence. "They want BDSM? I'd love nothing more than to redden her ass…"

"Absolutely fucking *not*," Max's voice was low but held zero room for argument.

Looking up with a dazzling smile, Delta replied, "You're not the *only* one skilled with a whip, Max."

"Understand this: you won't *touch* Sarah with leathers of any kind. I've seen your work. You aren't delicate enough."

Frowning, Delta tilted her head. "Ezbeth is smaller and lighter - I haven't hurt *her*."

"It takes three days for the marks to fully fade after you work together so I refute that statement. Ezbeth also identifies as a submissive both personally and professionally. Sarah does not."

"Sounds like you just don't want me touching her. Being a little possessive over someone who eats other women's pussies for a living, aren't you?"

Paige and Ezbeth gasped. Rolande crossed her arms and I could see there was a lot happening behind her still expression.

Max said nothing. She maintained eye contact until Delta murmured, "Th-that was uncalled for. My apologies, Sarah." I didn't move or speak. The woman cleared her throat. "Anyway, how do *you* feel about it?"

How I *felt* was I wanted to slap her in the mouth but I'd already slapped two other assholes in Viv's condo and figured I'd exceeded my quota.

I considered my words carefully after counting yet again. "I don't trust easily. Not at all, actually. I've been the dominant in *every* relationship but one."

Vivienne added, "And a rather good one, Sarah."

"I trust Max. I wouldn't want to be vulnerable in a room full of strangers if Max wasn't the one watching my back. I could have a panic attack. I'd be unpredictable and that's not safe for anyone."

"You freak out or something?"

I held her gaze and let the silence draw out until she started to fidget. *This bitch thought she was dominant.*

She wasn't.

"I don't respond well when I feel threatened - particularly in a sexual scenario. We've barely spoken, Delta. We *clearly* don't like each other. Not exactly a proper foundation to make a domination and submission scenario workable."

"You can *fake it*, right? Don't you fake it with your clients all the time? I mean…come on."

"I *never* fake orgasms. It's the coldest form of lying to another person." I didn't know what her problem with me was but I had plenty with her. "Also, BDSM isn't a *party trick* for someone like me. I'll pass."

Delta smirked. "Yet Max can do whatever she wants. Are you two fucking outside work?"

With a frown, I asked, "Why is that *any* of your business?" I sat forward on the seat I'd been relaxed in. "You asked how I felt about the proposal. I told you it made me uncomfortable. We've done shows like this in the past. I declined those as well."

Shaking my head, I kept my eyes on hers and didn't blink. "You're gettin' *personal*. You don't know me. You know nothin' about me."

"Uh…her accent," Walker whispered.

"No one can get to know you if Max is always being your bodyguard or something." Delta's voice got louder. "I mean, what's the deal with you two?"

"You know, I can't tell which of us you're hung up on - Max or me. Either way…Max is the *only* dominant person I trust - male or female. Based on how juvenile you behave in every way, you'd never even make my goddamn list."

Standing, I shrugged on my jacket and bent to pick up my pack and helmet. "Max is a bodyguard to every person at this agency and if you don't realize that, it's because you've only been here five minutes and don't know dick. Our relationship outside work is none of your concern."

"You're having a tantrum..."

Walker exhaled on a low, "Oh, shit."

Rolande said something in Patois and then in English added, "Sarah, most people *adore* you. It is the weak who *envy* you. How many must you fuck up before they stop pushing you?"

"What is *that* supposed to mean, Rolande?" Delta asked sharply.

Max turned her head to face her directly and said, "Simply stated? It means fuck around and find out. You're messing with the wrong woman. I suggest you stop."

I walked a few steps and crouched in front of Delta. Her entire body tensed. I'd already won this little pissing contest.

"Not sure what your fuckin' issue is with me but it's been there from the start. I'm not like anyone else here. I come from a different place. Stop what you're doin', Delta. You push hard enough and you'll *need* Max to protect you."

"Are you *threatening* me?"

"I never make threats." Getting to my feet, I stared down at her. "As for eatin' pussy for a livin'...if that's how you describe this job, you're in the wrong line of work. Screw your apology. I'm done with this discussion and I'm done playin' nice with you. You wanna be the resident country girl? Have at it, sweetheart."

I leaned over and she flinched. "If it's *Max* you covet, I suggest takin' a different tack. Your *mean girl* schtick isn't gonna impress a woman like her."

I headed for the door and ignored Vivienne's frantic efforts to call me back. There were raised voices and arguing but I tuned it all out.

I was done.

Downstairs, I revved my motorcycle and backed from the space before tearing out of the exit going way too fast.

I needed to go home.

I needed to decompress.

I needed to be alone.

Without conscious intent, I found myself at Max's place instead of my own apartment. The woman herself pulled up seconds behind me.

CHAPTER 40:
Maximum Release

Max placed her hand at my lower back and guided me through the parking garage to the elevators. She didn't say a word until we were inside her apartment.

Pressing me to the wall of her foyer, she pinned me with her body and stared into my eyes for a long moment.

"It's time for our talk, Sarah." My lips parted to respond and she shook her head once. I closed my mouth. "I want to hear *everything* you've kept locked up in your gorgeous head. You'll hide it from me - as you've done for over a year - unless I take complete control."

I shivered remembering the moment during our first night together when I trusted Max enough to submit.

For hours, she drove me over the brink of climax until I was open to her - voluntarily vulnerable in a way I'd *never* been with anyone in my life.

I was terrified.

I'd begged for more.

"Trust is more powerful and addictive than any drug. You gave me a full hit the night I touched you for the first time."

Max's fingers wrapped around my throat and she held me still for a devastating kiss. Our tongues slipped and curled as she stole my breath and gave it back. She sipped at my lips and finally lifted away.

"Since that night, you've kept me on an IV drip…giving me maintenance hits of your trust. Surprising me each time you gave me more. Infuriating me when you pulled back and denied me."

Another kiss and she wrapped an arm around my torso, holding me tight to the front of her body.

Max was the strongest person I knew but she was so fucking *careful*…every single time she touched me. Her ability to exude power and remain gentle fascinated me on every level.

"You will show me everything, tell me everything, and I'll *prove* why you can trust me with the knowledge."

Had I searched for a way back to this moment…?

When Max took the anxiety, pain, and indecision out of my hands and *commanded* my submission yet again?

The silence was heavy between us and I realized she waited for my *consent*.

"I trust you, Max."

She smiled and it was easy to see the victory in it. "Thank you, Sarah."

Turning, she took me with her across the apartment to what she'd always called a storage room.

Unlocking the door, Max guided me inside and I discovered it was actually another bedroom.

Smaller than her master suite or home office, the walls were pale pink with multiple track lights along the ceiling. The floor was bamboo, polished to a high shine. One entire wall featured windows that looked east over the ocean - the same view as the one from her bedroom.

There was a massive platform bed in the center draped with white sheets. Above it, several heavy ring bolts blended into the pale gray of the ceiling alongside a track that led into a narrow panel.

In the far corner was a chaise lounge I recognized from one of my single appointment clients - though we'd never used it. It was also draped in a white sheet. I knew it moved to accommodate multiple sex positions while avoiding strain on either partner.

Three lit cabinets lined the wall opposite the windows. The first held bottles, books, and statuary. The second held a collection of fake cocks in various sizes, shapes, and materials. The third held leather of all kinds from cuffs to nipple clamps to whips.

This room was intended *solely* for pleasure. My body heated, dampened, just seeing the contents.

"I bought this apartment four years ago specifically for the layout. Until last year, this room was empty. The walls were white, the floors poured concrete."

She looked at me. "After I met you, I knew exactly what to do with this space. It had to be naturally bright, well-lit even if the sun wasn't out, and wide open. With each incremental reveal of your tortured past, I knew I'd made the right choices to ensure you could be comfortable here."

"You decorated it…for me?"

"Entirely," she answered simply. "It was the best decision I ever made." Holding out her hand between us, she waited. I placed mine in it. "Your safe phrase is *I need a moment.*" I nodded. "That will tell me you require time to process what you're feeling. Your safe word is *stop*. That will tell me I've pushed you past what you feel you can handle. Do you understand, Sarah?"

"I understand, Max."

Lifting her other hand, she tipped up my chin and kissed me lightly. "Let's begin."

She waited while I put my phone on *do not disturb*. Stripping me slowly, she folded my clothes and placed them on a slim table next to the door. I stood a few feet from the bed and waited.

"Seeing bruises from other peoples' fists on your skin makes my soul scream, Sarah."

"I'm sorry."

She shrugged off her dress shirt to reveal a black tank top that formed to her torso. Removing her pants showed me her preferred boxer briefs, also in black.

Beneath the clinging fabric was the outline of the silicone cock she always wore under her clothes.

I once asked Max if she identified as male and she shook her head. "Just jealous of the *one thing* a man had that I didn't. It was easier than I imagined to rectify the situation." The answer always made me smile when I remembered.

"I'm going to suspend you. You may struggle initially with panic. Talk to me and I'll help."

"Alright."

Walking to the cabinet holding leathers, she removed several long strips of pale brown leather.

"Hold out your wrists." She bound each in the soft material and my heart raced. "Stay like this for a moment. Get accustomed to the feel of them on your skin."

Opening the panel, she attached rings on the opposite end of the straps to bars inside. Flipping a switch, I watched the bars travel up the wall and across the ceiling until they stopped above me.

Standing a foot from me, Max asked, "Are you ready, Sarah?"

"Y-yes."

"I'm right here and I will *never* betray your trust. I'd die before I harmed you."

The words stilled my panic. I exhaled slowly and nodded. "I know."

"Wrap your fingers around the leather above your hand. You'll feel more secure."

Using a remote, the bars turned, slowly rolling up the straps until I had no choice but to lift my arms. When they were above my head, a bit wider than shoulder-width apart, the pulley stopped.

My legs were slightly spread and there was no weight on the heel of my feet. Any higher and I'd have to lift completely to the front balls of my feet.

Tossing the remote to the bed, Max wrapped her arms around me and pressed the side of her face to mine.

"I know you're frightened. Let's stay like this for a moment." Trembling, I nuzzled my cheek to hers. "You'll always be safe with me, Sarah."

Bit by bit, my mind and body settled.

She murmured, "Alright?" I nodded. "Tell me your safe phrase and word…" I repeated them, my voice trembling. "Good girl. Use them if you need to. We go at a pace that *pushes* but doesn't *scare* you."

I left a kiss beneath her ear. "Thank you, Max."

She stroked her fingers through my hair and hugged me firmly. Then she let me go bit by bit and took a step back.

Placing her palm over my heart, she whispered, "This…*this* is what I want. I have to go through your pain to reach it."

She flexed her fingertips and released me.

Gesturing to the displays, she told me, "Every item in this room was purchased for you. It's never touched anyone else's skin."

Unable to stop my gaze from drifting to her groin, Max's smile was slow as she gripped the fake cock I knew intimately.

"Even this, Sarah. I purchased it the day you woke up beside me in the guest room and we talked for the first time."

My eyes widened.

"I'm sure men wish they could restart their cock's history so easily." I laughed, tugging my lip between my teeth.

From the cabinet, she took a flogger made of the same leather as the bindings on my wrists. It was about four feet long. A shiver of fear arced through me but I swallowed it.

"These tresses are soft." She stroked them over the skin of my belly. "Even soft material *will* eventually sting with prolonged contact. I need to *learn* your thresholds so I don't *cross* them."

I took a deep breath and she left a gentle kiss on my mouth before moving beside my suspended body.

The first lash across my ass made me gasp in surprise. I processed how it made me feel. It wasn't fear but it wasn't pleasure either.

Ten seconds later, another lash landed. The sound of the leather connecting with the skin of my ass was loud in the silent room. Less startled than the first time, I allowed my eyes to close.

Max worked the leather slowly up my back - using the same pressure each time.

As the twentieth lash landed across my shoulder blades, something *dark* slithered loose in my mind.

I was swamped by flashes of the worst moments in my childhood - those that left the deepest scars - and the flood of emotional pain was almost *unbearable*.

Resting my cheek against my elevated shoulder, tears flowed over my face. Max took me in her arms and murmured, "Tell me why you're crying, sweetheart."

"S-scared to sleep. Always there. Always." My sobs were wracking, painful, my words incoherent. Disturbing images flickered in my head over and over. "Max…Max, please."

"What can I do, Sarah? Let me help you."

I was bound in a position I *could not* escape, completely naked, and more vulnerable than I'd been to another human since I was ten years old.

And yet…the physical sensations - the sting over the skin of my ass and back - forcefully lanced a black and oozing psychological wound at my core.

Gathering my courage, I whispered words I didn't truly understand but couldn't hold back.

"Don't stop…"

Gasping against the side of my head, Max's arms tightened around my body until I couldn't inhale fully. Leaning back, she cupped my face and wiped my tears with her thumbs. She left kisses on my cheeks, lips, and forehead.

"Alright, Sarah." I lost her touch but a moment later, felt the sting of the flogger across my upper back. "It's time to let it all go. Bleed it out and let it go."

Another lash…

Another…

I cried for the little girl I never had a chance to be and leaned into the contact from the only person who'd been able to give me an ounce of true relief in all my life.

Every second in Max's arms disconnected me from everything but the now. I could *be still* in her presence and quiet the chaotic emotions that filled me almost constantly.

The lashes moved down my back and up again as I wept harder than I ever had.

Poison drained from me in the form of uncontrollable tears. While I knew the pain *would* build again, I felt genuinely *empty* of my rage and sadness for the first time in my memory.

My head fell forward on my shoulders and I went limp. "S-stop, Max."

She instantly held me against her to support my weight. Quickly reversing the pulley, it enabled her to loosen the straps. When my wrists were free, Max lowered me to the bed on my side.

Removing her tank top, she wiped my face of tears, snot, and my own saliva. I felt like a child but didn't reject the assistance.

"Thank you. Thank you, Max."

"My brave girl…rest now."

I was asleep in seconds.

* * *

It was late afternoon when I woke up curled tightly around Max's upper body.

I felt…different.

I wasn't magically *healed* from a decade and a half of sexual, physical, and emotional abuse…but I felt as if I could *breathe*.

For years, I'd used sex, dancing, running, and fighting strangers to keep my demons at bay so I could function as a normal human.

Pushing my body physically as far as I could to numb the ache I endured in every waking moment.

The night I was jumped and overcome by my rage, I'd wanted bloodshed. As it had been for years, I didn't care if I was the one who did the bleeding.

I didn't actively *seek* death…

I didn't *shy* from it either.

Max was awake. I needed to talk and knew she would listen. It would be hard to look into her eyes while I did. Instead, I stayed where I was with my head tucked beneath her chin.

"Before I was ten, I'd been raped by five adult men. Three of them were married to my aunt - two were the *brother* and *father* of her last husband."

"Those fucking *animals*. Oh, Sarah." She held me tight to her chest and let me talk.

The lump in my throat made it hard to swallow. "I ran away the first time when I was seven and managed to get five miles on foot with my backpack and a bag of camping gear. I was locked in a pantry and starved over three days for the *inconvenience* my show of defiance caused. No matter how many times I ran, I couldn't escape."

Max's body trembled around me but she didn't loosen her hold.

"She actually *loved* the last monster and let him come back. What they did to me always stopped eventually but she let *him* - the worst of them - back in the house. That time, I didn't run. I took my softball bat and destroyed tens of thousands of dollars in antiques in her house."

"Outstanding."

"I would have killed one or both of them if they'd come near me and I believe they knew it was no longer safe *for them* to sleep under the same roof with *me*." After a long pause, I whispered, "They were right. I would have murdered them in their bed."

Pressing my face to her skin, I inhaled deeply of Max. It gave me strength.

She inhaled deeply. "I would have killed them. No doubt. No hesitation, Sarah."

"The cops took me away. I spent a week in juvie and never said a word to explain my behavior despite being asked over and over by people who promised they had my best interests at heart."

"I imagine *many* people had pretended not to see the signs of abuse you showed over the years. It would have been *impossible* to trust anyone in authority."

"Yes…it made me paranoid, confused, so I stayed quiet. Other residents jumped me an hour after lights out the first night. I *beat* those broken kids like they were nothing - without a shred of mercy. One girl said she saw the devil in my eyes and crossed herself. They left me alone after that."

"You're an amazing brawler…for a long time, it seems." I nodded.

"The day I was released, I was sent to Florida and met Paula for the first time. I scented her insanity in seconds and weighed my options. It would be *easier* to disappear in a bigger population but…my brothers needed food, clean clothes, and routines. So, I stayed."

Max's fingers slipped into my hair and curled tight at the base of my skull. "Of course, you did."

"Two weeks in, Paula's husband grabbed me, tried to take me down. I held his balls in a vise grip until he cried like a child and begged me to let him go. I wanted to rip them off and watch him bleed to death. I described in detail how I'd bind him while he was sleeping and take his dick one inch at a time with shears. He left three days later with what he could pack in his Mustang. He looked like he hadn't slept a wink."

Max's heart pounded but she let me purge all the ugliness. If my confession could change how she saw me, it would be better to know from the beginning.

"For five years, I let her beat me. It was the vice-principal at my high school who introduced me to Monica. I-I told you about that."

I exhaled slowly. "On my own, I'd date someone for a few weeks, a month or two, and use them to decode normal human interactions. I didn't love them or let them get too close and had to maintain the upper hand at all times. There was always *relief* when it ended."

Thinking back, I remembered my one bright spot.

"Campbell was my first friend. I'd known him for almost two years by the time I left home. Paula read my journal - knew I'd had sex with him the weekend before. I *hated* her knowing about the first beautiful thing to happen in my life."

"She had no right…"

I hugged Max hard. "I loved him and he loved me. We knew he was gay and…got through the realization that we'd *never* fit romantically a little at a time. Being around him too much was hard. It reminded me how lonely I was. I kept him at a distance…until I started s-spending time with you."

"I'm so fucking glad you have him, Sarah." Max leaned back to look into my eyes. "You know we're *dating*, right?"

"I mean, I was an escort…"

"Yeah. I don't care, Sarah."

Moving lower on the bed so we were eye to eye, she kissed me. It was a gentle kiss - filled with warmth and acceptance - that made my heart pound.

"How do you feel physically?" She asked the question softly.

"You mean my back?" She nodded. "Barely feels like a sunburn. Within a couple of hours, I doubt I'll feel it at all." I placed my hand on her cheek. "I feel different…inside. That's what you meant before - about delivering pain I needed without hurting me."

"Yes. I never want to hurt you but I can give you controlled release whenever you start feeling like you're going to rattle out of your own skin."

Max frowned. "When you let people who don't care about you *beat* on your body, there's no guarantee they won't do permanent damage. Let me be the one to give you what you need."

"I need *you* now."

Without a word, she rolled me to my back and settled between my legs in a smooth motion that made me gasp.

As she set her cock at my pussy, I sighed. When she pushed inside, my eyes went wide.

"You're using…" The rest of my sentence was lost in a moan as she smiled and turned on the low vibration.

"Now you need a different kind of release, Sarah. Allow me."

I touched as much of Max as I could while she drove us up and over one orgasm after another. Her kisses went deep, touching a place inside me I'd never known existed.

At the peak of another climax, tears slipped from the corners of my eyes and I cried out, "Love you…I love you, Max."

"Fuck…*yes*." She held me hard, pressed as close to me as she could get, and said, "I love *you*, Sarah. I have since the first time you gave yourself to me."

"I'm afraid…"

"That's okay. You're the bravest person I know. Be afraid…and do it anyway."

Laughing through my tears, I nodded. "Okay, Max."

CHAPTER 41:
Ebb & Flow

Eventually, Max carried me across the apartment and lowered me into the soaking tub. It felt amazing on my exhausted body.

"Stay here. I'll be right back."

I drifted a bit and opened my eyes when she returned with a tray of sliced fruit, cheese, and chocolates.

She placed two plastic tumblers of ice water with orange slices on the edge of the tub and slid into the water behind me. It felt incredible to recline against the front of her body. We stayed like that a long time, snacking in silence.

"Max?"

"Hmm?" She slid her palm across my belly.

"I didn't like Delta flirting with you. I realize that's hypocritical considering…"

"Let me stop you there. You've been a great escort, Sarah. Your clients rave about you - even the one-offs." She kissed my temple. "You helped many and gave all moments of happiness they'll remember for the rest of their lives. I'm proud of how you handled the job. You should be, too."

I drank some water to give myself time to figure out what I wanted to say.

"I, uh, don't want… *that* anymore."

Her smile came through in her voice. "State what you want clearly. Be as fearless with me as you are in every other area of your life."

Inhaling slowly, I rushed out, "I want to be the only one to touch you. I don't want to touch anyone but you."

"Done."

I turned and knelt between her legs. "Really?"

"Yes."

"You won't feel…restricted?"

"Will you?" I shook my head. "There you go. Easy."

Climbing over Max's lap, I sat on her thighs with my knees on either side. "Can I touch you whenever I want?"

"Don't you do that already?" she asked in surprise.

"Sometimes…but not always."

Her hands rested at my hips and the expression on her face was quizzical. "When do you *want* to touch me and hold back?"

"I want…to hold your hand more. Um, to hug you when you laugh. You have the best laugh."

"That sounds wonderful."

I felt the blush spread on my skin. "And, if there's a movie moment, I want to go with it."

"A *movie* moment?"

"Mm hmm. Like if you have a little ice cream on your lip…I'd lick it off. Or, you know, if your tie gets crooked, I'll straighten it and pull you down for a kiss. Like they do in those silly

Hallmark movies. But sometimes, those moments really happen."

"You haven't shared movie moments with Campbell? I imagine the two of you would notice them right away."

Lifting my face, I smiled. "We do but…we make our reactions super dramatic and funny. We end up hysterical. Most *assume* we're a couple so our antics make people confused."

Quietly, I added, "I want people to *know* we're a couple. If that's alright. Not be weird about it and end up on some website but…you know?"

"I do. You want to live openly in your relationship with me."

"Yes. If you're okay with that."

"Yeah." Max cleared her throat. "Yeah, that's more than okay with me, Sarah."

"I figure we're strong enough to fuck up anybody who doesn't like it." My grin felt too big for my face. "And plenty *will* like it because we're smokin' hot as a couple."

Pulling me close, Max made love to my mouth and palmed the back of my head.

Eventually, I fed her pieces of fruit and cheese, bits of chocolate, and we finished both glasses of water. We took a long shower and she blow-dried my hair for me.

We were relaxing naked on her couch as the setting sun behind her building turned the sky beyond her window to brilliant pinks and oranges.

"Sarah, I'd like to take you with me to visit my parents next month."

"Y-your parents?"

"Your entire body just locked in complete terror. My parents and brothers are goofily normal. Watching my parents is like old family sitcoms from the fifties. Come to think of it, you'd probably witness a lot of movie moments with them."

"That sounds nice." Turning over, I braced my hands on either side of her waist. "You have *brothers*?"

"I have *four* brothers. The one closest to me is five years older - then two are seven, and the oldest is nine. I was their surprise child."

"Wow. Are they nice to you?"

"Ohh…that's a hard question to answer. They'd say yes, for sure. They love me. They also torture me. Three are married to women and Brandon dates men when the mood strikes. Between them, there are…" she counted in silence and said, "eleven nieces and nephews."

"Where do they live?"

"The family home is in Newport News, Virginia. Dad's based at Langley Air Force Base. Mom runs the equivalent of an in-home manufacturing plant to send care packages to military serving overseas. She does a ton of fund-raising."

"What do your brothers do?"

"Wesley is the oldest. He followed in Dad's Air Force footsteps. Neil runs a bed and breakfast in Vermont with his wife. His twin Simon became a Marine. Brandon is a financial guru based in New York. I idolized Simon since he gave me lots of silly attention when he was home on leave. My parents were *horrified* that their only daughter followed his example."

"What did they *want* you to be?"

"Chess grandmaster…"

I blinked. "Shut up."

"I'm serious. The problem was once I was good enough to compete at an international level, I was bored with the process. I wanted to use my *body*. I switched my focus to kendo, judo, and archery." Her eyes flicked down and back to my face. "Your nipples are hard, Sarah."

A little breathless, I admitted, "I knew you were smart. I didn't know you were *competitive chess* smart."

Max stared into my eyes for a long moment. "You naughty little sapiosexual…"

I kissed her skin from one hip to the other while holding her gaze. "I *am* partial to a sexy brain."

Moving lower, I dragged my tongue through her folds and watched her body tighten in need.

"You're also a badass and look goddamn gorgeous in a suit. A delicious pussy - in addition to a cock that *never* disappoints - certainly doesn't hurt. I want to feast on you, Max."

Settling in, I licked and sucked silken flesh that was too often overlooked as she repeatedly fucked me into a sexual stupor with her magic dicks.

The first time I made her come, she started to reach for me. I put my palm in the center of her chest.

"I need more. Let me have more of you. Eating you makes me happy."

I drove her up again and her trembling fingers went into my hair to hold me against her slippery skin. I moaned as I lapped lazily at her release.

Using two fingers, I thrust slowly as deep as I could get inside her. The skin tightened on the back of my neck at how wet she was.

"Dripping for me. God, yes."

Sucking her slickness from my fingers, I pushed my tongue into her pussy and it quivered around me. It made me moan and my eyes drifted closed at the pleasure of having her at *my* mercy for once.

Aching to consume all of her, I said hoarsely, "If you were over me, I wouldn't lose a drop. The next time you heat my back with leather, lay me down and fuck my face, Max."

Imagining it made me groan and I slid one hand under my body to stroke between my legs.

I devoured her pussy as I played with myself and by the time she gasped, arched from the couch, and came a third time for me, I joined her.

Resting my cheek on her inner thigh, I whispered, "I love everything about you, Max. Everything."

Still panting from her climax, she lifted enough to drag me up her body. Hugging me hard, she held my face against her chest.

I fell asleep stretched out on top of her.

* * *

I spent two weeks meeting my former clients for one final dinner date to say goodbye - without sex. They brought gifts, cash, and begged me to reconsider.

Keeping the cash and gifts…I didn't change my mind about leaving the life of an escort.

All but two - Monica and Juliana - asked if I'd be willing to see them outside the agency in a kept mistress arrangement.

I declined all offers graciously but firmly.

Though I hadn't decided what to do about Viv's offer, I didn't really see myself staying with the agency in any capacity. I needed to talk that through with Max and give the madame my final answer.

* * *

In early May, Max took me to meet her family for Mother's Day. It was a standing tradition that the siblings gathered to celebrate their mom. The brothers descended with their significant others and children in tow.

I was blown away by how *normal* they all were.

They were welcoming and kind - a little silly, as promised - and I smiled a lot during the four days we stayed in their huge Colonial.

Max's twin brothers - Neil and Simon - and their families took up the bedrooms on the second floor. Brandon's sanctuary was the bonus room over the garage that had been converted into a small two-bedroom apartment. Wesley and his brood stayed in the guest house behind the pool.

Max's childhood bedroom was in the finished half of the attic. I explored what felt like another world in fascination. There was a lot of floor space.

When I mentioned it, she said, "Mom wanted me to have room to practice without knocking shit over. She made this my room when I was eleven." Watching me examine her various trophies for chess and athletics, she asked, "Does it bother you to see families like mine?"

"You mean loving and non-toxic? No. It makes me happy. It would be terrible to think *my* experience was the common one. Campbell's family is normal, too." Wrapping my arms around her neck, I kissed her. "They're amazing. Smart, funny, kind. Thank you for bringing me."

"It's a first." Tilting my head, I wondered if I misunderstood what she meant. She immediately clarified, "I've never introduced a partner to my family."

"You're *thirty-two*..."

"I am. Yes." She held my chin between her finger and thumb. "It took me a while to find you. Probably because my ass was almost *twelve* when you were born." She crossed her eyes and I laughed.

"The age difference doesn't matter. Not even a little. When we're old..."

"You want to get old with me?"

"Silly question. When we're old, we'll use the chair so I can still ride your cock without one of us breaking a hip..."

"*Nice*," said a male voice. Glancing over my shoulder, I blushed at Max's brother Simon leaning in the doorway. "I bet hers is bigger than mine."

"Hmm. Admittedly, she has every size, shape, and function so a girl doesn't have to settle." Kissing Max lightly, I turned but kept her hand in mine. "Call me Goldilocks because my bear is always just right. What's shakin', Simon?"

"Presently pondering if my cougar would enjoy add-ons... since I'm *probably* the little bear."

Not getting suckered into a conversation about your dick, Simon. Nice try.

"She would because variety is the spice of life. Keep her guessing…but don't call her a cougar. It's cringey, man."

Simon walked across the room and pinched my cheeks. He was a couple of inches taller than Max. "You are so stinkin' *cute*. My baby sister did good."

"Thanks." All her brothers made me laugh but Simon was a *riot*.

"Did you see all her trophies?" Simon brandished his hand like a magician and I nodded. "I have photos. So many photos…"

"I'll drop you *right here*, Simon," Max warned softly.

"Oh, yeah." I nodded happily. "I'm gonna need to see those. Now, please."

The siblings got into an all-out wrestling match in the center of the room. It went on for a frightening length of time.

I ended up distracting Max by flashing my tits so Simon could get me the goods. He hauled ass for the door and slammed it behind him. Smart man.

Pinning me to the floor, Max growled, "That was a dirty trick, Sarah. My honor is on the line…"

"But my nipples are *hard* from watching you move and I wanted you to suck them." Kissing her roughly, I raked my nails down her back and gripped her ass. "Play with *me*, Max. It's my turn."

"Fuck, you slay me."

We didn't make it downstairs until dinner and Max's family smiled at us knowingly as we took our places side by side.

I liked how everyone talked around each other. Topics changed rapidly and there was so much laughter.

Since *Mrs. Huxley* was the one who presented me with several photo albums of her youngest child and only daughter - Max didn't have a leg to stand on.

Simon was a cagey one.

I spent hours paging through them and asking a hundred questions.

By the time we left her childhood home, I was more in love with Max than ever.

CHAPTER 42:
Important Decisions

June 2011

When we returned to South Florida, I took a bunch of groceries to Viv's condo to make everyone dinner. As I cooked, I chatted with whoever passed through the kitchen. Delta wasn't around.

Viv sat on a bar stool to watch me and I officially declined her offer to stay with the agency.

"I'll still be around but…I can't work here."

"I understand. I hate it but I get it." Vivienne came around and pulled me into a tight hug. "Don't forget your old Viv."

"You aren't old and don't get dramatic."

She stroked my cheek. "Max is leaving me, too." My eyes widened. "She didn't tell you?" I shook my head. "Found someone to fill the position and has been training her for a week."

"Vivienne. What have I told you about telling other people's business?" Max tugged me from the madame's arms. "This isn't high school. Act right."

With a pout, Viv returned to the stool on the other side of the island. "Fine. I don't know what I'll do if Walker abandons me."

"He won't. He secretly loves you as much as you love him." Max's hand slipped along my lower back and down to squeeze my ass. "If the two of you ever grow up…"

Viv waved her hand. "Don't curse us. We'd burn each other out in six months. Neither of us have brakes or common sense."

I kissed Max's jaw and washed my hands before turning to the brisket I'd allowed to rest after taking it from the oven. I used a Brazilian recipe I learned from Juliana.

"Interesting," I murmured.

Leaving a kiss on the nape of my neck, Max said in my ear, "This has been going on for *years*." Straightening, she added, "That smells incredible."

"Thanks."

"I *love* your cooking."

"That makes me happy, Max. Your mom's cooking is a *lot* to live up to. I had serious performance anxiety after tasting her food. She's like Julia Child."

She held my jaw. "You're in a class by yourself. You compete with no one."

Vivienne breathed, "Oh, my god…you two are *in love*. Like, *really* in love." We turned our heads to look at her. She fanned her face as her eyes filled with tears. "I *hoped* but wasn't *sure*."

"You know," I replied, "you're *way* more emotional than anyone would guess, Viv."

"I want to be your big sister like Monica. It's only fair…" Her voice was playful but I heard the seriousness of her request.

Placing my palms on the counter, I stared into her eyes. "When I let people close, I take their safety seriously. I worry about their futures, health, and overall happiness. It's not a small thing to me so be sure you want that, Vivienne."

"I-I want that."

"Alright. You're my other big sister."

"You mean it?" she asked softly.

"I do."

"Thank you, Sarah."

Over the next few years, Vivienne faltered in her own life many times but I stayed true to my word. I always came when she needed me and didn't pull my punches when I explained what she was doing to fuck herself up.

Eventually, she figured it out. I breathed a sigh of relief when she finally got sober and found love.

* * *

A few days later, I answered my phone with a frown.

"Can I sublet your place until I go back to school?"

"You know you're welcome there anytime." I could tell Camp had been crying and was instantly on high alert. Sitting at Max's desk on my laptop, I asked carefully, "What's going on?"

"I met this guy and it seemed great the last few weeks. I found out two days ago that he has a *wife*, Sarah. The man is *married* to a *woman*. He won't leave me alone and knows where my parents live."

"Don't worry about anything. I'll help you move before school starts again." It was critical to question him carefully. "How did you meet this guy?"

"Faculty at my school. Don't even *say* it...I know. He wasn't in my department so I thought it would be okay. Man is taking the books he teaches a little too seriously."

Lit professor at Camp's college.

Nonchalantly, I asked, "What kind of car does he drive so I can keep an eye out while you're here?"

"A Mercedes SUV - which should have tipped me off but I was an idiot." He exhaled roughly. "I'll drive down after my last class. I had everything moved to storage yesterday. My bags are in my car."

"I'll see you when you get here. Don't worry, Camp."

"Thanks, Sarah. Sorry I'm a mess."

"You've seen me in worse shape more times than I can count. Don't think about that."

After we disconnected, I walked rapidly through Max's apartment and changed into black jeans, t-shirt, and boots.

Grabbing my pack and helmet, I sent Max a quick text about making sure Camp was alright and then hauled ass north.

I made it my business to know my best friend's class schedule and the layout of his campus. I found a spot in the shade to park where I could see his car and got off to wait while I drank a bottle of water.

Around five o'clock, I saw Camp walking across the grounds with a group of his classmates. They were in a serious discussion as they reviewed pages of notes.

The Escort: In the Service of Women

They paused and chatted before going their separate ways at the parking lot. Camp looked for his keys in his messenger bag and I watched a Mercedes SUV cruise past his car and park on the opposite side.

"You're so innocent, Camp. You aren't even paying *attention*, babe," I murmured aloud.

An older good-looking blonde man got out and walked around the back of Campbell's car, startling him when he spoke. He jumped and dropped his keys. The man crowded my best friend against the side of his vehicle, talking low.

Camp wasn't the *only* one not paying attention.

I moved behind him and gripped the muscle of his shoulder as I grabbed the wrist closest to me and twisted. "Be still and listen carefully or there's going to be a scene, professor."

"Who the hell are *you*?" The blonde was angry but careful not to draw attention. "This is a private conversation."

"Not anymore." I squeezed the muscle and he gasped in pain. "Camp is my best friend. He's gentle and wouldn't expect you to stalk him but I'm cut from a different cloth. I always suspect men might be rotten shits and here we are."

"It was a misunderstanding…"

"Was it? You're *not* married? Know that I'll check."

"It-it's over…"

"Does *she* know that?" He didn't respond. "I thought not. You want *all* the cake, you greedy bastard." I turned his wrist enough to make him whimper. "Camp is not going to be your side piece. Whatever you might have had is over now. It's clear you were lying from the start."

"But I love him!"

"Not as much as you love yourself. If you don't take my advice and leave him alone, I'm going to blow up your entire motherfucking life. I will leave you *nothing* - personally or professionally."

A tablet appeared in my peripheral vision and I met Max's eyes beside me. On the screen were all the personal details of Frank Littleton - professor of literature and driver of a Mercedes SUV.

I grinned and she winked. "Professor Littleton." The man jerked sharply when I referred to him by name. "Should we move our talk to your house at 1135…?"

"No! Okay. Okay, I'll leave him alone."

Releasing him, I stepped back. "A wise move. It was unpleasant to meet you. Goodbye now, prof."

"I really *do* love you, Campbell…"

Shaking his head, Camp replied, "That sucks for you then because we're done. You made me part of your *adultery*, you piece of shit. I'd never do that to someone. Never speak to me again."

The man walked to his car and drove away.

Campbell released a heavy sigh. "His dick was amazing…and his after-care game was no joke. Fucking *asshole*."

Then he was crying and I gathered him close. "I'm sorry, Camp. I'm so sorry."

After a couple of minutes, he scrubbed his face and leaned back. "I need to calm down so I can drive."

"No need," Max told him. "My trainee will drive your car and you can ride with me."

"Th-that would be great, Max. Really." Campbell rested his head on my shoulder and I gave him soft pets. "You always come when I need you. Thanks."

"We show up for each other. That's the deal. Now Max is part of the deal and she's more badass than me. You'll be even safer, Camp."

I pressed a kiss to the side of his head. "Max will stop and get you a coffee, maybe a snack. Maybe…don't order a croissant. I almost gave her an aneurysm with the unavoidable crumbs. They're so *flaky*."

Camp chuckled and straightened. I wiped his tears and hated seeing them on his pretty face. "I love you and everything is going to be okay."

"You're my best friend. You have to say that."

I held his cheek. "No. I say it because you're strong, brilliant, and beautiful. One of the most loving people I've ever known. The right person to appreciate everything you have to offer is out there. Don't settle for anyone who tries to give you less."

Camp put his hand over mine on his face and closed his eyes. "It gets lonely, Sarah."

"I know, sweetheart. No one knows like me." I planted a kiss on his lips. "Summer at the beach…just what you need." He nodded and I gave him a smile. "Let's get moving. See you there."

Max bent to pick up the dropped keys. Several spaces beyond my bike, a woman in a tailored suit got out of Max's Audi and passed Camp with a nod.

"Sarah, this is Yvette. She's taking over driving the limo for Vivienne and the girls."

I figured her to be about Max's age but her short, sleekly styled hair was full silver. Lifting her shades to the top of her head, ice blue eyes held mine.

She held out her hand and we shook firmly. "Call me Vet. I've known Max since basic. Heard a lot about you but wasn't prepared for the reality. Nice use of pressure to the joint. Have you been professionally trained?" I shook my head. "Just *life* then?"

"Yeah. Pretty much."

"Impressive. You've never heard about me, huh?" I shook my head again. "Figures. Not sure I'll forgive you for this one, Max."

"Get in the fucking car, Vet."

Leaning close, the driver said in a low voice, "Until next time, Sarah…"

Max growled. "Keep flirting with my woman right in front of me and there won't *be* a next time."

"So…*out of your sight* then. Check." Laughing, Vet caught the keys Max tossed and slid behind the wheel of Camp's car.

"We're meeting at Sarah's place. I'll text you the address." There was a long pause and Max added, "She doesn't really *live there* most of the time."

The message was clear.

"I get it, Max. See you on the other end. Sarah, it's a real pleasure to meet the woman who thawed the ice queen. Can't wait to tell the unit."

She drove away a moment later and I met intense green eyes I adored.

"Your friend is a lot like you." I smiled. "You called me your *woman*. I like it. A real *marking your territory* vibe." Stepping closer, I whispered, "I'm a little tense from dealing with that asshole. How about later you do some marking of a *different* kind then fuck me unconscious?"

"Excellent plan. Once we get Camp settled, I want to take you away for the weekend. You up for that?"

"Can I crawl all over you at this new location?" She nodded. "Then I'm down. Let's hit the road."

She kissed me stupid and we did just that.

Max didn't complain once about Camp's crumbs in her car. My bestie and I *loved* croissants.

* * *

Three days later, Max took me to a beach house on a quiet stretch of the Treasure Coast that was out of sight of any other residents. We spent our time playing in the water, fucking everywhere, and eating the food we cooked together.

On our second morning, we watched the sunrise from the deck outside the second-floor bedroom and spotted a pod of dolphins thirty yards off the shore. It was breathtaking and made me emotional.

I turned to Max and she held a jeweler's box in her palm. The sun lit her eyes like emeralds.

"I love you. Marry me, Sarah. In every way we can and then all the ways that become possible. Stay with me. Let me love you every minute of life I have left."

Tears slipped silently over my cheeks as I took her face in my hands. "Talk to me if you change your mind one day…"

"I won't."

"If you get bored…"

"I won't."

"If you get tired of my problems…"

"I *won't*, Sarah. Never."

"I love you, Max."

"I know. Say yes."

Nodding, I whispered, "Yes, Max. I'll marry you."

She pulled me in hard and devoured me with her kiss. I was instantly breathless, overcome with emotion, and aching for her.

Backing me forcefully into the room with her body, she took me apart with pleasure.

When I woke up in the early afternoon, I stared at a beautiful diamond band on my left hand.

Curled against my back, Max whispered, "I love you more than I thought it was possible to love another person. I'll make you happy, Sarah."

"You already do." Swallowing hard, I added, "I never thought anyone would love me. Not anyone who could be mine."

I turned in her arms and she held me as I cried.

Even happiness sometimes comes with tears. I hoped I would cry a lot of happy tears in my future to offset all the painful ones in my past.

A future *with Max* that suddenly shone bright with possibilities. I'd never let the woman who managed to pull me out of the dark go. I would fight like a demon to keep her with me always.

Thankfully, she knew the crazy she signed up for.

CHAPTER 43:
Peace at Last

August 2011 - January 2015

I officially moved in with Max two months later and she made space for me in her life in ways I'd never imagined.

Changing the layout of her office, she created a beautiful area for me to write and brought in a carpenter to build floor-to-ceiling bookshelves to accommodate my many books.

I started writing as my future *job* rather than an on-again-off-again hobby. The results were frankly incredible.

Max became my fiercest supporter but wasn't above gentle criticism when I needed it.

I appreciated her ability to be both.

It was strange seeing my clothes on one side of her closet. Hesitant to give up everything I'd gathered for my apartment over the years, I decided to put it in storage. It didn't suit Max's place but I loved the pieces I'd redone myself for sentimental reasons.

She smiled in understanding and helped me make it happen. "One day, when we have a house, we'll make a space for everything you love, Sarah. I never want you to give it up."

I continued to film my videos every two weeks and started including Max bit by bit to gauge the reception on my channel.

It was phenomenal.

In them, she wore full-body leather and a mask that concealed the upper half of her face. Not that it mattered. Her *face* was rarely in the frame.

We filmed in our pleasure room. A space no one ever saw but us...and eventually Campbell.

As she knelt at my feet, put my leg over her shoulder, and ate me...donations *flooded* in. I was stunned to make over seven thousand dollars in a single session.

Each time she suspended my body and delivered lashes to my skin, I forgot we were on camera.

The subscribers never did.

The first time she fucked me live with her fake cock, subscribers contributed over ten grand.

My channel became my primary source of income overnight and I insisted on splitting the proceeds with the other person featured in them.

"I don't need the money, Sarah..."

I shrugged. "Neither do I but we're making it together so we'll split it."

Several adult video producers reached out to me but I declined their offers without hesitation. I wanted complete creative control and the ability to walk away from it the moment it was time.

However, it was true I didn't need the money.

I'd accumulated almost a quarter of a million dollars in fees alone over my eighteen months of being an escort. Naturally, I made that money grow with careful investing.

Before I became an escort, I'd saved almost fifty-thousand from amateur stripping, fighting, and playing cards.

There was double that from my videos.

In my safety deposit box was another seventy-five thousand from cash tips and jewelry valued at another hundred large. It was my *rainy day* fund - the only assets I possessed that weren't on *anyone's* books.

From the start, I'd kept my living expenses low enough to pay entirely from my day job alone - first at the grocery store and then working for Monica.

My bike was paid for and cost almost nothing in gas. I had no debt nor did I entertain expensive habits.

The day I laid it all out for Max, she was stunned into complete silence.

"You've just been…*accumulating* money for four years?" I shrugged. "This financial portfolio is *insane* for someone your age. Viv was right…you're going to be a millionaire." Eyes wide, she whispered, "Can I tell Brandon?"

Confused, I asked, "Why would he *care?*"

"Oh…he'll care. He lives for numbers and few things truly surprise him."

Two days later, Brandon appeared at our door and didn't bother with greetings. "Show me everything."

Laughing, I did.

I kept the fact that Campbell had followed my lead in *many* things to myself.

* * *

The following January, Max and I were married in a simple civil ceremony with Campbell and Monica as witnesses. We held it on the two-year anniversary of the first night we spent together.

A night that changed so much for me.

It wasn't a legally binding marriage but it meant *everything* to us. That was all that mattered.

When it became legal to marry, we vowed to do it again properly.

We held our simple but elegant reception at a hotel in Miami. It was attended by Campbell and his parents, Max's large family, many of Max's friends from the military - including Jake and Tracy, Monica and Jade, and everyone from the escort agency.

It was a night spent dancing, laughing, and filled with more physical affection than I'd ever experienced at one time from so many people.

Campbell appreciated the eye candy presented by all four of Max's brothers and quickly developed a heavy crush on her gay brother Brandon.

Unfortunately, it was a dead end.

The man was in a long-term relationship with someone who didn't seem to fit him *at all*...but they lived together in Manhattan and shared a life.

A secret part of me wished anyway. I wanted Camp well-loved so I always knew he was safe and happy.

The Escort: In the Service of Women

* * *

A few months later, Vivienne announced she was selling the escort service to a madame based out of New York City.

It had apparently been in the works for years but she'd been quiet about it.

Everyone was in complete shock.

Everyone but Max.

"I'm tired," Viv told us over an extravagant dinner. "I've been doing this for a long time and I'm ready to stop."

Reaching out, I placed my hand over hers. "Paige and Ezbeth leaving hurts. Doesn't it?"

The couple announced their plans to take a year away from everything and decide where they wanted to set up their new life together.

They'd been gone for several weeks.

Vivienne took it hard. They were her most frequent lovers other than Walker. I suspected she felt left behind.

"I want…" Her voice shook and she tried to firm it. "All of you are finding happiness, fulfillment, and people to love. I'm *happy* for you. Truly." With a painful expression, she added in a whisper, "I want that. Maybe…I can find it if I stop fucking for fleeting satisfaction."

Rolande planned to assist the new madame with her girls. It wouldn't surprise me a bit if she ended up running the Florida stable.

Vivienne put the elegant Jamaican in charge of recruiting not long after the major changes. Rolande found four new escorts of outstanding quality within two weeks.

Sonja finally accepted the offer of the Bettencourts to live with them when she discovered she was four months pregnant with the husband's child.

She outlined what she wanted and they granted every request in an iron-clad contract. Should any of them ever tire of the arrangement, she received a home and settlement that would take care of her and her child for the rest of their lives.

Unlike Nadia, she genuinely *loved* her long-time lovers and was excited to have her baby.

Delta had no qualms about working for the new owners and immediately bought a new car and a pricey condo. I still couldn't stand her ass.

Most of the support staff also stayed on. Mrs. Quincy would transition the business operations and then retire.

She planned to move to a small villa she'd purchased in Jamaica with Rolande's help years before. Something told me she wouldn't go alone. I'd noticed the quiet relationship between her and the good doctor for a while.

Sex was a hot commodity.

It would always be in demand.

Vivienne was done being the primary distributor.

I wondered what the changes meant for the mercurial relationship between Vivienne and Walker. Neither seemed inclined to share those details.

It took *years* for Viv to find her footing but when she did, it gave her a new lease on life that she never took for granted.

Those of us who genuinely loved her breathed a collective sigh of relief.

The Escort: In the Service of Women

* * *

In November of 2012, six months after winning a three-million-dollar civil suit against my biological mother that had dragged on for two years, DHS finally removed my younger brothers from Paula's home.

I was incredibly emotional about it.

Max thought I should petition to get custody but I knew that wasn't what would be best for them.

"If I take them, Paula will *never* leave them alone. She's a horrible, neglectful mother but hatred makes her violent. The hatred she has for me will transfer to them. They need…they *deserve* a fresh start."

Ultimately, they were placed with a kind older couple who allowed me to have regular visitation.

I followed the Schmidts for weeks out of sight to ensure what I saw on the surface was reality.

Joshua and David *blossomed* under their care. They were good kids and smart. Having a stable home life would change everything for them.

They were in therapy, regularly attending school again, and physically healthier than I'd ever seen them.

It was more than I'd dared to dream and gave me peace of mind I never expected.

With my accountant's help, I set up small trust funds for them that they would receive as adults.

And then, there was our *mother*…

Paula did not fade quietly into the background. Max took every precaution to erect an iron wall around my privacy.

My mail went to a post office box that was then forwarded to the apartment. The building was provided with her photo and copies of the restraining order so if Paula showed up, they had the responsibility to immediately call the police.

When she couldn't get to *me*, she made *Campbell* her target. I wanted nothing more than to destroy her.

It wasn't necessary in the end.

She did a fine job destroying herself.

Eventually, she was thrown off all social media, issued multiple restraining orders, and embroiled in a second civil suit filed by Campbell's family on his behalf.

Drastically overestimating her own cleverness, at last she made a mistake big enough to take her down.

She and several members of her radical church picketed in the quad on the day of Camp's college graduation in the summer of 2014.

I was ready to dive into the fray but Max held me back. "Not this time, Sarah. Wait."

They carried signs with his photo and name along with horrible slurs. I vibrated with rage as my friend stayed within our circle of friends and family.

Max's brothers came with her parents - without their extended families - and formed a protective barrier between my friend and the bullshit.

Paula hadn't warned her fellow lunatics about her pending legal troubles that included restraining orders that should have kept her well away from either of us.

None of them understood the most basic concept of *free speech* versus *hate speech*...or even how private property worked.

The Escort: In the Service of Women

The entire group was arrested for trespassing, violation of multiple restraining orders - since his parents and I were near him - and disobeying previous warnings from the judge presiding over the civil suit.

Campbell pressed charges for hate crimes, stalking, and reckless endangerment.

For the first time, Paula would do hard time for her careless choices. It might not be for anything she did to me but I didn't care.

Two years of her life were to be spent in prison before she would be eligible for parole.

She ended up serving less than a quarter of it.

Paula found out she had stage four lung cancer less than three months into her sentence. It had metastasized to several vital organs in her body.

I did not visit her before her death.

I did not mourn her after it.

However, Max and I found reason to celebrate with my little brothers when the Schmidts officially adopted them. They didn't care that Joshua was fourteen and David was twelve.

Rebecca Schmidt smiled through tears at her new sons as her husband Roger took another dozen photos to commemorate the day.

"It's never too late to find a family."

I could not have agreed more.

* * *

In January of 2015, gay marriage was legalized in the State of Florida at last.

I married my beautiful partner in the eyes of the law within days. Like my brothers, I left the name Kent behind and took Max's last name.

We spent three days celebrating and she couldn't stop calling me Mrs. Huxley. I never tired of hearing it.

We barely left our apartment.

CHAPTER 44:
A Different Life

December 2015

I rushed around handling last-minute details for the guests who would soon descend on Max's parents' home to celebrate the holidays.

Max and I arrived two weeks before anyone else. I'd been helping Fiona - also known as *Mom* - decorate the house, ready all the guest rooms, shop for food, and brace for the very real impact of two dozen people under one roof for ten days.

Trying to keep her from overdoing it after her recent knee surgery and *not* strap her to a chair wasn't easy but I was determined to make it happen.

Her rehab wasn't faltering on *my* watch.

Wes - or *Dad* as he preferred - was around more since he'd officially retired the year before.

Max did her best to occupy her father in physical tasks such as buying and putting up the tree, hanging wreaths, and supervising while she put lights on every outdoor structure.

Simon was the first to arrive with his wife, son, and adorable twin girls. They were in two rooms on the second floor - one fully equipped for the kids.

Brandon showed up next - alone and brooding more than usual. He dropped a kiss on my cheek, as well as his mother's, waved at everyone else, and disappeared into the small apartment he used away from the hustle and bustle.

Wesley and his wife entered like a circus with their four children and two exuberant dogs. I quickly ushered them out to the guest house they preferred to use when they visited.

Neil and his wife appeared last with the four stair-step siblings they'd adopted a decade before. They took the other two bedrooms on the second floor. The kids had two sets of bunk beds and shared a bathroom with their parents.

Max and I would be far from everything in her attic room that we'd updated together on our last visit.

I was giving everyone time to get their balance before I started dinner and working on a new story when she hugged me from behind.

"Not trying to interrupt. It's so *loud* down there."

Chuckling, I told her, "I could use a break myself."

She lifted my face and kissed me deeply. Moaning, I wondered if we had time for one of *our* breaks.

"Can we work in a quickie?"

"Hell, *yes*. Brace yourself on the desk…"

"You two are always so *dirty*," Simon announced from the doorway. "I keep catching you *in flagrante* on every visit."

"Because you *try* to catch us, you pervert." I laughed. "Don't you have chaos to attend to? Don't you dare let Fiona lift a finger…"

He gasped. "I'm *telling* that you called her Fiona."

"I will *end* you."

"Fine." With a funny expression, Simon snapped his fingers. "I forgot. There's someone downstairs for Sarah. He is cute, cute, cute and Brandon is circling."

"Fantastic," Max said with a grin. Looking at me, she added, "Campbell is here."

"What? *Here?*" She nodded. "You invited him?"

"I did. He's like a brother to you. I wanted him to feel included in our family traditions. He's been away for so long and you're used to seeing him for your birthday and Christmas."

"Wow. I fucking *love* you." I leaned up, kissed her lips, and took off running for the first floor.

Camp stood in the foyer chatting with Brandon when I hit him like a missile. Laughing, he caught me because he always did.

"I haven't seen you in almost three *months*! Hi!"

He held my face and squished my cheeks together as he spoke in his annoyed voice. "The Munich project took longer than expected. Why is everyone in finance so damn *stuffy*? Ugh. We can be *brilliant* and still have *charisma*. Jesus." He narrowed his eyes. "You're *extra* pretty today." I received a smacking kiss on the mouth.

Max appeared beside us and they fist-bumped. "Glad you could make it, Camp."

Dropping an arm around my shoulders, he said, "Thanks for the invite. My stuff has been in storage for half a year - again - and I have no clue what the hell to do about it. Apparently I'm a *nomad* now. I will never have a permanent home again. Avoiding it and hanging out with you guys is better than adulting."

Resting her hand on Brandon's shoulder, Max asked, "You remember my brother?"

"Of course. It's *still* disconcerting for there to be *male* versions of you, Max."

"Crazy, right? They're all involved..."

Brandon interjected, "Not *all* of us."

Campbell and I turned to him in sync. "Interesting," I whispered. "A fairly recent development?"

"A few months. It was long overdue."

"I'm sorry, Brandon."

His gaze moved from me to my best friend. "Don't be." He bent and picked up Camp's suitcase. "Let's get you settled before Mom sees you. Then she can fawn over you properly."

We went up the stairs as a group and Brandon turned down the hall toward his apartment over the garage.

Max frowned. "Sarah made up the other..."

"Perhaps, but *the apartment* has better light and Sarah's *dearest friend* won't have to share facilities with all the kids. Hush your face."

Entering one of the bedrooms, Brandon placed Camp's bag on a bench at the end of the bed. Cheerfully, he mentioned, "That's the bathroom door. My room is on the other side. Sarah stocked drinks and snacks in the kitchenette."

Crossing her arms, Max offered, "Cozy, bro."

"Unnecessary comments are, by definition, unnecessary, *Maxine*."

She flinched with a low growl and I muffled my giggle.

Brandon extended his hand and Camp placed his in it. After a *long* pause that gave me a bit of a shiver in memory, Max's brother said, "Welcome, Campbell. Let me know if you need anything." With a light squeeze, he released him and left the room.

I breathed, "Knowing another person does that like Max makes me happy."

"Makes *me* weak in the fucking knees so give me a second. Damn it." He focused on Max. "Did you invite me here to fix me up with your brother?"

She shrugged. "I wanted you here for Sarah. It's been too long since you had time together and it was making her sad. If you *happen* to score, consider it a lucky coincidence."

"You're diabolical. I like it."

I put in my two cents. "I mean, he's pretty, intelligent as fuck, and probably possesses at least a modicum of emotional skill. The other brothers are damn gooey on the inside."

Camp murmured, "You're not wrong." Releasing a small sigh, he added, "It's hard to be a rebound lover but…I've had a soft and silly crush on Brandon since your wedding." He held up his hands. "Not that I was wishing for his relationship to end…"

"Calm down, Camp. You're not a warlock." I snorted and Max grabbed his shoulder. "That pairing always felt a little forced to me anyway…like Brandon got tired of looking and settled for the least troublesome man in his orbit." She gave him a little shake. "Feel free to provide some trouble to his orbit."

We left him to get his bearings.

Just outside the door, my eyes met Brandon's from where he'd been listening. He put his finger to his lips, winked, and ducked into the kitchen as Max joined me.

Our hope for a quickie evaporated as the kids poured from their rooms on the second floor and asked us to play games.

"Later, Sarah."

"I consider that a promise, Max."

For ten days, we celebrated occasions, birthdays, and milestones missed while the entire family had been apart since May.

I watched Camp and Brandon circle each other and knew my bestie would fall easily. I hoped Brandon would be gentle because violence never went over well at family gatherings.

Caught up in Christmas Eve fanfare, I was cleaning the kitchen, considering Camp's love life, and making plans in my head for the chaos of Christmas morning.

I was stunned when Campbell and Max grabbed me between them and ushered me out of the house.

Brandon was behind the wheel of Fiona's SUV and Max helped me into the backseat before getting in the front passenger seat. Camp slid in beside me.

"Uh, where are we going? I have so much left to do…"

"Christmas lights. Hot chocolate. Ice skating…"

"Uh, Camp…we don't know *how* to ice skate."

My friend nodded serenely. "I've been told it's easy. Also, you're one of the most athletic people I've ever met. We got this."

Turned out, we did *not* have it. At all.

We ended up in the emergency room. Camp for a sprained ankle. Me for a sprained wrist received trying to break his fall.

The Huxley siblings felt horrible.

They made up for it in spades.

Campbell and I let them.

EPILOGUE

December 2019

As I sit in our apartment facing the Atlantic, I feel awesome anticipation about the future.

I'm writing this final piece of my story from my desk in the office that Max and I share. By *share*, I mean she sometimes keeps me company while I work by silently reading stretched out on the leather couch.

I like her presence. It keeps me focused and I can ask her random questions.

"Max, if you pull a weapon, is the hand movement to the trigger part easy? How proficient do you have to be to make it look natural…?"

Or…

"If you strangled a grown man," she always looked up and gave me her complete attention, "like, a *big* guy…could you do it with just your hands? Okay, maybe not *you*…someone like Vivienne's size."

Or…

"Hear me out. You poison your spouse," she made a funny face, "I need ways to get the body out of a high-rise that *don't* include dismemberment."

"It's the *little* things that make me feel better, Sarah."

She's the most incredible woman I've ever met.

We've packed most of the things we can't bear to leave behind and the rest will be here when we visit what will now be a vacation home.

We decided to buy her childhood home in Newport News when her parents talked about moving south where it was warmer.

The two of us would officially maintain the home base for the next couple of generations in her family.

Her parents turned around and bought a condo down the hall from Max so they'll keep an eye on the place. Originally, they offered to buy *her* condo but...we couldn't let it go for many reasons.

The Virginia Colonial is too big for us alone.

Of course, it is.

The night we celebrated eight years together, we caught our breath after a marathon session of sex.

Max asked, "Sarah...how do you feel about children?"

I couldn't hold back instantaneous tears.

For a couple of years, I'd been noticing families and their children more than I ever had. I was afraid that perhaps I'd hurt Max with something we couldn't have together.

"Hey, sweetheart...no need for tears. It's nothing more than a fishing expedition on my part. I was curious. Wanted to test the waters. We don't have to…"

"Wait…wait. You *want* a child?"

She tilted her head. "Um…? I'm not sure how to answer that question."

I gathered her hand in both of mine and whispered, "Honestly."

We maintained eye contact for a long moment. Then she said, "I love you. So much that sometimes, I'm overwhelmed by the power of it." Max squeezed my hand and pulled me closer. "I would never ask you to do something that hurt you…"

"I know, Max." I kissed her and pulled back to look at her. "I never thought about having a child because I felt damaged - maybe even dangerous. I didn't want to expose a child to that. When I thought about the future, I didn't think about another person. I always saw myself alone. Everything is different now."

"Would you? Have a child with me?"

"Yes." Max grabbed me in a painful hug. "I'm terrified of being a bad mom but I can do anything, learn anything, with you by my side."

"You'll be an incredible mom."

After a few minutes passed of just holding each other, I asked, "Wh-what about, you know, the other half? It makes me a little nervous."

"I get that. Random sperm freaks me out, too. How would you feel about asking Brandon?"

I couldn't help but smile. "That would be a good thing for us *and* him if he'd consider it."

"My thoughts exactly."

I wanted three months to prepare my body and I didn't want a bunch of wild card hormones in my system.

"You already have twins in your family. I'm scared I'll pop out a litter by dosing up on fertility meds."

After some back and forth with Brandon - who was both thrilled and honored - we decided on the turkey baster method. A little awkward but less than doing it all at a clinic with multiple hands in my business.

We even found a kit online. He provided the goods and Max inserted them.

The first attempt failed but Brandon returned to South Florida a month later.

We were nothing if not invested.

That time, it took. She swore it was due to us making love for an hour afterward. Logically, her fake cock pushing the very real sperm deeper into my cervix was likely what made it work.

I'm currently eight months pregnant with twins, trying to get our lives moved to Virginia, and Max follows me around like I'll shatter from a stiff breeze.

I keep telling her I'm strong as an ox but she is relentless. When I get annoyed, I call her *paranoid papi*.

Pretty sure she secretly loves it.

Life isn't perfect because humans aren't but Max and I find our rhythm daily. We always remember to speak to each other with respect.

No matter how irritated two people with strong personalities might get sometimes.

We argue over wet towels on the floor or whose turn it is to do the laundry.

She hates it when I forget to come to bed because I'm caught up in my writing.

I want to throw a hissy fit when she meets up with her old unit and comes home smelling of beer and cigars.

Max is a brat when she gets sick - which is thankfully rare. I hold a grudge when she nods off during a movie we've been waiting to see.

Normal human stuff.

People being people.

I love her more than I love myself because I know she feels the same way about me. I know because she shows me day after day.

She never forgets important dates, brings me flowers for no reason, and holds me when I wake up in a cold sweat from an occasional nightmare.

Perfect imperfection with my beautiful Max in a life I never expected but could never live without now.

Selling my body was a temporary occupation.

The love I feel for my wife, our unborn children, and the people in our circle…is permanent.

The lost girl…not so lost anymore.

© Shayne McClendon

EXTRA:
The First Night (Max)

The first time I met Sarah, I thought to myself, "What the hell is a girl like her doing in this life?"

I watched her carefully during her introduction to the escorts, her dustup with Walker, the photo shoot that had her crawling out of her skin, and all the other cautious steps into the world of a paid escort.

Within those four hours, it became painfully obvious that the bright and happy smile Sarah wore for the world was largely fake.

Perhaps...*pretend* was a better word.

She pretended to be happy, to love life, and did it *well*. Every person who entered her orbit responded effortlessly to it.

In reality, she *overflowed* with darkness that was slowly and steadily eating her alive. It was apparent in those moments when no one was looking. When she believed herself to be completely alone.

All the light went out of her face and she looked like she'd be just as content if she suddenly died.

She didn't trust men and it wasn't hard to figure out why. She didn't trust women either but tolerated them more easily because of her strength advantage over the majority.

Sarah didn't trust anyone.

From the very beginning, I wanted her for myself. I didn't care that I was almost twelve years older. I didn't care that I'd been an escort or she was currently one.

For the first time in my life, I looked into the eyes of another person and *knew* they were meant for me.

She kept her heart walled away to avoid injury. I didn't know the details of her past then…but I knew it was ugly, mean, and that the scars she carried might never fade.

For months, I watched her heal one client after another from insecurity, uncertainty, and loss. Observed the way she could light up an entire room and immediately fade into shadows.

I touched her whenever I found a reason to. I let her touch me more than any lover I'd ever had.

Originally to get *her* addicted.

Then to feed my *own* addiction.

I listened to her voice, her laugh, and the sounds she made in the midst of passion…

And I wanted all of her.

Every single piece.

My own life had been charmed in comparison to Sarah's. My family was stable and involved. I kept in contact with friends I made in high school and the military.

There was never an obstacle in my path other than the day shrapnel hitting my back took out a kidney, my spleen, and twelve inches of bowel - causing me to lose the career I'd trained my entire life to have.

Even then, I landed on my feet because I was surrounded by people who made sure I did.

I had no reason to become the person I am other than nature asserting its own dominance over my biology and psychology.

The first and only time I allowed a man - one who surpassed me in physical size and strength - entry to my body, I wished I was the one fucking him. In fact, I had to imagine that scenario to make myself come.

I never made another attempt.

I knew it was pointless.

The first woman I slept with made me think, "This is closer…but not ideal."

When I was on leave in Europe, I went along with a few Marines from my unit to a sex club. I watched men and women perform all night.

Some dressed in leather.

Others wore nothing at all.

With every kiss of a whip on delicate skin, my heart raced. Each moan attesting to dark ecstasy made my body throb. I didn't know why it affected me as it did. I simply knew it gave me something nothing else ever had.

I wanted more.

I left aching for power, control, and a need to know everything. Little by little, I educated myself.

Instead of envying men's cocks…I got one of my own.

By the time young Sarah appeared in Vivienne's luxury condo on South Beach, I'd spent *years* honing my craft as a dominant who worshiped women.

I left lovers boneless, breathless, and incoherent in my wake…and never looked back.

I didn't want to learn about them or give them access to what made me tick.

With *her*, I wanted both.

Little by little, I drew Sarah closer to me. I interacted with her in small ways whenever our paths crossed and I waited. I didn't overpower her or chase her as some of the other escorts - and Walker - did.

I gave her room to learn more about herself, time to grow into the woman she was meant to be, and someone to confide in when she was troubled.

All the while, I slowly, ever so slowly, gentled Sarah's mind, heart, and body to my touch.

There were so many times I thought the wait would drive me mad. Moments when I wanted to pull her out of the escort life and install her permanently in my house and my bed.

But…I didn't want to own her.

I wanted to watch the street fighter who survived against all odds lay down her weapons and bare her throat to my teeth…knowing I'd *never* draw blood.

To witness her confidence that she would *never* have to fight me, defend herself against pain I caused, or heal from wounds I inflicted.

To willingly - without caution or fear - place herself into my hands.

Her submission.

Her trust.

Her love.

It was a goal worth waiting to meet. I knew and accepted that there would be few chances to taste her pleasure, to hear her cry out my name, to watch her fall apart in passion.

Fate handed me an unexpected opportunity in Tricia Draper.

The client who mentally exhausted me to the point of leaving life as an escort myself…needed a replacement.

Sarah needed to be trained.

I would teach her by example.

I stand six-one in my bare feet and six-two in most shoes. Sarah was five-eight and built strong enough to handle anything the world threw at her.

She was a natural submissive with severe trauma that affected her ability to trust - the cornerstone of any Dominant/submissive relationship.

There was no guarantee at all that she could find pleasure under the circumstances I wanted to expose her to.

Under the guise of *training her* to be dominant with Tricia, I greedily accepted the opportunity to touch her. It was our first night together. In all my fantasies, I never expected her to react so explosively.

Every moment, she followed my lead but didn't shy from her own curiosity.

As we entered the hotel suite after the best evening of dinner, dancing, and real conversation I'd experienced in sixteen years of dating, I kissed Sarah until she moaned between my lips.

Her body trembled in my hands and I told myself to be careful with her, be gentle, take it slow enough for her to adapt.

I'd been desperate for her for hours.

Holding her close, my fingers clenched in her soft hair. I wanted to feel it all over me.

In her ear, I whispered, "Everything will be okay. I won't hurt you…I'll never break that promise." Sarah inhaled deeply and I heard the way it shook.

This was not the confident escort who'd blown away clients and a seasoned madame alike.

This was a young woman who never showed vulnerability…baring her soft underbelly. It would take time for her to believe in my intentions. I understood.

"Your safe phrase is *I need a moment*. Things will pause so you can process." She nodded against me. "Repeat it."

She did so.

"Your safe word is *stop*. There's no continuing once you say it. The conditions don't matter. You're fully in control."

"Alright."

I hoped she never felt the need to use it. Lifting my face, I stared into her eyes and saw her nervousness and uncertainty. I knew it was rooted in how others had touched her, treated her.

Slowly stripping her clothes away, I took a moment to appreciate the utter beauty of a woman I knew could hold her own in any situation.

A natural fighter…

In every voluntary sexual scenario until now, I had no doubt she was the predator. Always the dominant partner, the one in complete control.

The Escort: In the Service of Women

A natural lover...

With me, she consented to be prey. Though I was uncertain exactly how or when I'd won her trust, I was grateful for it.

Sarah was the perfect package for a woman like me. She fascinated me on every level.

Shrugging off my jacket, I folded it over the back of the sofa. I took my time because Sarah was a person who followed movements carefully.

Removing my vest and tie, I opened the top two buttons before rolling up the sleeves of my dress shirt.

Turning, I held out my hand. She placed hers in it without hesitation and I'd *never* felt more powerful.

Leading her to the bed, I urged her to sit and she did. Back straight, body tensed, she expected me to take pleasure from her...to have her *serve* me...to use her.

I was not a client.

I was not a man.

I wanted her submission, not her services. Using demands and strength against such a woman would give me nothing more than token acquiescence.

Sarah was stronger than most.

In a life and death scenario, I had no doubt she'd be stronger even than me. All my training and experience would be no match against her teeth and claws if she were truly fighting for her life.

Her will would never *break* and I had no desire for such a thing.

I wanted her will to *melt*.

Kneeling at her feet, I saw the surprise in her eyes. I gently separated her knees and she spread her legs wider to accommodate me.

"Many have told you that you're beautiful." I didn't expect a response and she didn't provide one. "Many have found pleasure in your body." She tilted her head a bit. "When *you* find pleasure, what's going on in your mind, Sarah?"

Eyes wide, her lips parted before closing again.

"When you're touched, kissed, taken…when you fall over the edge of climax…what are you thinking about?"

I smiled, placed my hands beside her hips, and raised myself enough to be eye to eye with her.

"It's different, isn't it? Intimacy as compared to sexual gratification."

Her hazel eyes were almost green and I knew something buried deep was responding.

"Think about it tonight. Examine how you feel while I touch you. What goes through your mind and why? When you feel comfortable, share the answer."

I kissed her for several minutes, slipping my tongue along the pink delicacy of hers, enjoying the plumpness of her lips, the warmth of her breath as she exhaled against my cheek.

Only my mouth touched her, only hers touched me.

Lifting my head, I smiled. "Kissing you feels almost magical, Sarah. Unique from every other kiss I've given or received."

"I…" Her voice trailed away because her natural defense mechanisms refused to share too much.

"There's no pressure, no rush." I kissed her again before trailing my lips along her jaw and down her neck. "You'll know when you can trust me. Don't push yourself. I'll wait patiently for what I want. Allow me to show you."

Spending long minutes worshiping her breasts, I used one arm to support her back so I had better access to my treats. Her body trembled in my arms as small sounds of desire escaped.

I knew each time she almost touched me, held me against her, and each time she forced herself to still, uncertain of the protocols.

It was a battle that said much about her and yet another key to her inner self.

Sarah would rather deny her own pleasure than disappoint a lover. Since she was unfamiliar with D/s, she didn't want to cross boundaries or break rules she didn't know.

Oh, how I wanted this woman.

Moving pillows, I gently lowered her to the bed, elevating her upper body so she could watch every touch I delivered. Lifting one leg then the other, I placed her feet on the edge and allowed gravity to display her for my perusal.

"Your gorgeous pussy…wet and quivering for me already."

Bending, I licked her slowly from her pussy to her clit, swirling around the throbbing nubbin, and her fingers gripped the bedding beneath her. I kept the flats of my fingers over her folds, rubbing lightly while I watched her inner thighs contract.

"A flavor I could become addicted to…as I thought."

"M-Max…?"

"Yes, Sarah?"

"Do...I ask p-permission?"

Moving over her with one knee on the bed, I kept my fingers between her legs, sliding lazily over hot, wet flesh.

"Do you want to come?"

"Please."

"I would love to make you come, Sarah."

I watched her face and she didn't look away as she released her body bit by bit from self-administered restraints. I found myself amazed yet again at her self-control.

"Don't stop..." she begged softly.

"Never," I assured her, maintaining the pressure and speed I would utilize every time I touched Sarah like this in the future.

Her body arched from the bed and I relished the expression on her face at her most vulnerable.

Eyes barely slits, jaw clenched, and body taut...as *fierce* in her pleasure as she was in everything else.

Sweat beaded on her skin as her climax went through her in a wave.

Open. Honest. Spectacular to behold.

I watched her ride it, take everything she could from it, until she relaxed against the bed again and exhaled roughly.

"Would you like another?"

"Yes. Please, Max."

"How would you like to come, Sarah?"

"In any way you want me to."

Everything about her made my body pulse to match her rhythm.

"Mm. Such a brilliant answer."

Slipping my hand along the back of her neck, I held her still to devour her lips. She moaned and again fought against her desire to touch me.

There was nothing I wanted more.

"Domination and submission are different for every couple…and I want you to take everything you need from this experience, Sarah." I continued to play over her clit and she panted into the silence. "If you want to touch me…you can." I wanted her touch everywhere.

Instantly, her fingers were in my hair, raking through the length, loosening the knot at my nape.

"As soft as I've always imagined. Like petting a beautiful cat."

Such innocent words shouldn't have affected me as they did but she had magic coursing through her that I was unable to resist.

As another orgasm drew her body tight, she moaned almost inaudibly, "Kitty, kitty…"

I wanted to fuck her until she couldn't walk.

Kissing her because I *could not* stop myself, I watched her slowly come down from her second orgasm.

"Stay just like this, Sarah. Let's see how high I can push you."

Stripping away my clothes, I set my sights on the peak of her pleasure and didn't waver. I ate her greedily as my fingers stroked deeply inside her pussy, curling *just so* behind her throbbing clit.

Discovering what her body was truly capable of achieving stunned her.

Her body flexed in an involuntary sit-up, both hands in my hair, and she gasped as her body released fully for the first time.

She whispered urgently, "Oh, god…what's happening to me? What's happening?"

I didn't answer because my mouth was sealed to her clit as she soaked my entire chest and the hand with fingers still rubbing a special place inside her.

Sarah came harder than any lover I'd had in my grasp, for longer than I thought possible.

I would have been smug had she not pulled me to her and wept in my arms.

"A-a moment, Max…I need a moment."

Holding her harder than I should have, covered in her pleasure, her heart pounded against mine as she struggled to breathe.

I petted her hair - damp tendrils sticking to her skin - and murmured soothing words meant to anchor her back in the now.

It took fifteen minutes for the aftershocks to slow enough for her to uncoil her upper body.

Another five before Sarah loosened her hold on me, shakily wiped her face, and met my eyes.

"I didn't…know my b-body could *do* that. It's never happened before."

Taking kisses despite my intent to allow her time to process what she'd experienced, she accepted them ravenously.

Only when she was satisfied enough to break the connection did I ask, "How do you feel, Sarah?"

"As if...I just came for the first time."

"What were you thinking about?"

"How much I wanted you to hold me so I didn't lose my way...and then you did. You did."

Tears slipped over her cheeks but I knew no matter how shaken she was, this was not the night she'd confess the fresh and fragile emotional attachment she'd formed for me or the sexual desire for what she now knew I could offer.

That was alright. I understood her locks and had the keys now. There would be others but the biggest one she'd told me herself...

Sarah wanted to be held.

Pleasure was something she understood - and wielded as a tool when needed in her own life. It was easy to grasp, simple to provide.

Touch was different. Sarah touched others and allowed them to touch her in brief intervals.

They didn't *hold* her, cherish her, and bring her back safely.

All her life, she'd battled all comers to protect herself as well as anyone in her orbit.

It was a core part of her personality but...she was tired. At nineteen, the world and other humans had taken and taken until she ran on fumes.

She wanted to be held - protected from the outside world - and safety wasn't something she'd ever ask another person to give her.

I wanted the assignment.

Gathering her in my arms, I guided her to the shower, removed my cock, and washed us both. When she was clean and dry, I pulled back the bedding and encouraged her to get comfortable.

Lounging on white linens, she was confident in her body and ready for more. She watched with interest, her lower lip between her teeth, as I reattached the cock I usually wore unless I was sleeping.

I wasn't ready to sleep.

Neither was my new lover.

I uncapped a bottle of lube and Sarah sat up to take it from me. Dropping her feet over the side of the bed, she murmured, "I've never seen one up close."

"Be my guest."

"You were conscientious about size." Her fingers wrapped around the silicone appendage and *stroked* in a way that made my teeth clench with need. "Big enough to ensure satisfaction without intimidation."

Her lips closed over the head and my eyes widened at the powerful visual she created. I thrust without conscious thought and she moaned softly.

Moving her hand up my thigh and between my legs, she explored the way the cock sat on my skin as she sucked it to the back of her throat.

Sarah's skills were well-rounded.

Her fingertips circled the entrance of my pussy and the *touch* combined with the *visual* hit different from any sexual experience in my personal history. My lips parted in surprise.

She pushed slowly into my body and deftly curled her fingers against the front wall. Lifting her gaze, she stared at me without blinking.

Sarah wanted me to fuck her mouth.

I'd never wanted anything more.

Holding her skull in my palms, I started to move, and she synced her strokes with mine. The skin tightened on the back of my neck as my nipples pebbled and the audible wetness of my pussy could be heard in the silence.

Her breasts framed my cock on either side and her dark pink tips were tight with need.

"Touch yourself, Sarah." My voice was hoarse. She instantly slipped her free hand over her belly and up to cup her breast as if to offer it to me. My mouth watered. "I'll suck them again. I love your tits." Rolling her nipple between her finger and thumb, she moaned around my cock. "Yes. Gorgeous."

She was going to make me come. I couldn't believe it.

Through gritted teeth, I said, "Play with yourself. Don't come until I fill you up."

"Mm hmm."

I knew the moment her fingers reached her clit. Her eyes fluttered and her breathing sped up.

"Licking your pretty pussy was magnificent, Sarah. Sucking your clit between my lips. Swallowing your come. I want more of you on my tongue."

Her fingers moved faster inside me and I knew there was no way to hold back my own orgasm.

"I made you come with my fingers. Again with my mouth." My head dropped back on my shoulders as I gasped. "Now I want you to come all over my cock." Groaning, I managed, "Sarah…fuck."

For the first time, I was in danger of truly losing control during sex. I came harder than I ever had and rode the pleasure as if it was brand new.

With her, it made sense.

Everything felt new and different.

Breathing heavily, I met her eyes. I slowly pulled my cock from between her lips and watched her suck the fingers she removed from my pussy.

Eyes glazed with need, she whispered, "Delicious. I hope you give me more." She scooted back on the bed, reclined with her legs spread, and added, "You won't need lube. I'm so wet, Max."

I fell on her like an animal and she met me as an equal. Sarah took my cock as if she'd done it a hundred times, touched me everywhere she could reach, and begged me not to stop.

There's no way I could have.

She was a fever in my brain, a pounding in my chest, and I would not stop until Sarah was mine.

I took her for hours in every position - using my cock, mouth, and hands to drive her through one orgasm after another.

Each time, I held her against my body, whispered softly to her, and allowed her time to recover in my arms before taking her again.

Twice more, she wept at the peak of climax and I knew it was purging something buried deep inside her that ached and burned.

I knew there would be more cathartic moments like this in our future and welcomed them.

The last word Sarah whispered as mental and physical exhaustion claimed her near dawn was my name.

I loved her.

I couldn't claim her yet.

There would come a day when *nothing* would stop me.

© Shayne McClendon

GOOD GIRL PUBLISHING

You should be reading…and this trio of writers is sure to offer something you love.

Check out Shayne's **LinkTree** (see last page) for all the ways to read incredible books right now!

Writing as Shayne McClendon
Members Only Series
Quiet Series
The Hollow Universe
Manhattan Madame Series
Wild & Unruly Series
Completely Wrecked
The Hermit
Quickies: Short Story Collections
And many more...

Writing as Sabrina Rue
The Others Series

Writing as Charlize Rojos
The Brotherhood Series
Eating the Cake

ABOUT SHAYNE McCLENDON

Shayne McClendon is the author of more than fifty published books and over five hundred short stories (and counting).

She writes heart-pounding romantic fiction as **Shayne McClendon**, thrilling paranormal romance as **Sabrina Rue**, and LGBTQ+ action-packed erotica as **Charlize Rojos**.

She spends most of her waking hours writing in one genre or another.

In the summer of 2022, Shayne abandoned her ten-year hermit lifestyle for a writing road trip visiting readers across the United States and Canada.

She's not sure she'll ever truly settle down…but the stories are coming faster than ever!

Coffee consumption is too high, the amount of sleep is too low, but the words always feel just right.

If you're looking for your next great read…you *need* Shayne McClendon! Her dramatic and erotic romances will grab hold and not let you go until the very last page.

Please join her on **Patreon** for exclusive stories and behind-the-scenes access. Follow her on **TikTok** for regular updates!

FIND ME EVERYWHERE

Find all things Shayne McClendon by hovering your camera over the image below. Just follow the link that appears!

Made in United States
North Haven, CT
18 April 2025